SAILING

TO

NOON

SAILING TO NOON

a novel

by

Hoyt Rogers

with

Artemisia Vento

and

Frank Báez

SPUYTEN DUYVIL
NEW YORK CITY

ACKNOWLEDGMENTS

In different versions, passages of this novel have appeared in *The New England Review, AGNI, Eunoia Review, The Summerset Review, The Writing Disorder, Axon, The Bitter Oleander Review, Offcourse, The Dillydoun Review, The Courtship of Winds, The Fortnightly Review, Isla Abierta, The Raven's Perch*, and *The Literary Review*. My sincere thanks to the editors of these publications for supporting my work over the years. I also owe a debt of gratitude to Jonathan Galassi, Siri Hustvedt, Edmund White, Paul Auster, Marco Genovesi, Robin Saikia, Frank Báez, Nicholas Callaway, Ricardo Bernardo, Anne Davenport, Nellie Barletta, Pablo Báez, Amy Bernstein, Michele Casagrande, Lena Papadaki, Peter Bernstein, Esther Allen, Bishan Samaddar, Marc Vincenz, and Anthony Seidman, who encouraged me along the way. For information about my other books, please visit hoytrogers.com.

Published by Spuyten Duyvil; maps and cover images by Mary Heebner; book and jacket design by John Balkwill and T Thilleman; supplemental editing by Joan Tapper.

Sailing to Noon, first edition, ISBN 978-1-959556-58-9, printed in the United States. Available directly from the publisher, or through Ingram, Amazon, and bookshop.org.

Library of Congress Cataloging-in-Publication Data

Names: Rogers, Hoyt, author. | Vento, Artemisia, compiler. | Báez, Frank, editor.
Title: Sailing to Noon : a novel / by Hoyt Rogers, with Artemisia Vento and Frank Báez.
Description: New York City : Spuyten Duyvil, 2023. | Series: The Caribbean trilogy ; Book One
Identifiers: LCCN 2023028801 | ISBN 9781959556589 (paperback)
Subjects: LCGFT: Novels.
Classification: LCC PS3618.O459 S25 2023 | DDC 813/.6--dc23/eng/20230710
LC record available at https://lccn.loc.gov/2023028801

For G, JL, and all the voyagers
who seek their 'untold want' on the open sea

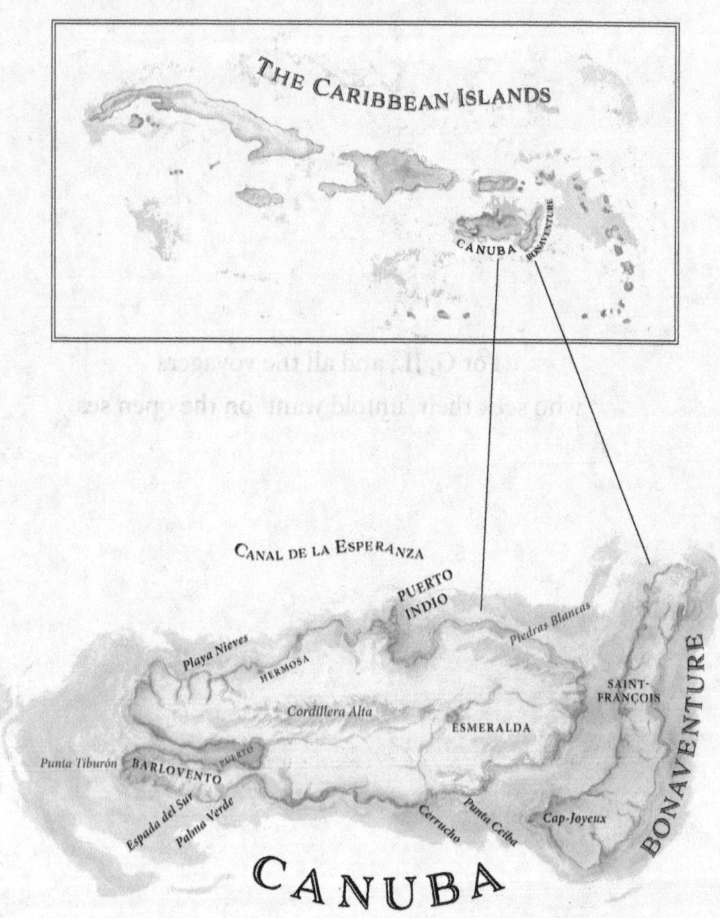

THE CARIBBEAN ISLANDS
CANUBA
BONAVENTURE
CANAL DE LA ESPERANZA
PUERTO INDIO
Playa Nieves
HERMOSA
Piedras Blancas
Cordillera Alta
SAINT-FRANÇOIS
ESMERALDA
Punta Tiburón
BARLOVENTO
PUERTO
Espada del Sur
Palma Verde
Cerrucho
Punta Ceiba
Cap-Joyeux
BONAVENTURE
CANUBA

ailing to Noon *draws on notebooks I received from a Sicilian journalist, Artemisia Vento, on the eve of her departure for an unnamed country in Asia. She was determined to live out the rest of her days in a cloistered retreat—whether Buddhist, Christian, Vedic, interfaith, or secular, she wouldn't reveal. Discrepantly, she also spoke of an 'environmental hermitage,' far from any contact with mankind. 'You're a translator and editor,' she said. 'These scribbles are a farewell gift to you. Make of them what you will.'*

Among her jottings, I found a lengthy narration. When pressed, she claimed it wasn't autobiographical, merely a record of 'wayward fantasies' she now disowned. In the pages that follow, various voices recount their story chronologically—though she hinted the action could also move backwards, forwards, or both. 'Tragedies and comedies take place in the course of time,' she explained; 'at some point, they happen to us all. But they're never the final chord: we constantly revise and transform the past. Our dead survive within us in the present. Memory is the surest form of resurrection.'

If readers choose to adopt her suggestion, they could start with the last of her monologues, and thread their way back to the first. Or they could skip from episode to episode, as in the randomness of passing thoughts. In that sense, this foreword might be an afterword—or simply an 'interword.'

Artemisia replaces quotation marks with periods, colons, or em dashes framed by blanks. Dialogues hover between the said and the unsaid. Her ambiguity was deliberate. 'Half our message is conveyed by our gestures and our faces,' she remarked. Because of her checkered background, her prose mixes British usage with American. Many of her notes are in other languages, ancient and modern, or in multilingual creoles and dialects. In translating those passages, I've kept a few key terms from the originals, as brushstrokes of linguistic coloring; but I've surrounded them with Anglo equivalents, so readers needn't worry they're missing a link.

The characters splice their mother tongues with English at will—just as occurs throughout the modern world, from Chile to China. I agree with Artemisia that hybrids like Spanglish and Germglish are idioms in their own right. Wherever they come up, I've slanted them heavily towards '-glish,' for smoother reading. To avoid other road bumps, I've limited the capitals and exclamation marks of 'emphatic' speakers to a minimum. Most importantly, I've ensured the authenticity of the island voices—under-represented much too often—by working closely with the noted Caribbean author, Frank Báez. When the satire flirts with stereotypes, it's self-parody: the cast making light of their own personae. Above all, we should bear in mind that—regrettably— ethnic, appearance, and gender sensitivity had not even reached today's low standard back in the eighties, four decades ago.

Artemisia urged me to emend her writings as I saw fit, or throw them away; in any case, she asked me to destroy them in the end. If I recycled them as fiction, she told me to use my own 'byline'—an allusion to her former career. She also wanted me to retain the copyright; she sincerely wished to 'vanish from the world once and for all.' I've preferred to acknowledge her by a pseudonym, 'Artemisia Vento.' The painter she most admired was Gentileschi; the wind was what she wanted to become.

—HR

SAILING TO NOON

With the early breath of the tropical morning, fresh and
fragrant from the hillsides, we slowly glided down the bay,
and were swept through the opening in the reef.

— Melville

Chiara Trigona, Puerto Indio, April 1981

Why did I come here? To fall off the planet, or jump on? For months I've strolled past these mottled facades—blue faded to grey, ochre bleached to white. Centuries of fierce sun, hurricane winds, and torrential rain have punished them past repair. Ferns sprout from crannies in the walls.

Here or there a balcony leans awry, as tipsy as the people on the streets below. Pocket-size grocery stores spill from crooked passageways, clogging the sidewalks. Their wooden counters double as makeshift bars where the locals drink themselves silly, shouting jokes to the blare of Caribbean tunes. Salsa, son, bachata, reggae, merengue, homegrown cambuca, romantic ballads, Latino pop—on the island of Canuba, all give their kick to a planter's punch of sound...

I never thought my hair would cause such a sensation. It's fairly thick, I'll admit. In Puerto Indio, strangers touch it with awe—like that sweet old lady just now. Here they call it 'good hair': the main symbol of beauty in Canuba. The other day, when I remarked on her lovely little girl, a mother sighed. — I wish she had 'pelo bueno' like you. Poor thing, she came out with 'pelo malo.' — 'Bad hair': appallingly, that's the Canuban term for buoyant African curls. White supremacy, diffused and internalized. Colonial racism at its worst.

As to complexion, islanders show more tolerance, even if for them, paler means better. Their creole boasts twenty-odd words for shades of skin, from freckly-white 'jabao' to wheaty 'trigueño,' from mulatto 'indio claro' to ruddy-umber 'tamarindo,' and from tawny 'amarillo' to jet-black 'indio oscuro,' a willful misnomer. 'Indio'—Indian—refers to the Taíno, the original inhabitants of the country. Though I seem average to my fellow Italians, here everyone tells me I'm 'hermosísima'—very lovely—with my pink epidermis and 'good hair.' Not that I agree, of course: I'm as ordinary as I've always been.

My house lies on Plaza Drake; I feel relieved when I exit the crowded lanes and enter the ample square. Postcards call it the 'Corazón del Barrio Antiguo'—the Heart of the Old Quarter. Unmistakably Victorian, a bronze statue of Sir Francis Drake looms at the center, atop a colossal granite pedestal. Drooping over the captain with a doubtful smile, an eagle-winged Nike can't bring herself to crown him. The laurel wreath withers in her hands, several inches above his head.

Canuba's fortunes have always been unstable, ever since Columbus first claimed the island for Spain. As usual in the Caribbean tug-of-war, the 'Catholic Kings' of Iberia were followed by the French: in the seventeenth century, France ruled the colony for twenty years, till the Spanish snatched it back in a gory battle at sea. The Office of Maritime Heritage is always dredging up a rusty cannon or two from Puerto Indio Bay.

The Indians, the Spanish, the French: typical enough—though the story is more twisted than that. Drake's brief invasion in 1586 foreshadowed the later British conquest; but Albion held sway for only four decades, from 1839 to 1880. During the final few years of that period, Canubans fought hard to win their independence. Fishing in troubled waters, the French did their utmost to regain control. They launched a ferocious attack from their nearby colony, Bonaventure, and their brave black infantrymen trounced Canuba. But after that final upset, the Europeans granted both islands their statehood, for all perpetuity.

My duty as a journalist—along with my bookish nature—impels me to read up on Colonial history: it's a convoluted tale. For example, I find it bizarre that Canubans consider Drake the founding father of their country. After all, they speak Spanish to this day—mixed with pidgin English and a soupçon of French. On the other hand, maybe it's fitting they chose a pirate for their Garibaldi, given their ethical adaptability. Hardly a moral paragon, Sir Francis...

This evening as every evening, a haggard crone stands at attention before the monument. She worships it with upraised arms, lifting one leg like a heron; her narrow nose, ruffled crest of hair, and unblinking eyes dovetail with an Audubon print. That pose must be a strain, but she holds it resolutely.

This isn't patriotism, I'd guess. More like religious ecstasy: she's praying to Drake with all her heart. She hasn't judged his character very well... But then the gods of the Santería pantheon, more or less paired with Catholic saints, don't cultivate the garden-variety virtues. In Canuba, angels and demons are sometimes one and the same.

The Colonial buildings in the Old Quarter, cobbled out of coral stone, never exceed two storeys in height. Rearing above them, a Belle Époque concoction borders the eastern end of the square; it's topped by a circular tower with round windows. Once a private clinic for wealthy patients, it now subsists as a boarding house for down-and-outs.

I already have a lease on a spacious house close-by. But a few weeks ago, I began renting the tower as well: at forty dollars a month, it was an offer I couldn't refuse. Though I call it my 'study,' I use it mainly as a belvedere, to dream away the hours.

Early evening is the peak time to revel in the view. With furtive delight, I unlock a small side-door and step inside; it takes my eyes a while to adjust to the dimness. Cautiously, I climb four flights of stairs: they angle off in odd directions, as dizzying as a Piranesi prison. I pause now and then to frame perspectives in my mind—pictures engraved on air.

Finally, I reach a cramped landing before a convex door. One turn of another key, and I enter my cylindrical room. Moonlight filters through the wooden blinds of the windows, a ring of oversize portholes. Crossing the silver disks they cast on the floor, I open the musty shutters.

Slim as an arrowhead, the peninsula is a hodge-podge of ancient churches, stone houses, roof terraces, unkempt gardens, and abandoned lots. To the north, east, and west, the Caribbean gleams, taut as a ribbon of navy-blue foil. A yellow quarter-moon has slipped above the horizon… it floats on the outer curve of the sea. At this latitude, its prow and stern balance on an even keel. It resembles a shiny boat… a child's primitive toy.

I'm reminded of the three small caravels from half a millennium ago. They must've astounded the Indians when they popped over the edge of the world, commanded by my countryman, Cristoforo Colombo—Columbus, the Admiral of the Ocean Sea.

At this height, the racket from the grocery-bars subsides to a muffled din. Plaza Drake is a pedestrian zone, hemmed in by steps of brick and stone. Though it seems like the perfect place for nightlife, there's not a single disco or club. On a Saturday eve in the Caribbean, you'd normally expect a ruckus. But the Archbishop, who's yielded to Mammon on the streets, defends his lakes of devotion in the squares. In each of them, one or two churches rest serenely at anchor.

All the same, this is still Canuba, where silence is anathema, and noise is the god of all gods.

Soon enough, a motorcycle shatters the quiet. Bucking

up the steps like a bronco, it zooms around Drake's statue, then screeches to a halt in front of my house. All I can do is whistle to myself: Oh well, another visit from my favorite madman. Not that I'm worried. Whatever happens, Amado will live up to his name—my Beloved, and my friend.

So that's it: a white Mercedes skids from one of the sidestreets, in hot pursuit of the motorbike. Blocked by the stairs around the plaza, it abruptly comes to a stop. The driver jumps out and runs across the bricks, shouting like a boot-camp sergeant; but instead of standing his ground, Amado ducks into my door. As British toffs used to say— or was it Tarzan?—'the natives are restless tonight.' A colonialist phrase, if ever there was one. Mea culpa, how awful! Whether I want to or not, I'll have to patch things up.

By the time I make my way from the tower to the house, my uninvited guest has wound himself into a conniption fit. As I approach the pool of mellow light, shed by a rusty lantern screwed to the wall, I note that he's wearing an antiquated tuxedo—double-breasted, with wide lapels. Even in his rage, as he bangs on the heavy door, he cuts the figure of a gentleman: virile and commanding, yet urbane.

To some, his outfit would seem ill-suited to the Caribbean—as travel brochures portray it. In fact, people dress more formally here than in Rome, Paris, or New York. Several neighbors have stuck their heads out, to see what the uproar's all about. Shrugging my shoulders, I wave to them apologetically. The blond fireball in the dinner suit spins around to face me, moustache bristling.

I try to disarm him with flattery. Ah! Héctor Méndez, our leading art critic. We finally meet again. I read your piece on Virgilio Miranda just this morning. You truly captured his mystique: 'Virgilio, the enigma of contemporary painting.'

The gambit calms him down. Canubans follow the same rules as Italians: anything goes, as long as you're polite. He limply shakes my hand. As before, his English has a transatlantic ring. Oh, it's you. I haven't had the honor since our chat in that bar last year. Remember how you owned up to all the murders you'd committed? I'm surprised they haven't put you away for good.

I was in a sorry state that night, as you know.

Deciding to spare me, he changes course: We have a lot of offbeat names in Puerto Indio. But Chiara is a rum one, even for us.

Badminton: a back and forth; if that's what he wants, I'm game. — I hail from an eccentric boot, like the shoe in Mother Goose. But Chiara is fairly common there. Especially in the North, where my godmother lives.

Humpf. Italy, the one and only.

No, the singular doesn't apply. There are many different Italies. Anyway, I'm not very 'Italian,' whatever that means. My family is international. I've spent most of my life in France, Germany, the States—all over the place.

He butts in with a non sequitur: Well, I'm ashamed to

admit it, but I've never liked Renaissance art.

I grew up in Sicily. It's almost Renaissance-free... except for Antonello.

Quite an exception. By the way, I read somewhere that Northern Italians call you Sicilians 'gli africani,' the Africans. Now you've moved to another island. Why?

Sicily wasn't far enough south.

With Amado, I think you've touched bottom. Though you're butch enough to be a top. With a prosthetic device between your legs...

Annoyed, I turn aside. — No need to be rude. I took you for a gentleman. I suppose you're looking for him now?

Looking for him? He led me straight to your door!

Making a scene won't help, Héctor.

All right, I'll leave. But promise me this: Amado will report to my gallery tomorrow, on time! I didn't give him a cushy job so he could hang around you all day.

It's his nocturnal life you're worried about, I imagine. I'll see what I can do... But I don't control him. Nobody does.

He kicks one of the motorcycle tires. I never should've bought him that bloody Harley!

An about-face, and he stalks off. Halfway across the square, he calls back in a courteous tone: Let's have a drink again some time.

Canuban inconsistency... just as in Italy, the 'Belpaese.'

It makes me feel right at home. I nod a vague yes, then wave good-bye.

With relief, I plunge into the comfy penumbra of my house. I've always detested overhead lights; I'd rather burrow through darkness like a mole. After all, I grew up in a man-made cavern. The ceilings were so high, you could hardly see them at night.

I click on a low-wattage lamp, perched on a tiny octagonal table. The only other furniture is a pair of rocking chairs, with cushioned seats and heart-shaped backs. Like sleeping animals, trunks with shipping labels hunker against the walls. The dim light barely picks out the wooden beams, fifteen feet above the worn brick floor. A lofty arch opens on murkier spaces, lost in the gloom.

As expected, Amado emerges beneath the vault. Against the blackness, his hulking form is only an outline. He growls in a low mumble. Héctor split already, ombe?

'Ombe,' the African-sounding variant of 'hombre': I love the way Canubans call women that, too. — Yes. So you don't have to whisper. Anyway, it hasn't escaped him that you're here.

I know. Ya lo sé. — His bass voice rumbles more loudly. — You think I'm stupid? — He pronounces it 'stoopid,' as I've often heard it said in New York. Many Canubans are translingual, equally at home in Spanish or English. I adore their hybrid language: it has a springy, expressive lilt. — That jerk shouldn't show his face on your street, ombe. No respect! He's a bozo, a fucking pendejo.

Well, just do your job and keep him happy. It's easier than squabbling, no?

He moves forward into the wan patch of light. Sometimes I can't believe my lucky stars. Almost twenty-one and of middling height, he has matted black hair, light-brown eyes, and clean-shaven skin. His face, slightly asymmetrical, is handsome but not too pretty. Even now, under the feeble lamp, his complexion gives off a golden sheen—a natural bronzing that sunlight can't produce.

He works out every day, for at least two hours. His T-shirt and jeans are bursting at the seams, though they don't betray an ounce of fat. His bulk almost gives him an overstated air, like the hero of a comic strip; but there's nothing trumped up about his strength. His barrel chest and corded arms aren't bloated by steroids. Thankfully, he's stopped just short of a Schwarzenegger's ungainly knots.

Don't hand me that crap about Héctor! He can't tell his head from his ass. And you don't care about me either. Coño! You don't give a shit if I live or die!

As before, I trot out the Italian ploy: dogged cordiality. Look how you're treating me, amigo. You haven't even said hello.

Mechanically, he plants a kiss on my lips. He drops the threatening note, turning almost boyish. Chiara, you gotta let me stay here tonight. My wife, she's driving me nuts.

Ever since I got that bike, she's jealous all the time. If I had half the women she says, I wouldn't have time to screw em all. Mujeres! There's other things I wanna do besides rapar.

I always have to remind myself that 'rapar' means voluntary sex, not rape. Maybe she thinks that's what you do best.

He flares up. Bendito! Lay off it, mi hermano! I need your help, and you treat me like dirt. You're always making fun of me.

Wide as a Taíno's, his eyes smolder with rage. 'Mi hermano,' like 'ombe,' is a unisex phrase; 'bendito,' too, more personal here than the Puerto Rican filler word. When he's excited, Amado's English comes straight from Queens, larded with savory chunks of Spanish. That's not surprising: thousands of Canubans call the borough home.

I mollify him once again. No, Amado, I'm concerned about you—that's all. I can't see how spending another night here would do you any good... By the way, you promised to give me back my keys. I'm afraid you might lose them somewhere.

He's not so easy to put off. Why can't I stay? No jodas! Don't fuck with me. There's plenty of room for both of us.

Sleeping is different. I'm an old maid. Besides, I'm not used to lots of people in one bed.

Throwing the keys on the floor, he strides to the door, jerks it open, and wheels around. Oh, and I *am* used to living in a goddam slum, with my family piled up like cucarachas. Is that what you think? You're no friend of mine. You hear me? Me oyes? You're never gonna see me again, never! Don't call me, and don't come looking for me. If you run into me on the street, don't say hello. I don't know you! I'm wipin you off with mierda de gato!

He slams the door so hard, I'm afraid it'll crack. But three-inch mahogany can take a lot of abuse. He revs up his motorcycle to an earsplitting roar. Through the shutters, I watch him bounce down the steps on the other side of the plaza. Swerving into a narrow lane, he vanishes.

Wearily, I sink into one of the rocking chairs. So now I've been 'erased with cat-waste': an ugly idiom for cutting me out of his life. Amado has his sterling points, but an even temper isn't one of them. He'll show up again, no doubt about that—as soon as he needs to moonlight, if not before... I always have a wall to paint, a bougainvillea to plant. That step-and-fetch-it job at Héctor's gallery barely keeps him afloat. He's always hard up for extra money— one of the drawbacks of fatherhood at an early age. Sadly, he also gambles; that takes a sizeable bite out of his budget. He's got some other pet vices, too, like giving expensive presents to girls he hardly knows.

He's been in legal trouble—nothing major, so he says. In the end, I have to believe what my instincts tell me: he may be careless, but he's not a criminal. He blows his stack from time to time, but I can be edgy, too. For me, he's as much a kid brother as a lover. I'm glad to listen to him talk about his troubles—with his parents, his wife, his boss Héctor, his creditors, his enemies, and 'la vida en general.' He seems tough to the rest of the world, but with me he's just a lonesome puppy. More than once, he's cried on my lap.

That's my second yawn… I need to turn in… Yes, Amado, you'll come back before long. What with your wife, children, and girlfriends—not to mention your male playmates—it's a wonder you find time for us. And then there's the gym: you spend hours there, too. Where do you get the energy?

I'd better take a gander around the house, in case a cat sneaked in from the patio; Amado might not have noticed. Beyond the arch, there's another huge room, equal in size to the front one, with nothing in it but a bed and a reading lamp. I was raised on the loopy arabesques of the late Baroque, but now I like a sparse décor. Further back, I check the main bathroom, the postage-stamp courtyard, the minuscule kitchen, the maid's room, the guest bath. The coast is clear—no felines tonight.

I take a leisurely shower, switch on the ceiling fan over the bed, and dip into the fresh, clean sheets. Tomorrow's Sunday, my housekeeper's day off, so I can sleep as late as I want. What a treat!

Sometimes Chiara really breaks my balls. Coño! She thinks it's all so easy, just cause she's got it made. She coulda let me stay with her tonight. I woulda fucked her like she won't forget. A good singada! I'm a real Canuban, a Canubano! Now I gotta hang in this dumb-ass colmado store, and wait for my wife to go to sleep. I like to drink, same as all my pals, but I'm short on dough. Guess I gotta stick to beer. The problem is it gimme gas, but what the hell. Otra fría! I tell the pint size colmadero. The guy must be fifteen, max. That next beer better be cold, like I said.

Chiara says I gotta lot going for me, but what does she know? Yeah, some of it's been good. Livin in the Apple, Nueva Yol, and freezin my ass off. That's everybody's big dream around here. I even made it through high school, with some help from my cousin on exams. Not my fault: they're mostly for gringos, anyway. The fucking English tripped me up, the whole damn attitude. Everything's gotta be just so. But maybe it was partly my fault. Hey, I'm a jock! I didn't study much. And maybe things are changing. My cousin Pilín, he did great. Got a scholarship to college. He's a total nerd though. Spends all his time on the books.

My mom owns a hair salon in Queens. My aunts, cousins and her are Ameribanos. What we call Canubanos with a visa, means they can work in the States. Most of em live in Miami, cause the gringos can't stand Espinosa. They say he's a dictator and maybe a communist, so we can claim asylum. But in my family, we don't need that gringo shit. On my dad's side, my granddad's got four hundred acres. A whole lotta tareas, is how we measure it. The farm's only thirty miles from Puerto Indio. Pretty big alright, and it goes back for five generations. On top of that, my dad owns a supermarket where the comparones live, the stuck-up kids. Not just a crummy mom and pop like this. He's got other businesses too, him and his brothers.

Chiara's always telling me I oughta work for my dad. She says if I play my cards right, I'll wind up with my own company one of these days. The problem is, I don't get along with him. He was mad as fuck when I hitched up at seventeen. Not legal with papers, I mean. Except for the jevitos, the rich dudes, for us it's ok living together, then maybe your woman starts havin babies. That's what happens when you like to fuck. I bet more than half the kids here get born with no papers, like mine. Till their dad declares em, if he ever does. I'm still twenty, I've already got two.

My dad thinks my woman is nothing but a country campesina. Your wife smells like leaves, he says, like hojas. He thinks Reina is just after money, and she trapped me cause my family's got dough. The joke's on her if she did, cause he won't give us a centavo. He says she got knocked up on purpose. Fat chance. I just forgot to wear my condom that night when we fucked. The natural way. Too much rum! Coño! Damn!

Reina's name would be Queen in English, almost like where my mom lives. I guess it's kinduva low rent name in Canuba. But why I like her is, she's a knockout. I'm proud to be with her cause she's got what it takes: tall, white and dumb. That's the best for guys here. I like Chiara too even if she's old, cause she's a fast learner. She might be smart, but I taught her everything she knows about fuckin and stuff, how to chichar. She's kinduva teacher for me too. Sometimes she makes me read outta books, English or Spanish. A loco book about whales maybe, or frogs and rats with cabins on a river, a río. Things I never heard about. Chévere, kinda cool.

Reina gets along fine with Chiara. I gave her Chiara's number one time when our phone broke, and I was gonna paint some walls in her house. After that Reina called her all the time. Coño, why? I got pissed off at first. Reina figures Chiara's too old and dried up to get in her way. Plus bein a foreigner, a gringa, she's gotta be loaded, so she can help out if we need a loan. Anyway, a señora like her won't be startin some kinda second family with me. That's not for Chiara, for sure!

When it comes to other women except for Chiara, Reina is jealous as hell. Always spyin on me everywhere I go. One reason she calls Chiara is she's sniffin around about my girlfriends. I've got a few. A guy's gotta have em, else life gets boring, aburrida. When Reina tracks one down, she goes through the roof. She beat up a couple of em really bad. That's why Chiara won't give her info anymore.

My wife's brother Sigfrido, my cuñado, he's a policeman. He protects Chiara's street for a price, not that I ever asked him to. People are always hustlin here for money: it gets kinda old. My cuñado, he didn't know how strong his sister is till he saw us in action one day. Sigfrido just happened to be there, and me and Reina almost totaled the fuckin neighborhood. The whole damn barrio! Hittin each other with whatever we could grab. Jerkin chairs away from old ladies sittin on the sidewalk, turnin over tables where guys were playing dominoes. We smashed walls fulla bottles at the bodega, banged each other's heads on concrete step, cemento walls, telephone poles. Kinda wild! But can you believe it, when we finally simmered down, we walked away with only a scratch.

Sigfrido's my pal, but sometimes he's an asshole. Chiara got after me when he blabbed to her. She thinks we musta racked up even more debt that day. Come on! I straightened her out. Hell no, the barrio we live in is used to that kinda shit. One of the toughest parts of town, amiga, San Sebastián. We call it Milk of Magnesia, cause it's so hard to take!

She didn't even crack a smile. One thing she's learned is Canubans love out to lunch nicknames, apodos. Even our normal names are way out. Round the corner from Chiara, a dude Rilke sells bananas. A few doors down, an old fart Rumpelstiltskin runs a baker shop. She's always explainin where names like that come from, but I forget. Too much other stuff to worry about.

San Sebastián is another beef with my dad. He calls it a slum, a barriada. He's always gripin about me holing up on the wrong side of the tracks. So what, if that's all I can fucking afford! But he won't help me, damn him. He says it's outta principle, but I think he just wants to put the pressure on. If I don't leave the campesina, I can just go to hell. My mom wants me to ditch Reina too, and go back to Queens and stay with her. She's a real Latina mother. Chiara says Italian moms are the same about their sons. Holding on, never lettin go.

My parents love their grandchildren for sure, their nietos. Either one woulda been glad to take em in, if they could get rid of Reina. But they aren't like the average Canubans. Most of us say we're Catholic, but we don't take it too serious. We just live and let live.

My parents aren't like that, nooo-ooo-ooo. They're Protestants, Evangélicos. They talk about doin good, but they don't. Around here they look at my dad as a leader, un jefe. He preaches at the Church of Prophecy. In newspapers, he writes a column, La Biblia Nos Dice Así—The Bible Tells Us So.

I don't think it's fair the way my folks blame Reina for

my problems. I've had a few run-ins with the law, I admit, but that's not her fault. I'm not a hard crook, anyway. I've only done a couplea months in jail, for minor offenses. Yeah, I sold some grass, some yerba, and I wrote a false check, maybe two. But both times, I swear I got framed. I just happen to know the people behind that shit cause they're livin in my barrio. When the heat turned up, they used me for a fall guy.

Both times I didn't stay in prison for long. The worst part was tryin to keep cool, not beat anybody up, else they make you stay longer. The prisoners were always givin me shit, tryin to stick their dick up my ass. But when I took mine out and showed em what a big pinga I got, they shut up in a hurry. I turned the table on two or three of em, just to get my rocks off. Served em right to get fucked. Hell, they probably liked it. If you're a macho like me, you gotta watch out for your image. Stay strong. Get people's respect. Sure, I'm a softie inside me. But if they want a hard ass, I gotta give em a show.

Well, I guess it's late enough to sneak in the house. I just hope the chicos don't wake up. I don't want trouble with Reina right now. She's mad cause we're behind on the rent. Coño! So what else is new? I do the best I can, but she likes to bitch. I don't know who's worse, Héctor or her! Or Chiara! Everybody's always gettin on my case!

Sure enough, Amado rings me at eleven this morning. He doesn't waste any words: I'm coming to see you tonight. It's gonna be good. — His tone tells me exactly what he means.

I've lounged around in bed long enough. Time for a cup of English Breakfast, a holdover from my nanny; I always postpone coffee till after lunch.

After I stow my pijamas away, I can't decide what to put on. On my first trip to Canuba, in 1979, I noticed that adults never wear shorts—not even bermudas—despite the tropical heat. By now, a year or so later, I copy the locals. Sometimes I still dress in black, Manhattan's signature hue. Come to think of it, that's the color Sicilian grandmas like, though they'd disapprove of my slacks and baggy shirts.

No black today: I'll skip the urban mourning. But I don't own any pastels, so popular among the women here. On me, they'd seem out of character. White is as far as I'll go—all white, down to my canvas espadrilles. In the mirror, I resemble a female orderly, or an acolyte. Either one would fit the bill! I often feel like a nurse in a holy madhouse. Especially on Sundays, when the Barrio Antiguo swarms with altar boys. Ptarmigans, minus the snow.

I step outside, heartened by the stainless blue sky... though I'm glad we have these stately trees, to shield us from the scorching sun. They're specimens of ficus religiosa, like Buddha's fig tree in Bodh Gaya—though nobody knows that here but my monkish friend, Horacio.

Lazily, I dawdle around the buttresses next to my house: as misshapen as the apse, they extrude from the cathedral like a monstrous tail. Turning into a wide alleyway on the other side, I survey the leviathan's full length. This is Our Lady of the Light Divine, known to Canubans as 'Luz Divina'—the second-oldest church in the hemisphere.

As always, I admire the rose-colored stone, the terra-cotta roof and lopsided belfry. The building dates from 1524, before an architect had reached the island, as you can tell by glancing at its walls. Here and there, dollops of crumbled brick bandage the mistakes. Pasted together in stages, the edifice seems weirdly out of joint. A bishop from Spain designed it—in an outmoded style, more late-Gothic than Renaissance.

It's amazing to contemplate, but the masons must have been Taíno slaves. Imagine them stacking up this massive pile in a virgin forest, where only frond-roofed huts existed before... In Mexico or Peru, the Indians had built entire cities of stone; the Europeans couldn't impress them. Here, the Taínos must've been dumbfounded—or filled with dread. And they were right: the worst was yet to come.

I hear the server tinkling the altar bells. The Elevation... I tiptoe through the entrance, watching the Archbishop raise the host. 'Hoc est corpus meum.' 'This is my body.' I've always found those words both simple and magnificent. They say nothing more—and nothing less—than the mystery of life itself.

Most Canubans don't go to Mass anymore. The nave is less than half full, so I can visit the first two chapels unobtrusively. One of them houses a life-size carving of the Last Supper, in brightly painted wood; it 'anticipates the masterpiece by Aleijadinho,' as the guidebook points out. True—but what about the 'sacred mount' of Varallo? Italy came first, then Brazil. Santiago Columbus, Christopher's nephew, commissioned the sculpture here from a second-tier Castilian, Julio Montalvo.

Montalvo only made a few sketches before his death—luckily for us, since the project was completed by Taíno artists. With Santiago's support, they blindsided the priests, modifying the work with many touches of their own. The Native American traits of the faces never fail to move me… Then there are the bracelets and feather belts… Judas Iscariot's Spanish crown, an outrageous dig at the conquerors… and best of all, Christ decked out as a Taíno cacique, a band of gold encircling his head.

In the next chapel, the same master craftsmen portrayed the Way of the Cross. Here there are seven statues, including one of Santiago himself. Kneeling to the left, dressed like a chieftan, he kisses the ground where Jesus just walked. St. Simon, St. John the Beloved, the Blessed Virgin, and St. Magdalen stumble by, racked by despair.

They weep as if their world has come to an end—as the Taíno's soon would.

Off to the right, a singular figure leans forward, glaring defiantly. Despite his Western robe, he wears a shaman's insignia: a scarlet cap and yellow-beaked mask, the totemic marks of the woodpecker clan. You can still make out traces of reddish-orange dye on his narrow, claw-like hands. Officially, he's said to symbolize the 'conversion of the pagans.' But that doesn't explain the ironic sneer on his lips…

As the faithful rise for Communion, I sneak back outside. A discordant Parisian building with an egg-shaped dome fills the northern edge of the plaza: the Invalides in miniature, down to the greyish-yellow stone. The French imported just enough ballast to lend the Ursuline Convent a thin veneer, as shallow as their impact on the country. They only lasted from 1670 to 1692, when the Spanish wrenched Canuba back from the Sun King's fleet. He had to accept the lesser island to the east, Bonaventura, as a consolation prize. His ministers promptly styled it 'Bonaventure'; its capital, San Francisco, became 'Saint-François'—though Canubans often insist on the earlier place-names.

Heading past the Belle Époque tower, I continue toward the square's eastern flank. Behind a wrought-iron gate, the Church of St. James nestles in a shady graveyard. The English founded this neo-Gothic chapel to celebrate their victory in 1839. Across from the portal, I sit down for a while on my favorite bench, at the feet of Captain Drake. From all directions, the pealing bells summon worshippers of every stripe.

It's marvelous on a day like this to bask in the greenish light... I love the way it sifts and ripples through the ficus leaves. Thank God I gave up my life as a journalist in the Big Apple. Too much pressure! Here in the tropics, at last I can relax.

Families amble by, the men in crisp white cottons, the women in organdy frocks. Like their parents, the children vary disconcertingly. Blacks with poker-straight hair. Blondes with cornrows of plaits. Redheads with Utamaro eyes... They drift along on a bubbly stream of laughter, like the curtain-raiser in an outdated farce.

Mamma mia! It's a quarter past one! I'm late for my lunch with Lamia. She'll let me have it, for sure. Oh well, never mind! In Canuba, time is elastic... And the restaurant's only two blocks away.

Lamia Metaxis, El Mediterráneo, the same day

My gonzo father picked such a boring place for his 'gourmet' joint. And I mean boooring. I've never liked the old part of town: too cramped, too run-down. And the trashy neighbors! I guess it reminds him of that Greek hole-in-the-road where he grew up. I'm glad my mother's Canuban: I got my sexiness from her—but without her pelo malo! I hate bad hair.

I'm not used to waiting like this. Who does that Sicilian skank think she is? She better move her ass right now! I'm usually late myself, come to think of it. But that's me, and this is her.

I wouldn't let on to Papa, but this outdoor café in front of the restaurant isn't so bad. The 'square' is more like a triangle, and the flowerpots are kinda cute. Pink and white hibiscus. Those creeps with their demitasses think they're SOOO chic… The tables look ridiculous, though. Clunky round stones. Oh, I get it: broken columns from Greece. Talk about obvious!

It's not classy to have that beanstalk César at the door. You can put him in a blue uniform and silver epaulets, but he's still a neanderthal. He grins so much I wonder if he's hitting on me. 'Don't worry, Señorita Lamia. The Italian lady will be here soon.' The nerve of him, addressing me that way! She must've told him we've got a date today. She has lunch here all the time, and she's such a blabbermouth.

Well, I'm not going to stand around outside. Maybe there'll be some action at the bar… This inside patio is a moonscape, except for a palm or two. A bunch of stone floors and arches, but no pizzazz. Only two choices. You can eat al fresco with the gringos, in their tacky shorts and tank tops. Or avoid the midday glare in this Flint-stone gallery: I've reserved the least awful corner, shady and cool.

Bingo! The bar IS worth it today. Seven young guys! And they're hunky too. When I saunter up, they start nudging each other. Men are all the same!

Hola, we're from Colombia! one of them says.

Must be from Bogotá.

Smart girl! How'd you know?

Been there on a concert tour. I was a huge success, especially with the dudes.

No me digas! I can see why!

I make a pirouette. They're not used to a woman being assertive. When I was in Colombia, they did seem kinda uptight. Compared to Canubans, everybody is!

Another one pipes up: Concert tour. Are you a singer?

No, better than that! I play the cello. Ever hear of it? — Only three of them know what I'm talking about. The rest just sit there with their mouths open. Men are so dumb! — I'm a world-class musician. I'd really be famous, if I practiced more.

Why don't you, then?

I'm too busy humping my boyfriends. — Now I've got their attention. They fall all over themselves, drawing up a stool for me. — So what brings you to Puerto Indio, chicos?

They start jabbering a mile a minute, but there's only

one thing on their brains: ME! They belong to a rugby team, they say. Here for an important match tomorrow. The Pan American Cup. They brag about how they're going to win, etc., etc.

I lead them on. 'Isn't that great?' 'You guys are something else!' You gotta feed their vanity...

Out of the corner of my eye, I catch sight of Chiara. She finally made it. César is seating her at our table. He always treats her like royalty, but he should remember who's who. Well, she'll just have to wait a while. It's not to get back at her, I swear! A little lesson, maybe. The boys swill their Canuba Libres, hanging on my every word. Rum and Seven Up: the sugar goes to their heads. I write down my phone number, then air kiss them good-bye. I let them get away with a frisky hug or two—just as a teaser...

Now I'm ready for Chiara. I know exactly what makes her tick, so I give her the FULL treatment. I pride myself on being a femme fatale. Fingering my blouse, I sashay across the patio. 'Undulate,' she calls it.

She busses me on both cheeks. Right, left, all'italiana. I'm implacable. One side in Canuba, you idiot. I was hoping somebody'd kidnapped you.

She clams up. I stick my lips out and pout: First you were late, and now you're making me miss those rugby dudes! I'm not going to share them, no matter how hard you beg. We're having lunch, just you and me.

She still can't manage a word. I try to pep her up a bit.

What's the matter, cat got your tongue? Don't you speak English anymore? Italiano? Français? Deutsch? You're supposed to be learning Español.

I eye her up and down. Hey, you're Marian the Librarian! Not the strong, silent type... Come on, SAY something!

She stutters. I'm j-j-just savoring the view.

All right, go ahead. I strike a few poses, and she leans back in her chair. Between the table and the wall, I hike up my skirt to my thong. Wispy as floss. Hilo dental, we call it. I keep my vagina shaved, and that makes her salivate.

I chatter away. Somebody's gotta talk! — My hair's lighter than before. But it's not bleached, in case you're wondering. Well, maybe just a teeny little touch... It's my new look... Anyway, your time's up. The waiter's getting a hard-on. Come to think of it, I should be charging you for this...

I'll pay anything... — Now she's made up for being late!

My price is too high. You can't even buy me lunch: it's on the house.

My father's a typical Greek—he says so himself: always hustling to make a buck. To hedge his bets, he dubbed this place El Mediterráneo. Couscous, Turkish meatballs, paella, bruschetta, lasagna, bouillabaisse. Whatever he thinks will sell. Chiara won't touch the Italian dishes. I don't blame her!

I order moussaka and Canuban beer for both of us. —

And make that SNAPPY! — You have to bullwhip these waiters, like any other men. — It's the fastest dish, Chiara. The cooks are from my papa's village. They keep that gunk in the kitchen to feed their faces.

What's the rush? she whimpers. Always hamming it up as poor little me.

I blow her a raspberry, and down a bottle of Papagayo. The local brew. Canuban-style, on the brink of freezing. When the moussaka comes, I pack it away on the double. I don't like to piddle with my food. Chiara's just the opposite. They take all day to eat in Italy. She's hardly finished half her plate when I lose my patience. I jump up and hurry her to the street. — Let's get outta here before my papa shows up.

As soon as I hit the sidewalk, I slow down. I always tell Chiara she walks too fast. It's a bad habit she picked up in New York. Here it's too hot. We barely drag our feet along, to keep from sweating. She says I move like a turtle. Well, she can kiss my ass.

THAT way, I tell her. We turn down a car-jammed street and stop in front of a small Colonial house. I stick my head through the window. Hey, Fulano! What's-Your-Name, the tubby butt with the long dick! — There's a hullabaloo in the back room. — What? Don't tell me you're screwing your wife for a change! Move over, we'll do a four-way!

His voice booms out. You goddam bitch, get outta here.

Bitch yourself! Takes one to know one. Serves you right for standing me up last night… — I've made my point, so now I'm ready to beat it. — I'll be back in an hour or two for the best part. Save me the concón for dessert!

The dried-up rice at the bottom of the pot! It's all so hilarious, I'm screaming like a guinea hen. But Miss Priss is upset. She purses her lips: That was a naughty trick.

Oh, just some bad, dirty fun. Don't be so serious. I throw my head back and shake my hair. I can't stop giggling.

In Plaza Drake, a dark-green truck pulls up near the steps. Why they ever put those stairs there, I don't know. Fucks up the traffic… Oh God! I don't want THIS driver to see me. Sure enough, he gets out. So now I have to introduce them: Chiara, Ángel María. Miss Boring, Mister Boring. — They know I'm not kidding!

Ángel María, she sighs lamely. That's an unusual combination these days, even in Italy.

The way she's licking her chops, I can tell she's got the hots for him. He's an old hook-up of mine, but I don't like him anymore. He runs out of steam, just when it counts the most. Oh, he's attractive, I'll grant him that. Curly brown hair, grey-blue eyes. His rugged jaw gives him a manly look. Swimming, tennis, polo. He even tickles the ivories! But he's not a hard hitter in bed.

Yep, he starts whining, right off the bat. — Lamia, Lamia. I just came from the restaurant. I was looking for you!

He's champing at his leash like a dog, per usual. I don't give him the time of day. — Maybe I'll call you next month, bub. But don't hold your breath. My fuck list is ten miles long.

Chiara cringes. She's such a little nun! As soon as we're out of earshot, I give her the lowdown. What a meathead that guy is! He keeps asking me to marry him. Sure, he's from an OK family, and he went to college in Gringolandia. Somewhere in Texas, was it? He's an engineer. Ambitious too. Probably makes piles of money. But who needs his dough, when I've got my own? As soon as Papa croaks, I'll be fixed for life. I don't have to sell my cunt! He can have it for free, now and then. IF I'm in the right mood!

I can tell what she's thinking. She'd LOVE to have a piece of me too. But out loud, she fakes it: He seems nice enough.

I have to set her straight: Oh, all he ever does is party, so he ends up plastered. Half the time he can't even get it up… Anyway, enough small talk. Tea time! Let's have a party of our own.

By now, we're in that empty house of hers. Oh, why tea? she pants. Don't you want something stronger? — She's dying to get me liquored up.

Hey, I was just kidding, dimwit. Tea! I can't stand the stuff. Here's what I mean by tea. It's the only damn thing that makes me proud to be Canuban. — With people like her, you have to take charge, they're so ditsy. I stick my hand in the cabinet and pull out a green, pear-shaped bottle. Ron Real—Royal Rum—the best on earth! Sold nowhere but here. I grab a couplea glasses too. I lob one to Chiara, to check her reflexes. Whoops! She almost blows it!

We step into the courtyard. She built an iron staircase in the corner, so she can climb to the roof like a tomcat. She's always wasting money. But the view isn't bad. When we reach the top, I hoot: TA-DA! Every time, I feel like I just discovered the spot.

She keeps some chairs up here—even planted some special flowers for the birds. I have to rib her a bit. Is that why you came to our stupid island? To watch the birds? We've got plenty of them! Wow, look at them suck.

Miss Particular, as always. Now she has to correct me. In English, they're called bananaquits, she says. Everybody likes flowers. Don't you?

No, I can't stand em. Too natural. I like 'birds,' though. Some of my best friends are 'ducks.' — The first thing I taught her was that here, 'pájaros' and 'patos' are queers. — Bananaquits! Yeah, once they get their claws on one, they never quit. — I lick my lips. — Yummm. Me, too!

The cat's got her tongue again. She sets the bottle on the table. We sit down and fill our glasses. I keep teasing her, to pass the time. — Why don't we plan an orgy? *A Midsummer Night's Dream*, right here on this roof? It's a real lovers' bower. As Titania, you could queen it over the fairies. And Amado would make a slam-dunk Bottom. On second thought, it wouldn't work. Amado is more of a TOP. — I laugh at my own joke; nobody else will. Then I knock back a double shot of rum.

She smiles a tired smile. Ha, ha, ha. Excuse me if I yawn. Héctor made that same wisecrack last night. — She's getting uppity. But I want to hear every detail: such a prime piece of gossip. Several of those gooey flowers plop on the table. She switches the subject. — I see why Canubans call them rain-flowers. They're always falling, like a shower. It's quite a job to sweep them up.

No grapevine today; all right, I give up. — That's why you've got your Light Divine. — I'm not talking religion, not that I ever would. Her cleaning lady's name is Luz Divina, same as the cathedral—like half the women around here. An old frump in her late fifties. She's stubborn as hell: I bet she gives Chiara a lot of lip.

Hmmm, I'd just as soon do without her.

You have to have somebody! You're right, though. Any Canuban would've fired her long ago. You mollycoddle that lazy hag. But as I always say, people get the maid they deserve. And you deserve the worst!

Sometimes she's glum, sometimes she chuckles. Once I start, I can drink till the cows come home. Today I gab the whole bottle away. After a while, she's not listening to me anymore. She's only staring at me, like a crocodile about to chomp. Hahaha. I know what she wants. The most romantic time of day is almost here… the pink douchebag of sunset. Well, TOO BAD. I'll have to excuse myself.

This was fun, Chiara. You sure know how to lay on the rum. But it's pretty late, and I've got a very heavy date tonight. It'll take me at least two hours to primp. I've got to look like a movie star. And put on my toughest diaphragm. Plus have an enema, just in case. A whole rugby team!

Yes… they might play rough.

She makes a frowny face. Hah! I bet she's got a date tonight too. Oh, she's a sneaky one! At the door, I air kiss her cheek. — Thanks again for the booze. See you soon, Chiara. I promise! — I flick my wrist, turn around, and whisk her out of my mind.

Chiara, Plaza Drake, a while later

Lamia: after we say good-bye, she edges forward like a glacier… or a tectonic plate. I loiter for a while, clocking her sedimentary progress. Front or back, the strata are superb.

I had a boyfriend once who went crazy over rugby. In my student years at Padua, it was seen as an exotic sport—a bit elitist and posh. Sometimes I'd watch him and his pals wallow in the mud… Maybe she'll take on the whole team. All fifteen of them. Mauls, rucks, and full-blown scrums. I wouldn't put it past her.

She can't doll herself up any more than she already has. That frilly magenta number with the yellow top was too much for lunchtime. As for her evening wear, it borders on parody, even for Canuba... Well, I hope she makes it back home in that dented beetle of hers: fire-engine red, of course. She's had so many fender benders, it looks like a squashed ladybird.

After the rum, I need some herbal tea before Amado arrives. Might as well enjoy the sunset! Clutching my pot of linden, I go to the roof again.

I love it up here. The tower vista is panoramic, but this view is more focused and refined. The cathedral and convent wink through the swaying palms. The clouds hang so low, they seem like a mist caressing my face—a Lamian steam... Good grief! Why fantasize about her, of all people! I try to knock some some sense into myself. I've never felt so smitten by a woman. What's coming over me?

I should dismiss her as nothing but an objet d'art—or Edelkitsch, kitsch with pretensions. Her beauty is totally screwball: her skin is as brown as a hazelnut, but her hair is platinum blonde. Her eyes mutate alarmingly from blue to green, amber to amethyst. She's from a different planet.

She likes to wear patent leather heels—high and spiked, as in the fifties. That miniskirt she had on today, and her half-buttoned blouse, would brand her as a 'puttana' in Sicily, a whore. Even by Canuban standards, she was overdressed—and underdressed—for early afternoon. Her mascara rivaled Taylor's in *Cleopatra*... But why should I quibble? In the tropics, everything is over the top.

More and more, I feel at home here. I was afraid leaving New York might hurt my career, but it's been just the opposite. It hasn't taken me long: now I'm an 'expert' on the Caribbean. What a laugh! In the travel mags, you can invent reams of lies, as long as you're glib enough... Anyway, it's amusing to write about these quirky islands. They complement my standby, the Eastern Med.

Manhattan was so hectic, so modern. Puerto Indio is soothing, like a tepid bath. Here I'm delving into a slower world, retreating into my past... It's like my childhood in Sicily. All over the Barrio Antiguo, bells are tolling for vespers, just as they did in Nodica long ago.

The Spaniards constructed many churches in their first years on the island. Gold-lust fueled the conquest, no doubt about that. But some of their envoys really wanted to 'evangelize the Indians,' as the Catholic Kings in Toledo claimed. Save their souls, not their bodies, you understand. Already on his second voyage, Columbus brought Dominican monks to Canuba. He named the harbor 'Puerto San Tomás de Aquino,' as a homage to Thomas Aquinas, their greatest theologian.

But that's where the plot begins to thicken—between the lines. The Admiral's nephew, Santiago, changed the city's name to 'Puerto Indio' in 1510. It seems he had deep misgivings about the 'Domini Cani,' the 'Lord's Dogs.'

After all, Dominicans staffed the Inquisition; maybe he feared they would torture the Taínos, using them as guinea pigs for their cruel techniques. The rack, the strappado, the iron maiden, the pear of anguish, the heretics' fork—or a new torment, 'la tortura de agua,' recently used in the Algerian War. As I understand it, you half-drown the victims, then jerk their heads above the water just in time.

Some historians have speculated that Santiago opposed the Dominicans because his mother, a Florentine, had suffered under their gruesome preacher, Savonarola. A closet Humanist, he preferred the learned Benedictines; at any rate, he was the only Caribbean governor who invited them to the region. In his correspondence, he praises the Franciscans, too. In the early sixteenth century, they Christianized many Taínos, a campaign they later extended to the native Mexicans. As a tribute to their order, Santiago christened the smaller island under his rule 'Bonaventura,' the Latin epithet for their 'Seraphic Doctor of Theology.' He granted its fledgling port, San Francisco, the status of a secondary capital.

Santiago was onto something: St. Francis, who gloried in nature, would have marveled at this virginal, unfallen world. Here he would have presided like Adam over Eden, bestowing names on the plants and animals. He would've embraced the Indians as his siblings, just as he eulogized his 'fratello sole' and 'sorella luna'—Brother Sun and Sister Moon—in the Umbrian hills.

As it turned out, the Franciscans dispensed more charity than Santiago had foreseen, and now they faced a dilemma. The Taíno were receptive to the Gospel; its message concorded with their peaceable ways. On the other hand, many of the colonists—the so-called 'Christians'—were gold-grubbing riffraff, who wasted no mercy on the weak.

On the nearby island of Hispaniola, Santiago's uncle Christopher had reduced the Indians to slavery. His rule was so pitiless that even to this day, Canubans dread that his name will invoke a curse—in Taíno, a fucú. They allude to him only as 'the Admiral…' Despite Santiago's doubts about the order, a Dominican priest, Montesinos, sounded the first alarm in 1511. He loudly denounced Spanish atrocities in the 'New' World: 'new' only to the European invaders, of course.

'Do Native Americans have souls?' Theologians argued the pros and cons in Valladolid from 1550 to 1551. Paradoxically—from Santiago's point of view—the Dominican friar Las Casas defended indigenous rights against a Humanist skeptic, Sepúlveda. By this time, in the Caribbean, the debate had become purely academic: the Indians' mortal flesh had already been destroyed.

Dark thoughts for a luminous evening… Night is coming on. I'd better go down the stairs while there's still enough light, and freshen up for my latter-day Taíno—Amado. His spirit is undaunted, and his flesh is blissfully intact.

Chiara conjectured she might accord me a visitation this afternoon, at some indeterminate, post-meridian hour. I ardently anticipate she will… Initially, I was irked when my brother fobbed her off on me; but now I have waxed quite fond of her, too. They were scholastic turtledoves when he was at the New York University and she was at the Universitas Princetoniensis; sooner or later, she was predestined to appear on our palmy, hedonic shores. Her inaugural 'weekend excursion' to Canuba perdured for a fortnight. Since then, on and off, she has sojourned on our insula for well over an annus. Catulo is always in such a commotion, he consigns the marginalia to me. I am the one who located her abode on Plaza Drake, and the turret she employs as a study—her cubiculum studiorum. She jubilates that combined, they amount to but a tertium of her expense for lodgings in New York.

I can easily perceive she is still enamored of my frater: his effervescent patter, his terpsichorean physique. She is not unique in this—though his snub proboscis must strike a high-born lady as déclassé. Ditto for his glabrous, penitentiary coiffure. Ditto for his lexicon, colloquial and obscene. By definition, Chiara cannot reverse the clock on their romance; nonetheless, unlike most of his quondam mistresses, she has remained an obeisant thrall. I wish I could profess the same of Lamia! She abhors Catulo now…

As a connoisseur of pulchritude, I can fully apprehend

why Chiara once beguiled her erstwhile swain. I might describe her as full-bodied—voluptuous though not Rubenesque. Her ankles and wrists are so svelte, I agonize that under torsion they might snap. I revere them on a par with her Phidian nose: corporeal emblems of her lineage, I daresay.

Like those optic orbs of hers... rotund and greenish grey. 'As glaucous as Athena's,' I often effuse, even if she chaffs me when I laud them. Her forebears worshipped the goddess: Sicily was a portion of 'greater Greece' in ancient times. Our father lectured us three boys on Magna Graecia, cartography in hand, when we were still but neophyte cubs. He was a learned classicist, albeit amateur, and he endowed us with our triple praenomina. 'You're my little Ro-*man* poets,' he liked to jest.

He inculcated us with Greek and Latin early on—and with an obsolescent English, too, his lingua franca as Canuba's 'diplomate plénipotentiaire.' I loyally deploy it to this day, with Miltonic grandiloquence: as a filial tribute, I have ossified myself into a rhetorical artifact. In our international institutes, we collected other tongues, wherever Espinosa sent him as Ambassador: Belgium, Taiwan, Austria, Botswana, Jordan, Denmark, Mongolia, et al. Between his postings, we always hied to our Alma Mater, the Colegio Jesuita in Puerto Indio; our education was variegated, to say the least.

Chiara's soul-searching gaze and contralto voice confounded me at first, but not anymore. Owing to the Normans' hegemony, blondes still proliferate in Sicily—or so I have been instructed. Though Chiara is not amongst them, her cheeks are peaches-and-cream. Her luxuriant mane is satiny, auburn, and fine as a mandarin's; alluringly, she unloosens it down to her clavicles. Now and again, she oscillates a tress with her tapering digitalia.

Our ancestry cannot compare with hers; all the same, in Canuba, our Miranda bloodline passes for august. For centuries, we have dwelt in our patrician manor on the Callejón del Platero. The silversmith who devised the structure must have prospered, since he erected six more in addition to his own. With the Ursuline Convent, they constitute the only relics of the French vignette in our island annals. Their facades are adorned with Grand Siècle motifs: pinioned dolphins, beribboned horses, seashells strung in garlands, parading sheaves of wheat...

We have converted the ground floor into a gallery of aesthetic vendibles: alas, we have to produce our quotidian bread somehow. Catulo thrives at his coastal caravansary, but Virgilio and I are idealistic wights, impecunious serfs of Apollo and the Nine. Our storefront comprises several windows, surmounted by a frieze depicting Artemis. On the left, she pines for the fair Endymion; on the right, she dismembers Acteon with her hounds. Behind the beveled, rectangular panes, I display a cornucopia of treasures: ligneous effigies, russet bottles from shipwrecks, and pumiced stones like nubile derrieres. You can never predict when a customer might meander past. We raise our ensign a mere five blocks from the Cathedralis Lucis Divinae, the celebrated fane of the Light Divine, and voyagers may chance our way as they navigate the tortuous Colonial maze.

While I await Chiara, I thrill to the choral music of Monteverdi: the most illustrious of all composers, barring none! She will auscultate his supernal genius, streaming through our oriel like a cataract. I am a musician to the marrow: alpha et omega, musicus sum.

I already detect her assaying the handle; to her perplexity, she ascertains that it is latched... Discreetly, she raps on the rosewood door. Three shorts and three longs: our cryptic code.

I am meticulously attired in tonalities of grey, as is my wont. Suede oxfords, tropical-wool trousers, and a silken Nehru shirt. She is arrayed in one of her snowy, garçonnesque ensembles. She makes mock of them as her 'Puerto Indio uniform.'

I uphold a certain formality. Instead of osculating her cheek, as vulgar Canubans would do, I plicate my hands in an aphonic Namaste.

She devolves the salutation. — Horacio, nobody would guess this is a shop.

Not for the nonce, my dear: I have occluded it for an interval. I was exulting in the harmony of the spheres;

and yet for *you*, I shall gladly relapse to the drab sublunar plane.

I bow to her amenably. She curtseys in response. This is part and parcel of our pantomime: a ritornello in our courtly score.

I admit her to our bazaar, and diminish the quire's full throat. The *Vespers of the Blest Virgin...* Chiara has doted on them since infancy, and so have I.

After some picayune palaver, she harps on a hackneyed theme. — Now that your health is better, Horacio, could you introduce me to the Third Person of the Trinity?

'The Trinity.' That is how the conoscenti advert to us. I am a conductor, and Catulo is a danseur. Since we are performers, we qualify as public entities. But our sibling Virgilio? As elusive as the Holy Ghost... We are convinced that he is an image-maker of superhuman caliber—although only Catulo and I have ever beheld his works.

Is her insistence fraying my nerves? I succumb to a dire tussiculation. — Better? With this cough? How lamentable that Virgilio cannot hail you with a reverential 'Ave Chiara.' He is amassing geo-specimens in Piedras Blancas.

Aporetically, she nods. Virgilio always has me obfuscate his whereabouts: his solitude must not be compromised.

Star-crossed Chiara, I regret that you must muddle through with me, your abject servant. — I cordially incline my head. — I still cannot penetrate why you grace us with your presence. A sophisticated Sicilian grandee—from Apple-upon-Hudson, Novum Eboracum!

Don't be ridiculous. You're the cosmopolites, not me. Anyway, I'm not certain I'm going to stay.

Come now, I susurrate to my internal audience: she is rankly deceiving herself. In the past few months, her passion for Amado has blossomed. And now the voltaic Lamia has galvanized her, too.

Dolefully, I shake my weary caput. — Incertitude, incertitude, my dear... You and I are affixed to the same hermaphrodite brig. Rudderless, we deviate across the watery globe; like you, I cannot disentangle the quandary of myself. Especially my illnesses: they never grant me a nanosecond of repose.

Sometimes she turns peremptory, but not today. I promulgate the wretched gazette of my ailments. The principal symptoms are anxiety, extenuation, and oversensitivity. I can only rely on two benedictions: the tonic properties of herbs, and the salvific potencies of prayer. Lately I have vested my aspirations in a Nepalese guru, who arrived just last month. He does his disciples 'a Himalaya of good,' as he declares in his kaleidoscopic brochure.

Chiara is overwhelmed by her own vexations, assuredly: the violoncello prodigy has martyrized her with concupiscence. Now she vituperates the seductress again. — I know Lamia was Poseidon's daughter, but the name has atrocious overtones. Didn't her parents ever read Keats?

I tap my enlightened cranium. — You allude to his opusculum about a serpent, who masqueraded as a woman? That must be why Catulo decries her as 'the Snake.'

Abruptly, in medias res, I hearken to the drumroll of knocking. Oh, the evening selection! With unaccustomed vigor, I locomote to the door.

Three maturing adolescents troop into the premises: two comely males and a delectable nymphette. One of the youths is obsidian and lanky, the other alabaster and thickset. Fortuitously, the damsel falls between those piquant extremes. All of them are nonchalantly at their ease, neither brash nor diffident. All are 'majors,' not minors—I have implemented my due diligence on that. And all are depraved: that seems auspicious, indeed.

Chiara is no simpleton. She must have inferred why I secured our emporium with lock and key. I present the striplings as 'Dakar Prince, Picasso, and Stalina.'

She rebels. — I know the nicknames here are outré— but aren't you pulling my leg?

All right, I fabricated 'Dakar Prince.' It beseems him, no? The other fellow is Pablo, so why not christen him 'Picasso'? He favors the artiste as a hirsute, twentyish pooch. And Stalina—her progenitors confected that moniker, as she affirmed through the telephonic device. I am gratified that she eschews her precursor's ominous 'moustaches.'

They grimace at us inanely; besides Antillean Spanish, stevedore English is all they comprehend. Please be so kind as to inspect the merchandise, I urge Chiara, while I determine my agenda with this triad. — I shepherd them to the rear of the corridor, to negotiate their emoluments.

As I contend with them sotto voce, Chiara canvasses our current miscellany. The varnished cedar shelves proffer our statues and masks, wrought from sylvan stuffs by consummate Bonaventurans. A few are polychromed, like the monuments in the Light Divine. She tarries before a substantial coffer of tinctured rocks. Some are ovoid, like those in the windows; others are oblong and flat, like flagstones propped on edge.

She has pored over most of these exempla before; but I have laid an ambuscade for her. The designs on our petroglyphs are usually abstract; yet today she will encounter a diptych of glove-size landscapes. I happen to know she composes poetry on the sly. These miniatures will entrance her, I ween. She will feel transported to a whitewashed hideaway, adrift on a sea of autumn leaves… and then to a hamlet at sunset, its mauve afterglow seeping through hill and dale.

Deserting my flock for a moment, I adjudge her temperature: Did you alight on anything you like?

Yes, these two landscapes.

Ergo, my dear, they are yours. — As I expected, that was an effortless transaction. But I desired her to acquire them out of altruism, too. I scrutinize her celestial visage. — In the entire repository, Chiara, those are the only nonpareils by Virgilio. He contributes a masterstroke to our repertoire now and then, when some flibbertigibbet leaves me in the lurch.

Though she feels rhapsodic, she refuses to let on. I only have twenty dollars in my pocket, she elucidates drily. That's a little less than thirty escudos. I'm sure they're worth more than that.

Infinitely more, my Minerva redux; they are utterly invaluable. — It titillates me to watch her squirm. — I shall conserve them for you, rest assured. Why not bestow a minute down payment? At the moment, twenty dollars would suffice. — I camber an eyebrow suggestively.

She forfeits the sum, and I secrete the exquisite gems in a cabinet. — Rapunzel, unless you require this venal trio for antics in your tower, I must animate them here.

No thanks. Amado and Lamia are more than I can handle, as it is.

We exchange our Namastes again, and she perambulates along the thoroughfare. I temporize for a while at the threshold. The gloaming: deliquescent, like me... On their way homeward, my neighbors agglomerate in the inconsequential grocery-bar, stridently braying the vox populi. Crepuscular umbrae spiral down, on distended wings...

Chiara must be deliberating what further monies I might exact from her. Twenty dollars more than the minimum, at any rate. That will hardly offend our bounteous patroness—no, not one whit. She is all too cognizant of our Miranda foibles: with us, vile specie incinerates to ash, puffed away by those rapacious zephyrs, our creditors. Yet we always have some face-cards up our sleeves to furbish the lucre again, like a phoenix renascent. Our Sicilian amica has probably heard that I ply a lucrative avocation on the side… as a brujo, a sorcerer deluxe. Unlike most, I concentrate on the high-end market: the educated and the affluent. They are the catechumens who covet mirabilia the most.

Low-end brujos are a tuppence a dozen. Not that they are worthless! Their glorious traditions hark back to Africa. They can cast puissant spells: induce a courtesan to fall in love with you, or pressure a fiendish foe into hanging himself.

I bedazzle my clients with beneficent magic: the healing arts. I transmogrify the age-old potions with a panoply of modern trends—crystals, astrology, imaging, auras, vibrations. Mutatis mutandis, I regenerate Antillean witchcraft in my own eclectic mode. Ah, if only I could cure myself!

As to the 'evening selection'—as Chiara must intuit—I would never dream of defiling those callow idols. What they do amongst themselves, whilst I keep vigil: that is their own affair. When Catulo is out of town, his procurers resort to me, his penniless fratellino. I confer half the orthodox stipend merely to 'look on beauty bare'—to the tintinnabulation of the gamelan, or of muted Tibetan bells... I forego physicality—in particular, the liquefying genitals—on ascetic grounds. Or so I like to allege. Verily, I say unto you: I nurture a phobia of venereal infirmities. I cannot hazard those, for heaven's sake, superadded to my other maladies!

Toi toi toi, as we melomanes exhort. Back to my lissome instruments: it is time to arrange a three-four minuet.

Chiara, on the way home

Horacio and his bag of tricks! I'm syncretic, too—as happy in an ashram as a Carmelite cell. I've been on dozens of retreats over the years, in Vedic, Catholic, and Buddhist communities, from India to South Korea to Japan. Meditation and prayer are closely allied, no matter what the outer trappings may be. But this New Age nonsense doesn't convince me.

If only I could meet Virgilio, I'm sure we'd see eye to eye. He revels in his inner exile, his hermitage of colors and shapes—of blanks and amorphousness. No manmade creed can house the universe, even if it creates the mosaics of Monreale, the Pantokrator of Cefalù. Our cathedral in Siracusa rests on Doric columns, robbed from a pagan god.

My parents value the Church 'less for function than for form,' as my father likes to quip, with a flippant moue. As for me, I cherish its essence but not its bigotry. Rebelliously, I endured an ultra-Catholic youth. 'Picciridda, let's go to Mass!' the nursemaids would say. The maudlin processions, the backbiting priests in Nodica... There I was everyone's 'little girl,' always being dragged to the Eucharist.

But at least it was still in Latin: I treasured each aureate syllable, preserved 'in saecula saeculorum,' or so we believed. Our cousin, the Bishop of Tragusa, taught me the grammar when I was six, and my uncle followed up with the *Eclogues*. After middle school, I wanted to enroll in our 'liceo classico,' to study Greek. But at fourteen, my parents packed me off to a convent academy near Lyon; it was ruled by a honey-tongued Mother Superior, Mère Angélique—no more sadistic than most.

I've chafed at the pettifogging hypocrisy of one and all. Isn't it strange that I've ended up in an enclave of clerics? I suppose I like to be in the thick of things. As I cross Plaza Drake, I can survey Caribbean history in a nutshell. A Spanish archbishop, French nuns, a British vicar—and hot on Europe's heels, the American boot. As elsewhere, incursions by the gringos taught the country who was boss, though they paid lip service to its 'sovereign independence.' A plaque on Drake's pedestal marks the latest US-Canuban pact.

I sometimes wonder why Washington tolerates the local strongman, Manfredo Espinosa: he's held power for decades. A bargain with the devil, no doubt… He may consort with Castro, but he allows for a mixed economy; it's state-directed without being communist. And there's gobs of corruption for the sycophants at his trough, including foreign investors. Above all, he kowtows to the Pentagon; his generals bark hup-hup when its orders descend from on high.

After the marines, Bible-thumpers brought up the rear. Mormons, Seventh Day Adventists, Jehovah's Witnesses, Pentecostals—pick your poison. Converts like Amado's parents lapped up the 'old-time religion' from them. In my opinion, Santería and Vodou have more to recommend them, since their roots run so deep: nothing could be more 'old-time' than African animism. Classicists don't want to admit it, but it closely resembles the cults that deified every stream, forest, and mountain in ancient Greece.

Readers of my articles often ask me: Are Canubans European or Indian, African or Latino? All I can reply is that they're Taíno and Spanish—thanks to Indian intermarriage with the early colonists—blended with a jambalaya of later arrivals. African, first of all. But also British, French, Chinese, East Indian, Japanese, Danish, Dutch, and on and on: the spicy ethnic stew of the Caribbean. A variant of Spanish is what stuck, though Canubans speak some English, too.

The elites julienne the languages constantly; the rank

and file shuffle them like well-thumbed cards. The Anglo words they've adopted are often hard to decipher: 'Vivaporú,' for instance, their euphonic version of Vicks VapoRub. Sometimes spellings conflict, according to the source. Orthographers would write a slangy tag for phallus as 'güevo,' with a diaeresis; laymen pronounce it 'gwaybo,' but scrawl it as 'guebo' on bathroom walls. Or so Catulo informs me. 'They don't mean "gay-beau," darling—or maybe they do!'

The 'freely elected' dictator, Espinosa, extols 'Iberian culture'—with a blatantly racist intent. In one of his early administrations, he even changed the currency from pesetas back to 'escudos,' a term the Mother Country abandoned in 1868. He disdains 'African additives,' especially from Bonaventure. Immigrants from the other island are often called 'Bonos' here for short, with a condescending edge. But this seems better than 'prieto,' the Canuban equivalent of the n-word, as far as I can tell—though many people claim the harshness depends on the tone. As to 'moreno,' all agree it sounds more neutral, a throwback to the Moors of Spain.

Why are whites so resentful of blacks, when we're the ones who've enslaved the entire world?

The riddle pursues me as I make a stiff drink, then clatter up the steps to the roof. Darkness permeates the knotted strands of corollas and leaves... Night tips the scales on the brazenness of day: not a threat, but a fulfillment.

I guess I'll take pity on Chiara, and leaven her prosaic routine. She deserves some theatrical relief. Horacio dilutes the Miranda family charm; I dish it out full-strength!

Oh, I know what's afoot. He fancies he's making headway with Chiara, but he's wrong. I keep telling him to ditch those gold rimmed glasses. Maybe he should try some contacts: it might help a bit, I don't know. He's so damn bloodless and frail! His 'skin' is more like onionskin. His strawberry mouth and beady black eyes make it look even paler.

He could do something with that frizzy hair of his, at least. Slick it down—or shave it off, like me. It's the same color as those freckles on his nose. If I weren't used to him, he'd give me the creeps. And that voice! It's like a little boy's—or a little girl's—piping up and down. His sick-talk and stilted English don't fool me. Underneath it all, he's tough as nails. When it comes to vocab, I'm a fuddy-duddy and a punk, an 'Ancien' and a 'Moderne'; I like to mix and match.

I honestly wish I had more time for Chiara. Sure, I invited her down; but I never dreamed she'd loaf around so long. Her thing for me goes way back, ever since we were in college. We even audited some courses together at NYU; she got credit for them at Princeton. One on Melville, another on Jacobean drama. Back then, I was into that scholar baloney, footnotes and all.

There's been a five-year gap, but we're still close friends. I don't want her to get too slushy, that's all. In New York, we often made love, drowning out the police sirens with Wagner. It was grandiose—almost a Liebestod, or 'Liebesleben'—but now I find her too tame. Pomona's my steady woman, when I want one. Knock-down-drag-out, the way I like em! Brünnhilde—not Isolde.

Our lovelorn Chiara is a pinched, congenital spinster; flounder though she will, the Vatican maimed her as a tyke. She's a female castrato—unfit for the choir, since her voice still broke, falling to sub-alto. If I say so myself, it was clever of me to shunt her off on Amado. Now she thinks she's tripping the light fantastic! In fact, it's just the night-light bombastic. Topsy-turvy, and the devil catch the hindmost. To me we're all just balsam marionettes, jostling at the Kleist cabaret!

Chiara takes me back to New York in the seventies, when I spawned the Florence F***ing Jenkins Operettes. As Norma or Turandot, I was the draggiest queen of them all. And our chorus line: every night, we outdid the blooming Rockettes! That's how I got my start as a chore-ographer. Oh well, that was then...

I hope Chiara doesn't misread me when I hug her, poveretta—poor little lamb! Unlike my two brothers, I'm touchy-feely by nature; I can hardly keep my hands to my-self. I'll adapt to anything, high life or slums, as long as I can flirt. Canuba isn't Lapland, so everybody takes me in stride.

For the hotel biz, I dress like a preppy—Brooks shirts and Church's shoes. At the office I'm as square as Clark Kent, with a poker instead of a pecker up my ass. Oh yes, that's natural to me, too. I swear by you, Cosmic Walt, bard of the Americas: 'I am large, I contain multitudes.' If you scratch my water-cooler veneer, you'll bash into a superhero—or superheroine. I'm a wild thang, as wild as they come!

It's a shame I have to eke out a pittance at the Hermosa Beach Resort, eighty miles from town. 'Hospitality management'—it doesn't get any duller than that. But it's the only way I can make ends meet. Dance doesn't bring home the bacon—not in Canuba—and I have *very* expensive tastes. Thank God I still commute to the capital twice a month, for face time with our associates. Chiara's on my Rolodex as a 'tourism maven'; and today's her providential day! Mine too: around her, I can strut my stuff. Yeah, it's not hip anymore to act like a flamer. Yada yada, Mary Beth, I know: we're all machos now, even the fems. But for me it's fun to play a sassy onnagata again—like on our Operettes stage, near Sheridan Square...

Soon as Chiara opens the door, I sweep her off her feet to our theme song, 'Light My Fire.'

She feigns annoyance: Put me down, you maniac! — I'm swinging her around like a ragdoll. She's always said she's dumbstruck by my strength. But in modern dance, 'wiry' is our middle name!

She keeps it up. — If you love me, you'll let me go. And beg me to forgive you.

Love? What's that? — She's looks so bereft, I might as well indulge her. I set her down and kneel, blinking my soulful brown eyes. — Oh mamma, I've been a bad little catamite. Molto cattivo. — I press my face between her legs, and spoof a few sobs. — You want me to commit hari-kiri? Like Madama Butterfly?

No, I'd rather kill you myself. — She pats my gleaming noggin. Back in the day, she used to call me her 'cue ball cutie.'

Why don't you get me drunk instead? It's almost the cocktail hour.

Oh, all right! You're a lost cause.

Hail *Mary*! But that's the only one I'll say!

She snags a bottle of Absolut, while I bring the glasses and ice. Once we're semi-crocked on the deck upstairs, I start my skit again.

Girlfriend, I just can't decide! Who should I be when I grow up? The Queen of England? Or the Pope? They're both the poohbahs of goofy cults, with oodles of bells and smells. They've both got drop-dead palaces, outlandish gowns, and beefcake guards in campy duds.

Don't forget the castles, for weekend getaways...

And the cash. The Crown Estate. The Unholy Spirit

Bank. — I smack my lips. — Mirror, mirror, on the wall. Who's the queerest of us all?

Self-satire on steroids: she lets her hair down, too… — Let's see. Maybe you'd do less damage as the Queen. Besides, you're halfway there.

I jump up and swagger around: Come on, you shiftless puttana, you have to carry my train. — She tags along behind me, lifting my velvet caboose. — That's it, Chiara, all six yards! Heave ho!

Oh darling, what's a girl to do? The Queen's outfit is fab. But she only wears it to Westminster once a year. Mostly she slogs around at Balmoral in rubber boots. Too stodgy for me! Now the Pope, he's in drag all the time.

True, but then he barges into people's bedrooms, telling them what to do. — She collapses back into her chair.

I bless the faithful from my balcony, singing a tune: You got rhythm, you got rhythm. Who could ask for anything more? — Then I stoop to mundane prose. — Gimme a break, girlfriend! Nobody pays attention to that hokum anymore. Not here.

They do back home! And it's not just birth control. If His Holiness hiccups, Italians tout it as a revelation. Divorce, abortion, same-gender marriage, sexual freedom, women's lib: it's all one giant taboo!

Boo! I echo, wagging a papal finger. Boo-hoo-hoo. Merry munchkins, you merit somebody better than that humbug, the Pontifex of Oz. You know how much I love the Belpaese. The people, the art, everything.

You couldn't love Italia more than I do! I may be your mamma, but she is mine.

Of course, bimba-babe, but you're right about the hang-ups. On the map, your worn-out boot seems more like a syphilitic cock. Cazzo! It's falling apart! Maybe I should stick to Queenery. — I parade around for her again, waving the little wave.

She snickers: Oh, but you're a he-man, too. That's what makes this place so unpredictable.

Damn straight, and I'm not just hamming it up. Maybe I'm really Joe Palooka. — I flex my muscles, like an alpha baboon. — I'm Popeye the sailor man, I'm Popeye the sailor man! — Then I switch to plainchant, crossing myself. — Pope-eye, to the Curia, et in saecula...

She cuts me off: Spare me! Can't you keep still for a minute? You have the attention span of a two-year old.

I do? What did you just say? — I wiggle my ears, to get her goat. — Oh mamma, tell me a bedtime story! Dai, pretty please!

I lay my head on her lap, and she tucks me in for the night. — All right, tesoro, my love. I'll tell you a joke I heard from Lamia. What's the difference between a straight Canuban and a gay Canuban?

Great balls of fire, she stole that one from me a century ago! — I raise my hand like a teacher's pet. — I know the answer, Miss Brodie: Two beers! Or two escudos!

Two escudos? That's a twist! Do you mean gay for pay?

Hah! You need to step out more, girlfriend. Those words mean nothing here—neither one of them! If money changes hands it's only a pretext, just like the beers.

We sing-along together this time: You maaaade me doooo it. I didn't wanna do it, I didn't wanna do it…

That's it, Barbie doll. Here everybody's gay, and everybody's not. To put it another way, even the maricones are bi! Just ask my mistress, Pomona. As to pay, what's two escudos?

Depends on how poor you are. But no, seventy cents won't keep the wolf from the door.

Grrrrr… You mean me?

I make like I'm driving a car, hunched over the steering wheel. — Vroooom, screeeech! I haven't told you about the taxi-driver I met today. He was too chubby, and waaay over the hill. I didn't sit up front and shift his gears, if you know what I mean. But holy cow, was he talkative! Twenty-eight kids, with six different gals. From there, the dialogue quickly veered to sex in general. For kicks, I took on a nerdy tone. 'You know, sir, I was shocked the other day when I read a scientific study, based on millions of surveys. It proved that one hundred percent of Canuban males have had… mmm… intercourse with other men.'

It's painful when an airhead tries to be an egghead! — She peers at me over fictive glasses.

Screw you, Principessa: I hear that's all a Princess ever

does. The point is, the driver believed me, and he was up-set. 'No, no, no!' he went. 'The professor's wrong! I'd say it's only ninety percent.'

Chiara laughs and laughs, like a Looney Tune.

Me too! I wanted to lose it. Instead I kept my ladylike composure. All I said was: What about the other ten per-cent?

And?

The old coot hung fire. Then he replied: Well, señor, I guess some men are just too ugly to fuck.

She whoops: Now I've heard it all!

Ho-hum humdrum in Canuba, sweetie-pie! Here 'magic realism' is everyday life.

I bounce her around in a seismic cambuca. She needs a lot of dancercise, she's so out of shape. When she catches her breath, I break the news: Sorry, Chiara. My carriage is about to pumpkinize. I'm outta here!

She tweaks my nose: Itching for greener pastures?

Once we're downstairs, I strike up my leitmotiv. — Ahem! So we've agreed! Shag Land awaits you tonight! — I'm dying to cruise with her on the Malecón, our steamy ocean boulevard. — Come on, sidekick, we'll make a Dy-namic Duo! 'Debutantes Do Dallas'!

No thanks, grazie mille. — She gathers her hair in a prim mega-bun. — Too rich for my blood. Besides, we're not debutantes.

Well, for a tight-assed dyke like you, there's another

place we could go. Very PC: ecotourism, out in the wilds. Parque Espinosa!

At night?

Oh yes! It's better than La Rambla. Even better than the Ramble! Safer, too. Miles and miles of trails, bushes, and trees. Enough light to see the crotches. And it's not just men, there's lots of women too. — I shield my eyes with a cupped hand, scouting the terrain. — Much people, Kemo Sabe. Today's Saturday! The paths'll be crammed with thrill-seekers. Male, female, and everything in between.

Ah. What Whitman called the 'she-harlots and he-harlots.'

Don't forget the 'she-he-harlots'—and the 'we-harlots.' You can't pull that comp-lit jazz on me. No, smarty-pants, it's more like 'singing the body electric.'

All for a fee, I suppose.

Ladies, you never know. Gentlemen and in-betweens, as I said: the bottoms are free of charge, but the tops want two escudos. That way, a macho can claim he's an entrepreneur! A hustler! You know, a 'bugarrón'!

Aha, the derivation is clear.

Right, cf. 'Bulgaria.' I tell you, we're living on Melville's 'Buggery Island'—he just got the coordinates wrong. But mind you, a bugger might turn passive for a change, to explore how it feels. By the way, there's a classic porn film about that charming trait. It's set in the Caribbean. The girlfriend catches her man with two guys, frigging him fore and aft…

I can guess, Chiara says. She pants in a gutsy bass: 'Conchita, I'm only doing it for the money!'

I chirp in a high falsetto: 'Fantástico, Carlitos, we'll go shopping when you're through!' You nailed it, dear one. Conchita gawks at the triple climax, then skedaddles with Carlitos to the mall!

We double over, hee-hawing like donkeys. When we come up for air, I waggle my hands and make a ghoulish sound. Ooo-woo-ooo. Trekking by starlight? Aren't you tempted?

I'll pass, she sighs.

Then how about an 'outing' tomorrow with Freud und Jung?

I've told her about my forays with Jaime and Pichipín; both of them are psychoanalysts. Their trump card is a pink Cadillac, a magnet for country folk. Hayseeds don't bother to nickel-and-dime their lust. A spin in the car, then a sweaty coup de grâce against the hood. And Chiara would be appetizing bait. She's not bad-looking, plus she's a gringa! That always helps.

Damn it, she's no fun. She grazes me on the cheek, a schoolmarm peck: class dismissed. No, Catulo, no shrinks for me. I want to hang on to my last inhibitions.

I know, Casta Diva! — I slap her behind, and waltz to the door. — The Mother Superior gave you too many spankings. And you got off on them—even more than she did!

Chiara, Plaza Drake, later that evening

I spend hours on this bed, mesmerized by the ceiling fan. I never daydreamed much, until I came to Puerto Indio. I was always too industrious, too bent on improving myself… Here I can finally let go.

I grew up on a fabled island, and now I live on one again. I reached it after wandering on every continent. It had to be an island, even if it's different from my own. In the midday of my voyage, I've sailed much further south, all the way to noon: the mezzogiorno, we call it in Italy, the meridian.

For me, no continent could ever be a life. A continent seems boundless: it distorts the human scale of time, as if it might never end. On an island, there are limits. Before long, you come to a cliff, a beach, the mouth of a river.

On maps of an archipelago, the shorelines reign supreme. But the sea around them always choruses the same refrain. Here you stop and go no further, not on your own two feet. You have to leave yourself behind. Flow like water or air. Change into a sailfish, a frigate bird. Waft above the breakers like mist…

I've changed a lot over the past few years. To the nuns at my French boarding school, I was a pest—kooky, outspoken, heretical. But they could never have guessed how 'loose' I would become. In my first months on the island, after all the pent-up dorms and claustrophobic flats, I more than made up for lost time. I devoured every color, every size that landed in my lap.

Canuba is headier than a candy shop—it's more like an open bar. I've sampled drinks that only the Caribbean can serve, just by stirring its ethnic mix. Some of those cocktails I'll never forget, even if I sipped them for only a night or two.

Francisco from over the river: chocolate and sinewy, with golden fuzz on his forearms and calves. Too bad he married that Canadian nurse... Or how about Elpirio, the baseball-player I met at the hardware store? Cinnamon-brown with wavy hair—and that bat of his, what an appetite! The Triple-A League shanghaied him to Kansas: a homerun for him, a strike-out for me. And then there was Mario, a bit on the pudgy side. That olive skin, redolent of Topkapi: an Ottoman prince! Too much of a sultan, all in all—bossy and demanding as hell.

Maybe the handsomest was Hitler: his sinister 'nomen' was not an omen, just an uncle's ignorant whim. A talented crooner, he belted out ballads of cloying love, the sorgum Latinos adore. Even Pelops would have envied those shoulders of his: pallid as Carrara marble beneath his glitzy, sequined shirts. The sun hadn't speckled him, thanks to his mother's vigilance. His sumptuous glutes, his sculptural feet, his molded back and thighs... every inch of him was 'niveous,' as in a fin-de-siècle quatrain. But his parents kept tabs on his movements, day and night; like a greyhound at the racetrack, he spun through concert tours to bankroll their garish house.

Of all my easy conquests, Ramsés and Hamlet were the most devout. Ramsés: Ramses the Great, I dubbed him. His complexion was almost reddish, like the temple paintings in Thebes. A statue from Abu Simbel come to life, he surpassed all human dimensions—starting with his member, a rock-hard pillar of strength. But he also had a softer side: when he attended a potters' workshop in his barrio, he brought me misshapen bowls as offerings. They could've been made by a tyro along the Nile—or a Taíno apprentice on this island. According to Genesis, all of us are fashioned out of clay, from the beginning of time.

Incredible but true, Hamlet favored his namesake, too: always down in the dumps, and unsure how to clamber out. He claimed to be the bastard son of a Venezuelan ex-President, Juan Pablo García. Luscious and slightly sallow, like a bowl of Devonshire cream... with his waspish waist, shapely legs, and blond goatee, he could've posed as the Swan of Avon's 'Mr. W. H.' When he threw off his clothes, the unsullied sheerness of his skin took my breath away; it was hairless except for a silky tuft at the midpoint of his chest.

Sooner or later, all my paramours confessed that besides their bevies of women, they'd also had men 'para vacaciones'—'for a holiday.' As the active partner, of course, or so they said. They laughed at my European notion they must be 'bi': in their estimation, if they stayed on top and didn't kiss too much, they were unimpeachably 'straight.'

When I consulted Lamia, she said their wives and girlfriends would agree. 'Most island women have had sex with women, so why shouldn't men have sex with men?' Was she speaking from experience? She grinned and kept mum. I objected that females can fake an orgasm, but males can't. She batted her vinyl lashes. 'Sure they can, in a porno film. Hahaha. Nobody's FAKING anything! What's the big deal, dumbo?'

Everyone here finds me comically naive. Though a macho's pleasure with other men might be authentic, Catulo explained, it has nothing to do with his identity. He can be passive physically, but active inside his head. 'It's all just a sleight of hand, girlfriend—or other dangly parts, if you will!'

'Mens virilis in corpore inverso,' as Horacio summed it up: 'in an inverse body, a virile mind.'

Even when making love with women, the male license to 'invent' knows no bounds! Truly—davvero—luckily for me...

The very idea of anilingus seemed disgusting in my early youth; but over time, I've become an adroit practitioner.

To me it's the gender-neutral version of cunnilingus: from behind, we're all the same. I love how a red-blooded man will coyly resist me in the shower, as I carefully wash him front and rear. I tell him it's no more than a prelim to fellatio. I begin with that, all right, to warm him up; but then I slowly spread his legs as I browse from the scrotum further down, further in.

He might try to brush me off at first; but after a minute or two, his scruples melt away. Writhing and groaning, he submits as I tongue his anus like an overripe fruit. His buttocks dimple around his rectum: it's like a ravenous mouth, puckering just for me… His ass tumesces into a face with no eyes and no nose, only swollen, quivering cheeks. Gently, then roughly, I slap them again and again. No matter how manly he tries to be, I've transformed him into a bashful, compliant virgin—the outdated cliché of his own erotic dreams. And before he knows it, he longs to be deflowered.

The next step is only a matter of course… On Lamia's advice, I've added dildos to my arsenal, either hand-held or pelvis-strapped. It may take some coaxing, and a bit of commandeering; but sooner or later, I can break the will of even the flintiest stud. The pendulum-swing of roles—top and bottom, he and she—restores our sexual balance: it renders us both complete. I'm a feminist to the nth degree; we've always had to struggle for equal rights. The rolling flipflop of gender conventions—inside-out, outside-in—

elevates women and men to a universal partnership. If we can achieve that, we'll defeat the scourge of sexism once and for all.

Ramsés did some repairs on my house as soon as I moved in—and one thing led to another. For several months, he was my loyal companion, my noble Fido. Ramses the Great—the great dane. I feel guilty about dehumanizing the boy, but he really did lope around with worshipful, canine eyes, tracking my every move. Like most Canubans in private, he far preferred nudity to clothes: a Taíno 'flashback'—an atavism, or so I like to imagine. At day's end, lounging on the patio, he would stroke his pole until I noticed him.

He was courteous to a fault—an archetypal campesino from the Cipango region. Quaintly, he still spoke with its gracious accent. Once, in the delirium of climax, he politely inquired: 'Tá gozando, mi doña?' In English, it might've come out as: 'Takin' your pleasure, maa'm?' His archaic formalism made me shake with laughter, to his bafflement.

I know that to him, I was from a 'higher' social rank; but distinctions like that, so important to my father, mean nothing to me. Thank God for the pill, anyway: we weren't in danger of having babies, like the ones my ancestors sired with the women who tilled their lands. History has totted up a few small improvements, at least.

It didn't bother me that Ramsés trolled the beach for

men now and then—business as usual, I'm told, in tropical climes: in Jamaica, it's known as 'being on the down low.' But we did cross swords about something else. I was shocked when he let drop, off the cuff, that his live-in girlfriend was only thirteen. He was such a colossus, for heaven's sake—and he wielded a battering ram to match. How the poor muchacha could endure such onslaughts, I couldn't fathom: I'd had to resort to gymnastic contortions, and I was pushing thirty. I was incensed the girl had lost her maidenhood—and let's face it, her childhood—at such a tender age.

Her parents didn't see this union with a pubescent minor as anything untoward, Ramsés assured me. They needed a strapping son-in-law to man their delivery truck, and their daughter was head over heels for him. 'In other words, they've sold her into slavery,' I fumed, as I frogmarched him to the door. The next morning, when he didn't drop by, I assumed he was miffed at my remarks.

After a week, I rang a number he'd left me—at a neighbor's shack, since he didn't have a phone. 'Who? Oh, Ramsés? An electric wire snapped while he was fishin down at the river. It fell right on top of him. He got fried!' The funeral had already come and gone. His relatives hadn't notified me. How could they? For them, I didn't exist...

Hamlet buzzed into my web a few months later, when I was shopping for guayaberas—the pleated shirts worn by

Caribbean men. For him it was a gas to watch a girl dress up like a guy; perched on a stool outside the changing room, he tut-tutted at the show. Chatting nonstop, I tried a dozen colors and designs, asking his expert advice. In the end, I bought a classic white one: unbeknownst to him, a foregone conclusion. After that, he tagged along to my house for a beer. He had nothing better to do, he admitted.

Once we were up on the roof, we both fell prey to a gloomier mood. I cried over Ramses the Great's untimely death, and he rehashed his perpetual spats with his father. Even after leaving office, when the mini-scandal of Hamlet's birth was long forgotten, his deadbeat dad had never flown him to Caracas to meet his half-siblings.

Hamlet dropped by fairly often over the next few weeks. Then, one evening, our affair began in earnest—at his initiative. He was such a mercurial boy, I suspected him of taking drugs. But I'm no judge: as Catulo once japed, I'm a 'chemical dunce.' I accepted Hamlet's mood-swings at face-value, whether he was laid-back, hyped-up, or strung-out.

After my bludgeoning pharoah, Hamlet seemed airy and droll, manic and edgy—like Ariel or Puck. The golden wisp on his chest glimmered in the moonlight, or under the candles he brought along as gifts. For hours he admired his own nakedness, in the full-length mirrors I'd had mounted on several walls. His reflections, and the pictures I snapped of him au naturel, aroused him far more than the porn mags in his rucksack.

Then the nightmare recurred. Hamlet missed a date, and disappeared for over a week. I dialed a number he'd scribbled in my address book. A female voice trickled through the line—drowsily, as if she'd been asleep. When I asked to speak with Hamlet, she sighed. 'No, amiga, I haven't seen that chico in a looonnng time… But you can try this number.'

It turned out he'd given her mine. Rivals should stick together in times of need, and so we swore a pact: whoever heard something first, would let the other know. A few days later, she called me back, almost choking on her words. Hamlet had drowned at Cambuca Beach, trying to rescue a foreigner.

All alone, I went to an upscale bar that weekend; I hoped the noisy crowd would serve as a fillip—not a solace. That's how I struck up a conversation with Héctor, who'd studied art in Boston and London. He told me he was a friend of the Miranda brothers: unsurprisingly, in the ingrown world of Canuba. When I mentioned Hamlet, he filled me in on the details of the tragedy.

Hamlet had been a well-known fixture of 'café society,' Héctor intimated with a leer. At a dive called The Summit he'd met a spongy, middle-aged German, who'd shelled out a fortune in rentboy fees. During an afternoon at Cambuca, they'd tossed back wallops of whiskey and speed before they swam beyond the breakers. The flailing tourist had been seized by a fit of cramps. When Hamlet attempted to save him, he dragged the younger man down, buoying himself on his shoulders… so Hamlet was the one who'd landed in the morgue.

The double wave of grief loosened my tongue. The bereaved always prate about the dead, no matter who's listening. Without really meaning to, I told Héctor about Ramsés as well. As soon as we became enemies—in his mind, not mine—he launched a bitchy bon mot that made the rounds: 'Touch Chiara and die.' Not long after that chat at the bar, Catulo set me up with Amado; I still had no inkling he and Héctor were an item.

Ramsés and Hamlet had vaporized like morning fog, leaving me in limbo once again. But toward the close of my first year on the island, Amado brought me back to earth. We swiftly attained a flawless equipoise. Always aiming for the grand effect, Catulo unveiled him with the words: 'Amado *is* the flesh.' The phrase annoyed me; it smacked of the meat-market, Catulo's stomping ground. He rolled his eyes waggishly. 'Believe me, girlfriend, I know.' Soon I realized he'd hit the mark. Amado wasn't just another Canuban macho-man, much less a 'bugarrón.' He shipped on a mysterious sea, where nothing seemed definite or direct.

That evening, he didn't betray any offense at Catulo's gibe; in fact, he beamed with satisfaction. Why shouldn't he? As I've learned 'to the hilt,' he's proud of his accomplishments. Amado is that rarest of beings, a carnal virtuoso; he gladly doles out lessons to beginners like me. He says he acquired his skills from an older woman, Dulce, when he was only twelve years old. Now he returns the favor, sharing the bounty of his perennial feast.

I've never encountered anyone so fully at home in his own skin. It's as if his body, organ by organ and inch by inch, is his entire self. He's not vain—though not modest, either. Unremittingly incarnate, he's at one with the physical world. The garden of Eden was devised for his fulfillment; and as far as I can tell, he's never felt the slightest twinge of guilt. He offers himself the apple, and eats it, too: he relishes each morsel, and consumes it down to the core.

When I lie jackknifed under his thrusting weight, my assent becomes a gradual ascent: I rotate upward in a vortex, on the verge of blacking out... At first I rise in tandem with the rhythmic, delicious pain; but in the final quietus, Amado pervades not only my flesh, but every recess of my mind. Or is it the other way round? Between us there's no man or woman, no up or down, no you or me.

Amado, I travel deep into your memory: I chart a map of every mountain, every valley, every rock you've ever seen. I revisit all your ballgames and fistfights; your salsa, meringue, and cambuca steps; your jobs waiting tables or sweeping floors; your runs on the beach and your workouts at the gym; your drunken horsing around at the

corner bars; your mother's hugs and kisses; your shouting
bouts with your father; your indolent mornings, groggy
between the sheets.

But also, like a sea-swell: all the paintings Héctor ever
sold, all the bench-presses Reina ever repeated, all the
dance-moves Catulo ever plotted, all the children Dulce
ever daydreamed of bearing in her womb, all the billions
of flashes through billions of nerves, the trillion sensa-
tions pulsing through me and all your other lovers, past
and passing and to come. And eddying down, I reunite
with the grasses and seeds and shoots that animals have
cropped, pecked, and nibbled, from generation to generation, back to plankton, to microbes, to the primal stirrings
of life on earth.

As you reach your goal in spurt after spurt, a second
heart throbs inside me, more essential than my own. I'm
grounded, planted, rooted by your sex; but you also set me
free from the body, sailing into limitless space. Soaring
and held, floating and gripped, I'm a shuddering kite you
reel in and out with your practiced, forceful hands.

Amado, San Sebastián to Plaza Drake, a week later

Héctor says he did me a humongous fuckin favor, buying
me this Harley. But it's not the top of the line. I wanted an

Electra Glide and this is just a Sport. It's not worth all I gotta put up with to deal with him, even if he gives good head. Qué va, the bike's ok, better than nothin I guess. Sure beats takin a motor-taxi or a shared jalopy. All I gotta pay is the gas, and it's only twenty minutes to Chiara's house from mine. I'm already late. I better speed up and go between the cars… Whoa! I almost hit the side of that Honda. I gotta slow down, give me some time to think.

I need to see my granddad sometime soon. When I was growin up I used to spend every summer on his farm. He's still a womanizer, but back in the day he was a champion. He fucked the campesinas whenever he wanted to. In a bean field or tool shed, didn't matter to him. But only if they were up for it, don't get the wrong idea. It was a game. They'd keep warning each other: watch out, Don Quipo's gonna catch holda you!

Chiara says from my stories he was like her granddad who had a lotta land. He screwed the country mujeres too, but he loved to gamble, too much! He lost most of their land that way. Musta been a shithead. My granddad's not like that: he's stingy, stingy as they come. Well, I gotta admit I love to gamble too, I just don't have the dough to do it with.

Anyway, that's somethin me and Chiara's got in common, the country life. We like it out in the campo, ever since we were children. She says I remind her of her brother Giuseppe. I wouldna pulled her hair and kicked her like he did. But I probably woulda teased her for a dork, same as him. Books! Libros! Always reading too much! She'll put her eyes out like that.

The thing is Giuseppe and me, we're just regular dudes. Me, I like what all the guys like, and I'm always the best at it too. The leader of the pack. I used to ride bareback, especially the horse my granddad gave me, Blanquita. I loved her. She was white with just a spot of black on her tail. Fiery as hell, but I handled her. I can handle fuckin anything. Nobody else was brave enough, but the other boys watched me climbin up the ceibas. We call em God trees, cause they're the biggest on the island. Some of em go up a hundred foot high.

I was always the head honcho on the baseball diamond too: el jefe. My pal Winston and I set it up near my grand-dad's house. The cows kept the grass down low enough so we could run the bases fast. The boys on the next farm over played against us, but we usually won. We used to beat em at tugawar too. We had a long rope for it, a soga. I loved that game when it was good and muddy, after a few days rain.

Nobody ever cared how dirty I got as long as I washed off in the río, right before dark. The men came in from the fields then and we all washed together in that river. The women and girls in another part, where they washed the clothes. The men were always tellin us not to pee there, or we'd turn into women too. When it got real hot me and the boys would take a dip in the swimmin hole at the river. We had a swing we made with an inner tube, and I'd swing high up in the air. Higher than anybody else, then I'd fall in the agua with a bigass kaboom.

We learned about fuckin early in the campo. For us it was just like riding a horse, somethin you wanna do as soon as you can. Sure, ombe. But like everything else, I'm the top dog when it comes to that too. I was only four when I started rubbin dick with some of the muchachos two times my age. I had dreams about girls and was comin in my bed when I was ten, maybe ten and a half. And I was only twelve when I started singando with a woman, Dulce.

I never told Chiara this, but Dulce wasn't the first female I had sex with. Hahaha. I gotta tell her sometime what really went down. She'd get a kick out of it. Sabes? Know what I mean?

One morning I decided to go fishin, all by myself. I dug up some worms and picked up my fishin pole, figurin I'd go down to the río. But then I got the idea of tryin a smaller little stream that runs through the farm. It's kinda deep in some places, nice and clear, clarito. I only wanted to catch a few tilapias. When I walked up, I saw her standin there in the water, up to her knees. She didn't shy away. She was young and still a virgin señorita, I could tell. Flirty, too, the way she set her head on one side, with a funny spark in her eye. A little coqueta. I didn't need encouragement. My dick was hard as a cucumber, so fuckin hard I was afraid it would bust out of my shorts. So I pulled my pants off and threw em on the grass. That's all I had on, anyway.

You know how it is when you're that age. I mean, it usually happens a couplea years later. But already when I was eleven, my feet and hands were bigger than the rest of me, and my cock was big for my height. A pingaza. There was a little breeze blowin, a cool brisita, and I remember how it tickled my pinga, my cock and my ass and balls. Drivin me bananas. I never had much hair on my body, but whatever I had was standin on end. Sure felt good. Man was I horny. Recio as hell!

I eased myself into the water, squeezing the pebbles with my toes. The piedrecitas. I didn't wanna scare her off. Noo-ooo. Then when I got close enough, I grabbed her by one leg. I drug her in the water, and she lay back just like a slut. I started fuckin her like loco, and she was goin Ehh, ehh, ehh.

I'll never forget it. The sun was shinin down through the pomarosa trees, and all the fuzzy pink flowers were floatin in the río all around. Tickling my cojones and my butt. All of a sudden I'm comin, viniéndome. But when you're a young dude, one time is nothin, so I did it again. Dos, tres. By then she'd had enough, and she ran off, tail in the air, as proud as could be.

I always say I was lucky, my first time. She was cute, and she was soft inside… just like any cabrita goat! I screwed a lotta different animals after that, even hens, gallinas, but cabritas are the smoothest of all. Suavecitas. Chiara says if I'd lived in the old days I woulda teamed up with a god of Pan. Pan—I guess cause sex is like bread to me. Fuckin! Culiando! But what do I know? Doesn't make sense, half of what she talks about! I listen and go along as much as I can.

When summer rolls around the next year, I'm already rapando a real woman. A mujer for sure. Dulce Lorenzo, the mamá of one of mis amigos at school. Even if he's a sissy little dude with glasses, espejuelos. I never meant to hook up with her. I was only twelve and she was thirty two. It's somethin my granddad got me into, a kinda accident on purpose. He's alway funnin around, playing jokes on people. Hahaha. You gotta laugh!

He had it in for Dulce's husband, her marido, cause he cheated him at cards. We call em barajas. The guy's name is Pipo Lorenzo, and he travels for work, sellin things. My granddad sent me to take care of his house and family while he was away. Said he just wanna be a good neighbor. Yeah, sure.

I heard em jawing about it. Pipo wasn't buyin it just like that. Amado's tall for his age, Don Quipo. But can he really look after a house?

My sonuvabitch granddad was puttin his arm around Pipo's shoulders. — Don't look a gift horse in the mouth. He's just doing you a favor cause your son's his best friend. His mejor amigo. He's as strong as an ox. Don't worry, he'll look after your boy, and your wife. Your esposa, Dulce. It's a job for un adult, important. But he won't charge you much. Que dices? Whaddaya say?

So there I was stayin at Pipo's house six nights a week, while he was huntin for customers all over Canuba. My granddad thought it was fuckin hilarious Pipo was even paying me to take care of his esposa. I looked after her alright! But after a couplea months he made a mistake when he told my dad the joke. Fuck, man! He didn't think it was funny one bit. Chichando somebody's wife goes against his religion. He got mad as a toro seein red and brought me back home to Puerto Indio, kickin and screamin. Hell, school hadn't even started yet. Coño!

My dad and his dad were always fightin hard about somethin. My granddad's more like me, and he always defended me. He likes the women, so do I. My dad's a Protestant, somethin my mom got him into. He says sex has always gotta be for having a baby. Evangélico stuff! But my granddad says that sounds like Catholic bullshit he heard when he was a kid, and he never believed it then, neither. Men and women are here to have fun, he says, the same if they're makin a chico or not.

Anyway, a couplea years went by before my dad would let me stay on the farm again. And that was only cause he wised up, seein there was plenty of trouble with women in Puerto Indio, same as in the campo. And Nueva Yol, the Apple, forget it! That's the best place for gettin your rocks off. El mejor!

Great, I'm finally here. I've got Chiara trained now. I can leave the Harley inside her house, so nobody steals it. Just inside the door. Why not? Porqué no? It's a double door so there's plenty of room to get in, and no grease drippin on the floor like she was afraid of. Hey, man, this is a fuckin Harley Davidson! And I always keep it in good shape, just like my bod, my cuerpo.

I'm still thinkin about Nueva Yol. Gives me a boner. Soon as I give Chiara a kiss, I start kiddin her. — I don't see why you had a problem gettin laid in New York, mi hermano. To me it was the same as here, in the part of Queens where I lived. And the whole fuckin ciudad! We even gave it a Spanish name: Nueva Yol. I was never hard up for a wild night out, bendito. Never!

All she's got on is that see-through pyjama top. Drives me halfway off my rocker. And she knows it, the putica. — That's just because you can seduce anything that moves, she says.

I pull my clothes off and take me a quick shower. Smoke a little grass I brought along. When I come back, she's already in bed, naked like me, both desnudos. Oh, it's not so easy gettin some kinda women, I tell her, noo-ooo... — For fun, I'm standin beside the bed and making my pecs jump. — I don't know why, but the rich young cunts can't stand me for long.

She sits up on the pillow: Thanks for calling me old!

Women are always tryin to trip you up with shit like

that. So I shift the gears. Hey, you're not rollin in money, señora! That's all I mean. But it's better that way. When you help me, I know it counts for a lot.

She punches me in the belly. Bet it hurt her hand! Well, don't push your luck by asking, she says.

Don't push yours! — I mess up her hair. I love it, so fucking straight and liso. — I'd be better off with a little rich chick than with you!

You'd leave Reina, just like that? — Who's she tryin to kid? What she's really afraid of is, I might leave her.

Coño! Mind your own business for a change, I tell her. Reina and me aren't married. — I can feel my jaw harden up. — If I leave her, I'll always go see the children, my hijos.

She won't shut up: But rich girls would want you to have a degree, a job—what they call a future.

I gotta laugh. She comes up with some screwy ideas sometimes. — You mean they'd be wantin dough from *me*? Presents, sure. Claro. Why not?

She's on a fuckin jag today. And it's not even her time of month yet, todavía. They'd want more than presents, she says. They'd want security. A man who's responsible, who pulls his own weight. A decent husband who can help them bring up their kids. Because once a girl leaves her family, she depends on you. At least for half the income.

You gotta be joking! Not if she's got dough. Cuartos!

Oh, I guess some women don't mind living off men.

But most of us would feel ashamed, the other way round.

Or maybe they're just stingy. The young bitches I know won't even pay for a movie or a coke! A fuckin cocacola.

I don't mind. But I'm old and poor, as you say. And foolish, too! Anyway, no need to be defeatist. Why don't you go to college, and learn a profession? Do it here on the island, in Spanish, so it won't be so hard for you.

There she goes again. I try to keep smiling. I wasn't all that smart in school, I tell her. I always hated it. Besides, all that kinda crap gets in the way of my fun! I need to gozar. Go to the gym, spend time with you.

Ha! Not just with me. If you want to date young girls, forget the gym. They don't like bodybuilders. They want you to be slim like them. Even shave your chest and legs. But women my age might go for you.

Yeah, and what if I get old myself?

You, never!

No? Well, I was hopin to live a couplea more añitos. A few more years!

I got her now. She's biting her lip, real nervous like. To lighten things up, she hits me in the stomach again. Men will always go for you, too, she says. Not just old ladies like me, who think they're still young.

Coño! I wish to hell she wouldn't talk about shit like that. Que vaina! — Men, how would I know? But one of my pals says they come in handy sometimes. More fuck and less flak! — I put my hand over her mouth and drag her closer up on the bed. — You're ok, if you'd just shut up. So how about let's get down to business? Tá bien, Chiarita?

Just don't come at me from the wrong side. I'm still sore.

I get off on that, Italianita. Understand? I'm only gonna stick it in a little bit lower. Tá bien? I know how you like it. I'll warm you up, then you'll be ready. Nice and lista.

I stick my tongue up her cunt for a long time. What a toto, it tastes so good! Then I stick it up her cheeks even longer. Alluva sudden I grab both her ankles in one hand, pushin her legs in the air and goin for her asshole. Her culito. Shoving my pinga in, good and lento. Nice and slow. She's makin like it hurt, but after a couplea minutes all I hear is she's lovin it. Le gusta!

A lotta women are sloppy in the cunt. Some of em are born that way. Some of em get that way after a lotta action. Me, I like the hole to be tight. Real estrecho. The tighter it is, the more friction to your dick. It just feels great. The asshole's always better, unless the girl's a virgin. Dudes, same thing—course the ass is all they've got. And they suck better too. They don't call em chupapingas for nothin. Even if I like women more, tá claro.

Front or back, while I'm doin it I always look em straight in the face. Straight in the eyes. Chiara, she's good at that too. Like now, she's starin in my eyes. Look at me, Chiara, look at me! I'm inside you, going deeper, deeper, about to come. Casi me vengo. But I'm holdin it off long as

I can, making it last. Ay ombe, there's nothin better than this!

Chiara, Miami to Puerto Indio, two months later

I should be reading about St. Gregory of Nyssa for my next article... But I'd rather daydream by the window instead. The plane's so high I can't see anything but clouds. It always astounds me to fly above them, watching them drift, collide, and buckle like continents.

I'm glad my job takes me away from Canuba now and then: it makes me appreciate the island even more. And Amado, of course... While I'm gone, we both develop a voracious appetite. I'm sure he feels relieved to get me out of his hair. When we meet again, I don't give him unsolicited advice—not for a week or so!

Maybe I should ease up on him: he knows what suits him best. He's smart all right, but not in an academic sense. He has a knack for learning by osmosis, absorbing his lovers' knowledge through his skin. And the same thing happens in reverse: he pours himself into us—in more ways than one. That's why we'll never forget him; through him, we multiply our lives.

After they broke up, Héctor claimed Amado was just 'a book he'd read, a movie he'd seen.' But the truth is, he'll never dislodge him from his memory. Amado leaves an after-image: he's the noonday sun you still perceive with eyes tight-shut. He's a Van Eyck you can always recall, down to the last detail.

Work of art, force of nature, or both; anyway, a piece of work... He likes to enter his lovers from behind—but with me it took a lot of persuading. At almost thirty, back there I was still a vestal. My mother once told me that many Italians took that route in the old days, so they could have their cake and eat it, too: no contraception, to obey the Church; but with the added tang of a more heinous sin. When I was at university in Padua, I was much too namby-pamby for shenanigans like that. Ramses the Great and Hamlet both mocked me for cleaving to the frontal pose, since I was so 'experimental' when it came to them. But Amado wouldn't accept no for an answer! Well, I don't mind anymore, as long as I do it face to face and feet in the air: 'missionary pole-vault style.'

In Canuba, I jumped off a cliff into the dark—or the blinding glare of noon. I've always been plagued by indecision; but as soon as I spent my first hour with Amado, I upended my existence without a qualm. A few weeks ago, the penny dropped: my 'trial period' in Canuba was over, no bones about it. I went back to New York with a single purpose—to move to Puerto Indio as soon as possible, this time for good. In my line of work, I can churn out articles anywhere, if I stay in touch with the magazines by phone and fax. As it is, I'm offered so many gigs, I have to turn half of them down.

After terminating the lease on my flat in Murray Hill, I made the rounds of every travel editor in town. I either donated my paltry sticks of furniture to friends, or left them on the sidewalk. Packing my souvenirs and books into three stout trunks, I consigned them to a shipping agent. Who knows when I'll lay eyes on them again...

I got sidetracked on my journey back to Puerto Indio; but it's just as well, since my bank account was running low. Out of the blue, *Now, Voyager* sent me to Cappadocia, to write a piece on the underground cities. With the return fare, I contrived to change my flights, and visit my mother in Sicily for a week.

At my childhood home near Nodica, I loaded up four more trunks, and dispatched them from the port of Augusta. Switching planes several times, I winged my way from Catania to Puerto Indio, via Frankfurt and Miami.

Thank God this is the last leg of the trip. The clouds are thinning out as we coast above the Bahamas, in the waning light of late afternoon. The flat, greenish islands glint like copper parings, scattered across the ocean. Soon enough, night will solder them together, and that will be Canuba...

As the jagged scraps slip past the window, dulling to grey, second thoughts begin to assail me. Maybe it's rash to give up New York's cultural goodies, and abandon all my friends there. One of them said he was worried I'd bog down in 'a provincial morass, as stifling as the Sargasso Sea.' A trifle melodramatic. But he's a dyed-in-the-wool Manhattanite, who scarcely sets foot outside 'the city.'

A Brazilian colleague said something that rattled me much more. You have no idea what you're letting yourself in for, he insisted, taking my hand in his. I grew up in São Paulo under the junta, and several times we found a corpse outside our door. — There was a tremor in his voice. — Espinosa and his cronies may *seem* less brutal— for now. They pretend to be 'democratic,' to hoodwink the UN. But under pressure, they'll go back to torture again, and assassinations too. Don't let the balmy climate mislead you. In Canuba, you're playing with fire: you might be risking your life!

As the plane lands at the spartan airport of Puerto Indio, his words keep haunting me. But as soon as I reach the house on Plaza Drake, with its airy spaces and picturesque views, I feel reassured. Thanks to a phone call the day before, Amado is here for dinner, as eager to make love as always. After a copious banquet of the senses, he leaves me long after midnight, sated to the point of torpor.

I wake up at nine this morning—very much against my will. It's Sunday, Luz Divina's day off, and I'd planned to slumber till noon. But there's a tapping at the door, feeble and sporadic, like a mouse skittering inside a wall. Then I hear a high-pitched voice through the window, almost gasping for breath.

By the time I open the shutters, Horacio is quaking with impatience. Chiara, where on planet Terra have you been? You averred you would be gallivanting for a fortnight, and it has been a lunar month. I praise the elysian pantheon that you have returned! Frederica is holding a resplendent soiree tonight—in your honor.

Who, the Countess? — Charily, I omit to say 'the so-called Countess'; if she is one, it's only by marriage. I poke out my chin in annoyance. — She doesn't even know me.

He simpers. — Knowing me is knowing you—quoth she.

He probably put the woman up to the idea... — Well, it's very generous of her: I'll allow her that.

Hear, hear. No necessity for embarrassment. Frederica entertains hebdomadally: she rejoices in celebrations. And she is very desirous to have the pleasure of your acquaintance.

He's on the brink of neurasthenic collapse. Alarmed, I invite him in. — Here, sit down while I make some tea.

He shrinks: Not English Breakfast? I can hardly imbibe anything that apocalyptic.

Pazienza, I tell myself. — I know you can't, but I need a fix. For you, I've got chamomile.

As I set the cups and teapots on the table, he scolds me. — Forsooth, Chiara. I must upbraid you for this. I endeavored to obtain your parental telephone ciphers from Luz

Divina, but she was paralyzed by discombobulation. What if an emergency arises?

Like a reception, you mean? Please!

I detest the way Horacio fawns on the rich. He reminds me of my father at times, the bogus marchese. Keeping up with the Joneses—or in his case, Lampedusas—he's frittered away my mother's land. Only a couple of hectares are left: the seedy garden around the villa, and a corner for the tool sheds. I've always been fond of the place, though it's a middling example of the Sicilian Baroque.

Nowadays my mother keeps her husband afloat by renting out the house and grounds for weddings and other events. But in my childhood, we could still afford an English 'governess,' Miss Pinfold. She was a crotchety harridan, but I owe her my love of nineteenth-century novels. If I sound somewhat like her at times, I come by it honestly. I missed her after she left, to my astonishment. Thanks to my father's profligate ways, my mother was forced to let her go…

Horacio seems crushed by my testiness. An abominable happenstance could befall you, Chiara. Or Luz Divina might be stricken by an indisposition. Please do not be refractorily pervicacious.

I relent: You're right, Horacio, I've been negligent. I'm grateful for your concern. I should keep my mother better informed about my whereabouts, too. She's always griping, just like you.

He stares at the floor. Ineluctably, my goddess: we are preoccupied with your eudemonia.

That's very kind of you. You're both maternal, and I need your affection. Especially with the worthless father I have. — I didn't mean for that to tumble out. The very thought of him sickens me: his rubbery face, his insincere chortles, his mincing walk. — I'm sorry, you must have wondered why I was away so long. First, I had to do some research for a magazine. Then I stayed in Sicily for a week with my mother. Poor woman, she's stoical, but sometimes she just can't cope. My father left her alone again while he went off sailing.

Not to be an inopportune quidnunc, but does he commit such affronts with any frequency? — Like most Canubans, Horacio thrives on gossip, even about people he's never met.

I may as well satisfy his curiosity, for once. Often? All the time! His nouveau-riche patrons take him everywhere on their yachts. The Aeolians, the Tyrrhenian coast, as far away as Greece.

He nods at me with a knowing air: They must feel flattered to have a titled guest aboard their vessels. Incontestably, he *is* a marchese.

Now I'm truly put out. — I never should have told you that! I'm afraid you're a fop, just like him. His father scrounged the title from Mussolini, in return for licking his boots. It doesn't amount to a hill of beans: there's no heraldry to back it up.

Horacio smirks. Indubitably, his protecteurs do not seize upon his emblazonry, if they are lowly commoners themselves! — He must think of my father's antics as an Alberto Sordi comedy: well, maybe he's right.

Even if they did, I tell him, they'd probably applaud his cheekiness. That's the kind of people we're talking about. Right-wing morons! While he's gone, my mother is repairing the roof of our house. It's an onerous project, and my father shouldn't be shirking his duty. After dealing with the laborers day after day, she's entirely worn out.

Horacio probes a little more: It *is* a historic villa, is it not? It must be perforated by leaks. Could your brother lend his assistance?

That's another sore point. — Giuseppe? Oh no. He decamped to Uppsala last year with his Swedish girlfriend. But he's so mammone, he'll return before long. Italian men can't survive without their mammas: it's like here, only worse.

My mind races back, and I relive how my timorous, forsaken mother was always clinging to the boy. No wonder Italian paintings compulsively depict 'la Madonna col Bambino.' For one another, she and Giuseppe are gods; but I love them as more than that—as human beings. My brother will always be an endearing, feckless child; and my mother will always be my closest friend.

Horacio persists, like a pesky mosquito: Is there nothing you can do to succor her?

Davvero, no. Giuseppe is the heir. She wants him by her side, not me. I'm too frank! Only veneration will do. I could tell you a tasteless joke—a barzelletta—if it weren't so sacrilegious...

Now you absolutely *must*. I beseech you! Pleasantries are my Achilles' heel!

All right, but I'm only quoting. And it has to do with culture, not faith. It goes like this: The greatest man of all time must've been Sicilian. Why? One, he believed his mother was a virgin. Two, he believed he was God. And three, she believed it, too!

Mentally, I cross myself, though Horacio is unperturbed. — Heheheh. Exceedingly humorous, my dear. — There are limits to my irreverence, I find; but in his magpie creed, there's no such thing as blasphemy.

My saucy Uncle Totò used to treat us to that one, I tell him—to my grandmother's horror! She would call him a 'picciottu malu'—a bad little boy—and clack him with her ivory fan. Anyway, when my parents banished me to Lyon, I said farewell to the villa. Though I have to admit it's come in handy for storage. After I received my degree from Padua, I stowed my books and papers in the cellar. I didn't feel like lugging them all the way to Princeton. But the basement's as porous as the roof, so half my things got wet. On this visit, I assembled whatever I could salvage. Plus some china my grandmother left me. I sent four trunks from Augusta, our commercial port: one of the roof-workers drove them over in his truck.

That is a momentous disclosure for us! — Soundlessly, Horacio claps.

It's not the first time I've pulled up sticks. But it may be the last.

Ojalá! Godspeed! Besides Sicily, where else did you divagate?

To Turkey, on my assignment. And New York before that, as you already know. Three more trunks are on their way from the States. I've given up my apartment, Horacio. From now on, Puerto Indio is my home.

A signal accolade for us. Benvenuta! — He makes a ceremonious bow. — Till later then, dear Chiara. I shall collect you at eight.

After unpacking my suitcase at a leisurely pace, I scare up some lunch, take a long nap, and pamper myself with a bubble-bath. Soaking in the tub, I recall my first glimpse of Frederica's house, on my maiden voyage to Puerto Indio. When I emerged from the broad alley beside the cathedral, I came across another handsome square, almost as large as Plaza Drake—with one big difference: it was utterly bare of trees.

Stendhal was enamored of the Belpaese, but he was right to remark: 'Italians hate trees.' Especially on a piazza... As I later learned, a Sienese designed our Plaza Catedral in the early 1500s. Catty-cornered from the church facade,

I noted a trio of imposing palaces—all from that period, too.

The escutcheon on the middle one singled it out as the Archbishop's residence. Well-proportioned, but a trifle severe for my Sicilian taste… The building to the left was also austere, though several of its windows held bonsais in grey ceramic planters. As Horacio later told me: 'that domus belongs to a socialite, yclept Carolina Del Río.' My English may be a bit dated, but his is antediluvian…

The mansion to the right was far and away the most colorful of the three. It was studded from top to bottom with boxes of yellow jasmine, and their scent suffused the air. That was Frederica's house, Horacio said. Both these grandes dames are my confidants, he went on, clearly enraptured with himself.

I can almost whiff the perfume, as I watch the suds swirl over my breasts… Ah well, it won't be so bad. I need to see how the other half lives. But come to think of it, what half do I mean?

…Goodness, I can't believe I fell asleep in the tub. Time to get a move-on! Thanks to my Condé Nast office job, and the family hand-me-downs, I own a small stache of formal clothes. When eight PM rolls around—the Canuban 'drinks hour'—I'm gussied up in a black Chanel suit, white silk blouse, and two-tone Bally pumps.

Horacio has donned his usual sober greys, though he's made a special effort with his grooming. I tell him he's never looked more dapper. Naturally, he rejects the compliment. — How can you iterate such a thing, when I feel so moribund? The habit does not validate the monk. I cannot guarantee I shall survive the fete, however splendiferous!

Frederica von Gesichtseck, Plaza Catedral

It's always gratifying when my guests stream through the portal! I've done my best to make this place inviting, not just imposing, imponierend. The illumination is low-key at night, to match the rest of the plaza. Brings out the faded rose-color of the tiles. I've always thought the irregular windows add a fanciful touch. They're Late Gothic, I'm told. Spätgothisch, we say in German. The walls are so ponderous—more than a meter thick—you need some adornments to lighten them up. Like the gay yellow jasmine I've planted along the facade.

I shouldn't be so loyal to my staff. Wilkin deserved the axe years ago, that time he let some hippies through the door. How foolish! How törricht! He's so weedy, a grasshopper could knock him down. But he's improved lately, I guess. At least he recognizes most of the habitués. In his scarlet jacket with gold buttons, he doesn't look so bad. A Bonaventuran might be more stylish though: red on black.

Mulattoes like Wilkin project an anemic air. And he's always terminally bored. The uniform livens him up a little. Gott sei dank! Thank God! Of course, like all Canubans, he firmly believes he's the cat's meow. Or is it the cat's pyjamas? I guess that's what comes from being spoiled when they're small. Children need love, but here they're lionized. Every Canuban is a superstar.

Aha, there's Horacio now! And that must be his friend Chiara. I'm glad she made it. Supposedly, the party's in her honor, but any reason will do. I love splurging on my friends. And I've acquired the ideal locale for it now. When people see this palace from the street, they imagine it's a grisly fortress inside. Wrong!

I can tell from Chiara's expression she's like everyone else: amazed at how I've tarted the mastodon up. The rooms are so enormous, jawohl, yes indeed. And those huge mahogany beams hang so heavy overhead. But I soften them with lamplight and candelabras. That gives warmth, gemütlichkeit. Another gimmick is lots of vegetation. All three courtyards are awash with bougainvilleas in different colors. And my five-foot Chinese vases full of fresh-cut flowers, too: orange lilies ruffed by greenery. A spray of orchids here or there, preening on a polished table. It all strikes a festive note!

Horacio and Chiara are inching closer. Of course, I have to greet the people in front of them first. I always stand in the entrance hall to welcome everyone. Wagging my head and raising my arms to each and all—it makes them know they're valued.

Sometimes I feel self-conscious. I know I'm too plump now, but I'm going on a diet soon. Ach, that's what I keep telling myself. When you reach a certain age, maybe it's good for your face to puff up: it irons out the wrinkles. My shoulders are so wide I can carry the weight, I believe. Like a Wagnerian soprano in Bayreuth! I hide the bulges under loose, flowing shifts; the one I'm wearing tonight is crimson velvet. Besides, the portlier you are, the more Canubans love you: 'gordito y rosadito,' 'chubby and rosy,' that's their greatest compliment. They think it means you're healthy and well-off, with lots to eat. Men here have a fetish about fat, so women cram their bottoms with silicone!

I hope I'll make a positive impression on Chiara. From what I've heard, she understands what Europe's like—in higher circles like ours, I mean: in höheren kreisen. She can probably tell what inspired my beehive, piled in a pyramid on my head. Portraits by Boldini, the artist I always try to emulate! Even if my hair *is* dyed these days—the price of maturity—there's still some natural black. Horacio told me she's wild about art. Me too! Art über alles! She's already staring at the pictures on my walls. One of them is a real Goya from his Bordeaux phase, she'll sleuth that out. The others are just daubs. As the Graf, my late husband, used to say: Only experts can tell the difference;

to the peons, they're just swatches from a fabric shop. My homely little Count had his moments.

That charcoal-grey Nehru suit. Can't Horacio afford another outfit? He's so officious, he tickles me. He's basking in the party mood now. It always floors me how he blooms into a spry gadabout, when he claims he's at death's door. Na ja! Whatever! As soon as he presents us, he leaves Chiara to me…

She's a superior person, much as she tries to conceal it. I have a practiced eye. This tête-à-tête is only the prelude to many, no doubt! I clasp her hand and won't let go.

Chiara! Welcome! Willkommen! I hear you've moved to the Barrio Antiguo! From New York! And your uncle was a Sicilian prince! — Maybe I'm too pushy, I reproach myself. The Graf always thought so. When I went a little too far, he'd say: What the devil, woman, anybody can see you're not a born aristocrat.

She pulls back. — Horacio is a mythomaniac. He must've made that up, Gräfin—I mean, Countess.

Please, call me Frederica. You can't deceive me, dear one, meine liebe! I sniffed out your whole family in the *Libro d'Oro*, the Italian nobility guide. — I cluck my tongue. — Your maternal great-uncle was the Principe di Mazara. Am I right, or am I right? — I try to be likeable. She dismisses me as crass, but I'm breaking the ice.

You're right, she gives in. Zio Totò was not just my uncle, he was my godfather, too. A sweet-tempered, quixotic bachelor: I owe him my love of books. He also bequeathed me a tiny income.

A splendid thing to do! Herrlich! — I rub my hands together, brandishing the carats on my rings. It never hurts to have money, no matter what these decrepit families say. — Your annuity will go much further here than in the States.

True, Countess. I mean, Frederica. There it only made me 'independently poor.' But here it gives me some leeway.

I nod at her shrewdly. She must know from Horacio that I'm a businesswoman, first and foremost. — So now we're neighbors, nachbarn! Welcome home!

People nitpick that whatever words I use, they sound like an exclamation. I'm enthusiastic about life, no harm in that! There I go again… I spent so many decades in Vienna, I still think partly in German. I never put the capitals on, though: too hard to keep track. When I was only sixteen, I ran off with an Austrian ski-instructor. We met at Cambuca Beach, and I eloped with him to his beloved heimat, his homeland. He diddled away all his savings on me, the sad little chump, and then I discarded him. I wanted to scale the heights! Ganz normal! Par for the course! I was very curvacious then... And from man to man, bed to bed, I slept my way to the top.

I never bring that up here. In Puerto Indio, I suffer from total amnesia. I forget about my humble origins, too. My mother couldn't read or write, and she auctioned me off for food—out of desperation, she had no choice. She died of tuberculosis long ago. These days everybody calls me la Condesa, the Countess. For years I had to settle my husband's debts by 'leasing' myself to his snooty, unhygienic friends. Ekelhaft, disgusting! Now that he's finally bitten the grass, I've earned the title at least. To be fair, his second cousin, the Prinz von Feigenblatt, did invest a sizeable sum in my company...

We chew the fat about an assortment of themes, but Chiara is rather wishy-washy. Sits on the fence too much. I have decided views, and I don't mind saying so! Zum beispiel, for example, I can't abide background music, even a live quartet. A practiced hostess doesn't need that. If the guests are well-suited, I lecture Chiara, their lively chatter reduces all else to a nuisance. You either talk, or listen to Bach; you either read Hegel, or make love—some things demand our undivided attention.

I emphasize my opinions as much as I can. Why not? Warum nicht? You never know when a stupendous concept will realign the universe. Marriage, too: it changes people utterly, from bottom to top. Look at me! As I intimate to Chiara, matchmaking is my hobby. Many a romance has germinated in these patios, behind an elephant-ear or a bamboo palm.

Ach Gott, how I wish I could work my alchemy on Gustavo—turn his brainpower into gold! He's my only child, as misfortune would have it. I don't want to run him down to my new Italian friend, but he had a fine opportunity to wed Leandra. What a catch! She's Carolina's daughter, my neighbor two doors down. Instead, he doodled his time away in Europe—universities in Spain, Switzerland, and who knows where. Doing one silly degree after the next. Leandra is the best match in town, I tell Chiara. Not too bad to look at, and steinreich, filthy rich! We old families should never turn up our noses at a healthy transfusion of cash.

She lets out a cryptic hmmm... Chiara knows nothing about the social set here. I can fill her in on some juicy tales. For privacy, I sweep her up a hidden staircase to my boudoir. I even show her the seven-foot bathtub, where I contemplate a privileged view. Right below is the Archbishop's cloister. Sixteenth-century columns. Very pretty, sehr hübsch!

Finally, the girl perks up. — Beautiful, Frederica. I love the dim lighting. The columns seem to glow... from within.

She's vaunting her good taste: swanky, distinguished. I'm onto that game, and I can go her one better. — Ja, dear friend, here's where I hover with the angels at night, and forgive His Grace for his sins. He's a notorious skirt-chaser, you know... I can spy on him, but he doesn't see me. Only the happy few have surveyed this paradise of mine. Not when I'm actually wet, mind you!

False, hahaha. But I like to keep up with the klatsch,

not be a topic of gossip myself. My boarding houses for girls are only in foreign countries. In Puerto Indio, I'm a model of propriety. After we retreat downstairs again, I angle towards the kitchen, my pride and joy. I assure Chiara she's gained my confidence. Ordinary guests never 'ascend to the heights' in my house. But I'm legendary for spoiling them with food and drink. — I trust you'll come back often, meine liebe, my dear one!

She goes off to corral a flute of Veuve Clicquot, while I supervise the staff. As she'll soon find out, there's no set date for my parties, such as Christmas or New Year's. The occasion might be a Venetian masked ball, a pow-wow for the Diplomatic Dames, or nothing in particular. I've something of a talent for orchestrating events, if I do say so myself! And the wherewithal to make them pic-ture-perfect—ganz perfekt.

Idle ambassadors congregate bei mir, at my home: they have nothing better to do on this God-forsaken island! The most winsome member of the corps right now is Arnaud Fontaine, the Belgian envoy. I adore Fátima, his slinky Brazilian wife! Writers, artists, musicians, dancers—they never reject my invitations. There's Horacio, Catulo, La-mia, Héctor, and the rest. But on the whole, I've been quite disappointed with the old-guard families. Unless they're intellectuals, they turn me down. Snobs! In Europe they'd be nobodies!

Come what may, there's always fresh blood, like Chiara

tonight. Oddballs filter through the city in a constant dribble; if they're presentable, I take them on board. I've had a Zambian who pens thrillers about the mafia; and then there was that expert on arachnids from Borneo… cross-eyed, bless his heart. The antique map dealer from Slovakia, he's always mooching free drinks. I've even had a John Cleland specialist from Chile. I'd never heard of *Fanny Hill* before I met him. Unglaublich! Unbelievable! Such a naughty book! It reminded me of my youth. Very edifying, ahead of its time. I've lent it to the girls at my boarding house in Amsterdam.

Here in Puerto Indio, I keep everybody guessing: who'll shuffle through next? The cuisine I serve is unpredictable too, God help me! That drives me mad, completely ver-rückt. I can't get a decent cook. Partly because I don't want women: they're too capricious. I like to hire teenage boys, mostly from the countryside. They're hardy and obedient; they can double as gardeners too, in a pinch. Horacio calls me a 'pedophile.' I was shocked till he explained he meant an ancient Greek ideal: paideia.

'I said -phile, Frederica, not -erast; philia, not eros. Loving the young chastely, with a view to their ameliora-tion.' Yes, that's how I feel about my boys. The problem is they resign at such a rapid rate!

Maybe I'm too strict, zu streng. I'll try to let up. I en-courage the waiters as they pass by—Nelki, Gregorio, Almondjoy, Parménides. My current chefs, Usnavy and

Tico, acquit themselves well for a big party like this, a cocktail for hundreds of guests. The task is easier, since I fall back on traditional snacks. Local tidbits, and foreigners appreciate them too. Tonight there's casabitos—cassava thins toasted with olive oil, garlic, and salt. Croquetas de carne—yucca rounds with meat, instantly fried so they're chewy and crisp. And pasteliños—turnovers stuffed with spinach, pork, and pumpkin seeds. They all look irresistible on my Moroccan brass platters. Ducky and delicious! Ganz köstlich!

I have to be honest, though: dinner parties are a challenge for my boys. I do them in two different ways. Groups of six to twelve are seated at my oval table from Innsbruck. I use eighteenth-century silver and heaps of candles. Heavenly, himmlisch! When I have suppers for the 'petit comité'—the small committee, my pet phrase—I limit the place-settings to four, on a round glass table in the courtyard furthest back. All you can hear there is the fountains, gurgling contentedly behind the ferns. From both vantage points—to keep my eye on what the cooks are up to—I leave the doors to the kitchen slightly ajar.

Sometimes I worry when I hear them conferring. 'Is this the sauce with basil, or parsley?' 'Where's that gadget she told us to use?' 'What did she mean by pasta al dente— toothpaste?' 'She says I'll mess up this dish; but hey, I can make it better than you.' That kind of thing! If I weren't a seasoned hostess, it would make me scream. Dreadful! Schrecklich!

The wisest course is to distract the guests. I propose toast after toast, to prime the chitchat. 'Except for the edibles, everything you see before you—from silverware to candlesticks—is from 1789. It's my banner year, the last gasp of the Ancien Régime.' Or maybe I've ordered flowers from the mountains, to match the decanters of Margaux. 'Wunderbar, my friends! As Oscar Wilde exclaimed: a table red with wine and roses!'

I'll try anything to stall for time. No matter! Macht ja nichts! If the delay goes on too long, I have to jump up! Catulo has a wicked tongue. He and Horacio always natter about music. Catulo says I'm a prima donna, overly theatrical! He calls it opera buffa when I steal into the kitchen 'like an adultress about to get caught.' But 'ach Frederica!' he jeers. 'It's *Götterdämmerung* when the curtain descends on a pancake soufflé, incinerated fowl, or botched bavaroise.'

As the night dwindles, I groan about my troubles to the last survivor, usually Horacio. — Damn it all! If only these ignoramuses could grasp what I've achieved! Who else could come up with real mozzarella or Scottish salmon on this öde insel, this dreary island? And also, auch noch. Did you notice that smudge on Almondjoy's glove? No, I guess not: because to top it all off, he was serving from the *wrong side*!

For me, a faux pas like that is the ultimate crime. But I know I only make it worse by berating my boys in German. The more high-strung I get, the more my Viennese side comes out. I feel like I'm back at the boarding house, ordering the stupid girls around, the dumme mädchen! The ones who're still wet behind the ears, and never cuddle up to the clients as they should.

It's better when I take the helm myself, for two or three of my closest friends. We can yak while I work, with only a scullery boy to do the chopping. I do hope Chiara will join the 'petit comité…' Oh, there she is!

What took you so long, meine liebe? I ask. She tells me she ran into the map seller from Bratislava. Yes, he does gabble on!

I guide her around my kitchen. I call it my 'temple of cuisine,' and I'm very proud of the way it turned out. I've lined it with mahogany cabinets and shiny copper pans. Over the stove hangs a canopy carved in oak. It's from a palace in Palermo—where one of the Graf's forebears lived.

Oh, she lets drop. The Two Sicilies. Maria Theresa must have sent him there.

You know all about it! Maybe we're related. — I'm overjoyed, but she only accords me a brittle smile. The little minx.

I like Chiara, even so: she's not haughty, nicht hochmütig. I find myself lapsing into a confessional mood. — Between us girls, I wasn't always so grand. I used to run a boarding house for young ladies in Austria; and after the war, we were starving. It was awful! People say they're hungry on this island: they haven't a clue. They mean they don't eat meat every day—but we didn't even have a potato, a kartoffel.

Chiara clears her throat. Yes, Catulo tells me you've expanded that establishment into a worldwide chain.

Her tone is neutral enough, but you can't bank on the Miranda brothers. They're devious! Undoubtedly, the shameless rascals tattle behind my back! I throw up a smoke-screen right away.

It's a mission for me, liebe Chiara! Young women should be well nourished. They rave about 'fusion cuisine' nowadays, but I've been making it for decades. I mix dishes from all the countries where I operate: Austria, Germany, the Netherlands, Italy, England, Japan, Argentina, and so on. Believe me, I can stir up kaiserschmarrn like a hausfrau, but my gnocchi are scrumptious too. I age my plum pudding for a proper year. And my miso soup! You'll have to come back for a cozy little dinner next week. What do you say?

We set a date. I'll have Horacio, and Catulo too if he's in town. Boy-girl, boy-girl. Oh, it's only after meals for a few choice friends that I can truly relax, I tell her. The courtyard is so quiet, so serene. At the end, I like to kick back my heels and sip a glass of vintage port. How pleasant! Wie angenehm! You'll laugh, but every time I make a solemn vow: No more big parties! I'll never, never invite hundreds of guests again!

Chiara purrs like a cat: Oh yes, Frederica. And I'm sure your 'nevers' hold good... for at least several days.

Quick! A pot of tea and some plain toast for breakfast. I need a liter of water, too. I'm hung over—again. If Frederica's going to ask me to dinner so often, I'll have to restrict myself to one glass of wine. And my God, those lethal Negronis! Her Germglish is as chunky as Amado's Spanglish; diced with Canuban creole, it must make a heady sauce for her 'boys.' On her invitation cards, below an embossed coronet, she writes the German nouns in lowercase. They should be capitalized: I can sympathize, I feel decapitated, too!

I don't know how she keeps that gigantic barn in such impeccable shape, feting day after day. It's a far cry from our crumbling villa near Nodica, where I woke to flakes of fresco on my sheets. That's the power of money, I guess: Frederica is the quintessential parvenue. Still, she has a magnanimous side, as long as you don't tread on her toes.

As for her social pretensions, they're transparent and naive, like Horacio's. Neither of them knows that in Sicily, a baron can rank higher than a prince: the baronies date back to Norman times... She's detected that I speak German. The way she latched onto my uncle, I'll never tell her about my Wittelsbach cousins; I used to spend my summers with them in Bavaria. They only belong to a cadet branch of the royals, but she'd look up their titles in the 'Gotha,' the Teutonic answer to Debrett's.

Aaargh, I can't believe I'm thinking all this. It's exactly the kind of nonsense I left Europe to escape. Sometimes I have to wonder: why doesn't Canuban snobbery repel me as much my father's? Maybe because it doesn't affect me directly, so I can let it go with a laugh.

That's the advantage of living in a foreign country: you feel a certain indifference, a sense of 'je m'en foutisme.' But somehow, Canuba seems familiar to me, too. And not just because it's an island, like the one where I was raised. After all, Indonesia spans eighteen thousand islands, many of them alluring—Salawati, Ampat, Celebes, Flores, Bali, Lombok—but I couldn't adapt to any of those. A Caribbean island still belongs to the Western world: I want to stay close to Ithaca, the eternal myth of home, even though I know that 'home' doesn't really exist.

All my life, I've defied the Sicilian cult of 'la famiglia.' Do relatives share deeper values, merely because they're linked by their genes? It's a lesson I've forced myself to learn. When you cleave to your household gods, you never accept your exile. You keep looking to your childhood for protection. To be resilient, we have to devise a shelter wherever we go: the sheltering sky, the sheltering earth—even the sheltering sea.

The archipelago I've chosen lies cradled between the green Atlantic and the blue Caribbean. Because of its latitude, Canuba floats entirely in the blue. Almost as much as Sicily, it's been a hub of conflict for centuries. Like the language of my childhood, Canuban creole bears the stamp of various empires: it's a verbal palimpsest. While both islands have declined into little more than outposts, their layers of history still endure.

Yes, Italy seems far away... Gratefully, I've settled into my modest house, with its cool brick floors and white-washed walls. Neither a villa nor a palace, thank God, it's the optimal size for a single wordsmith. To me, it offers a haven from the past.

Here I can muse away the hours, like a boat bobbing beside the dock. But there's no danger I'll lose my moorings: every morning, Luz Divina jerks me back to terra firma with a scowl. She treats me like a hostage, not a boss.

Morally, I look askance at depending on servants. I'm happier fending for myself, as I did in New York. When I said as much to Horacio, he reprimanded me in no uncertain terms: Indefensible, my dear! The neighbors would conclude you were avaricious, if you attempted to extemporize without a domestic. You would be recriminated for not commiserating with the indigent.

A flimsy excuse for exploiting cheap labor! I harrumphed. I used to hear the same argument in Sicily. — But then I raised my hands in surrender. — All right, I give up.

I'd scarcely arrived in Canuba when a dozen women knocked at my door, one after the next. Fresh from the beauty parlor, they all touted their housekeeping skills. By the time Horacio brought Luz Divina along—introducing her as an 'aboriginal factotum of our gens Miranda'—I was glad to enlist her to keep the others at bay. She's such a virago, the Mirandas must have jumped at the chance to pawn her off on me.

She does make a concerted effort with her Spanish. In her 'employment interview,' since Canuban drops the *s*'s, she overdid it by putting them where they don't belong. When I asked her if she could read and write, she screwed up her face. No conozco las lestras, pero sí conozco los núsmeros, she pronounced: I don't know the letterses, but I do know the numberses. Horacio had alerted me that she likes to 'hablar fino,' talk la-de-da. She's poles apart from Amado, whose Stateside years have supercharged his Spanglish into a rollicking Engspan. Not that I care, either way: I'm not 'normative.' To me, as a Sicilian, all vernaculars are languages, not mere 'dialects.'

I've offered many times to teach Luz Divina to read, but she rebuffs me with scorn. While she busies herself with her chores, I absorb the island newspapers over breakfast. I'm keen on learning Canuban, a mixture of Taíno, outmoded Castilian, and American slang, flecked with Briticisms and crinkles of French. It also borrows from other Spanish variants: a marbling of Puerto Rican, Cuban, Dominican, and Venezuelan. Linguistically as well as geographically, Canuba lies at the crux of the Hispanic Caribbean.

At Horacio's suggestion, I'm picking my way through

the Gospel of St. Mark in a local translation. When he heard that, Catulo sniggered. How characteristic of my saintly brother! Saintly for a warlock, that is. But maybe he's right. After all, girlfriend, you already know the plot! Personally, I would've dunked you headfirst into our greatest Caribbean author, Lezama Lima—sink or swim!

I have to contradict him: That would be too ambitious! — On the surface, I tell myself, Cervantes might be easier—purely as a narrative. In the fullness of time, guided by the dictionary of the Real Academia, I'll thread through every feat of the deluded knight; a noiseless, patient spider, I'll retrace the intricate web.

Given my mother tongue—plus my knowledge of Latin and French—I'd presumed Spanish would be a cinch. But my childhood lingo in particular hinders me as much as it helps. Sicilian and Castilian are easy to confuse, because of our lengthy subjugation to Spain.

As I've gained fluency in Canuban, Luz Divina has turned into a chatterbox. She regales me with stories about her childhood in Cipango—the inland region Columbus mistook for Japan, when he 'discovered' the island. She labored in the fields from an early age, and never went to school. From my side, I tell her about the customs of rural Sicily, similar to Canuba's in many ways. Here's the paradox once more: the Caribbean portends a break with my past, but a homecoming as well.

After two or three months, I'm fed up with leaving my

trunks stacked in the sala. At last, I'm getting bookshelves built. Lamps, tables, and chairs have also begun to clutter the rooms.

The other day, Horacio mildly voiced his disapproval: You are evolving precipitously from Zen to Late Victorian, my dear. Soon you will undertake a major renovation. I would classify you as the nidification prototype.

Minor, perhaps, but major? I wouldn't dare, Horacio. This is only a rented house. Besides, what would the owner say?

No obstacle, goddess. Don Belisario asseverates that you can reside here forever, and dispose of this abode as you please. Although he roundly contemns the Barrio Antiguo, he inherited several properties here. And he revels in optimal vitality, unlike me. Moreover, his son will respect the concordat, if he becomes your landlord one day. He is a man of honor, and an amicus in excelsis of the Trinity—our paramount friend.

I should meet him! So far, I've been dropping off the rent at a notary's office.

When I feel equal to the exertion, I shall solicit an audience on your behalf. — Horacio wheezed for effect. — On further reflection, you could not opt for a better contractor. He would be highly meticulous, dedicating himself to a paternal asset. And he is exceedingly attached to Lamia—by one appendage, at any rate. So that should provide another guarantee that he will do his nec plus ultra.

Attached to Lamia! Another victim—among the thousands. What's his name?

Ángel María Gonzales.

Oh, I may have met him already; the diva introduced us herself. He was driving a bottle-green truck. Very good-looking.

That is the paragon de facto! Sursum corda! Lift up your hearts! The ascendant architect, dilettante pianofortist, slayer of ladies' hearts, nature aficionado, topflight athlete, and lifeblood of festivities. He even composes poesy, to utilize a superannuated term. Believe me, to know him is to worship him, Horacio sighed. We all do, sub rosa. Omitting Lamia: he is far too gallant for her.

A week went by... And now, just my luck! Ángel María *would* turn up this morning, when my head is stuffed with mothballs. Without consulting me, Luz Divina brings him back to the patio. To her perverse amusement, he's caught me in my pyjamas, still flopping around at eleven AM. She's a grimalkin, all right.

Brimming with energy, he firmly shakes my hand. Caramba! The small world of Canuba. When we met, I didn't realize you were living in this house.

No? Funny Lamia didn't tell you.

She must've forgotten it belongs to my father. She doesn't focus on details!

In his grainy baritone, he prattles about the latest political news. He's even more striking than I remembered:

steel-blue eyes, a swimmer's build, a golden-brown complexion, wavy chestnut hair. And last but not least, the indispensable moustache of the debonair Latino. His jaw is somewhat heavy, but that lends him authority. It's easy to picture him running a vast hacienda, heading up a right-wing junta, or waging a guerrilla war in the jungle. Any cliché would fit him like a glove—to coin a phrase.

I tune back in. This house is a disaster, he's saying. An overheated cube. What you need is cross-ventilation. — He points to the end of the sala. — We can put a new window there. You'll have a terrific view of the apse, to boot. This is a National Heritage area. We'll need a permit from the watchdogs at Patrimonio Nacional, but I've got friends in all the right places. Their headquarters is just up the street from here.

I fiddle with my hair, hoping he'll notice my best feature. — Oh yes, Ángel María! Oily 'amiguismo.' 'Friendism' greases the cogs in Canuba, the same as in Italy.

Right: two of the rustiest claptraps on earth! No wonder Canubans and Italians are so easy-going. We have to be simpático, just to get by.

I chuckle softly, dialing up the charm; maybe it's not so bad that I'm in dishabille… — Well, I'm all for ventilation. And vistas. My favorite part of the house is the terrace on the roof.

He takes the hint, and follows me up the stairs. — Wow, way out! If I lived here, I'd put a Hitachi on this deck, and barbecue T-bone steaks.

How American, I mutter to myself, how suburban. I'm about to say something arch, but I bite my tongue.

Back downstairs, Ángel María bustles about, inspecting the rooms. — My father always assumed a couple would rent this house. That's why we modified the chopped-up Colonial plan. Since you're on your own, we could go a step further. Didn't you tell me your maid doesn't stay here, unless you're out of town? The whole place could be like a loft. You only need doors for the closets and baths.

Coquettishly, I egg him on. We brainstorm with abandon. Wooden partitions melt away. Patio windows morph into full-length doors. Modern masonry yields to wrought iron. The façade will be restored to its historic symmetry.

I agree with him on every point. — Excellent, Ángel María. That last touch will open up the visual axis.

Dead on. From the entrance clear to the courtyard.

He offers to charge the minimum for labor and materials—with no fee at all for himself. But his crew will show up only when they're not busy somewhere else. He pats me on the shoulder. — That will tide me over a bit. I still have to pay them, even when they're idle.

I paw him back: Sounds like a deal!

We better get started, before I reconsider! You've probably heard about the Synorix syndrome. He was a Taíno, an Indian chief.

Yes, I know. He did everything for the Spanish, and

nothing for his tribe. We 'gringos' have been bilking the Canubans ever since. — I hesitate for a moment. All the same, I may as well be blunt. — I'm sorry to bring it up, but one thing bothers me: this house isn't mine. Why should I invest in it?

My father doesn't care for the Old Quarter. And neither do I, for practical reasons: parking is too difficult! Rent this place as long as you want. Forever, for all we care. — He seizes my hand in his. — You can count on our word, even more than you can count on a gringo's.

That's a relief, because I wouldn't count on a gringo's. Especially not an Italian's. — I stall for time; I don't want him to go just yet. — To us it's pretty daft, the way Canubans call Europeans 'gringos.' We think the word should apply only to Americans. Well, the French might be offended, but I don't mind!

I like that: a gringa who isn't conceited. Besides, any friend of Lamia's is a friend of mine. — His face hazes over. — What a woman! But she's a wild card. You can't predict what she'll be up to next. She used to play duets with me: I dabble at the piano, as a pastime. But lately she says I'm cramping her style, not allowing her to 'grow as a musician.' Huh? Pendejadas! Nutso talk!

I disguise my joy, as we say good-bye. If Ángel María gives up on Lamia, I might stand a chance with him—or with her. Or with both! In Canuba, you never know.

I go back to bed for a while, despite Luz Divina. — How

can I change the sheets? Gonna lie around the livelong day? — Closing my eyes, I riffle through a deck of lurid fantasies. I have to laugh at myself out loud. Ángel María? Lamia? My plate is already full—with Amado!

Chiara, Plaza Drake, March 1983

As the months roll by, the rain-flowers flourish; I refuse to have them pruned. I love the way they weave a canopy, snaking above the patio to the terrace on the roof. Their lavender corollas sway in the breeze, flaunting buttery yellow stamens. Bananaquits swing on them like acrobats, siphoning the nectar with their sharp, curved beaks.

To Luz Divina, the flowers are a nuisance; they rain down constantly, day and night. It takes an endless round of sweeping to stem the flood. In the evening, when I'm having drinks with friends, the fleshy blossoms plop around us, or land on the table like heaven-sent gifts. By breakfast time, they've carpeted the courtyard, and Luz Divina's Sisyphean task begins anew.

As a child, I gave no thought to 'la servitù,' the servants. In spite of our family's waning fortunes, three crabby, bent retainers still lived at the villa, tucked away in an annex at the back. Every morning, my grandmother gave them their orders: here in the Caribbean, that tawdry role has devolved to me. I hate the idea of subordinates! It's an offense to democracy as a whole.

Besides, I'm not equipped to cope with Luz Divina. She sets her own schedule, whether I like it or not. Condescendingly, she clocks in at a quarter to eight—except for Sundays, her day off. She stays till two PM, and not a minute longer. Most maids drudge till six or seven; but only a dire emergency would make her continue till three. If the truth were known, I count myself lucky she's not around for long…

One day I asked her why she rushes home so early. She answered me matter-of-factly: I don't like all those vegetables you eat. I'm not a rabbit like you. Un conejo! When I get home, my cook has a *real* meal laid out for me, with lots of meat.

Horacio often quotes his mother. 'Her axiom is: in Canuba, even the servants have servants. That is why for islanders, my dear divinity, humiliation is never implied; tomorrow, it might be your turn to don the pinafore!'

Luz Divina has reams of self-esteem, no doubt about that. First-off, she's sniffy about her pious name, 'Light Divine.' She won't answer to the usual diminutives, like 'Lucita' or 'Divi.' But I suspect that vanity prompts her more than religion. She highlights her bust with a fifties-style brassiere; her breasts project like traffic-cones, despite her age. Whatever the cost, she swears by quality make-up—stuff that never runs, even in the dogdays of August.

At breakfast, on the flower-strewn patio, I practice my Spanish in our casual chats—though I can't foresee where they'll end up. This morning, for example, she catches me off guard.

I had a dream about you last night, she says. Soñé con usted. At the moment, I'm fixated on my tea: it's an opaque brown, almost a sludge. This has gone on far too long. — Do you really have to make the tea this strong?

Luz Divina understands, but doesn't deign to react. She's used to my Sicilian-Castilian by now—and my caprices, too.

I've adjusted to Canuba with gusto—maybe too much. At times, I'm afraid I'm losing my grip. I've just turned thirty-three, and my age is creeping up on me. After a night of rum-and-sodas, two postprandial javas, and an afternoon of beers on a sun-blasted beach, last week I had some scary palpitations.

Examining my EKG, the cardiologist reassured me: Your heart is fine. If you stay out of the sun and skip the stimulants, you'll be back to normal in no time.

But Luz Divina keeps brewing English Breakfast full-bore; the way she makes the blend, it's as inky as espresso. She packs the pot with so many leaves my cup could almost walk. Meekly, I've been beseeching her—por el amor de Dios!—to lower the dose: for the love of God! Today I have to take a stand. In my condition, carburetor tea is too much to bear.

Luz Divina, I can't drink this! I've told you a million

times: it's bad for my heart!

Again, she pretends she hasn't heard me. She dilly-dallies from plant to plant, pinching off withered leaves and dried-up twigs. I've collected a dozen flower-bushes in large clay urns, and she tends them with aplomb. She brags about her green thumb, like all her other talents. Now she pauses in front of a rare, burgundy hibiscus. The plant has bloomed again, after several weeks of 'rest,' as she calls it. 'Cada flor tiene su tiempo,' she's fond of saying: every flower has its time.

She beetles her brows. A new pearl is about to drop. — Look at this rose—how pretty.

It's not a rose, it's a hibiscus.

Well, maybe I'm stupid. But I know one thing: the heart is like a flower. When it opens too wide, it falls apart. Maybe that's what's happening to you.

She sizes me up. Discomfited, I gaze at my casaba toast. After a while, she brings me some pale, propitiary tea…

I'm on the verge of asking about her dream. But my train of thought is derailed by Marino, the handyman. He bangs on the door till Luz Divina lets him in. With his toolbox clanking, he marches straight to the courtyard. No rest for the weary!

As with her, I've kept him around mainly to ward off the others. At twenty-two, he already has five children to support. — You have to give me work, he says. I've got a family to feed. — Not for the first time, he makes it sound like *my* fault.

Today, as on other days, I can't think of a thing for him to do. But Marino always knows how to invent a job. — That mosquito net needs replacing. And while we're at it, let's stretch it on some sticks clamped to the bed. — Before long, my shallow pockets are plumbed once again.

Luz Divina resents having Marino in the house; she goes out of her way to mistreat him. I guess she fears he's a threat to her livelihood. If he scrubs the floors today, maybe he'll water the plants tomorrow. And what if he brings his wife along, to wash the clothes and cook?

To make matters worse, though he was born on the island, his parents are 'Bonos.' To Luz Divina, he's an 'invader.' She disdains his African features—especially his hair. Straight as a poker, her lush mane befits the Canuban ideal of 'pelo bueno': 'good hair.' It's lustrous and black, without a thread of grey. Her elongated eyes lend an Indian cast to her face. I've always surmised that in her, as in many of her countrymen, the Taíno genes live on.

Given her filbert-brown skin, in Europe we'd consider Luz Divina 'black,' no less than Marino. I've told her this several times, trying to squelch her prejudice, to no avail. Here, if you have a drop of European blood, you're 'white.' In the States, I used to observe, if you have a drop of African blood, you're 'black.' Racism is patently absurd! And deadly when it taints politics...

Luz Divina seems to be bristling more than usual. I

hear her grouching under her breath: Marino's nothing but a Bono. A prieto. The police should send him back where he belongs.

'Prieto' is uncomfortably close to the 'n-word,' when said in that tone of voice. I don't know if they'll lock horns in the next few hours. But I'm beginning to dread the worst.

Luz Divina Mota, Plaza Drake, over several days

As soon as I get here this morning, Chiara starts in on me. She's been turning the house upside-down, looking for a stupid camiseta. Some people call em T-shirts, some say playeras. To me they're just camisetas, the chintziest kinda shirt. I know which one she's talking about. For a camiseta, I guess it's a special one. Dark-blue, almost black, with NEW YORK in silver letters across the front. That's where everybody wants to go around here. I can see why.

If you don't feel like working, in the States—'los países,' we call em—the government gives you money: el golfeo. A check every month! Here, you could starve to death, and nobody would care. Yesterday was Sunday, my day off. Now the closet's a mess, with all the clothes pulled out on the floor. I don't see why she cares about that dumb camiseta. She's got so many blouses, she doesn't need it.

She blabs about 'what a great gift it would make for the neighbors' son.'

Sure, I get it: Melvin's about to turn fifteen. The biggest birthday for us, cause it marks the coming of age. Your maturity, your *madurez*. Chiara wants to give him something nice so she won't have to go to the party. Claims the music would be too loud! Why can't she just enjoy herself? Dance a cambuca for a change! If you ask me, it's too quiet in this house. When she listens to anything, it's música de muertos, music for the dead like at funerals.

She looks me in the face. I know what she's thinking. Luz Divina, she whines in a phony voice, I saw that shirt just a week ago. What do you suppose might've happened?

Que vergüenza. She should be ashamed. I've worked for her a couple of years, and I've never pinched a centavo. I'd say she owes *me* something, not the other way around. What really burns me up is how she lets that Marino into the house. If anybody stole from her, it would have to be him. He's always picking fights with me, I don't know why.

Chiara's acting like those detectives on TV. She's so rich, why should she care about a camiseta! Besides, what would I want with it? I'm a single, middle-aged woman, with a grown-up daughter, no sons, and no boyfriends. None she knows about, anyway. She should have more confidence in me than a Bono with children to feed. I've spent a lot more time around the house than he has. I come to work every day, and he's only here once a week.

The way I see it, she should trust me, not him.

But here she goes, nosing around. Says she wants to 'question' me. I'm not gonna let her get under my skin. If the shirt's gone, I tell her, it's gone. Don't cry over spilt milk!

It just seems strange to me, she says, in that fake voice again. Don't you want to check the closet yourself? Seems like you already know the shirt's not there.

I let her have a piece of my mind. — Oh, I can tell what you're up to. But why would *I* snitch a tacky camiseta? I'm a doña, a Canuban lady, not a dirty Bono. Besides, I can ask you for anything I want. If you don't need it, you'll hand it over—pim-pam-pum. Like that broken saucer you let me have, the other day. The one that got chipped from just sitting in the cupboard. You complained I dropped it in the sink, but that's not true. It wasn't much of a present, but that's why I asked you for it. I wouldn't expect you to give me anything valuable. That's how I am: así soy yo.

She's batting her eyes like she doesn't believe me. But she should know better by now.

Remember what happened when you first got here? I tell her. The plumber's kid-brother was helping him, while I was doing the wash, and he made off with one of your blouses. The next day you pinned it on me, but then you learned your lesson. I felt insulted—yes, señora, I did. But I've forgiven you. That's how I am: así soy yo.

When it happened, that muchacho bamboozled both of us! Only twelve years old, but already smart as the devil. While my back was turned, he snatched a wet blouse off the clothesline and slipped it under his shirt. It was so hot that day, the water-marks looked like sweat. He gave the blouse to his sweetheart for Valentine's. His only mistake was joking about it later with his brother. The plumber was afraid he'd lose a client, so he came running to Chiara. He didn't apologize. Why should he? *He* wasn't to blame. The girl had moved to Esmeralda, and the blouse was gone for good.

From the look on her face, Chiara's still not convinced.

I just can't figure out what happened, I go on. All I know is this: the only person here besides me was that soot-face hoodlum, ese tíguere prieto. I'm not calling him a thief—but just think about the last time something got pinched. At least you can be sure it wasn't me!

She bites her lip. — I never accused you of taking the T-shirt, did I? Let's forget all about it.

What a blockhead gringa! She's not getting the point. I raise my voice. — No, no, no. You can't forget about it. If you let that no-good prieto come here again, he'll grab more of your stuff. Up till now, it was only a camiseta. But next time it'll be the stereo. Or your pocketbook. — I wag my finger at her. — You've got a lot to learn.

Bien, bien, Luz Divina. That's enough. I'll decide what to do.

No, I won't drop it there. I remind her about something

else that happened a month ago. I overheard the whole thing. That punk Marino begged her for an American camiseta—and she ignored him. Later she told me she was tired of people asking her to bring them this or that, like a special shampoo from Brookli. Or tennis shoes from a store in Queen. Two barrios in Nueva Yol. She didn't have time to be an errand girl. So then the NEW YORK camiseta comes along, and guess what? It was just what Marino wanted!

When she hears that, she's impressed all right.

I listen to them talking on Friday, when he shows his ugly mug again. Chiara warns him she won't put up with any more of his stealing. Marino won't back down. He's got no shame. — Doña Luz and I were both in the house, so it had to be either me or her. But *I* wouldn't do something like that, Señora Chiara. Just ask my old boss, the engineer. Or Father Flores. Or my uncle, Jean de Dieu. He's worked at the French embassy for years. They can tell you I've always been honest.

Chiara's hashing it over, for sure. She knows an engineer can't keep track of all his employees. Priests are easy to con: we've talked about that before. As for that uncle of his, who can believe a relative? Especially if he's just another Bono! Through a crack in the door, I can see Chiara staring the little jerk down, the pendejo. She dares him: I'd like it so much better if you'd just admit you did it. If you tell me the truth, and return the shirt, I'll forgive you—I promise.

I wonder what he'll say now. Maybe he'll go away—I hope. But he defies her, the filthy prieto. Oh, I understand, he says. You believe the doña because she's a pelo-bueno with good hair. I've got bad hair. But what can I do about that? It doesn't mean I'm dishonest.

Chiara is real upset, who knows why.

The low-life prieto won't shut up. — Just come with me right now to my house, and you'll see for yourself I don't have that shirt.

She's not going to that rathole where he lives! He must be loco.

Oh well, she says. It doesn't matter that much, does it? Probably some youngster climbed down from the roof, and yanked it off the clothesline.

That could happen pretty fast in this part of town. Boys are always prowling from roof to roof, especially when the mangoes get ripe. But Marino's not so dumb after all. She's already let on the shirt was brand-new, still in the package. That means I've never hung it out to dry. He knows she's brushing him off.

She crosses her arms. — Anyway, there's nothing for you to do today. I'll let you know if something comes up.

She points to the door. But soon as he's outside, he starts gabbing again: Wait, señora, let me say one more thing.

No! She closes the door. There's no work for you this

week—that's that.

I sneak back to my ironing board. Chiara walks around in circles. She ends up in the kitchen, where I'm hard at work. It serves him right, I grunt. Lying and stealing like that. Que ladrón! What a thief! It's bad enough to rob you, but then he had to go and lie. I've always said he was a crook, that prieto.

I mash the iron down on a sábana. I feel like it's Marino's face: I'm scrunching his nose and frying his eyes. Except the sheet is white, and he's black! — That's the end of him around here. This time it was just a camiseta, but next time it woulda been something big. It's a good thing you canned that prieto, before it was too late.

She's mad at me, not him. You figure. — Please, Luz Divina. Don't use that word 'prieto.' Don't you realize you're black yourself?

Me? With my light skin and straight hair? Chiara's a loca de remate, crazy as a goat! But I don't care. I'm just glad I got back at Marino!

A while later, it turns out different. That damn prieto rings the bell again. I'm still ironing, so Chiara goes to the door. Oh, Marino, I hear her say. You won't give up!

His voice is louder now; I don't even need to sneak any closer. — It's about Doña Luz. I talked with my uncle, Jean de Dieu. He says if you're treating me this way, *she* must've put the idea in your head. You're right, one of us stole the shirt—but it wasn't me. Let me ask her, and you'll find out.

Chiara is out of her mind sometimes. She lets him in, and he hoofs it to where I'm ironing.

Señora Chiara is right, he says. If the shirt is missing, one of us must have taken it. I know it wasn't me, so it has to be you. — He starts shouting at me. — You did it! You did it! You know you did! I'm telling you right to your face! And you tried to make her believe it was me. Look me in the eyes, and swear you didn't do it! Swear it on your mother's grave!

I'm terrified. Why did Chiara let him in? He might hit me. My voice comes out weak as a kitten's. — I never said you did it, I never even thought it. — My eyelids are twitching. I'm about to faint…

Well, he hollers. One of us stole that shirt, and it was you, doña, it was you.

I can hardly talk, I'm so afraid. — No it wasn't, Marino, I swear! It wasn't me, and it wasn't you.

Thank God, Chiara's had enough by now. But I can't believe it when she tells him he can work here, just like before. To top it all off, she puts the blame on both of us.

I'm sure nothing in this house will ever go missing again, she says. You can spy on each other to make sure. If something else walks away, both of you are going with it.

I don't know why Héctor exhibits gobbledygook like this. Awesome 'artwork'! Buckets of mud with nails on top. It's a good thing he's not here today, or I might do a Dame Edna on him. Really speak my mind about this folderol. Political art needs to be tougher than this. More in your face…

Look, here's Chiara breezing through the door. What a coincidence! I was going to drop in on her tomorrow. Amado quit the gallery several months ago, so maybe her cat-fight with Héctor is over. Plus she's always keeping up with the Next Great Thing. Sorrrryyy, buckets of mud aren't it!

She spots me and prances over. After some sub-romantic hugs, we agree about the 'art,' lickety-split.

It's supposed to 'symbolize the exploitation of Bonaventuran construction workers,' the catalogue gushes. Chiara, I've had sex with quite a few of them, and this doesn't do them justice. Their tools are much bigger than nails, and a hell of a lot juicier! They're right up there with Canubans.

Oh, I thought Bonaventurans weren't your cup of tea.

No, they're not my cup of Twinings, but they *are* my cup of Illy. The stronger the better! You and your teacups, Alice! I'm not a racist, I'm a patriot. Aesthetically, I love the rumpus of ebony and ivory in bed.

She tells me she's got a *real* ethnic clash going on, between Luz Divina and a Bono.

That's run-of-the-mill on this island, I shrug. Bonaventurans versus Canubans, and Canubans versus Bonaventurans. The half-black versus the all-black.

She zeroes in: Or the part-white versus the non-white. Thanks for not using that distasteful term 'Bono,' anyway. For once!

You're welcome, girlfriend. But it's just a form of shorthand, like 'prieto.' Haha, don't cringe! Now go ahead: I lend you my ear.

It's all I can do to keep a straight face! She blathers on and on about the maid and the handyman, and how they've 'turned her into a monster.' Just because of a Gotham City T-shirt, for crying out loud. Now she knows how her grandmother must've felt, she moans. Running a household makes you 'inhuman.'

Caro Catulo, she bleats, I know it's all pap for cats—just because Luz Divina prides herself on being 'white'!

George Wallace in brown-face drag! And to the princely young Bono, 'black is beautiful.' So retro, so kumbaya, I say to myself: American treacle she sopped up at Princeton. Ahhhh, how Chiara longs for the 'self-reliant virtues' of her former life in New York. Dadadee, dadadee, dadada.

I can't believe she's taking it all so seriously! She views this camiseta bagatelle as a moral Armageddon. — Anyone who pilfers will also lie, she laments. So I can't expect a straightforward answer.

It's even worse, girlfriend, I reply with mournful gravitas. Thief or not: in this country, it's always someone *else*'s fault.

Davvero! Canubans never own up to anything, no matter how insignificant.

The common people, you mean. Even if they break something right in front of you, they say 'se rompió.' As if objects could implode by themselves!

Acridly, she agrees. Yes, it's like one of those newfangled gumshoe stories. The perps never confess, so the mystery's never solved.

I souse the flames with kerosene. No, it's more twisted than that, girlfriend. The suspects will go on blaming each other. Things might turn vicious, and spin out of control. Pretty soon you'll have a race riot on your hands!

Upping the ante always brings people back to their senses, I find. — Don't exaggerate, she says in a calmer tone. Who cares about a silly old T-shirt?

Poker-faced, I hector her: It's not about that. It's the principle of the thing! Didn't the nuns instill you girls with a code of ethics?

Oh, now you're just thumbing your nose at me.

Who, moi? Never, darling Chiara. But I have to confess, I'm not surprised by any of this. Luz Divina and I go way back; she looked after me when I was just a tot. A kerfuffle between the two of you was in the cards.

Why? She's not some harebrained teenager. After all, she's close to fifty.

Don't tickle my funnybone! She's sixty, if she's a day.

Chiara tugs on her Peter Pan collar. — She claims she doesn't know her age.

Ha! She used to say she was born during Hurricane Elena. She can't be ten years off the mark. But then, she's always been duplicitous...

Now I've really pushed her buttons. Duplicitous?

I pause for effect. Oh, nothing beyond the pale. She used to make off with the usual things: my father's socks for her boyfriends, my mother's undies for herself. She liked to wait till repairmen or shoeshine boys came round, so they could take the heat.

And the T-shirt, then?

Oh, poveretta! You can be sure she committed the crime.

But why would Horacio recommend a thief?

Don't be such a puritan! Be happy she's just a petty thief. She won't steal anything exorbitant. As we always say: Everybody's got to have a thief; just make sure it's one you can trust!

The conversation turns to theater and dance: Robert Wilson, Pina Bausch. But Chiara is only half listening. She can't take her mind off Luz Divina.

She starts obsessing again. — You're right, Catulo. I guess I'm a real 'cabeza cuadrada.'

A 'square-head.' That's what we call tight-assed foreigners, who don't relish the zest of immorality: now she's wising up.

Right, girlfriend. From the island point of view, Luz Divina's behavior is utterly normal. She believes you're Imelda Marcos, with clothes to spare. So why shouldn't she swipe a few of your fabulous togs?

I'm so careless with cash and jewelry! Chiara admits. I guess it could've been a whole lot worse. I've lived in the States too long. And Germany, too. If I think like a Sicilian, I'll loosen up.

I frame her head with my hands. — Enlightenment! A bulb went on in there! Me, I can image Luz Divina, boobs a-bouncin'! — I do my Dolly Parton impersonation. — She's dancing the cambuca with an underage hunk! And he has NEW YORK emblazoned on his pecs!

Luz Divina, Plaza Drake, three weeks later

I don't know why Chiara can't believe me. Even if I did take something—and I didn't—she doesn't need it. All she does is sit around staring at books. Wish *I* could loaf like that the livelong day! A while back, she claimed she couldn't find a camiseta. After that, there was a brand-new blouse she'd bought. I wish I had enough money to buy one… but I don't!

At first she didn't say anything. Wash day is every Friday. I know she must've counted the clothes in the hamper the night before. Friday morning she checked the clothes-line where I was hanging up the wash in the patio. I only string it up on wash day, cause she says it's too ugly to hang it up all week. The extra work she makes for me, all for her batty ideas!

She pretended she was looking at the pink hibiscus. Then the yellow one. But I could tell she was counting the blouses.

I snorted at her. Six blouses. Don't worry, they're still here.

She played dumb. What are you talking about?

Oh, I counted them, too.

She snapped at me. Why should I care how many there are?

Good question, I thought to myself! Seis blusas or five, it's still too many for one woman. But I held my tongue.

When I left that afternoon, she was half-asleep in one of the rocking chairs. It was so hot anybody would've dozed off. A book was slipping out of her hands... I opened the door, ready to say good-bye, when I saw her sizing up my handbag. It's a fat one, all right: red straw with purple handles. One day she asked me why it has to be so big, if all I need to carry is a work-dress. Well, she doesn't know a thing about make-up, and how much space it takes up. She runs around like a three-year old—with no lipstick, even!

I let her know she wasn't fooling me. Would you like to look inside?

Why should I want to?

Because that way you can be sure. Since you don't trust me, we better keep things clear. That's how I am: así soy yo.

I had to let her have it, didn't I? Then I slammed the door behind me, hard as I could...

Now this morning she's talking about another blouse she can't lay her hands on. Says she was dressing for dinner last night—dinner with some millionaires, I bet. She's in a tizzy cause she couldn't find that blouse with embroidery on it. I know the one she means. Has little stitches of blue and grey. Always says it belonged to her great-grandmother, her bis-abuela. She only wears it now and then, for special nights out.

She's like a cat when she gets her claws on something and won't let go. I'm not surprised when she brings up that worn-out blouse again, just when I'm trying to go home. She says she wants me to sit down in the other rocking chair with a back like a heart, a wooden corazón.

I don't like this a bit. It's one thing to talk standing up in the patio—but not on a chair in the sala. I'm no friend of hers, one of those ladies who flop around drinking tea and jabbering all day. I feel embarrassed. My eyelids start twitching, like that time Marino was so mean to me.

She's eyeing me with her priest look, like she can see right through me. — Luz Divina, as I told you this morning, another blouse has disappeared. I don't know how you did it. I've even put a lock on the closet, but I must've left it open.

I noticed that lock she bought the last time she mislaid a blouse. No trust! But I check it all the time and it wasn't open yesterday, not while I was here. I feel like I'm coming out of a nightmare, just waking up. I can hardly hear myself talk. — I didn't do it, I tell her. I didn't do it.

She sounds like a judge on TV. — I was sure you'd say that. Please, Luz Divina, you stole the T-shirt and the other blouse. Now you've stolen this one, too. Why don't you just admit it? You don't have to return them. Just tell me the truth. That's all I care about, the simple truth.

My face feels like it's bulging: a balloon about to pop. Chiara gets up. — So you don't have anything to say for yourself? Bueeeeno.

I can't stand the pressure anymore. I fall to my knees on the floor and grab Chiara's legs. I'm crying like a baby. — I didn't do it, I didn't do it. I took the T-shirt and the other blouse, but I didn't take this one, so help me God. I swear it on my mother's soul, el alma de mi madre. I didn't do it, I didn't do it.

I'm bawling like a crazy loca, swaying back and forth. She's got to believe me!

It's all right, she answers in a guilty voice. I believe you, Luz Divina. Stand up. Please stand up. — She's crying, too, dabbing her eyes with a handkerchief.

All the way home I keep thinking about it. That woman should feel ashamed, the way she's going on about some worn-out clothes she doesn't need. I can hardly watch TV or listen to the radio, I'm so upset. I shoot the breeze with some of my neighbors for a while, but I can't stop wondering: what happened to that blouse? I spend the whole night praying to San Antonio. He's the patron saint of lost things. He's helped me before, and he'll help me now. I light some candles for him. I remind him how Chiara says she lived in his hometown, Paduba. So he's got to do something for her—and for me.

The next morning I go to work without any breakfast, a lot earlier than usual. I bring some things I only use when a hurricane is coming, or when Chiara goes away and I stay at her house alone. That great big house is too quiet for me. Somebody could break in one night and rape me, even murder me!

I unpack the candles and holy water. Give them velas and agua bendita, my mother taught me, and the saints will always love you. I put their pictures up in the pantry.

San Miguel has a sword in his hand, and he's squishing a fat red snake with his foot. San Tomás is looking at Jesus, feeling the wound in his side. Santa Magdalena—I don't believe she was ever a puta, no matter what they say. If she was a whore, she's sobbing about it now in an orange dress. She knows how it feels to do something wrong, and then feel sorry for what you did. If San Antonio forgets to help me, the other saints might pitch in…

When Chiara wakes up, she sees the candles burning. That'll show her how wrong she is. Somebody who prays as much as I do wouldn't steal anything.

She yawns and stretches her arms: When I was a little girl in Sicily, they used to take me to Mass. There were lots of statues and pictures, even more than here in Canuba.

They're not statues and pictures, they're the saints! I tell her.

She nods and shuts up; she better not talk any nonsense today.

I make the breakfast she likes, watery tea and toast with that orange marmalade. Bitter naranjas with hardly any sugar: how she can stand it, I don't know.

She reads the newspaper for twenty or thirty minutes. That's how she 'practices,' she claims. When she got here she couldn't talk, not anything you could understand. Now she makes sense, some of the time.

I'm clearing the flowers off the patio, or else the drains get clogged and the house might flood if it rains. It's happened several times already. All of a sudden, she speaks up.

Luz Divina, my mother called me last night. You know how my madre loves to talk; I don't mind, I like to listen. She always ends with a big hug for her 'lovely joy,' me: 'un fortissimo abbraccio, bedda gioia...' And then 'ciao, ciao, ciao.' Italians repeat that word three times, or else the phone call isn't over.

I don't see why she's telling me that junk. I don't know what chau means anyway. Nothing, I bet.

I'm tempted to leave you in the dark, she goes on. Ever since the spat over the T-shirt, you've been doing a better job. The tea's not too strong, and the food's not too salty. You don't even leave those unsightly dustcloths on the chairs.

I never did! I shout.

She closes her trap for a while. Then she pipes up again, from behind the paper. Guess what? My mother told me I left that blouse at her house, when I was there last month...

I'm pushing flowers into a clump with my broom. I don't pay her any attention. Serves her right. Finally, she can't take it. — Luz Divina, oyó? Did you hear what I said?

I turn around. I'm standing as straight as the broomstick in my hand. — I heard you, all right. God answered my prayers. But you accused me of lying. You didn't believe me! Usted no me creyó!

She should be sorry, but no. You've got some nerve, she says. What do you expect, an apology? Why *should* I believe you? You stole the T-shirt and the other blouse. And you lied about them!

Chiara is a terrible person sometimes. Maybe they're like that where she comes from, but I'm glad I'm not from there. I took them home with me, I answer. But then I told you I took them. That's not stealing or lying!

She can't argue with that. So she changes her tune. — Oh, I give up, Luz Divina! In all this time, it's completely slipped my mind... A few weeks ago you said you'd had a dream—a dream about me. Do you still remember it?

She's always putting me down. Sure, I say. How could I forget a thing like that?

She sticks out her lips. Oh, of course! Your memory is perfect.

I have to explain it to her again; she's like a baby. Look, dreams give you numbers for the lottery, so I always try to keep them in my head. In this one, you were helping me make a big fruit salad. — I shoot her a dirty look. — You've never done that before, have you?

You wouldn't let me if I tried!

We chopped up mangoes, papayas, pineapples, and bananas. The salad must've been for a party. We chopped and chopped till we filled a great big bowl. — I've got to tell her the whole story now. — We said good-bye, and I closed the front door behind me. In my dream, your street was different: long and empty. I kept walking, and soon there weren't any houses. Up till then I thought I was go-ing home. Instead, I was walking in the country, the cam-po where I grew up. After a while I came to a river, the widest river you ever saw. There was lots of mud, but that didn't stop me. I took off my shoes, and when I got to the water, I kept on going. The funny thing is, I walked right on top of it. I didn't sink. I just kept walking, all by myself.

Gotta ride in the taxi share now, ever since the Harley got totaled. I try to sit up front with the driver. A build like mine, I can't fit in the back seat with three more pasajeros, like I have to right now. When there's a cute-looking chick, I put her on my lap so she can feel my dick under her butt, if she won't start squealin. No luck today, just a buncha old folks, but at least they're skinny.

I coulda told Chiara it wouldn't work with that Bono, Marino. First she has a run-in with him about stealing shirts. But then it turns out that old bitch Luz was the one liftin em! For a while the guy was workin hard, extra careful so nothing else would happen. Chiara was always talkin about what a good crico he was, even if she never said that word. But once a Bono, always a Bono. The trouble started when he was making a date to come around, then maybe he would get there late or maybe not at all. Pretty soon she realized he was drinkin all the time. He banged on the door any time of day, stinkin of booze and tryin to con dough outta her. The worst part was, he was doin risky things while he was drunk, borracho, like cleaning the gutters or maybe the water tank. After he almost got killed a couplea times, Chiara up and fired him: so long amigo, adiós.

But that's not the end of it. Nooo-ooo. A few weeks later, a radio went missing. Luz Divina's not even there that day since it was Sunday. Chiara went out a minute, and it musta been carried off by somebody sneakin down the stairs from the terrace, la terraza. A neighbor said he saw Marino prowlin on the roof that morning. But Chiara never reported him to the police. She was afraid they might beat him up. Y qué? So what? He fuckin deserved it!

The job at Chiara's house came just when I needed it. I finished with Héctor and ditched his goddam ass. Coño! Fuck! He only used me at the galería to push a few crates around so his chupapinga friends can watch me. To show the cocksuckers he got a hot guy. I don't mind long as they keep their paws offa me. But then he blew up when I wrecked the Harley. It's not my fault! Some other guy drove right in fronta me and I jumped off the bike before it hit a tree. Anyway, I was lucky to only get a sprained wrist and a couplea bruises. He never even showed me simpatía, so I quit at the gallery. He felt bad later and he wants me back. But no way, I say—not even to chichar. He's a good enough lay, for a guy, but I've had better. And how!

Chiara keeps me busy, in bed and out. Fuckin, culiadas: she helps me pass the time. Soon as I start workin for her, I see one project that's really urgent. So I've been repaintin the entire house, inside and outside. Hasn't been done in four years, since before she moved in. And the water sweats right through the wall in an old house like that, so the paint peels off. A leak que no tiene madre: so bad it never had a mother. Leakin up to your ears!

I know she was worried when she took me on. Sure, great havin me around for screwin, for fun-time rapadas, but am I too lazy for anything else? She was scared to end up in Héctor's shoes, fightin with me all the time.

Ha, she shoulda known it's different with me and her. For one thing, she's not jealous, so she never gives me grief all the time like Héctor. They say with men more fuck and less flak, but he was almost bad as Reina! Chiara's so busy with her books and stuff, she hardly pays attention to me most of the time. With nobody breathin down my neck, I'm glad I'm puttin in the hours. I like to work! Me gusta trabajar!

I'm a lot neater than she figured too. Paintin's a messy job, but I don't drip, even when I'm doin a ceiling. I built myself some tall wood ladders, so I can brushpaint the spots I can't get to with rollers. It's kinda cramped when you paint between the big wood beams, and it's high off the ground, muy alto. She almost had a fit one day when she saw me fallin on the bricks, all the way to the floor. She oughta remember I'm an athlete, everything from baseball to wrestling, pelota to lucha. I did some gymnastics too in Queens. So that day I landed in a somersault, and rolled to my feet like it was nothin.

That's when she started callin me el Gato, the Cat. In a way that's true. Not just about fallin but how a cat shuts up all day and only goes loco at night, de noche. I don't sleep in the day like they do, they're so lazy. But it's true

I just keep workin and don't bother Chiara by talkin like that bitch Luz always does, runnin her mouth! Later, when Chiara and I finish workin about six, a las seis, we have a drink and hit the bed for sex.

Yeah, I'm gettin a boner, right here in the carro público, the taxi share. What an ugly creep: that old pendejo next to me is lookin at my crotch. I better think about somethin else, so I don't bust his face.

One thing I like about Chiara's house is she keeps it neat, ordenadita. That's what I'm always tryin to do in San Sebastián, but Reina is such a slob she drives me nuts. My children are still little, so I don't wanna explode in front of them. But sometimes it just happens. No aguanto, I lose it. I take Reina outside and give her a talkin to, and we start hitting each other on the sidewalk. She's a strong bitch, spends more time at the gym than me. Liftin weights, mainly. And she's quick. We give each other a run for the money and waste a lotta dough, cause we have to pay for stuff we bust up in the barrio. Chairs, tables, bottles. Hey, nobody's perfect!

For a guy, I really care about the place where I'm living. Sure, it's a crappy neighborhood, but inside my house I want it lookin nice. I'm the only person on my street with a lotta plants in pots and plastic fundas. I put tiny holes in the bags, so the roots get to breathe, respirar. I always bring lotsa seeds from my granddad's farm. Not just veg-etales, some flowers too to brighten up the place. Cayenas, trinitarias: Chiara calls em hibiscoes and boogievilles.

One reason I like to work at Chiara's house, she's got a real garden, not just pots and bags but deep earth where the matas can grow big roots. I wish she'd let me keep animals in the patio, but she's not down for that. What am I supposed to do with them when you're not around? she says. Yeah, they'd be jumpin on her and gettin in the way. But how about a turtle? I ask her. Tortugas don't make any noise. She just ignores me.

Chiara never messes things up like Reina. The only one that causes trouble is that bitch Luz Divina. She does it on purpose. She thinks she can call the shots, but I'm not a chump. She tries to boss me around the way she does Chiara, but the old puta better watch out. She oughta be grateful, agradecida, cause I clean up in places she can't reach. Anyway, the best way for not buttin heads with her is me showin up in the afternoon when's she's already gone.

That's a great schedule for me, cause I can put in two hours every morning at the gym. The gimnasio is my life! Chiara never gets much exercise herself, but she likes me to stay in shape. And at the end of the day, she can give me a massage for my muscles, especially the biggest one. Hahaha!

The way I keep a house clean, I like to keep my bod clean too, mi cuerpo. A lotta times when Chiara goes up to the azotea and reads a few hours, she catches me washin up in the patio when she comes down from the roof. It makes her laugh when I do some weightlifter poses while I'm rinsin off, poses de fisicultura. She says I look like a statue in a fountain, a fuckin estatua. Ok, whatever flips her ship. I go on like that for half an hour, and sometimes she sits in a chair and we talk. The darker it gets, the more I like to jawbone. I get in the mood.

Like the other day I'm sayin how I always tell the guys you gotta rinse yourself first, with a lotta plain water: agua, muchachos, agua! After that, you sudsy up with the soap. Not before, never: no antes, jamás. Never in the life.

She teases me cause at the gym a buncha young dudes follow me around. They're only fifteen or sixteen, somethin like that. Lookin for tips about working out. She calls em my fan club.

Bad advice from Coach Paniagua, she says. Sounds like a waste of water to me.

No, Señora Chiara, I tell her. Canubans gotta be careful. Most of us never got cut. We gotta scrub our pingas good, else we get infected.

I pull my skin back to show her. I'm gettin hard, and she's already hungry. I can tell by the look in her eyes. Greedy like. Ya le conozco, I know her like my hand back.

She's takin her time though. Same as in Italy, she says. I bet your muchachos don't have as much to scrub as you do. Have you ever measured yourself?

Sure. Tá claro, amiga. Nine and a half inches, and then some!

I got a humongous cock and I know it. I'm pingón. She

laughs at me, calls me 'Amado the horse' sometimes. She's always comparin me to animals. It's okay by me cause I love em. They got more sense than people any day. Mucho más! I'm a tiger when I jump all a sudden, she says. But mostly I'm a dog. She says I'm faithful like one, and that's for sure. And I'll defend her anytime, bite somebody's fuckin hand off with my teeth. Don't ever mess with me! Funny, now we're together a lot we get along great. Not like with Reina or Héctor, fightin all the time. I used to hate it when she never let me stay for the night. Now I don't care. She notices the difference, she says.

Yeah, I tell her, you and me. It's special. Muy especial. You're the only damn person who likes me the way I am.

Sometimes I surprise her by leavin a note on the kitchen shelf, or in the gaveta of her desk. The drawer where she keeps her pens. I write it the best way I can. It's harder than talkin, for sure.

The other day I left one that says: You're a real señora to me Chiara. I never loved somebody so much, jamás. I don't know what I did for Dios to help me knowin you, pretty lady.

Yesterday was: You don't want me to live with you so I gotta wait, esperar for tomorrow. To see you again. Chiara, I'm sayin your name for to make me feel better, and I'll never leave you, always and siempre lovin you.

Round the words I like to draw little hearts, maybe with wings. Corazoncitos con alitas. Kinda romantic that way.

People don't understand the more macho you are, the more romantic you can get. Coño! You just gotta let go and be yourself. Fuck what anybody thinkin.

Most of all, I like my hours at the gym. I like to feel the burn in my muscles, when I push myself harder and harder. I get off on that shit! A lotta people say I could be a bodybuilder champion if I wanna. A real fisiculturista. But that's the thing, I don't care about that stuff. I don't run round in a tank top or lycra shorts like most of those dudes. I just like the disciplina, the burn. Maybe that's the only disciplina I got! Hahaha. When I'm exercisin, I get excited. My whole body's like one big dick. A pinga enorme.

Well, here I am at Chiara's house, and it's time to work. I gotta wash down the roof and clean the drain up there, where the fuckin flowers clog it up. Damn em to hell. That's one thing where I agree with Luz Divina. The friggin flores are such a pain, fallin down all over every day. What a plaga, worse than the clap!

After that I gotta climb on the tallest ladder, and limpiar the dust off the ceiling fans, clean the abanicos. If you don't do it a lot, they start to rust.

Finally, I'm through! While I hose myself in the patio, Chiara comes to watch me. Get naked, mujer, I tell her. You can't be lookin at me like that if you're not desnuda too.

She gets undressed and sits in one of the green metal chairs, the sillas verdes. I feel like talkin now, so I ask what she's been up to, all and nothin. I get a charge outta hearin her talk about the people she meets, la gente. That Frederica lady's always introducin her around. The ones I wanna meet are the rich young bitches, las jevitas. Maybe richer and younger than Chiara. I'll never ditch her, I love her too much. But there's always room for more. I've got a jumbo appetite. Un apetito!

She usually dodges outta my questions about the jevitas, but today she says I'm not their type.

Huh? I'm leanin back on my heels and laughin. Oh yeah, I tell her, that's the trouble with this fuckin country, este maldito país. The women with all the dough don't want the machotes, they never like the strongest dudes. They're only interested in wimps, flojitos. But they get what they deserve. The same weak little chotas they say they like get turned on by machos like me!

And who turns the machos on?

Good-lookin women, obvious. Or anybody's got a throat, a garganta, and the plata to buy some Canuba Libres. If you stay on top, amiga, you're still a macho no matter what.

You mean a bugarrón.

She's pitchin me a fuckin curveball. All I say back to her is this. I don't like it when you talk dirty. Catulo musta taught you that word. Coño!

So, she says. What's the big deal? If they do a good job

in bed, don't macho guys like a present? A silk shirt, maybe? Or even a motorcycle?

What got into her today? She tryin to fuck with me? Not everybody's so greedy, so interesado, I tell her. I'm flexin my biceps, remindin her who's who. All I know is, long as you act like a man, you're not a pato, a queer. Sorry for talkin trash in front of a lady. But Héctor always says, a man who fucks a man is twice a man.

Chiara's about to laugh, but I tell her off. Look, ombe. You're not a man, you're a woman. And you don't have to worry about gettin a bill from me, if that's what's eatin you.

I need to calm down. She's just havin fun with me, I know. Wants to be in on things. Hmmm, I say, to make up. Maybe you're not so out of it after all. Half the time you seem like some kinda monja.

Monja? With what we've been up to! Not just you, though: a lot of people here think I'm a nun. The little old ladies in the street always say 'Good morning, Sister' when I go by.

That's cause there used to be Italian monjas in the barrio here. They wore regular clothes. Like anybody else. And they were serious, like you.

Hahaha. I'm no saint—not by a long shot. I don't need to tell you that. But I'm not much of a sinner, either. It's just too exhausting! After our evening 'massages,' I feel tuckered out.

I'm thinkin I want more, not less. No, you're wrong, Señora Chiara, I tell her. It's like exercise at the gym. Believe me. The more you do it, the more energy you get. My strongest muscle is between my legs. And you know how they say in Nueva Yol. Lose it or use it!

Yes, Amado, you pumped that muscle like you pumped your biceps. With a million repetitions! But I wish you'd stop calling me señora. I'm only about ten years older than you. We're close friends by now, at least.

Ha, what she does she know? — I'm just showin you respect, I say. Around here, I'm the crico, and you're the boss.

There you go with your slang again: I love it! I've tried to figure out what that word means. Horacio came up with 'employee.' But the way you use it, it's more negative than that. Catulo claims crico derives from Crisco. It's an American grease for cooking, and at first it was expensive here. Only wealthy women could afford it, and they sent their maids to buy it at the fancy grocer's. The maids called it 'crico,' so they became 'cricas.' You Canubans are always dropping the inner *s*'s, and the final ones too! So now it's a pejorative term for the working-class—or for anyone who's 'vulgar,' so it seems.

She's goin on too long, as usual. — Employee. Yeah, I guess. You're always talkin about stuff like that. I can be brainy too, when I wanna. See, recepcionistas and waiters, they're employees. No, a crico's more personal like. Más personal. Somebody who washes your laundry or polishes your shoes. Look at me now. Here I am, sweaty from cleanin the roof in the goddam sun: todo sudado. And you, you're fresh as a petunia.

After all that rinsing, you look clean to me. Anyway, you're right, there's no such thing as a crico in English— or Italian. Not anymore. There used to be nasty words like that. Flunky, servo. But nobody says them nowadays. They're undemocratic—though maybe we're just being hypocrites.

Right, hipócritas! Coño! That's nothin new for gringos, Chiara. In Canuba we like to face the facts, los hechos. Most people around here *are* cricos. That's what we all hate about this place. It means we're inferior.

I don't look down on you at all. See what you just taught me? Now I understand why Lamia was cracking up the other day. She'd seen a homemade movie called 'La Criconauta.' The crica astronaut!

A crica's only a maid. How come an astronauta?

Oh, one of Lamia's pato friends did the cartoon, and a film studio produced it. The criconauta had steel hair-curlers shaped like a helmet, and they shot her into space.

I gotta laugh out loud. Yeah, they wear curlers all day, gettin ready for the disco! But who cares if they're cricas or cricos. They wanna blast off friggin anywhere, even to the moon, if they can leave this hellhole behind. Here there's nothing, no hay na!

She gets that look on her face, like she's gonna tell me the cuatro verdades, the four truths. That's what I don't understand, Amado. You can move back to the States any time you want. Half your family's already there. Instead you stay here, in the slum of San Sebastián.

That's cause I love my country, bendito. Amo mi país. Even if it's a hellhole. Besides, you goddam gringos treat us like shit in Nueva Yol, como mierda. Okay, you didn't grow up there. Maybe you're different. I'm just proud of Canuba, proud to be a Canuban, and prouda my family too. Mi familia.

She's still got that look. Why don't you work for your father, then?

I already decided, I'm not gonna get mad at her today. You know the story, I tell her. He never liked my wife, and he says I'm too wild. My mother's the same. She never liked Reina either. Damn Evangélicos.

Maybe I'm gonna get mad after all, but not at Chiara. She's on my side.

Catholics can be just as narrow-minded, she says.

Not here, except maybe the Arzobispo. But he's more like a politician, and the Papa in Rome tells him what to do. Most Católicos, they say caramba, who cares ? Let it be. In secret, the Archbishop does what he feels like, when nobody's lookin. He chases women all the time.

If the Protestants want Canubans to change their ways, they've got their work cut out for them! she laughs.

Hey, the little slut. La putica. She's already got her hand on my pinga, strokin it up and down.

Yeah, Chiara, mi hermano. Just let em try!

I've got a total hard-on now, and I'm almost ready to jump in bed.

But anyway, I tell her, how do you know what we're like? No sabe nada, not a damn thing. All you do is read all day long, or blab with stuck-up pendejos. I can't stand em. Fuckin dickheads! Why don't you go out with me, and see how real people live?

Sure, Señor Amado. It's a deal. Anywhere you want… anytime.

I'm not listenin anymore. I'm rubbin her tits. Sus tetas. They're still pretty good, not too sloppy for her age. I shove my dick in her mouth.

Let's get down to it, mujer.

She pretends like she's shocked, escandalizada. What else does she expect me to do, when she's makin me so horny? Coño! Coñazo!

Chiara, San Sebastián, September 1983

I didn't know how to react, when Amado said he'd squire me around the city. I figured he'd drop the idea soon enough. But before he left that day he shook my hand like we were making a solemn agreement. I had to wince, he squeezed it so hard.

Remember, we gotta deal. — He swept me up in his arms. — Hey, señora, maybe I love you after all. Tal vez.

That's what the notes you leave me say—unless you're lying.

He kissed me on the lips: Shhh. It's a secret. Un secreto. Smiling like a little boy, he set me down.

That was several months ago, and we've seen a lot since then. For our first outing, he invited me to a baseball game at the Cayonaiba Stadium: the Estrellas versus the Leones. Compared to a match I saw in the US during grad school, this one was faster and more free-wheeling. In Canuba any kind of chore, even walking, proceeds at a snail's pace. But baseball is like dancing, drinking, or making love. By speeding it up, you can pack more pleasure into every second. Almost shattering my eardrums, Amado yelled through every inning. My back and legs took a beating; when his team scored a point, he thwacked my shoulders or clenched my thighs.

There've been so many excursions since then, they're almost a blur... Centinela Beach on the Malecón, where tween boys surf in polluted waves... Jaula del Papagayo, a hangout that boasts the coldest beers in town... Cruz del Monte in the mountains, where two rivers converge at a mammoth swimming-hole.

I'd been to Playa Cambuca before, with sybaritic Catulo: we lolled on the terrace of an opulent hotel, sipping prosecco from Valdobbiadene. When I went back with Amado, he made me lie on a beach-towel, wedged between hoi polloi Canubans. Each of them came armed with a squawky boombox. No matter where we happened to be—town or campo—Amado horsed around with his pals, flirted with the best-looking girls, and rippled his muscles for the 'ducks.'

Catulo needles me about our 'camaraderie,' as he puts it. Deep down, he's jealous. He'd love to share an hour of simple companionship, unmarred by self-deflating irony.

One day he drives into town from Hermosa, and discovers me at my desk. — I'm flummoxed you're here writing, girlfriend! I thought you'd be noshing camburicos at a curbside stand!

We bear-hug for almost a minute… Ah, if only… These days, all I can do is reminisce. We were a couple once, even if it didn't pan out. Catulo should take me for another spin, after my postdoc in sexuality! I'm not the awkward 'geek-essa' I used to be.

Regretfully, I tear myself away. — Camburicos! I'm soaking up pop culture with Amado, not attempting suicide.

Look on the sunny side, dearheart. We don't need to kill ourselves. — He caresses my back. — Sooner or later, the Grim Reaper does it for us.

For the time being, I plan to survive. And Amado pulls

my nose out of the books.

That's fine and dandy, carissima, but don't delude yourself. He's rooked you with the censored version so far.

Oh really? What's he leaving out?

For one thing, the people's religion—and I'm not talking about the Church.

You mean Voodoo, I suppose.

Voodoo? Come on, Chiara! Have you been hiding under a rock? The hip nomenclature is Vodou. It's similar to Hispanic Santería. Whatever you call it, it's a force to be reckoned with.

As usual, I can't decipher his tone. Cynical, or sincere? — Don't be so pedantic. That was a slip of the tongue, smart aleck. Yes, I know it's Vodou. I've heard of Santería. And Amado will teach me more. Any other suggestions?

Why not go from the sublime to the sublime? Strip joints, whorehouses, seamy discos. I bet you haven't been to a drag show yet.

That's not a priority for me.

But it *is* for Amado. — He spreads his arms, like a danseur at his curtain call.

Oh, he likes to kid around. But he's a red-blooded he-man, if ever there was one.

That's exactly what I mean, girlfriend. Machos love lip-synch. If you propose a drag show, you'll see how his ears prick up.

When I relay Catulo's list the following day, Amado

shrugs. Sure, you wanna meet a mambo? Pointedly, he overlooks the other items.

Now that we're actually headed for the shrine, my main sensation is fear. Not of 'evil spirits,' but of San Sebastián, the barrio where Amado lives. He's cautioned me that any gringa will attract rapists and muggers, so we're moving through the streets in a taxi, not on foot. As long as we keep the windows rolled up, we'll avoid machete-thrusts, or hands lunging for my purse.

The distant gunshots I've heard once or twice hardly reassure me. A bullet might zing through the windscreen any moment, x-ing me out before I know it. Except for a few squat houses built of concrete blocks, the shacks we pass have been thrown together from sheet-metal, vinyl siding, and cast-off wood.

At Amado's command, the driver skids to a stop before a putrid alleyway. Wait for us here! my friend bellows.

We plunge into 'la parte atrás,' a rabbit warren for the poorest of the poor, 'the part behind' the run-down houses on the street. We zigzag past slapdash huts, festering puddles, and rubbish heaps. Finally we arrive at a door of corrugated tin, painted a pristine white. Without knocking, Amado flings it open.

If he weren't here to protect me, I'd never step inside... It's so dark I can't see a thing. The place might be a dog-fight pit, a safe house for hit men, or a torture chamber for Espinosa's goons.

Somebody strikes a match: whoever lit it must've been been lying in wait... But instead of hoodlums, a ravishing priestess stands before us. Her blue silk turban, turquoise pendant, and white linen robe set off her burnished black skin. With her full lips and long, graceful neck, she resembles an Egyptian bas-relief. Murmuring in a cultured, melodic voice, she lights several candles.

Chiara, I've been dying to meet you. Bienvenida. Welcome. Or should I say bienvenue? Amado tells me you speak French, as well as a dozen other languages.

He looks away. I've caught him bragging—about me.

Oh, that's a flattering fib! In five, I can muddle through. But I can read the menus in nine or ten.

A useful talent! she titters, taking my hand. Let me introduce myself. My name is Diana. I'm Bonaventuran on my father's side, but my mother is Canuban.

From what I understand, that's the wave of the future.

Don't bet on it, Amado growls.

Diana is unfazed; she continues in French, to exclude him. — Don't say things like that where Canubans can hear you, Chiara. They don't want boat people like me getting uppity. I was raised in Saint-François, the capital of Bonaventure, but the channel isn't wide.

So that's why your French is so good.

She goes back to Spanish. — No, not really: we call our language Bonavent. It's a mixture of French, Spanish, Taíno, and English, along with words from West Africa.

You wouldn't understand it very well. I learned 'normative French' in Paris, where I did my Master's in history on a scholarship—my maîtrise. English I picked up by interning with Oxfam in Ghana. I've been back to Europe a couple of times since then for...

Amado glowers at her. Why didn't she finish her sentence? She seems terribly urbane for a Vodou mambo—though no doubt that only shows how much I need to learn.

We don't have any more time to chat: the faithful are filing into the temple. Many of them are dressed in white like Diana, and some of them carry drums. As my eyes adjust to the dimness, I see that her sanctuary is spacious and well-appointed. The packed-earth floor has been neatly swept. In the center, an altar overflows with candles, costume jewelry, statues of animals, pictures of loas and saints, sprigs of herbs, festoons of ribbon and lace, tin figures in vibrant hues, and bottles with strings of lentils. Chicken feet, too—some fresh and some decayed.

Once her followers have all trooped in, Diana leads a rousing incantation, mostly in Bonavent. Like any journalist worth her salt, I've boned up beforehand on Vodou. I can't follow the language, but I distinguish several names I came across in my research: Erzili Freda, the spirit of love; Damballa, the spirit of wisdom; and Agwe Tawoyo, the spirit of the sea.

Taking her time, Diana anoints the ground with molasses, perfume, and rum. She scatters cornmeal in elaborate patterns. Then she shakes a beaded gourd-rattle tied to a bell. Her congregation watches her raptly, swaying to the tomtom of the drummers. At the climax, she falls into a swoon, possessed by one of the loas. Delirious, she rocks back and forth in the arms of her female disciples.

When she staggers to her feet, the frenzied drummers start pounding even harder. Amado whispers in my ear: Vámonos. This is the part they call the palos. It could go on all night.

Once we're safely in the taxi again, I ask him if he believes in Vodou. He gives me a sidelong glance. — My abuela made me wear a resguardo when I was growin up. Kinda like a double string they tie around your waist. I was fallin outta trees, ridin bronco horses, and blowin up a lotta fireworks. But hey, ombe, I'm still alive, so the thing musta worked! — He snickers. — A few months ago, Diana put a wanga bag around my neck. Said it would keep my wife from being such a pain. It had some caña de azúcar to sweeten her up—some sugarcane—and some ice to cool her down.

What happened?

The ice melted and the caña rotted away. What else? My fuckin wife, she's still jodona as ever. — He tosses his head back roguishly. — So who knows about this stuff? Maybe it's mumbo-jumbo. Anyway, you're about to meet the bitch in person, if you can stand it. My house is right round the corner. We'll grab us some food there, ok?

Three or four streets away from the temple, we get out of the taxi. The driver promises he'll wait for me outside; I pledge him something extra if he does.

So this is where he lives... Amado's plywood shack could barely withstand a gust of wind, much less a hurricane. But he's lined up five flowerpots on the swaybacked porch, to spruce it up a bit. Inside, he's nailed some pictures on the wall. His mother, his son and daughter, his wife. Not his father—predictably enough.

Reina is long on smiles, but short on words. Since I'm her husband's employer, she offers me the chair of honor. It's the only real one, in fact—the rest are soda-pop crates. I can see why Amado complains about her being slovenly. The doll-size room is littered with broken toys, though she must've tucked the children into bed an hour ago. I can hear their gentle breathing behind a flimsy partition.

Frowning at Reina, Amado rakes the bric-a-brac into a corner. She seems indifferent to his anger; her moonlike face, haloed by blue plastic curlers, beams at me vacantly. Brawny as a wrestler, she trumpets her assets with bikini underwear—her evening outfit, tout court. Amado is always denigrating his wife, but he's sacrificed a lot for her: his parents, his US green card, his future. There must be more to her than meets the eye. If Reina makes love as energetically as she works out, that might explain her appeal... I kick myself. I'm beginning to think like a

Canuban, with a one-track lascivious mind.

After a while my hostess comments flatly, to no one in particular: I didn't cook today, but there's some conflay in the cupboard, and leche en polvo. That's what me and the children ate.

It's her longest speech of the evening. For dinner, corn-flakes and powdered milk. Whamming his fist against a shelf, Amado bangs it loose and storms into the street. After a hurried 'hasta luego' to Reina, I have no choice but to follow suit.

Amado, all over town, a few nights later

I coulda killed Reina the other night. I told her I'm bringin Chiara to the house, so she better clean up, or else. Instead it was a mess, as fuckin usual. If Chiara hadna been there, we would've had a big fight for sure, a pelea en grande! Out on the sidewalk, to keep from wakin up the kids. I don't know what Reina did with the food I bought so she could make us dinner. Maybe she gave it to those no good sisters of hers, her hermanas. Always comin from the campo and bummin somethin offa us. Like vultures, buitres!

Anyway, Chiara picked up the slack, the way she always does. My exercise routine means I gotta eat. She told the driver to take us to Casa Madrileña. An old timey Spanish place where they cook carne and sausage caldos. A lotta protein for my weightliftin diet. Even if Reina fucked things up that day, Chiara promised me she'd go out again this weekend—at night. Great! she said. A tour of Puerto Indio de noche!

We meet up at ten on Saturday, and I flag down a taxi close to Plaza Drake. A tin can piecea junk. I tell the driver we wanna go to Club Caribe. No address needed, for that. The beatup Chevy heads through Damasco. Not the richest part of town, but a helluva lot better than my neighborhood. And more goin on than where Chiara lives. At least in Damasco people are sittin around outside with their radios, tappin their feet and havin some fun.

She covers her ears cause of the noise, la bulla. But I'm not gonna let her off the hook. I'm singin the chorus to my theme-song cambuca, good and loud. Eres el amor de mi vida! Eres mi amor fatal! Hey amiga, I tell her, you hear how the music is revvin up? It's comin from the houses and the cars, even from the goddam sidewalk. Come on, let's dance in our seat. Forget that cemetery where you live, if you can call it livin. Olvidalo!

Pretty soon we're in the money. Ortega sector, the big-ass casas of the millonarios. Club Caribe is a bar where jevitos go, young rich kids. It's kinda cool, cause it's divided in four levels round a waterfall, a cascada. The chick who thought it up still comes to look at it sometimes. Caramela Sosa is her name, and she's kinda famous now. What you call an architect. Half the queers in town wanna be architects! She's sittin over there right now in a torn-up camiseta, with her arm around a girl.

Yeah, it's always a mixed-up crowd. The jevitas in miniskirts with no bra and the jevitos in suits with no tie and no socks, some old-timers too. Most of the chicas got their dates in tow, dudes they lead on a correa like dogs—we call em chotas. But you count more dudes and pájaro queers than women, plus some of the women are pájaras too with short hair and leather pants or jeans. Or going the other way, girly as hell. Different folks for different strokes, they say in Nueva Yol. Fine by me. In Canuba we just say no problema! You can be one way, another way, or all kindsa ways for all we give a damn.

Chiara's laughin cause everybody's shoutin out my name. She teases me I got more friends than anybody she knows. Well, I like people and they like me back. Y qué? So what?

Hey, that big tit waitress just goosed me! Don't tell me, the morena says. You lookin for a job again? Or a loan?

That's somethin Chiara never knew about. When I chucked that asshole Héctor, I tell her after a drink or two, I worked here for a while. You know, bartender. A good kinda job. Before you took me on fulltime.

She stares at me like I'm loco. Three hours a day is fulltime? she asks.

She better not give me any backtalk, or she'll end up

like Héctor. She's drinkin her usual, Ron Real and club soda, and I'm suckin on Canuba Libres with a straw. Double on the rum. Makes me kinda talkative. You know what, Chiara? Héctor kept comin here night after night, all that month. Gatuseando, like a cat wantin his head rubbed, butterin me up. Yeah, he'd smack five hundred escudos on the bar. This is for an hour's worth, he'd say, if you go home with me right now. But I just gave him the finger every time. Not so fast! No es así de fácil! I'm not so easy, man!

I shouldna said that. I back up some, real quick. No joda! I mean, I wouldna worked in that bastard's gallery again, not even for quinientos escudos an hour!

Chiara's got a funny smile on her face. Ok, she's right, nobody'd ever offer that much. Not for hangin a picture, anyway. After a while, she says: Speak of the devil. I look over my shoulder, and here comes Héctor headin our way.

Good evening, Chiara, he says, oily as can be. Como una culebra, like a snake. It's been a few years, but I told you we'd get together for a drink. And here we are.

He eases himself on the barstool I'm jumpin up from. He won't look me in the eye. And me at him, neither. He can go fuck himself. I move a few seats down and start talkin to the bartender. But I'm listenin to everything they say.

Chiara's tryin to get away from him. I'm sorry, Héctor. I'm out on the town tonight, so I'll have to run along.

He's bustin for an argument. Oh, you mean you're with him. He can wait till hell freezes over. What's wrong, afraid he'll go out back for a quickie? With somebody his own age?

The nerve of that guy. Coño! I could smash his face in, but all I'm doin is listen. He butts in on me and the barman, callin him over like he owns the place. A double Stolly cold, young man. No rocks please. Plus a double Real and soda.

Drunks like him can always tell what brand somebody's drinkin from the smell. So why are you hanging around with what's-his-name? he asks. Lousy little fucker, like he forgot my name. He pours the booze down his garganta in one friggin gulp. I thought you were having a fling with Lamia, our female Danny La Rue. To quote our motto: Once you go black, you never come back; and once you go brown, you never come down!

Chiara's keepin her cool. So I keep mine, too. What if I trash the bar, and she gotta pay the damage? Racist rubbish, she says. I like all kinds, don't you? Amado's just a friend, by the way. Lamia, too. Hey, she's really takin him for a ride!

Héctor starts seein red. So you're everybody's little friend. He's slurrin halfa what he says, the hijo de puta. Gettin plastered outta his mind. Why don't you crawl back under that African rock you came from? You're nothing but a jinx. You know what I tell my friends? And they're *my* friends, not yours: Touch Chiara and die.

She looks hurt, like she's about to cry. If she does, he's fuckin done for. I shouldn't have confided in you that night, she says. Of all people. Believe me, I didn't know about you and Amado when I met him.

Que pendejo! Héctor's such a jerk. All you had to do was inquire, he laughs with his nose in the air. Anyway, I couldn't care less about you and your toy-boy. As I always say, he's a book I've read, a movie I've seen. You hear me?

Chiara stays calm: What I hear is the alcohol yapping. And by tomorrow, the hangover's going to howl.

By this time she's had enough of his shit, and I'm makin for the exit. Chiara takes a detour to the ladies room. I look back and see him grabbin the ron con soda he ordered for her. He kicks it back sloppy like, all over his moustache and down his chin. Rum on toppa vodka. Rayos, man! He's on a binge.

When Chiara catches up with me, I'm clownin round with a chick on stiletto heels, tacos altísimos. Fifteen years, maybe. Sixteen max. She kinda wobbles into the bar, like she's about to fall down. Nothin I can do for her now! I rub Chiara on the neck. Let's go, mi hermano, I tell her. This dump is already dead.

The next taxi I flag is only a Honda Civic, but at least it's in decent shape. Pretty soon we're at another joint. The owner calls it a gentlemen's club, and he tries hard livin up to the name, Diosas. Some of the strippers look like a goddess, long as they keep their mouth shut. But they don't know crap about dancin. Ni en pintura, not even in a picture.

Chiara, I bet you never been to the strip joints in Nueva Yol. They're great, a maravilla! Not like here. This is the third dancer, and she's the worst. Somebody oughta teach these girls how to shake their booty!

Why don't you apply for the job? You could bill your-self as El Profesor.

Hahaha, not a bad idea. But the pimps would probably stick it to me. They're right over there, the chulos.

There's two of em hangin out in the corner. Hair slicked back, cheapo suits. I can spot em a mile away, from leguas. The short one is watchin me, and I know why. Account-ing, contabilidad. His main girl is prissin over to our table. I had her before, and she's not so bad. Green eyes, ojos verdes. A pretty color to her skin, like honey and miel.

Amado, cariño, long time no see, she says, kissin me on the lips. Where's Héctor? Oh yeah, and who's your gringa friend?

Meet Chiara. She's just here for the strip show. Right? Verdad?

I look at Chiara, hopin she'll play along. Héctor used to pick up the tab with these chicks. We'd do a threeway, and wow it was awesome. I'd fuck her, fuck him, and the other one would eat my ass while I'm doin it. No luck with Chiara though, la monja. She clams up like a nun.

I pat the chica on the butt. Well baby, gotta go, nos fuimos. We jump in another taxi, and I can tell Chiara's havin a second thought. I know she's got a thing for Lamia, and she's not the only one. I've been with her a couplea times, and she's hot. But way too bossy for me. Too mandona! Anyway, I don't know if Chiara's into mujeres, or just that one. Too late to find out, right now.

Hey, Chiara says. What's the rush?

That stripper got my motor goin, bendito. If you're not up for a trio, I still need a piecea ass, some culo! And I guess it's gotta be free.

We end up back in Chiara's part of town. Where are you taking me? she asks, confused. I walk down this street all the time!

Uh huh, and I bet you never noticed this little sign.

Kinda curley cue, in blue neon. MOMENTOS, the name of the place. Flashin on and off, like a strobe light. No, she goes, I never did. I guess you can only see it at night, when I'm already in bed.

You're such a damn monja! I tell her, slappin her ass.

Inside it's dark as Diana's temple, but no mambo's here to strike us a match. I push Chiara down a pasillo crammed with people. At the end of the hall the music is goin for bust, loud and fast, a lotta fuckin noise the way I like it: bulla! A hundred sweaty cuerpos sudosos jivin to the music, stuck in together. Tá timbí! Packed like sardines! You can smell the perfume and cock and toto, the pinga and cunt. I set Chiara down in a plastic chair at a little table, with a soft kinda light. You wait for me here, I say. I'll only be gone for twenty minutes, max.

When I look back, a hand's bringin her a beer, and takin some escudos outta her fingers. Now she's coverin her ears! What does she expect from a disco?

I'm squashin my way to the pista de baile and lettin the crowd rock me, every way but through the floor. Some kinda gringo stuff is playin, dudes with high voices, I've heard em before. But the rhythm's OK. All I'm seein is my watch dial, the radium lucita bouncin around. I feel up whoever's in fronta me from behind. Yeah, a muchacha with a bigtime ass, a culón! My hands start swipin all over her. She's got tetas grandes too, humongous tits.

Coño! I'm in luck cause we're right next to the mattress. The guy who owns this place keeps a kingsize colchón turned on its side and nailed to the wall. I bump her back against it and she pulls up her skirt. I whip out my pinga, put a condom on, and fuck her right there. Nobody can see us but if they do, qué va, who cares? We keep on dancin all the time, never missin a beat. Que mamacita! What a babe! Ohhh, that's so greeeeeat, cheverísimo! Estoy en el cielo! I'm way, way up, in the fuckin sky! I shout when I'm comin, and nobody hears me it's so goddam loud.

It takes me a while pushin back to where Chiara's been sittin. A record, amiga! I tell her. Just fourteen minutes to grab a mujercita and rapar. I screwed her standin up!

Wow. Vámonos, let's go.

Out on the street, I'm still fired up, calentado! I did it with a real perra, a slut! They've gotta whole wall that's a mattress in there, Chiara. You oughta try it sometime, your house is so close.

See, she pinches my butt. My barrio's not so tame after all!

Hard to find a taxi now. I finally get a rundown jalopy to stop for us, a cacharra. This time all I say is the address. The driver turns round and winks at us, like he's in on somethin. Tá claro. Sure, I know, La Cumbre.

Wiseguy, sabihondo. Chiara's pretty tired I guess, so I give her a little massage in the backseat, a masajito. She says she's never been to most of these streets. Hahaha. How could she, if she never goes out? La Cumbre's kinda off the beaten track, alright. They call it The Summit cause it's a penthouse, on toppa an old, broke-down building. Any guy who's got what it takes and needs some fast cash, this is the place. All the pájaros hang around here, the queers who're ready and willin to shell you a fair price. The bugarrones hunt the patos, and anything can go down! If you don't wanna take somebody home, you can do it right here. In the rest rooms, or they've got a couplea balconies with curtains you can close. Or you can let people watch you, if that's your thing. We say 'para los gustos son los colores': everybody's got a favorite color to their own!

Sort of a relief havin some light after Momentos. Here

it's still kinda dark, but at least you can see your dick in fronta your face. Thing is, they've got three kinds of customers. The pájaros in regular clothes, havin drinks. Might be local queers, might be gringos or both. The hustler bugarrones in tight jeans and camisetas with no sleeves. And the drag queens, petites or grandotas. Some of em are six foot tall! A lot of em got plastic fingernails, uñas two inches long, and they're all wearing a jewel necklace pretendin it's real. Some of em got a tiara on toppa their wig, a coronita. Oh yeah, I almost forget, there's a few regular women too, mujeres de verdad! Some of em are dykes, and some of em just like a man who can bat both ways. When you come down to it, mostly us Canubans swing left and right. Depends on who we meet. So what the hell? No problema.

Everywhere I've been with Chiara these last months, she's always teasin me about my fans. What can I do? I know a lotta people. But here they go fuckin ape, I gotta admit. The drag queens are all screamin when they see me, and the buggarones are slappin me on the back, giving me palmaditas.

When we find us a table, Chiara starts in on me. I guess you used to frequent this dive with Héctor, too.

Sometimes she's hard to take! I put her in her place. Héctor who? No, ombe, you got it wrong. Reina's the one who loves this club. We even got married here. It was some kinda crazy party! Qué locura!

She laughs. Not an official marriage, I suppose. The day you set up house together, no?

I don't say yes or no, and she yaks on. By the way, is Reina a part time lesbian? You can't shock me. Wouldn't that go with the territory?

Chiara and her ideas, sus ideas. Coño! You just do stuff, you don't talk about it. She shuts her mouth when the mujer herself shows up. Our surprise guest, I tell Chiara.

Hahaha! Reina can hardly get her thighs under the table, she's been pumpin iron at the gym so much. I smack her on the cheek with my hand, but not too hard. For once in your life, perra, you made it on time. The three AM's about to start.

Chiara's hard to please. Tells us she's seen some famous drag shows in London and Bangyacock. Whatever. Yeah, the lip synchers miss a lotta words here, cause they don't know much English. But they've got gasolina in their engine, a helluva lot of gas! They jump around the stage like a buncha goats. The funniest to me are Las Tres Suizas, three old maricones from Swissland. They flew here for a week and never went home!

But I gotta agree the next six strippers dance shitty: una mierda. Eighteen or maybe twenty years, jovencitos. Skinny Canubans and Bonos. They think all they gotta do is throw off their shorts and flap their XL pingas around. Chiara calls em mangueras, fire-hoses. They're not sexy anyway para nada, not one bit.

I'm kinda wasted by now, after five double Canuba Libres. Reina had a few too. Fuck, I tell her. These dudes are even worse than the chicas at Diosas. I've had it with em, big time. I sock her arm. Come on, bitch. Let's teach em a thing or two!

The whole room's been waitin for this moment. I was knowin that all along: we're always the stars of the show. Soon as we get up, everybody starts yellin. Amado y Reina, Amado y Reina, Amado y Reina! The stripper muchachos scram to the back, waggin their tails in front of em. Reina and me climb up on stage, nice and slow. No hay prisa, no hurry.

The DJ puts on a salsa to warm us up. But he changes it pretty quick to an old-time cambuca, kinda funny. The letters go Ay señorito! No lo tienes chiquito! About a small little guy with a great big cock. I look over at Chiara. Her mouth's hangin open. Spite of being so built-up, me and Reina are always amazin people how fast we can boogie. We're spinnin around like fuckin basketballs, a couplea baloncestos.

The DJ switches us now, from cambuca to disco beat. He starts with the Hermanas Pointer, I'm So Excited! Everybody knows that one. They're all roarin like lions in a Tarzan flick, in Spanish, English, German, who knows what, no importa! The message comes through loud and clear. Take it off, take it off, take it all off!

Me and Reina flip our tennis shoes away and mosta

our clothes, never missin a beat. Now we're just in our underwear, and it hardly covers much. Mine's kinduva jock strap, and Reina's a hilo dental, a thong she wears at the beach. We're bouncin back and forth, up and down, sideways and every way. The audience is goin wild! After a few more minutos hammin it up, we fall down fakin we're worn out, agotados. That's the signal for the whole crowd to jump up and dance. Techno and hip hop are blastin through the room like a goddam ciclón, a hurricane.

So we're the heroes of the evenin! Nothin new, hahaha! We climb back into our ropa, sweaty and happy as hell. Borrachitos from all the drinks, we stumble down the stairs with Chiara. I can tell she's contenta too, feliz! Happy as a worm, a lombriz! Rayos, I can't believe our luck! A taxi down here is waitin for somebody else, but I give him a propina and he takes us instead. Tá claro, I only do it for you cause of the ladies, he says. Yeah, man, sure. But I sit up front and after a while he starts feelin my knee. Same old same old!

Frederica, Plaza Catedral, February 1984

I can't count on Chiara as much as I used to. Leider! Too bad! Before, I could call her anytime I needed an extra female to balance out my table. But now Horacio tells me she's traipsing around with her handyman, getting to know how the riffraff lives. For God's sake! I grew up with cretins like that, and I dumped them as soon as I could.

I'll meet her beau tomorrow on our whale-watching trip. I asked Horacio if Chiara and the odd-jobber are lovers, but he only smiled a weary smile. That must mean yes. Damn it all! Why is she wasting herself on some low-life type? Just because her uncle was a prince, does she believe the only way is down? She should stay with the PLU contingent: People Like Us. I can take care of her.

When I seat my guests boy-girl boy-girl, I try to smooth the path for them. A lovely girl with a rich boy, or a good-looking boy with a wealthy girl. Natürlich! Of course! It makes sense to me what Ángel María is doing now. He's lucky that loose mulatta jilted him—that Lamia. Thank heaven he's getting over her. Now he's taken up with Carolina Del Río's daughter, Leandra. My next-door neighbors, almost. Just the Archbishop between us, the schwein: he's such a lecherous pig.

Leandra's no beauty, mind you. All the same, she's a hard-working girl—unlike that shiftless nympho, Lamia. Leandra's face is plain, and her chin is much too pointed. She returned a while ago from her postgraduate studies in the States and France. She calls her field 'la philosophie de l'art.' People don't give me credit, but I get the picture! I've known lots of intellektuelle! The Graf and I used to host them in Vienna.

I've read about her pet philosophers, Heidegger and Derrida; they were both discussed in *Vogue*. One of them was a Nazi sympathizer. My late husband the Graf used to say almost everybody was, in Germany and Austria too. Hitler was the Graf's compatriot: Austrians were so proud of Adolf during the anschluss, when the two countries joined. Well, not all of them... The other one Leandra chatters about is French. I've tried them both, but I couldn't make much headway. Too pretentious!

Leandra is fond of music too, especially a character named John Cage. Just sounds like noise to me! She wrote her thesis on him. She composes little pieces of her own, tiny stücke—but more tropical, so she claims. The only one I heard was some coconuts and gourds she clapped together. Absolutely terrible! For a while she was at the university in Granada, exactly when my son Gustavo was there. She fell in love with him: he's the cerebral type like her. They used to go for walks in the Alhambra gardens.

But Gustavo rejected her, the dummkopf. A match made in heaven! He told her he 'admired her mind, but still preferred boys.' When I heard that through the grapevine, I was beside myself. Who cares what he 'prefers,' with a fortune that big. If he'd just keep his mouth shut, he could do whatever he wants—on the side. In German we call it 'side-jumps.' Seitensprünge. Instead, he'd rather weasel an allowance out of me. That's the only reason he ever phones me, now and then.

Unlike my imbecile son, Ángel María's got a head on his shoulders. Engineers are always practical. Since he can't have Lamia, he'll console himself with the Del Río millions. Realpolitik! Leandra doesn't like the way he curries favor with her parents. But she has to admit he's handsome. Anyway, he's won her mother over, by pandering to all her whims. Oh, he's very clever, that boy!

Carolina is the greatest supporter of his suit. I suspect she's in love with him herself. But she's no dummy either. He's got more going for him than just his looks. Though he doesn't have much capital yet, he's been very astute at advancing his career. He's already managed two large construction projects for Espinosa. Everybody hails him as the President's right-hand man.

All the ladies wonder how Leandra can resist Ángel María. To us he's the most eligible bachelor in town! But Leandra is always calling him 'bland.' I like what Chiara told her, even if it was somewhat pert. 'Bland, Leandra? Then it's true what they say: blands have more fun!' Those two are close friends now. Studied in some of the same places. I wish I'd gone to university; but I was too poor back then. Besides, it wasn't considered proper for a girl— so I turned to something else. As Mae West said about her diamond: goodness had nothing to do with it!

Chiara keeps me in the know about the affair. She calls it a cross between a Schnitzler comedy and a Venezuelan soap. Schnitzler, I know who she's talking about: I saw one of his dramas in Vienna. A gala at the Raimund Theater. Hervorragend! Outstanding! Chiara tells me Leandra looks down on Ángel María because he's 'too simple-minded for an academic like me.' She also complains that 'his designs are too clear-cut.' He only wants to marry her for her bank account—and her social prestige.

Well, what does she expect, as homely as she is? Good grief! Himmel noch mal! Leandra says Lamia will always be Ángel María's ideal, just as Gustavo will always be hers. To each other, they'll never be anything more than runners-up. But Chiara believes Leandra's 'philosophie' is slowly giving way to Canuban reality. She'll come to the same conclusion I did, long ago. Maybe it's very intellektuell to make a marriage of convenience, when all is said and done. I bet she's just wriggling on the hook.

Ángel María thinks so, anyway. He told Chiara that sooner or later, Leandra's parents will hand her to him on a solid gold platter. Wrapped and tied with a bow! Until then, he's feting his last months as a bachelor. He's still in charge of Espinosa's building sprees, but the President has also launched an 'umwelt' campaign, for the 'environment.' Says he wants to protect the whales! Ángel María convinced the old schnook they'll attract hordes of tourists. And that means income for the government, straight into the geezer's secret coffers.

First, though, our young friend wants to sow his wild oats. Have fun, vergnügen! Feel free as a bird before he settles down. He certainly does look dashing now. He's grown his hair a bit longer, and he's sprouted a dark-blond beard. Keeps it fairly short though. Thank God! Not like a deadbeat, a gammler. He's always swimming, boating, and deep-sea diving. A regular athlete!

He's been giving talks on whales at Carolina's culture club, her tertulia. It's the latest rage! People show up who wouldn't know a whale if they saw one on the street. The ladies are only there because he's so adorable. Leandra told Chiara she even noticed Virgilio lurking behind a bush. He's the Miranda brother who holes up like a hermit; but he came out of his lair for his former classmate, Ángel María. Looks kind of scruffy, from what I hear—a reclusive, pot-bellied bear.

Well, time for my bath, and then to bed. I'm very curious about the outing tomorrow—sehr neugierig! Let's hope we meet some whales!

Ángel María Gonzales, Barlovento Bay

It's the height of the mating season, the prime time for whale-watching in Barlovento Bay. For some of these people it'll seem like a long haul from Puerto Indio to the southwestern tip of the island. I'm used to it, after all these months of setting up guidelines for the marine reserve.

The President is always being lambasted in the overseas press—even vilified. Some have dared to criticize him in Canuba too, if only behind four walls. This initiative should boost his reputation both at home and abroad.

Today's trip is an advertisement for our project. Some of the island's movers and shakers have come along. I'd expected a few more takers to sign up, but at least we've enlisted the most prominent ladies, Carolina and Frederica. They organize loads of events; between the two of them, they exert a huge influence on public opinion. I've given five or six talks on the humpbacks at Carolina's tertulia, her lecture series: that has put the word out, loud and clear.

Carolina's husband tagged along today, too. Adalberto Peralta is a consort, like Prince Philip, since he has no fortune of his own. But he does descend from one of the oldest families on the island. I think he's opposed to my courting his daughter Leandra, so I'd like to win him over. Carolina's already in my pocket. She wishes she could get into my boxers too… Fine by me, but only after I marry Leandra.

My future fiancée also joined the excursion—reluctantly. Grumbles that she's doing me a 'tremendous favor.' My strategy is this: I won't pay any attention to her today. Sometimes you have to make women jealous; or men, same thing. As my 'Captain's special guest,' I've brought along Palmoliva, a 'grade-A groupie.' That's what she called herself in the letter she sent, with her picture clipped to the CV. Very cute—and definitely hot to trot. She's only nineteen, the choicest age—not too green, and not too ripe. Wants to report on the whales for a newspaper, she claims. But that's only an excuse.

Catulo is a rising big shot in the hotel business; I'm glad he accepted. I'd like to establish whale-watching tours for the guests at resorts like his. Get them away from the beach for a change… Chiara's a welcome addition, too. She loves hiking and that kind of thing, and maybe she'll pen some articles about the humpbacks. She insisted on bringing her boyfriend, Amado; says the outing will make him understand *Moby Dick*! Fat chance. I had to read that book for our humanities class at Texas A & M. Boring as all get-out. I like poetry more, as long as it's moon and June and spoon.

Amado's a pal of mine from way back, though nobody knows it but him and me. He understands I'm in the all-stars now, so I'm sure he'll bug off—not act too familiar… What truly set me on my heels was when Frederica answered my flier. Not exactly an eco-nut! I guess she can't stand for Carolina to outdo her—even by chasing a pod of whales. Women! Always competing with each other. Well, I love winning too, in polo and tennis anyway. With men, life *is* a sport; but we're not catty like the ladies, just doggy. Or so we like to believe.

We departed Puerto Indio at five AM, and folks are

still snoozing in their seats. It's been three hours now, and soon I'll have to wake them up... This bus is ramshackle, I'll admit; Leandra's been complaining about it since dawn. Complaining is her number-one activity. I'm not going to baby anybody today—much less her. She runs me down so much, it's her turn to roll with the punches. These wusses have to realize: ecotourism isn't for sissies. I want them to confront nature in the raw.

I tap on the microphone. Time to start my talk on cetology. That should keep them entertained for an hour or two, till we get to Barlovento. I know the speech so well, I could recite it in my sleep. While I'm droning on, I'll watch the landscape flow by. Chill out for a while... The trees, the valleys, the shoreline... The whales are stamping through the hills like elephants... Huh? I'm seeing things! I must've given this talk one time too many... 'The humpbacks are the most gameful and light-hearted of the whales,' I hear myself saying, to finish up. That blurb from Melville has Chiara all stoked, I can tell: I stuck it in there just for her.

It's about ten AM. We've reached Puerto Barlovento on schedule, more or less. The rinky-dink harbor doesn't look like much, just one slipshod dock. And Leandra's already bitching about the boat: it's a creaky sports-fisher, about fifty foot long. I wish it were more spacious, for a gang this size. But I searched high and low, and it was all I could find, this coast is so out-of-the-way. I see some glum faces and some scared ones too when we get off the bus, but it won't take long for the crew to energize the group. I've worked with the same sailors before, and they're always full of pep. The apple of my eye is Milkyway, a runty deaf-mute who's always the first to spot the whales...

Luckily, this morning we've already had several encounters, all with mothers and their calves. Another adult usually accompanies them, the escort whale: it could be either a female or a male, swimming a little further off. Not necessarily a blood relation, as the genetic samples prove.

Wow, the humpbacks are cooperating! They've gone through a bunch of typical behaviors, almost like they're showing off.

They've treated us to breaching, spyhopping, lobtailing, fluking, the whole nine yards. The babies are my favorites, the way they flip through the air again and again. Chiara says she's impressed by the 'footprint' adults leave behind when they sound: it's like an oil-patch floating on the water. Awesome, I agree.

Around noon, the sky starts clouding over. As we sail past the mouth of the bay, a strong southeaster kicks up. The boat's pitching from side to side, and it's not too long before Leandra and Carolina hightail it down to the hold. I advise them they should keep on deck and fix their sights on something stable, like the horizon or the coast. But they'll probably stay down below for the rest of the trip, throwing up in the head. All I can do is leave them to their own stupidity. Some landlubbers never learn!

The rain's shooting down in spurts. My cheeks and hair are spattered, and I can hardly see. The wind is throttling up to a gale. Makes me feel wild, like a maniac. Maybe Chiara's not joking when she shouts: Ahoy, Captain Ahab!

Now there's a sunny spell, just long enough for Milkyway to pinpoint a rowdy group. Sawing his arm due west, he screeches like an osprey, the only sound he can make. There they are: young males on a tear, cartwheeling just for kicks. I tell the helmsman to bear down on them, full speed ahead.

Frederica and Don Adalberto are right behind me, trying not to slide off their seats. Palmoliva hangs onto my arm, frightened to death. But Chiara, Catulo, and Amado are really gung-ho: they're scrambling around the boat, scouting out the clearest view. Not too safe—but hey man, this is Canuba, where we don't have any rules. They're clutching at whatever they can grab—ropes, winches, the splashboard, the gunwale. The squall is beating our faces and drenching our clothes.

The barmy threesome end up wedged on a shallow ledge, right below the prow. All of us are psyched, watching those blubbery roughnecks do somersaults on the waves. The sky brightens all of a sudden. The ocean bucks like a zebra's back, white stripes of sun with black stripes of shade from the clouds. It's like the whales are bounding through hoops. Or maybe running offense like I used to do in Texas, butting past the yard-lines, sun to shadow to sun.

Now they notch down the pace, and it's one belly-flop

after the next. Fantástico, amigos! I holler to the three goofballs below me: they're sopping wet, like stray dogs in the rain. Fantástico! That's the spirit! Whales go berserk in stormy weather!

If Chiara and Amado are half as fagged as I am, then they're pooped. Thank God we managed to claw our way to the deck without falling overboard. Staring up at the sky, we take a rest while the boat chugs back to Barlovento Bay. We're soaked like lovers who've had sex for several hours. That's what it felt like, the whales were so stunning! Male or female, who cares?

To cite Mrs. Slocombe, from my favorite British sit-com, 'I am unanimous on that': with humans too, the differences are superficial. We're reversible sock puppets, at bottom—the operative word. You turn the genitalia in-side-out, switch prostate and clitoris, et voilà! Trade the hormones, exchange the wardrobe, and you're cooking with gas... or ready to hit the sidewalk.

Ah, so this is the famed Cayo Encantado! A roundish island with lush vegetation, arching high above the water-line—high as a cat's back. I've always hankered to lend this key my presence, and enchant it even more! Viewed from the sea as we approach, it rests on the bay like a lump of jade on a table of blue glass.

Butching it up, Ángel María commands the crew to moor at a Lilliputian dock. Higgledy-piggledy, he doles out some stale box-lunches, utterly inedible to our rarefied group. Behind his back, I award mine to Milkyway.

We'll stop here till four, Captain Ahab warns us, then head back to town. If you're late, you're bait!

I accost him: The key is gawjus, but not as untrammeled as I presumed. Why all the flowers?

Espinosa, natch. Ángel María is tactful about the tyrant, so I listen between the lines. He confides that the island was a nature reserve until a decade ago. Then, on an autocratic lark, our Lizard of Oz sought to mine its 'tourist potential.' For months he could spit and sputter of nothing else. His engineers landscaped the island for a hotel they never built, since he scuttled his plans after less than a year. Too far away! Who came up with that lame idea? he demanded. Que idiota!

Just one more case of the need for better management, I reflect. Now if *I* had been in charge of this resort! Doing my stentorian schtick, I would've alpha-maled it into shape.

As it is, the Cayo is beyond picturesque! Abandoned to run wild, the bougainvilleas have multiplied: crazy-quilts of color spill down the slopes. They're fringed by wide, salt-white beaches, divided by corniches of coral stone.

Now that the cloudburst has lifted, a few vendors from the mainland set up refreshment stands near the wharf. Some counter-culture types from Canada, who just arrived in dugouts, eagerly sample their wares—albino Caribs on a raid. Gadzooks, those Quebeckers are sexy as hell! I groove on their earthy French. She's got the boobs, and he's got the piece. What contours! Their wet white swimsuits limn each and every innuendo. If we were alone on this celluloid shore, I'd sock-puppet their rumps from here to eternity.

The pax on Ángel María's eco-trip are mismatched, to put it mildly—save that we wear the rags most urbanites affect in the 'campo.' Never mind that country folk are always spiffily dressed!

Like our ecstatic trio at the prow, Frederica and Adalberto relished the jaunt. He's an equestrian: from stallions to bulls, not much of a stretch. But Frederica? Given her dimensions, perhaps she communed with the humpback cows. Nothing turns me on like corpulence: just ask Pomona, my grande-amie. Her delicious curves remind me of a roseate, unwrinkled walrus. The Gräfin's shelf-life hasn't elapsed; huddling behind our able-bodied Captain, she must've reveled in the thews of his stern.

Palmoliva, his perky First Mate—or Playmate, I wot— still gloms on his arm, just as she did during the storm. Oh, Ángel María, I was terrified! she repines. A convenient pretext, for both of them…

Pasty as fish-bellies, Carolina and Leandra can barely totter down the gangplank. If he meant to blandish his prickly heiress into a truce, Ángel María has achieved just the opposite. His insouciance reveals just how certain he feels of his game. When he exhorts them to join us at a rickety bar, they whinge.

Leandra squeaks at him testily: No, thank you. After vomiting all day, we couldn't even drink a glass of water. Carolina wanly concurs.

Well, we have two hours to wander around the key! he buoys them up. But don't stray too far, and miss the boat!

I seem to detect a dash of sadism in his breezy tone. No matter what their travails, the faint-of-heart will not be countenanced.

Making nice with her Prince Valiant, Carolina murmurs: Don't worry, we'll wait right here.

Ten yards away, she and her daughter crumple to their knees on the grass. Don Adalberto perches on a camp-stool beside them. He's doing his utmost to keep from grinning, the brainless jackass: it's not often he gains the upper hand on his willowy wife. She's an infamous Japan-freak. That multi-tiered, pseudo-Nipponic hairdo is one of her sillier conceits; alack for Edo fashion, now it sags in disarray.

Frederica is ruthless. Inflated to her full cetacean size, she gloats over her depleted rival. Her fuchsia muumuu balloons like a sensuous blimp, straining at the seams.

A speedboat whizzes up to fetch her, by artful prear

rangement. No roasting in the sun for me! she interjects. Too hard on my delicate skin! Espinosa awaits me in the city, for a tête-à-tête with the Queen of Denmark. Auf wiederschauen! Toodle-loo!

On principle, Carolina would never set foot in the Presidential palace, no matter who the guests might be. A boorish upstart, she calls Espinosa; to her familiars, she hisses the same of Frederica. But for now, the redheaded geisha is too kaput to reply.

Frederica barrels on. Frivolous, I know, but what can I do? Duty calls! I hear we're having quail eggs, and turbot braised in champagne. Anyway, what a charming trip. Atemberaubend! Breathtaking! Let's do it again, next week.

Waving to us regally, she steps into the boat with remarkable lightness, for someone of her titillating girth. A few minutes later, we glimpse her rounding Barlovento Point in the slim, teak-decked cigarette.

Ángel María slaps his thigh. That woman! She takes the cake. Chiara, Amado, and I hunker down with him on crates, leaving the sole plastic chair to Palmoliva. Here, sweetheart, I tell her. You mount the throne. Don't worry about Chiara. She may be long in the tooth, but she's just one of the boys.

Whistling for the barman, Ángel María orders a 'trago de dama' for his kumquat, 'tragos regulares' for Chiara and me, and 'tragos de macho' for Amado and himself.

What's this about a macho drink? Chiara asks.

The ever-manly Amado cues her in. A regular's got twice as much rum as a lady. Double the rum again, you got a macho. Come on, bendito, you didn't know that?

Chiara is soooo unobservant, especially for a travel writer. I prod her in the bum. Hey, girlfriend! Get with the program. You're a Canuban now.

Uh-oh: she's in a truculent mood. I'll take the challenge if *you* will, she declares. Catulo and I want machos, too!

All I can do is rise to the occasion. Su-u-u-u-u-ure, I flute with a tremolo. Of *course* we want machos—as usual!

Chiara, Cayo Encantado, forty minutes later

To avoid losing face, I have to glug down a second round. But after the third—partly to escape a fourth!—I tell them it's high time to explore the island. Three sheets to the wind, we follow a path of crimson and violet bricks. Snaking through clusters of blossoming trees, it leads us to the heart of the key. Before long, we reach a sun-dappled clearing, raggedy with uncut grass. At the edge, a lonely bench overlooks a bed of white impatiens—and beyond them, the blue-green mirror of the sea.

I flop down groggily. I'll stay right here for a moment, amigos.

The others sniggle, and continue on their way.

I dawdle on and on, hypnotized by the waves, musing about that 'footprint' the humpbacks leave behind them when they sound. It's like a sheet of paper drifting on the water. A letter from the deep....

In Nodica and Lyon, my punctilious teachers massacred *I promessi sposi*, *Polyeucte*, and scores of other works. It's hard for a classic to survive high school unscathed! I'm grateful I read *Moby Dick* on my own... How wondrous that Amado saw the whales with me today. He loves animals so much, his love for them will be whale-size, too...

I hear muffled laughter, and swivel round. Ah... Ángel María and Palmoliva. They're creeping up stealthily, almost like conspirators. I see he's imprinted his teethmarks on the girl's right breast: hastily, she rebuttons her grass-stained blouse. Captain Ahab is still suffused with the afterglow of conquest.

Looks like you haven't budged, he says. It's been about an hour. Did those tragos de macho do you in?

No, I was just resting. What a marvelous vista! Where did Amado and Catulo end up?

Ángel María gapes at me blankly, as if he's never heard of them. His bewilderment seems phony, like a pose.

Oh yeah. I believe they went to the nudist beach, to rustle up some gringas. Would you go collar them, Chiara? I have to whip the crew into shape. You know, for anchors aweigh. All you have to do is stick to the path. When it forks, veer left. See you later!

I feel invigorated now as I amble along, through tunnels of elephant-ears, royal palms, and majagua trees. Shortly after the bend, I pass a promontory, twenty feet or so from the trail. I can't resist a detour to take in the view. I have to be careful with the toeholds; but once I reach the top, I'm glad I persevered.

The entire bay spreads out before me, narrow and long, from the Río Infanta at its head to the sea at its mouth. Puerto Barlovento is reduced to a clump of roofs; it hardly makes a dent in the overarching greenery. As I know from my guidebooks, that must be Macaracha Forest to the north. On either side of the bay, low mountains line the coast in verdant, loping arcs. Above them, the wind shears cumulus-clouds into frazzled scarves, as the golden afternoon lumbers on.

Absorbed by the panorama, I scarcely pay attention to the sequestered cove below me. At this hour, the sunlit cliff where I'm standing has plunged it into shade. But once my eyes come into focus, I recognize two figures on the sand, only fifty meters away.

Amado is lying face up, naked and motionless. He resembles a statue of dun-colored marble: a Hercules, toppled from his plinth by barbarian hordes. The grains of quartz dusting his limbs reinforce the illusion… but only till he shifts to one side. Nude like him, Catulo kneels intently over the demigod's groin. His bald crown rides

Amado's cock like a lotus-bud, swaying on a stiff, fleshy stem. Even in the shadow, his pallor stands out strikingly against the hero's inborn tan. Synchronized for pleasure, the swollen phallus rotates under Catulo's unblemished pate.

What I feel isn't jealousy at all—more like a comic sense of projection, an autoerotic thrill. So that's what my lover and I might look like from above... only I would have hair, I remind myself impartially.

Suspended in dream time, the climax seems close yet far away... Amado's tongue curls wantonly over his thick upper lip. As far as I can tell, his eyes are shut: the watcher is not being watched. I hover over the scene invisibly, an Olympian spying on her fellow gods; without qualms or embarrassment, I glory in the spectacle. I mustn't spoil it by making a noise—dislodging a pebble or snapping a twig.

After a dozen more voluptuous twists, Amado braces himself. His thighs sprawl apart, as he quakes uncontrollably. He cups Catulo behind the ears and buries his face in his pubes, hefting his member deep into the older man's throat. For several seconds, the milky circle of skin pauses abstractly above the black triangle of fur... When Amado ejaculates, spasm after spasm, his groans echo loudly from the cliffs. He collapses into a heap, as if he's suddenly been shot.

Still crouched over the titan, Catulo mounts the detumescing pole as deftly as a cowgirl, lifting his wings like an angel homeward bound. Then he pumps his own sizeable tool—as familiar to me from long ago as Amado's is now. His lithe buttocks tautening, the dancer convulses in soundless euphoria. Exhausted, he keels forward on Amado's fraternal chest. Light and dark, gleaming with sweat, they fuse into a mythical, bicolor beast: an oceanic griffin, washed up by the surf and gasping its last.

When Amado opens his eyes, I dodge behind some trees. Leerily, I retreat to the brick-paved path. Pretending I've just arrived, I start shouting: Catulo, Amado! Where are you? It's time to go!

Amado yawps back in his lusty bass. It takes the two of them ten minutes or so to scrabble up the breakneck trail. Amado shoves Catulo in the rear, to keep up his momentum; our trim choreographer seems drained by all his sexercise. They must've rinsed off in the sea before they left the inlet: they're still wringing-wet under their clothes. They riff about the 'mamacitas' they 'scoped out' today, as though I might believe them. Why the act?

We're in a giddy mood when we catch up with the others. They're all on board already; but instead of huffing about our tardiness, as 'square-heads' would do, they welcome us wholeheartedly. Carolina and Leandra, the casualties of the day, even thank us for the extra time we've allowed them to recoup. They both seem much more chipper after their siesta on the grass; they endure the brisk sail to Port Barlovento with ladylike aplomb.

During the five-hour return in our dilapidated bus, Ángel María sits dutifully between them. I overhear him expounding his future plans for the marine reserve, and spinning tales of apocryphal corsairs. Canuba was a bountiful hunting ground for French and English pirates, when they infested the Spanish Main. Carolina poses eager questions, while Leandra nods distractedly from time to time. With calculated charm, our intrepid Captain makes amends for treating them so shabbily.

Don Adalberto beams at his presumptive son-in-law. Though not renowned for his intelligence, he's an expert breeder of horses—and Ángel María plays polo with dare-devil verve. I can just imagine what's seeping through his noodle. 'That boy sure knows how to tame the fairer sex. They're as feisty as headstrong mares. And he had his way with that filly too, I'll wager…' He dozes off, and soon we hear him snoring.

At the back of the van, Amado hits on Palmoliva. No inroads there: around middle-class girls, his seductiveness fizzles. No doubt he'll grump to me later that she's 'just like all the other rich jevitas—they've only got the hots for nerds.' Ángel María's whale-lore was enough to earn him that dig, in Amado's book. As for me, I tuck into a casserole of slander, served up by Catulo. Still knackered at first, he soon recovers his customary zing. And then it's 'girlfriend' this and 'girlfriend' that, to a fare-thee-well…

For the other participants that day, whale-watching was only a one-shot junket—but I've remained hungry for more. Since then, I've visited the bay many times with Ángel María, compiling notes for articles in *Ecotraveler*. 'Like birds,' I wrote last month, 'humpback whales have it all: grace, humor, distinctive markings, a gift for gab, and an endless repertoire of song.' Through underwater mikes, I've listened for hours to solitary males as they vocalize head-down, deploying a wider range of tones than ten Mahlerian orchestras.

As a special favor, my government chum has now invited me to spend a month at the brand-new marine reserve, Banco de Torres, a coral head sixty kilometers from the Canuban coast. This is where ninety percent of the North Atlantic humpbacks winter each year, in the halcyon Caribbean. Anchored at the midpoint of the sanctuary, a research vessel caters exclusively to zoologists, most of them imminent scholars from abroad. In their erudite company, I'm earning my keep as an interpreter. All these scientists know basic English, of course, but sometimes they need assistance with words like 'eerie'—not to mention 'magari,' 'plantureux,' 'zünftig,' or 'ensimismado.' Stopgaps like 'let's hope,' 'curvy,' 'darn good,' and 'engrossed' don't quite make the grade.

Our mother ship, the *Hipocampo*, is a sturdy metal tub

that belies its twee name, 'sea-horse'; it was lent to Ángel María by the Canuban Navy. The cetologists sally forth from the vessel in rubber Zodiacs, six to seven times a day. Through a systematic survey of the whales in their tropical season, they hope to record an expanded list of individuals, many of them never sighted before. Like fingerprints, the black and white patterns on each fluke and flipper are unique.

Waiting is what we do most: the whales are shyer here than in Barlovento Bay. Only once in the last two weeks have humpbacks sidled up to the *Hipocampo*—two young males, the experts agreed. In the teetering brine, they stuck close to the hull, spyhopping over and over; they were downright ogling us, so it seemed. Wagging their mugs, they rambled on like a pair of drunken frat boys, joking in beeps, tocks, thuds, whistles, and burps—'rowdies' after a raucous party.

Since the whales are reluctant to make contact, the biologists have to pursue them. From the Zodiacs, they scan the horizon for telltale spouts. The field of action at Banco de Torres is much larger than in the bay, and the specimens are legion—perhaps as high as four thousand. We can anticipate many encounters during the course of a day; the trick is coming close enough to glean good data on our skittish, wily targets.

A coral head is crisscrossed by alleys and canyons. In the steep, submerged reefs, the humpbacks have found a haven for raising their young, safe from predators like orcas or sharks. Yet to breathe, they have to surface; and when they're nurturing calves, with their much smaller lungs, they bob up with them more often. These are the optimal moments for detailed inspection. As I already learned in Barlovento Bay, the whales always travel in trios: like a sentinel keeping vigil from a distance, a second adult escorts the mother and calf. The baby's curiosity and relative slowness often afford us a longer look at all three.

The scientists soon acknowledged my snorkeling skills, honed during childhood holidays in the Aeolians. Even in heavy seas, I contrive to weave among the angelfish and tangs at the pinnacles—polyp-towers where the coral head almost grazes the waterline. After initial doubts, the team leaders allowed me to fulfill my greatest ambition: swimming with the whales. If a calf nears the Zodiac, I slide into the sea and observe it through my mask. The baby's companions pay scant attention to the black rubber boat above them; and they fully disregard the clumsy pink fish beside it, with no tail at all, and four misshapen fins.

Whale-watching from a boat is mostly piecemeal—a back, a flipper, the flukes: at best, it's hit or miss. Drawing near to the humpbacks underwater, and engaging them for a spell, is quite a privilege. If the whales head off, they seem to be spurred more by tedium than fear. It's incredible how swiftly the adults can disappear. I barely catch sight of their hulking shapes, further magnified by the ocean's lens—and then, in a flash, they're not there. I never actually see them swim away; instead, they cease to be... a split-second's vision, half-seized in a waking dream.

This afternoon, as I slither off the Zodiac, I foresee that something momentous is in store. The calf we've homed in on approaches me, ratcheting down to my sluggish pace, as if eager for a dialogue.

Angling my head to one side, I can read each flexion of your flippers and tail, each nuance of your pearl-grey skin, glistening in the wavy light. You're still an infant, no more than four meters long; perhaps your newness to the world makes you more trusting and unafraid. Whether you're a 'he' or a 'she' makes no difference. You convey a definite character: an alertness, a genial serenity.

We glide along in communion, breaking the barriers that divide your species from mine. Your right eye, narrowed to a slit in the brightness, steadily gazes back at me. We share amusement... tolerance... sunlit peace. Your languid wink, just before we part, seems to ask: 'After all, who is who?' And then you sprint away with a flick of your tail, suddenly beyond my reach...

All this while, I've been aware of the mother whale, looming to the left of her progeny. She has condoned our interplay with tranquil patience, her giant white flipper at rest against her monolithic flank. And now, after the baby has swum ahead, I note that the escort whale has trundled right beneath me, dwarfing my puny frame.

I don't feel the slightest trepidation. So far, I've glimpsed full-grown humpbacks only for a second. But the stillness of these whales brings time to a halt... Breathlessly, I dangle in the meditative space they've opened up around me. I sense my pulse completely stop. Whether this interval lasts for a minute or a year is irrelevant. I neither am, nor cease to be. I've never existed, and yet I always will.

The coral head fans out on every side—a labyrinth of lives, breeding and dying, all in a single instant. The sea congeals into a dense, temporal element, a lucid mass that holds me suspended, undaunted in my transitory smallness. Like the ocean itself, the whale below me heaves upward, levitating with a conscious power... a power I know will never harm me: a power to which I belong.

Darkness ascending, light descending in the half-dark language of the whales—and I am light... until they vanish like ghosts.

On the way back to the ship, several people ask me how it went. What happened on your latest round, Chiara? All I can do is equivocate—there's no easy answer. I can't tell them what I've witnessed, or where I've been.

My only refuge is the captain's private deck. Nobody uses it, not even the captain himself. I lie in the hammock and stare at the sunset. Am I delirious, or is the sky really wheeling through every color in the spectrum? The ponderous clouds sheer from red to gold, tilt from aquamarine to blue, slowly subside from indigo to violet, sink at last into limitless black… and then reignite, a cinder-cloud of stars.

Ángel María, near Palma Verde, April 1986

It was a piece of cake to do that rehab for Chiara several years back, and I'm glad I could give her a hand. She's been a pioneer in the Barrio Antiguo. Up till then only a few society dames like Carolina and Frederica had revamped historic mansions, even if the rest of the tony set saw them as kooks. Who wants to patch up a moldy ruin when you can buy a modern condo, or build a concrete bunker with a garden and pool?

The Mirandas simply stayed where they've lived for generations; Chiara embraced the Old Quarter by choice. Like theirs, hers is a modest house, not a drop-dead palace. She's started a trend, and now more foreigners are snapping up properties in the neighborhood. Restoring them has turned into a lucrative sideline for me. We're coming up on the Fifth Centennial in 1992, and the Spanish government plans to fund some ambitious renovations. They'd like to exalt the Madre Patria's Colonial past. Who will they turn to? The famous fixer-upper: me! Not only that, I'm the President's right-hand man. So I can get them any permit they need, without a hassle.

Chiara has done her bit for our Marine Initiative, too. She's always bumming a ride with me to Barlovento. Right now she's catching a few winks on the back seat, while I sit up front with my driver. You might say she leads a double life here in 'Lotus Land,' as Catulo calls it. Whenever she tires of the city's pollution and noise, she seeks fresh air and silence in the countryside. I've taken her to unpopulated coasts, mountain backwoods, and secluded valleys—places reached only by boat, horseback, or heavy-duty hikes.

I have her in mind for some long-range projects, and time will tell if I'm right. Maybe with her travelogues, she'll attract investors to Canuba. Instead of beach resorts, I'd like to design upscale ecolodges. They'd bring sustainable development to our island—and lots of cash to my bank account! I don't talk about the money angle with her, needless to say. I don't want journalists prying into my affairs. Ever since I married Leandra last year, my transfers to UBS in Zürich have gone off the charts.

I've tried to persuade Chiara to vary her menu, instead of sticking only to Barlovento; we've visited several other regions, with lots to recommend them. But Barlovento is her mania, by land and by sea. It's true that this province has always been a world apart; its isolation dates way back, to pre-Colonial times. In fact, Barlovento was still a separate island when Columbus sailed by: that's clear from a primitive map he sketched himself. He called it 'the most westerly of the windward islands.' Over the last five hundred years, the shallow channel he drew gradually filled in. Now the lesser island is a fish-shaped peninsula, nipping the Canuban southwest with its narrow mouth.

Despite that low land-bridge, the province hasn't lost its unique identity. It's still surrounded on three sides by the sea, which often becomes tempestuous. Steep crags and dome-like rocks also safeguard its remoteness. My colleagues in the public works ministry scratch their heads when I propose more infrastructure for the region. They object that there's no room for a major port, or that the cost of decent roads would be prohibitive.

Searching for solutions, I've studied the peninsula extensively. From a geological viewpoint, the saw-edged peaks of Canuba's central cordillera are youthful—still thrusting upward from the seabed. Barlovento's stumpy mountains date from a more ancient era: they've been disintegrating for millions of years. Half karst, half coral stone, they're as full of caves as a mammoth Swiss cheese. Porous cliffs front the ocean, interrupted here and there by sandy coves. In other stretches, the beach goes on for miles, sheltered by barrier reefs that teem with crustaceans. Spring-fed streams vein the entire shoreline; their icy waters mix with the tepid waves.

Most of Canuba swelters in the standard Caribbean climate—semiarid and broiled by the sun. But Barlovento's rainfall is the highest in the archipelago. I've heard

French travelers compare the landscape to Polynesia, with its waterfalls, rampant flora, and morning mists.

The region wasn't wholly pristine when I arrived, back in the seventies. Coconut groves had supplanted most of the native forests, and tourism was making its baby steps. The man who led the way was a hard-bitten German, Torsten. He runs the rustic Palma Verde Inn with Sandrine, his blonde Provençale wife. She's a dish—though I can't say the same for Torsten! He's blond too, but in a grizzly, unshaven way. Their kids' hair is almost white; they have two little boys and a girl, between four and eight years old. The villagers of Palma Verde are black as coal—descendants of runaway slaves from Bonaventure. They can't believe how fair those children are! They've nicknamed them 'los albinitos,' the little albinos. Local toddlers follow them around, gawking at them like freaks who've escaped from a sideshow.

When Torsten first rode his horse over the mountains, the milelong beach at Palma Verde was almost unknown to outsiders. After a grueling trip on brambly passes and switchbacks, he stumbled on denizens from the Stone Age. The great landowners lived in Puerto Indio or Miami, and never set foot in Barlovento. Their overseers, trustworthy men from the region, parceled out daywork to their neighbors. Every now and then, crude flatboats would drop anchor in the inlets, to onload coconuts from the overgrown plantations.

For the most part, the inhabitants subsisted on the margins of the coco trade. Whether fishermen or farmers, they employed a barter system: a red snapper for a chicken, a foal for a calf, a basket of sardines for a bag of yams. They didn't need escudos, since stores didn't exist 'de este lado de la loma'—'on this side of the mountain.' That's how they always referred to their settlement. Even when Chiara appeared on the scene, their indifference to filthy lucre still amazed her.

When I sent her to Torsten's, I told her he didn't take travelers' checks, much less credit cards—so cash would be the only option. After she signed the registry, she asked him to put her escudos in his safe. You'd better stow your money under your pillow, he said. If you give it to me, I'll leave it where I keep all my dough. He pointed to a rusty cigar-tin, lying half-open on the bar. This box sits here night after night. But in all these years, nobody's filched a centavo.

I often put potential clients up at Torsten's, when I showcase the southwest coast. The bone-jangling trip can try even the hardiest; but it's well worth the ordeal. In my government jeep, shoehorned between trucks full of coffee or rice, it takes us five hours to inch down the potholed highway. We break the drive by having lunch at Barloven-to Port, where the day's catch is served under breeze-raked palms.

From there, we double back to Torsten's iffy track,

marked by a faded wooden sign. He made the 'road' himself with a bulldozer—Teutonic grit! The trail winds through vine-choked valleys, past weirdly conical hills. Mud and boulders obstruct the pass over the crest. If there's a downpour, teenage campesinos pop out of nowhere to push the vehicle up an incline, or prevent it from skidding down a slope. I toss them one-escudo coins from the window, and they tussle for them with glee.

Torsten's seven clapboard cabins, raised on stilts, are spartan enough for the strictest eco-buff. They bring out the child in you, like treehouses in the woods. But the creature comforts aren't neglected. Most incredible of all: Sandrine offers you French cuisine for a song. She calls her vegetable soup a 'velouté,' and she prepares an unbeatable lobster with herbs; follow that up with chocolate mousse from homegrown cocoa beans. Ten times better than the recipes in *Gourmet*, that magazine my yuppy friends like to read! To irrigate the food, there's plenty of wine from her personal stock. The entire feast costs less than what you'd spend for a pastry in Saint-Tropez.

Torsten recounts an anecdote that sums up Palma Verde to a tee. On his first expedition, he was bushed when he reached his goal: the tantalizing coast he'd heard about for weeks. It was almost twilight, and he led his thirsty horse to the nearest stream, just where it flowed into the sea. As in a Charlie Chaplin film, the boys who joined him on the beach kept doing double takes. The smaller ones had never laid eyes on a white man before; they were afraid he was a spook.

He peered out at the reefs: the water was swarming with life. What's all that movement out there? he asked. A school of fish? No, señor, the oldest boy answered. It's just a bunch of lobsters. They're tough and nasty as roaches. Poor people eat em, when they don't have a chicken or a pig.

Well, time to say good-bye to Chiara and drop her off. From here she'll backpack to Torsten's on her own. Too bad I need to forge ahead to Puerto Barlovento. I'm founding an NGO there, so fishermen can earn some income from whale-watching tours.

Before she took her nap, Chiara was raving about the land she bought last month. Four miles west of Palma Verde, she came across a wide expanse of beach, dubbed 'Playa Grandota' by the villagers. What really fired her up was the three keys offshore. I've sailed by them once or twice, reconnoitering for our Marine Reserve.

It's strange, but they look exactly like whales, only twice as big. The fisherman call them the 'Islas Jorobadas'—the 'Humpback Islands,' what else? They could almost be a mother, calf, and escort when you catch sight of them from the beach, on a moonlit night or through an early-morning fog.

Chiara's a fuckin loquita at times, out of her mind. Don't get me wrong, I love her anyway, but I coulda found her some land much cheaper than this. And on a nice cold river, not on the crummy ocean. The water's too salty for me, but that's what foreigners like, los extranjeros. All she got was a hectare, what we call fifteen tareas, but the rich guy who owns the whole beach made her pay through the ears. And he's never even been here, the son of a bitch! Coño! That's how it is in our crazy country!

She had to throw away all her savings, just like that, and she's still shellin out. But at least I cornered some work outta the deal. At her house in the city, I've already done most everything, from a plomero to a carpenter. I'm what we call a todólogo: Chiara says it means a trader jack or somethin like that. As soon as she decided to build a cabin on her playa land, chévere, cool! I'm her man. The nearest neighbors, a fisher guy and his woman, live in a hut two miles away. Talk about a deserted beach! But I knew how to round up a construction crew outta nowhere. In Canuba there's always people, if you look behind a tree.

Kinduva dumb design. Chiara dreamed it up herself, so what can I say? Just one giant room with eight sides, and with coco logs holdin it up. From a farm a mile off, a pair of oxes drug em here one by one. They're about twenty four foot tall, and I chose em for the straightest I could find. The two bueyes kept sweatin, the logs were so heavy. I had about a dozen guys to raise em and easy em into place by buildin up big piles of dirt and sand, plus pullin em with ropes. Chiara said what we did was Egyptian style, working with our muscles and the sand, and she took a lotta pictures.

I put the downstairs level four foot off the ground, in case of a flood from a hurricane, or from an earthquake in the sea. The floor's made from cement, and in the middle I stuck the steps goin up in a circle. It was easy to make em by splittin some coco logs in two with an ax I brought from Puerto Indio, a big hacha. To make the other floor upstairs, we put more logs crossway. There's eight wide doors, so when you open em up you look in every direction. What a fuckin vista, rayos!

We set a roof on top with green tiles from the capital, carried in on a coconut truck. A helluva a hard job, and the guys almost broke their necks fallin off from up there. A lotta danger. But Chiara says the clay tiles remind her of Sicilia, except over there, they're red. The roof goes straight up high like a witch's hat from Halloween, like I used to see in Queens growin up. I put another row of tiles round the bottom floor, to keep out the rain.

The roof's about twenty foot high at the pointy top of the hat, all in those damn tiles, frog-green. Everything else is painted in what I call Chiara green. The hardware store calls it verde foresta, forest green. When we go swimmin in front of the house, Chiara talks every time about a pagoda, whatever that is. She says it's from China. From far away when we're swimmin, it looks more like a Nueva Yol water tank to me. But whadda I know? I've never been to China like her.

Bit by bit, me and my team have been addin things. A kitchen with a butane stove, a bathroom with a pozo séptico, a septic well, a room at the back for the look-after guy, a cistern for catching rain. Plus a terraza where Chiara sits and reads, right next to the ocean. The cabin started out as nothin but an empty shell, where we camped out in sleepin bags for several months. Now it's almost a house. I've been workin on the final part this past week: walling in the first floor with screen, stretchin it on a wood frame. That's where we gonna eat without the fuckin mosquitoes eatin us, if God wants.

I'd never admit it to Chiara, but I'm havin a lotta fun! It's cool being in the campo, with people like at my granddad's farm. But these guys are even slower and dumber, and that's what drives me up the bend. Coño! You gotta know how to handle em, cause they're not too big on gettin things right.

I always say my summers in the campo growin up helped me with my muscles, especially my legs. Chiara says I probably owe em to my Spanish blood, since the Indians had skinny legs when Columbus came, from the knee down like most Canubanos today. He wrote that down in a report. The Taínos, she's always got em on her brain!

When I was little I had a lotta animals, and now I've got em again. Around the cabin I'm raisin a big white goose, a blue China duck, and a macho black rooster. I'm always jokin the blue China pato reminds me of Héctor, grouchin all the time. Best of all is my funny brown horse. She's a mare, a yegua, scared of her shadow for sure. Females are always wantin to get outta control! But no problem, I know how to keep her goin straight.

Since Chiara bought her for me, I let her choose the name. No surprise, she went for a name out of a fuckin book, Rocinante. Who cares if the one in the book is a macho, she says. The campesinos fixed the problem by nicknamin her Rosy. Now she's got her two names, like all the rest of us! She's pretty lazy, haragana. Mostly all she does is munch on the wet grass back of the land, where it borders on a ciénaga swamp. But on clear nights with a moon, I mount her nude for a gallop down the Playa Grandota. Bareback, Chiara says with a wink, and bare ass!

After a while I come back for Chiara, and she swings up behind me. Only woman I know loca enough to ride on a horseback naked, like me! She hangs on to my waist while we're gallopin along the empty beach, jumpin over arroyo streams, and cuttin round the coco trunks. It's pretty the way the moon shines through the long coco leaves above our heads. When we slow down, the horse hide tickles my skin. Chiara's so shameless she reaches around and plays with my pinga till I'm hard as hell.

Then it's time to get down to business. We always go to the same secret place. A stream with a poza, a swimmin hole. You feel private in there, cause there's ferns on every side. But anyway, at night nobody's close, not even the campesinos. First we float in the warm water, where the cold stream from the poza hits the water from the sea. We take our time kissin and lickin and suckin, mamando y mamando. Then we do it again, again and again.

I take my time gettin inside her too, front, back, and every way. When you build up like that for an hour, it feels incredible rapando your woman in the water. Tu mujer. You hear the waves and feel the stream like fingers on your legs and ass. The sweet and the salty, like they're fuckin each other too, same as you and her. When you come inside her, it lasts forever, para siempre, and the water round you is comin too. Comin and comin.

One time Chiara was still in her period, her time of the month, but I wanted her so bad she let me have her. In the moonlight, I saw a red line in the water, like a hilo, a thread. It turned into a vein, kinda thick. After a while it looked like a long pink cloud, a nube rosada. Like Chiara was meltin away, washin out in the ocean. When I came I felt like I was goin out there too, going with her out into the waves. Coño, man! Fuckin wild!

When we're through, we always refresh us in the poza

pool, and Rosy drinks her fill. Thirsty, that girl! Her pop eyes keep lookin down at us like she's sayin: Glad you enjoyed it! Then she trots us back home on the sand where it's nice and firm, good and dura, right where the tide comes up. In the moon, our shadows are black, black as they can be. Blacker than in the sun. Like a dibujito, a TV cartoon with no faces, nothin but empty lines. Kinda creepy, you know what I mean? Like maybe they'll still be hangin around, a long time after we're gone.

Chiara, Playa Grandota, the following month

Ángel María ribs me at times. First you cling to the Barrio Antiguo, then you clamp onto Barlovento and won't let go! You're an undiscovered species, the Sicilian barnacle!

He tries to lure me to other parts of the island, and sometimes I go along. But even he has to concede that Barlovento is unsurpassed. The rock formations remind me of Sung landscapes, vaporous and green—though I don't get carried away: there's always Amado to bring me down to earth.

For self-styled Gauguins seeking 'natives' unspoiled by greed, the villagers of Palma Verde fit the bill. I've done my best to shield their innocence. Their ragtag huts, cylindrical and thatched, are no different from Taíno bohíos;

they blend into the scenery like ceiba-tree stumps. To Ángel María's annoyance, I've never covered the hamlet in a travel magazine. I want it to remain invisible, just as it's always been. For miles around the settlement, fractured hills cascade to the ocean, and hidden bays unfold like glistering fans.

In Barlovento, swampy wetlands meet tidal shoals, palms border hardwood copses, and steamy mountains give way to drier, scrub-decked crags. These ecotones host a broad array of wildlife, with avian species topping the charts. What I wrote about the humpbacks also applies to Canuba's birds. They too have it all: grace, humor, distinctive markings, a gift for gab, and an endless repertoire of song.

Unlike most islanders, Amado never dismisses a hike as pointless. During my early months in Canuba, several athletes pooh-poohed my intention to trek to its highest peak. Not me, amiga! they'd say. Why get sweaty unless you're in training?

Amado roves even farther than I do, his trusty shotgun nestled in the crook of his arm. He spends entire days tracking feral guinea hens along the crest; in the evening, he grills their savory meat over a campfire for our dinner. We complement it with roasted breadfruit, capping the meal with mangoes fresh from the tree.

Now that he's finished screening the lower floor, it's time to celebrate. As a boy he used to hunt birds with slingshots, and he still knows a lot of them from then. This morning, he may add a few more to his list: I've hired a spry old man to take us birdwatching on Río Negro. Like a Taíno dugout, his boat is carved from a single big trunk. With his aquiline nose and lordly bearing, Don Eneldo could play the cacique in a Columbus biopic. Many are being filmed for the Fifth Centennial; but luckily for his peace of mind, no talent scout has smoked him out. He's brought along two husky teens to punt for him, and now they ply the river with tree limbs stripped of their twigs.

Mangrove hammocks bracket the somber waters, which barely seem to flow. In the tentative light of dawn, birds emerge from every nook and cranny. Snowy egrets, limpkins, least bitterns, and night herons wade through the marshes in silence; they stoop here and there to pinpoint frogs or fish. Antillean swifts dart by, and 'cuatro-ojo' tanagers lurk behind leaves. Canuban piculets squabble in royal palms, their roots confined to diminutive islands. Fearless, hummingbirds zigzag close to our skiff—all three of the island species. The ranger's neck gleams with several colors, like an opal; the zumbador balances its scissortail, immense for its mothball weight; the cerulean featherlight, no larger than a horsefly, ranks as the tiniest bird in the world.

When city slickers deride the campesinos' ignorance, they only betray their own. Maybe Canuban peasants haven't mastered calculus, but they command a precise terminology for every plant and animal. Often they're Taíno words—another confirmation that the Indian heritage endures. Though his lads can identify birds from scores of meters away, Don Eneldo readily outdoes them. Even Amado is impressed by his knowledge of their calls, diets, nesting habits, mating rituals, and other lore.

When I applaud his expertise, he bows his head. — I used to know a lot more, doña, when I traveled with Don Jaime. — Like most elderly people in the countryside, he assumes all foreigners must at least be acquaintances, if not relatives. — You've met him, haven't you? Señor Bonde?

I'm floored. He means the *real* James Bond, renowned for his field guide to Caribbean birds (Ian Fleming, an avid birder, named his spy for the ornithologist). In the forty years since it was published, Eneldo has never seen 'Don Jaime''s book. When Amado pulls it out of his rucksack, the old man presses it reverentially, like the hand of a long-lost friend.

To brain the quarry with his slingshot, a bird-slayer needs to zoom in: like Don Eneldo's punters, Amado sharpened his eyesight as a child. But lately I've persuaded him that songbirds must be spared, and he's impressed that message on his adolescent 'fans.' Now he often shows off his early aptitude, as we stalk the feathered sylphs on our bloodless quests.

Over these past few months, he's taught me that in

the foothills, birding often prospers on overcast days. A slight drizzle draws a veil over the mountains and the sea, so only the trees along our path are visible. Then we can pause across from a ficus, gri gri, or sigua tree, stand with bated breath, and attend the avian parade.

We can always rely on the Canuban woodpecker, sporting his red skullcap and camouflage vest, splotched with brown and green. Often the jaunty, black-eyed king-bird will join him; or the salamander cuckoo, with her long chessboard tail. There might be a Bonaventuran thrush in her tan-striped bib, a frisky bananaquit wearing his robber's mask, or a tropical mockingbird flashing her wide white bars. Each of them treats us to a vaudeville act, gamboling in and out of tree limbs and clustered leaves. We hear their sarcastic hoots, their pe-tirí pe-tirís, their knock-knocks on hollow bamboo… their squonkity-squonks, histrionic wheezes, or coloratura trills. The mockingbird vocalizes like our European nightingale, a baritone; but here, he oddly sings a tenor part—and in fact, 'ruiseñor,' the Spanish for nightingale, is his island sobriquet.

At the end of the afternoon, when the patchy rain tends to lift, we loop back to the beach. Sometimes we'll sight a flock of thickbilled plovers, swerving over the waves; scores of them flip back and forth in unison, alternating their dark-grey backs and snowy undersides. They keep it up till nightfall, writing cryptic runes across the sky: black to white, white to black, black to white...

Lately we've started pursuing more fragile wings. In Barlovento, the meadows seethe with butterflies, so many that they seem unreal. The orange tip, brushed with marmalade. The flame, cooly singeing bush after bush. The doris, a tinier doris painted on her back. The cydno, stamped with cobalt and white. The clipper, with her snowdrops that melt into mauve. The starless midnight of the cattleheart. The smalt-blue morpho, edged with black and white. The swallowtail's tribal mask. No matter how long we trail them, we never tire of the hairstreaks, skippers, parnassians, satyrs, and woodnymphs; the fritillaries, sulphurs, zebras, crackers, heliconians, and brushfoots; the coppers, buckeyes, calistos, peacocks, julias, and metalmarks. What a heartbreak of extravagance, the way they flitter for a day or two, only to mate and die...

With snorkels and fins, we've widened our scope to marine 'lepidoptera.' I've often observed butterflyfish in Banco de Torres, Hawaii, and the Seychelles; but for Amado, the Taíno river-god, they're a novelty. Here along the reefs off Playa Grandota, they pullulate. In slow motion, we free-dive past the foureye's specs, the spotfin's yellow rims, and the banded's silver coins. Shredded rainbows waft beside us—the Quattrocento wings of angelfish: the queen, with her cadmium tail and aqua flanks, her lips electric-blue; the French, with his banana-peel scales, grated and shellacked; the grey, with her yellow pectoral and clipped square tail. The rock-beauty, a diptych of saffron and navy, poses for his close-up. Meanwhile, the plentiful tangs riff through their medley of blues; and despite his ugly name, the striped grunt unzips an underlay of gold.

The luminaries of the horde, the basslet, bluehead, and wrasse, iridesce like prisms on the move. Swimming in schools, other species weave their tapestries—green or salmon-pink, sepia or brown: billowing curtains of doctorfish, chubs, surgeonfish, and damselfish; of goatfish, sergeant majors, parrotfish, and trumpetfish. Once in a blue moon, we spy the rare Canuban lunafish, or fluster the puckish harlequin bass. Now and then a moray eel protrudes his angry head—or a great barracuda hurtles like a spear through the startled, liquid sky. But normally the reefs drowse in their timeless daydream, nibbled by starfish, lobsters, and crabs. Breathing in and out, in and out, they filter the wayward currents and migrant tides... a parallel Canuba, sunken and still.

Amado, Playa Grandota to El Silencio, July 1987

Unless we hitch a ride with Ángel María or one of his dudes, Chiara rents a car to drive to Barlovento. She won't let me take the wheel, since I don't have a license for a carro, only for a motorbike. I keep askin her to buy me one from a crook police, like everybody else. It's just a lousy piece of paper. But she's afraid I'd total a car like I did with the Harley, and get the both of us killed. Coño! Women are always worried about dumbass stuff like that.

My job makes me feel like a loser: fuckin read to her on the way. Gives me a headache, but I tell her ok, she's the boss. No, she says, you are. At least she lets me pick out the book, maybe a thriller in español or a murder story in English, a novel of detectives. Kinda hard for me when I started, but now I read a lot better. She corrects me when I say stuff wrong. I tell her to buzz off sometimes, but I know she's tryin to help me. She's like a sister, a hermana. Not just a cunt to culiar.

Ever since I know her, Chiara brings out my romantic side. I write little notes in the capital, but here in the campo I do it more. Face it, I got more time to waste! I hide my messages in the cabin to give her a surprise, a sorpresa. If they're stained with turpentine or paint, it's not my fault. Depends on what I'm workin on. I know it's maybe mushy, sorta sentimental, but I like to draw little hearts on em: corazoncitos. I used to do that for my Mom when I was a chico. Last year I bought a special crayons carton in different colors. Kinda makes me feel like I'm five years old again.

Back in the city Chiara is always funnin about the teenage guys at the gym. She calls em my fan club. Here it's worse, cause kids in the country don't have a damn thing to do. While I was buildin the cabin at Playa Grandota, I felt like an action hero, Flash Gordon or Captain America. The muchachos from all the coco farms were coming to watch me sweat. They said they wanted to help, but that was just crap, a cuento chino. All they did was blab and feel my muscles, askin for weightliftin tips—especially after I taught em how to make weights outta paint cans filled with cement. They called me Hulk, the Hombre Increíble. Biceps, deltoids. Hey Amado, how many reps? They were such a damn nuisance I had to run em off.

Once me and my crew finished buildin, we started on the paisajismo. Chiara calls it landscraping: grass and stuff. We sowed some ground cover, what the campesinos around here say is Chinese grass. Goes with the pagoda, Chiara joked. It's a sorta weed with thin little blades, and when it's young it's green as a rice field, an arrozal. I call it a goddam weed cause it sprouts friggin everywhere, even in dry sand. It clumps up like pillows even on stones and logs. Coño! You couldn't kill it if you tried.

The Chinese grass is growin like loco now, and the cabin's done. I don't need to do much anymore but repairs, just like in Puerto Indio. But even in the campo, things walk off if you don't pay attention. People always need wood or tiles for building their own house, and I wouldn't be surprised if they tore down our cabaña bit by bit. So I got Chiara to hire a guy from my fan club, hahaha, to look after things while we're gone. His name is Pingo, and he's only fifteen. I call him Chévere cause it's the only word he knows. Medio bobo, kinda dumb. Not good for much except keepin an eye around.

Me and Chiara have been comin here kinda regular for a year. Course, we don't live together in town, so it takes some gettin used to. Mostly for her, since she lives alone. Here we're almost a couple, I tell her one day: a pareja. I kiss her, too. But she's such a smartass, she has to give me some backtalk.

Sure we're a pareja, she says. A couple of bigamists! You've got Reina back home, and I've got my books. Except for that, we're pretty faithful. Around here, there's not much choice!

I don't hassle Chiara, when I know she's writin a article. To get outta her way, sometimes I go out real early, to hunt guineas. There's a lot of em runnin wild up on the cresta, the mountain. That's how I came across the cave at El Silencio, a big hill nobody knows about down here on the beach. On our next trip to Grandota, I make sure I take her up there for a look. I know it's gotta be her kinda place.

Like I plan, we leave Playa Grandota before the light. When we're passing Río Frío, where we always go swimmin in the poza pool, she says she been noticin a path to the hills. Maybe it'll lead us up there without being so inclinado, so steep, like where I walk to the crest. From the look of it, I see maybe she's right. Rosy is stubborn as a mule about goin uphill, so we leave her at the pool, tied to a tree.

I'm sure glad we did, cause after a hundred metros the trail gets kinda scary. You go between a tall rock cliff on one side, and on the other side it falls way down to the sea and more rocks, so tight there's hardly room for a burro—a horse forget it, ni hablar. The ground's all covered with shells, caracoles, and Chiara says they're fossils, millions of years old. I don't believe it, but she says the ocean musta come inside the land before the mountain started stickin out of the ground. You figure.

There's lotsa that weed she calls baby breath, respiro de bebé. She says people grow it inside apartments where she comes from. Leave it to gringos to grow a weed inside their house! Maybe in Italia. I never saw it in my mamá's part of Queens. Ni en pintura, not even in a picture.

When we get high up enough I raise my arm and show her where we've been going. Nobody walks up to these hills. Even Palma Verde's gettin bigger now, and there's more tourists every day. But up here, nobody, nadie. I always wanted a place like this, and I almost feel like I musta made it myself, just for us, para nosotros. On the left, nothin but the ocean at the end of valleys. On the right, the mountains, so high you can't see them for the clouds. After a while, the rain I've been afraid was gonna fall turns into fogs, low on the ground.

Here the path levels off some, and we're crossin a

buncha humps and dips. A dozen of farms used to be up here, but now they're all empty. An hour later you come to El Silencio, the Medina family place. Their huts are even smaller than the Palma Verde cabins, just chozitas. Cana roofs, round like a wheel, with floors of packed down earth. Chiara says they're just like the bohíos, the Indian houses a thousand years ago. Whatever.

The Medinas kinda suspect us, especially her, a gringa from who knows where. Think we wanna steal bat-shit abono, fertilizer from their cave. But two of the young dudes remember I've been huntin up here before, and that settles em down. Soon they're jokin the way of campesinos, about animals and fuckin and stuff. After asking their permission, su permiso, I shove and drag Chiara up a red clay path for goats, slippery as a rotten mango. It starts beside the cabañas, then ziggyzags every whicha way up a big hill, a loma. I pull off my shirt and pantalón and tie em to my codos, my elbows, it's so damn hot. Chiara's clothes get wet from sweatin too, not the usual thing for her, I gotta say.

All of a sudden we're standin right at the cave, the cueva. Chiara's amazed, I can tell. A huge fuckin higo tree with roots ten foot long is hiding the entrance. I gotta laugh at her for standin there with her mouth open. I point behind me again, showin her the vista. Since I discovered it, I feel like I own it. Like the Almirante, hahaha. Chiara says yeah, the Taínos probably saw the Columbus ships from here when they sailed by. I tell her I don't know, but I've seen the whales swimmin by alright when I'm huntin up on the mountain cresta.

Hangin onto the closest branch, we keep lookin at the ocean, all spread out. The rain stops for a while, and in the sun we see the whole damn bay, the Bahía del Holandés. Coño, so beautiful, man. There's a long beach and smaller playitas between the cliffs, but it all makes a big half moon. The Jorobada Islands off the coast look like they're swimming right at you. They're even more like real whales, real ballenas, from this far away. We take our time and like the gringos say, we slow with the flow.

When we go walkin through the mouth of the cave, and Chiara looks how big it is, she can hardly believe it. Two thousand meters if you square it, I'd say, and she agrees, and it divides into two tall rooms makin an L. I light some matches I brought along, and we make some spooky shadows on the wet green wall. Pieces of rock like sausages or pingas stick outta the roof and the floor. Chiara calls em stalatites and stalamites, somethin like that. The ceilings look like cúpolas, with hundreds of bats hangin like caterpillar cocoons. We call em murciélagos. Their shit never stinks, can you believe, it just makes a nice carpet on the ground. Chiara notices a few places with holes the size of tubs, bañeras. Probably the Medinas, diggin up the junk to fertilize their plants.

Once we get out again, she asks me if Taínos ever lived

in this cave. Indios! All she ever thinks about. I tell her
I heard from the Medinas a buncha guys from the capital were diggin up the floor one time and took away some
skeletons. A couplea statues too, like a whale and an owl,
a lechuza. If I was the Indians, I woulda made a bat not an
owl, they got so many in there.

Chiara just smiles. Archaeologists, or grave-looters?
she says.

What's the difference? I ask her. She's sorta simple
sometimes, sorta ingenua.

Soon as we scooch down the mud camino to the cabins, the Medinas start up on a sale pitch, like they gotta make a venta. They say all their neighbors already left,
so they're desesperados to sell their land and move to the
city. Palma Verde's only a hole in the road, but it's a city to
them! I guess they're right, cause the town's gettin bigger
every day. Torsten put in ten new rooms and he's got some
competition now, a couple other hotels.

The oldest Medina, the jefe, keeps workin his mouth
on and on. He's got a high voice, and he's real small, real
pequeño. He sounds like a cricket, and he looks like one
too: a grillo. The cave and the hills, he says, the tall rocks
next to the sea, el mar. But he really jaws about the fruit
trees. Bitter orange plus dulce, grapefruits, limones, sugar
lemons too, avocadoes and tamarindos. He takes us down
a path where he shows us buenpan bread trees and mangoes, some of the tallest and oldest I've ever seen. In the

center of the farm you've got a pasture, plentya grass for three dozen horses and cows, he bullshits.

Inside me I laugh. Sure, what can you expect from a campesino tryin to sell his land? But it's not that fuckin big!

Chiara keeps quiet, and she looks surprised when I speak up. The señora's not interested, I'm tellin the little guy. She's only here on vacations. But you know, maybe I could take the land off your hands, if you ask me a Canuban price. I'm not a gringo, so you can't cheat me. This farm's not worth much, next to nothin. Just look how run down it is, out here in the middle of nowhere.

I can tell Chiara wants the place, but I don't want her gettin screwed. After weeks and months, we negotiate, and I make a bargain with the familia. Chiara says it's almost criminal, twenty hectares for half what she paid for a hectare at the playa. She calls it criminal—I call it listo, smart. What's she fuckin know? She got cheated over at the beach. The Medinas would never get more than I offered for their weed patch, without a road. You can't even go there except by horses or on your feet.

Chiara insists on payin em more, and I say ok, ok. But I keep her from makin it too goddam stupid. She felt better once she decided to leave the place to me some day. I never asked her to. But sure, she knows me for a campesino in my heart, my corazón.

It took half a year of tussles at the land-court, it's such a quagmire; but at last we've laid claim to El Silencio. Now that the property is ours—officially mine, but one day Amado's—it enthralls me more and more. The primeval isolation… the cavern's L-shaped nave… the ocean you see far-off through its gaping, tree-shrouded maw. The pungent smell of guavas, when you crush them underfoot… the lazy sunlight, percolating through the leaves. The swatches of beach, torn to wisps by the pounding surf… or on calmer days, the hypnotic twitch of the sea… sliding back and forth on grey-green ledges of rock. The cove that fills with evanescent sand…

Tonight's our first time camping here in the pup tent. We've set it up in the half-wild orchard at the end of the pasture, where fruit trees struggle for sun under the giant ceiba's canopy. This is a different world from the unfertile sand and salty air of Playa Grandota, fit only for coconuts and sea grapes. Many species of trees thrive in these highlands, both endemic and introduced.

By dint of repetition, Amado has convinced me that fish need sleep, just like birds. I doubt that butterflies do—though he believes that, too. And now I've overheard him saying good night to the trees!

Come on, amigo, I object. You're going too far.

He balks, as usual. We all sleep, why not trees? He

might as well have said: We all sleep, except for you. Now and then, I'm plagued by insomnia, and this evening I'm having one of my bouts. Amado nods off beside me right away—though thank God, he doesn't snore.

The winds are violent in Barlovento. Far into the night, I hear the fig trees rubbing their boughs, trying to get comfortable. I listen to the mangoes toss and turn, heavy with kicking fruit. The mighty ceiba chugged down sea-shine all day long; now he moans to his stunted teammates, who've passed out between his roots. When I slip through the tent-flaps, I find them sprawled across his knees.

I ramble around the pasture, under a radiant gibbous moon—only a day or two past its prime. There aren't any clouds tonight, and everything stands out in incisive detail. I have to hand it to Amado: it's true the trees have changed. They seem more relaxed, more alive, more uninhibited... 'stoned,' as he might say.

The jobo sipped a thousand cups of solar tea: it filters through his wasted limbs; his mangy foliage lies scattered at his feet. The breadfruits dandle their hoof-like leaves; they yearn to graze in the pasture like cows, slurping the dewy grass. The royal palms imagine their own utopia: a kingdom where no weevils bore their skin, where no woodpeckers drill their flesh.

Swinging pink-tipped tassels, shy mimosas bump and grind, moonstruck out of character. The shaggy gri gri quavers in his nightmare: standing bare-trunk on a public hill. The bronze almácigo flaunts his bulging muscles, too self-satisfied to dream.

I haven't seen them sleepwalk, but I will.

At dawn, I poke Amado in the ribs. If trees can sleep, they have to wake!

He yawns; it's all so obvious to him. Sure, mi hermano. They daydream too. If you watch em a while, you'll see how their branches move with their moods. Happy sometimes, and sometimes sad, or angry too. Sometimes they don't care. The same as us.

I yank his hair. Oh, God! You're starting to sound like me. You're right. We've turned into a couple—a two-headed monster!

He puts his arm around me. Don't worry, Chiarita. The trees won't tell. They keep a lotta secrets. They're all alone up here, solitos.

Yes, I answer, just like us. Together and alone. The trees are alone with their branches. The leaves are alone with the wind.

Lamia, Plaza Drake, January 1988

Ever since Chiara bought that finca out in the sticks, she's completely lost her mind: what was LEFT of it! I won't go anywhere if I can't get there in a car. Fine for the Girl Scouts, but she's too old to be a Niña Exploradora. Might make a kinky outfit, though, come to think of it... Hmmm, I'll have to try it sometime!

The latest wrinkle: Amado and Chiara are Indians now, from before Columbus hit the island. She's shopped her way through Puerto Indio, San Juan, Santo Domingo, Havana, even Caracas, buying up funky books about their weirdo customs. Like Canubans today, they sure held some spaced-out parties. They called them areítos. They'd trash-talk a lot, get high on drugs, and have group sex. Hey, doesn't sound so bad!

Horacio and Catulo keep pouring cognac on the fire. The Miranda sisters, las Mirandas! They've been into this native claptrap since they were little, dressing up in their mother's clothes and doing Shakespeare! Columbus Meets the Indians, too. The Taíno outfit is a helluva a lot easier than ruffles and lace: you run around buck naked, or maybe in a jockstrap. Not that they needed one then—or now!

Here they are, parked at a table in Chiara's 'library.' Might as well call the whole house that, since every wall is lined with books. I don't read em, EVER. It's bad for your eyesight, and I already need my brand-new specs for far away. Not very sexy! Contacts, NO—they hurt too much. Today I'm wearing my owl-eyes so I'll look intellectual, like Chiara and las Mirandas claim to be. They asked me to 'preside' over their so-called 'seminar.'

Is this some kinda honor, or are they just pulling my

leg? I don't give a flying fuck! No concerts on my schedule this week. And now that I'm a MILF, the young guys expect a 'loan.' Pay for a lay! It's against my principles! Well, most of the time... I wonder, should I get a facelift? Or just a nip and tuck? How about liposuction for my cellulite? Depressing! God, has it come to this?

Lights, action! Maybe this gig will cheer me up. ALL RIGHT, I call them to attention. It always makes me moist to be in charge! I order Horacio to read that dippy story they wanna discuss. Yeah, pinhead, out loud!

At the dawn of time, the Earth was a loving daughter to the Sun and Moon. The Earth gave birth to mankind in a cavern called Jovovava, where the Sun rose and set, and where the Moon came to drink from a hidden spring. At first, the Sun felt possessive toward the humans, and wouldn't let them leave his mountain cave. If they tried to escape, he would punish them: he turned one into a stone, another into a mockingbird, and several more into jobo-trees.

But two men managed somehow to abscond—and to the Sun's disgust, they sneaked away with all the women, too. The females abandoned their husbands and older children, taking with them only their newborns. Wayworn after a lengthy trek, they reached a stream; there, they left their babies behind as well. Piping for their mothers' breasts, the infants shriveled into frogs. After a while, the women were deserted in turn: the two men set out on their own, travel-

ing to an unknown place. Finally, they were joined by the other males; and for a long time, they enjoyed a peaceful existence.

At first the men were content without any females at all; but as the years went by, they missed them more and more. One day, after bathing in a river, they noticed some timid beasts in the treetops. To their surprise, they resembled human beings. Bit by bit, the men inveigled them down to the ground, hoping to mate with them. But the slippery creatures had no orifice of any kind.

Luckily, some woodpeckers came to the rescue. The men bound the tree-dwellers hand and foot, and the birds punched holes in their bodies, near where a woman's sex might be. Now the men could make love with the creatures as much as they wished, and so they felt joyful again. The Sun smiled benignly on this new breed of humans; from then on, he let them roam free. Such was the beginning of the Taíno race.

I should've known he'd snivel like a priest, in that mealy-mouth voice of his! He's a disgrace to classical music: it should sing, not meow! Now he goes on, in the same annoying whine.

Ahem. The Taíno creation myth tells us more about the aboriginal cosmology than any other pre-Columbian legend. — Horacio gulps for air like he's gonna die: too BAD he's only faking! — Fray Ramón Pané initially annotated this apocryphal fable in Hispaniola, at the behest of Columbus. An anonymous friar chronicled more such sagas on a journey through Canuba, where the Indians lent credence to a similar phantasmagoria. What I recapitulated for you is the variant he dispensed to our governor, Santiago. — He starts wheezing again, but that doesn't snow anybody!

Chiara chimes in, with her usual nutty bunk. You'll caw like perico birds, but Jovovava reminds me of my cave at El Silencio. I've spent months there now with Amado, the ultimate Taíno. — She leaves us hanging. What a drama dyke! — Since the cavern faces south, the sun rises and sets over the ocean. When the moon is full, it shines all the way to the back of the cave. Water gathers there in a tiny pool. You never know: long ago, that puddle may have been a gushing spring...

Anybody can tell you I hate Catulo's guts. He's sucking on a cup of 'Lady Grey,' but I know it's spiked with vodka. Why does he bother with the bluff? I'm tossing Ron Real straight down my throat from a tall, fatso glass, but I don't have to JUSTIFY myself! On top of the fibbing, it gets my goat when he poses as Mr. Superior. Using words nobody ever heard of, like now.

Mere solipsism, girlfriend... Next you'll be hallucinating you've found Yaya's gourd; and that it belched the ocean out, right in front of your eyes.

That's not the myth we're here to talk about. But maybe it did. — Hahaha! Chiara is hopping mad, and I don't blame her!

That cunt Catulo crosses his legs. — Don't worry, professoressa. I'm on your side. Amado is certainly prime Taíno beef, as you and I both know. According to an early scribe, the tribes pampered their warriors. 'Young men of surpassing comeliness,' they whiled away the hours 'engaging in ball games, grooming themselves, and strutting like peacocks.' In the creation mythos, no wonder the males take care of each other's 'needs' for years on end! — He grins at Horacio. — All around us, nothing has changed. The Indian 'ephebes' are with us still.

There should be a LAW against two poofs being brothers. Or sisters, in fact! They're always at each other's throats, but oooh sooo refined! Horacio wipes his forehead with a dainty silk handkerchief. Grey, of course. And Hermès, of course. He makes sure I notice the brand.

You are fustigating my predilection for Greek Antiquity, Horacio mews. But I have cogitated that Taíno epos as assiduously as you have. In some unaccountable fashion, do you concord that it mirrors the *Symposium*?

Through a glass darkly, adelphe. Dig the Hellenic vocative, bro! Catulo looks very pleased with his answer: why, I don't know. All this Parthenon stuff is for the birds—the pájaros—in more ways than one. I'm a Modern Greek, and we've got bigger balls than all the fucking dead ones!

He prisses on. — Both texts express our yearning for

what's beyond us: our 'desire and pursuit of the whole.' Though in the Taíno tale, you could leave off the *w* and just say 'hole,' it's so grossly sensual. Now *that's* my cup of tea. — He jiggy-jigs to the cabinet, pulls the Stolly off the shelf, and serves himself some more. Up front about it, at LAST! — A far cry from Plato's Diotima, who dooms us so priggishly to beauty in the absolute.

Horacio rattles his Roy Boys, some kinda African tea he drinks. He flies off the handle, hissing like a kittycat. — Oh, there is infinitely more to Plato than that! Just recollect how Alcibiades satirizes Socrates for his unshapeliness. Or what about the elocution where Aristophanes, the magister of comedy, elaborates his 'woolly yarn'? Humoristically, as it were, he categorizes the three typologies of amatory attachment: female/female, male/male, and female/male. In the West, after two and a half millennia, we have yet to transpose those Ionian, Dorian, and Phrygian modes into a nuanced, polyphonic spectrum.

What they're jabbering about, I have NO idea. Sure, the modal scales I know from music school. But what the fuck happened to the drugged-out Taínos? I collar Chiara: Listen, woman. I don't wanna get bored to death by these two lunkheads.

She groans: Alas, Lamia, the 'opposing sex' is trying to steal the show. — She twiddles her hair, that dorky tic of hers. Doesn't turn me on, believe you me. — As to Aristophanes and his mirthful speech, she croaks, the chariot race wasn't on an even playing ground. The Greeks always awarded their prize to love between men—especially an older and a younger man. Their wives had to vegetate at home. Aspasia was the lone exception, and she was a courtesan. In the Indian story too, the men treat the women like chattel.

Right on, girl! I'm glad you got us back on the SUBJECT! I shout. — Even with my glasses on, I haven't jawed much. They won't let me get a word in edgewise!

Catulo taunts us, the scumbag. — They also manhandle the tree-dwellers just as they please. Feminists and dendrophiles, unite! All that machismo, ladies: so repugnant, then and now.

Horacio stares us up and down. — You are misconstruing the entire signification, my dears. The Taíno fantasia lauds something else. You might formulate it as 'indeterminacy'—a subliminal obfuscation of the persona, the peritoneum and otherwise. I predicate it still pertains to our population today.

Finally, here's something I get! I jump right in: From what I can tell, those slutty tree-dwellers don't even have a gender. And no 'orientation,' either. They just SCREW any goddam way they want. FYI, Canuba has more hermaphrodites than any other country in the world. And more 'transitioners' too. On top of that, we're mentally trans. Maybe that's what this story is about!

Chiara backs me up. — Yes, Amado taught me a saying

he heard from campesinos on his family farm. Females wash in one part of the river, males in another: a Taíno tradition, no doubt. To keep them in their area, the little boys are warned: 'If you pee where the rainbow drinks, you'll turn into a girl.'

Even that bitch Catulo toes the line. — Aha! I've heard that dictum in the campo many times. Does it reflect macho fears of becoming a 'little woman,' or does it let us in on a wish-fulfillment dream? Especially while bathing with naked, hairless boys. Either way, gender fluidity is epitomized by the river itself. And please observe: the tree-dwellers appear in a grove along its banks. After their immersion in those mutant waters, the men decide who's who. The Taíno story affirms male dominance, as you'd expect; but on another level, it's subversively undermined.

Chiara cozies up to him, moony-eyed. — Why Catulo! This reminds me of our academic phase, when we'd just met!

Who cares about their Jurassic love affair? I've had Catulo too, just like everybody else! He huffs and puffs, but he's an Ángel María: short on delivery, most of the time. Now that we're on a roll, I join back in. — The females are my heroines. They run away from their mates. They even junk their children. Women with brains in their heads! They don't wanna be COWS, homebodies chewing their cud—nothing but cooks and nannies. When you get right down to it, the males chuck that family bullshit too. To hell with being husbands, fathers, and providers! They run off to 'another place,' who cares where, and settle down on their own. — I top up my glass with three jiggers of rum, feeling like Alfred E. Einstein.

Horacio giggles: Absolutely, my dear diva. As in Plato, a liberating risibility informs the Amerindian narration. — I can't believe how NORMAL the sicky seems right now; he even forgets to cough. — What could be more hilarity-provoking than the woodpeckers' rat-a-tat-tat? Those ludic 'birds' perforate whatever apertures the males desiderate—with far more variegation than Aristophanes conceived. The 'slippery' eros of the dendroids confers a plenary emancipation on the females as well: henceforth, they never need rotate back to the males at all, unless they elect to cohabitate. Now they too can communalize amongst themselves.

YEAH, and make it with each other! Way to go! — I slam the table with my fist.

Chiara freezes up. — Please, Lamia: a modicum of moderation from the moderatrix, as Horacio might say… But yes, I agree. In the end, the humans emerge from darkness into day. Their new world of clarity projects no shadows: no fear, no regret—and above all, no guilt.

Yeah! I yell again, but without a bang. Goddammit, I can be a lady too…

Catulo purses his lips; he's still Miss Teach this afternoon. — I'd like to piggyback on your theological point,

Chiara. Colonial priests decried the Indians' nonchalance toward sin. Amazonian mythology still evokes magical beings who rove the forest canopy. But in the Taíno account, lured down to earth, they even go so far as to couple with men. With their multiple holes, they're literally 'open' to experience, and so are the humans who seduce them. Like islanders now, they want their carnality unconfined. Sex is their integrating link to the wholeness of creation.

I'm falling asleep, but Chiara's still locked in the classroom! — When Westerners crossed the 'Ocean Sea,' she drones in a fruity voice, they encountered the truly 'other'—for the first and only time. They didn't accept that soul-changing gift; in their dread of the unknown, they killed their potential mentors. Their petty dualities—God and Satan, Christian and pagan, good and evil, body and soul, culture and savagery, male and female, 'natura' and 'contra naturam'—couldn't rival the Taíno's overriding unity.

I'm drifting off; I push my glasses to the top of my nose. — Let's get back to the women, I demand. I don't like babies, OK? They ruin your figure and cramp your mojo! But there's one thing that's kinda hard to swallow. Sure, leave them behind: fine by me! But why turn them into frigging FROGS?

Elementary, my alliterating Watson—ye of the assonant rhyme! — Catulo always talks down to me, one reason I can't stand him. — To this day, isolated ethnic groups slay their children in times of dearth; then they eat them without compunction. For tribes in harmony with nature, people never die, they're simply transformed: into spirits, ghosts, beasts, plants, or even stones—as in our tale—since nothing is inanimate. Cannibalism permits you to fuse with another body; and it's much less 'heartless' than burial in a box!

Horacio takes the bait. You are far too extremist, Catulo, as is your assuetude. In the Taíno narration, human beings transmute into jobo-trees and mockingbirds—'nightingales,' to the Spanish. The infants also permutate to another species, without becoming petits fours. — He chuckles kinda nervous, like he's steering us away from the brink. — As with the woodpeckers, I apperceive whimsicality here: a folk-etiology of why diminutive frogs fife beside rivulets. You cannot take this too seriously, much less confuse it with societal mores. If females had abjured their child-rearing function, the clans would have yawed towards extinction.

Catulo vacuums his 'tea'; he's starting to slur his words, the sot. — I'd say the episooode suggests something else. Beyond the baaasics—such as perpetuating, or shall we say perrrpetrating, the race—all humans thirrrst for expansion. Instead of quailing in our cages—people versus naaature—we long to embrace a vaaast continuum.

Whatever that means! — HEY, you eggheads! I snap.

Let's get back to the Indians. Didn't the Taínos come here from South America? Just look at the Ameribanos today, split between here and Miami or Queens. Once you're an immigrant, you live in two places: not just outside, but inside yourself. I don't mean going to school somewhere for a while, but staying there half your life! Like Chiara might do in Canuba!

She seconds my point. — Right, Lamia. Once you've migrated, it's easier to straddle two spheres. Now you'll always be 'here,' but in that 'other place' as well. The Taíno had already voyaged from the mainland; then the Caribs followed in their wake; then the Spanish, the French, the British, the Lebanese, the Chinese, the Bonaventurans, and on and on. Though Africans were viciously hauled to Canuba against their will, they eventually mingled with the rest.

Catulo is falling-down drunk by now. He never COULD hold his liquor! — Yeees, amiiica, he drawls. Even the naaames of our island wobble. Like the tree-dwellers, they adapt to everyone's whiiims. Canuuuba, for the Taíno. Moriqueya, for the Caribs. Aquina, for the early Spaniards. Or our city. Puerto San Tomás, for Colummmbus. Puerto Indio, for his nephew. Thomas d'Aquin, for the Frennnch. Indian Harbour, for the Ennnglish. An agnomen for every taaaste, like a whore trying to please! Why not call our town Pueeerto Puuuta on Trollllop Iiisland?

He slumps on Chiara's shoulder, and she fondles his

arm. I've always found that lovey-dovey stuff disgusting! Who needs it when you can have SEX? — Even present-day tourists are migrants, if only for a while, she pipes up for his benefit. Like the guests at your hotel, Catulo. What visitors here always tell me is that they instantly feel at home. As former outsiders themselves, Canubans put newcomers at their ease.

Except when they have the misfortune of being Bonaventurans, Horacio tacks on. — He's a goddam Bono-lover! More pelo-malos to drag us down, that's all they are. It's the one thing Catulo and I agree on.

Yes, Chiara nods. Isn't the racism sickening? — She's a Bono-lover, too! — Though for anyone else, besides the hospitality, there's another magnet here. This island is twice as large as Sicily, where I grew up. To me, it strikes a perfect balance between shelter and openness.

Catulo is still coiling on her like a snake. From the sound of it, he's got the DTs! — You're riiight! Just think how different the Taíno myth is from Genesis, girllllfriennnd. In the Indian tale, humans free themselllves from the dank dungeon of a cave. They travel to wiiide horizons, never fully settling down. Instead of being expelllled by their god, they flee his tyranny and saluuute the entire world. They welcome whatever commmfort or trials they might discooover there. In their self-deterrrmined life, they merge the near and the far, the huuuman and the divine. They don't lose their paradise, they connnquer it.

They learn to walllk in the light, on their ooown two feet.

The Miranda she-cats are sharpening their claws again! Now it's Horacio's turn. — That may be one interpretation, Catulo. Not all of us conspire to transplant our ancestral ramifications, thanks be to God. But we assuredly *do* yearn to inhabit *ourselves*: the insula of an indivisible mind. — He buffs his gold rimmed specs. They're the two-bit philosopher kind. MINE are glitzy with rhinestone wings, sorta Zsa Zsa! Course, I'm a helluva a lot younger than that frowsy bag! — It would be facile to refuse those malodorous Castilians the accreditation they warrant. Remember, behind them were the Romans and the Moors, who had advanced the anterior cultivation of the Greeks. I do not emulate Hispania mawkishly, like Espinosa. And yet we would not be vocalizing its composite tongue, if Iberia had not organically revived the concatenation of epochs, once the Taíno expired.

SISTERS, after all! Catulo's eyes dilate. I bet he sniffed a lot of coke before he came! — I couldn't jiiibe with you more, hermanito. Cervantes presents his *Quijote* as a translaaation from the Arabic, to emphasize that chain of metamorrrphoses. As to the 'archives of La Mancha' he cites, they reveeeal that all facts are fiction, and all history a liiie, just as much as the kniiight's chivalric feeeats. And while the Spanish looked back, they also looked forrrward; they were spellbound by these 'ínsulas extrañas'—our 'outlandish islands,' to quooote St. John of the Cross.

Chiara, you called for surmounnnting duality: oneness suuurely pervades his great poem, and the fertiiility cults underlying his worrrds. 'La cena que recrea y enamora': the meal that enamors and restoooores. Eating and being eaten, like bodies in the act of looove. Anthropophagy, but also commuuunion… Everything is sacriiificed, and everything is gained. By reinventing the beloooved, we re-create ourselllves.

He lays his bald head on the table. Maybe he'll have a heart attack! THAT would liven things up. This talkathon has been such a drag! I'm almost grateful when Ángel María shows his face—though he's the last person I'd usually want to see. Well, next to last, after Catulo!

Chiara scampers to the door like a chihuahua. What a shameless skank! I'm more attracted to the bodyguard posted outside… a lot higher octane in his motor, I bet. — Thank you so much for dropping by, she yips. You'd never guess… but I know what the Mirandas will make of my little 'coup de théâtre'!

Namaste, Horacio bows. How regrettable that Virgilio is not present, Ángel María. He has always been your chosen one, your prima Miranda.

I have to yawn! That gossip is old as the hills. All three Mirandas were crazy about Ángel María in high school, at the Colegio Jesuita. Virgilio had the worst crush of all— and he's SUPPOSED to be the 'straight' one, whatever that means. Bromance, I guess!

Catulo hugs the clueless oaf, tipping him back on his heels. — Yes, you've always been our brooother's Alcibiades. And that's why he can taaake you—or leave you… Like Socrates in the miiilitary camp.

Ángel María draws a blank; he's as stumped as me! He can't unglue his eyes from my boobs… Sure, he's unreliable in the pinga department, for hard-core sex; but it's nice to get some appreciation for a change! Especially after wasting my afternoon on this queery-weery marica crap.

I'm knocking back my rum. Catulo's swilling his vodka. Ángel María brought some scotch along. Laphroig, it says on the label: smells like cigar butts to me. Well, to each his own! I herd Chiara and the guys up to the roof. We hook together in a conga as we go! Now we'll finally have some FUN!!!

Chiara, Plaza Drake, late that night

Thank God they're gone! I'm fond of them, one on one. But together they're wormwood, catnip, egomania, and persiflage: the standard Canuba Quartet.

I missed you, Amado. You went to your grandfather's farm this week, so you couldn't turn up in tandem with Ángel María. That had been my plan: one Alcibiades for the Mirandas, and another one for me.

During our 'symposium,' I kept recalling how you like to exult: 'No soy heterosexual. No soy homosexual. Soy todosexual!' You're not hetero, you're not homo, you're 'all-sexual.' You mean sex in itself. But now it's dawned on me that you also embody something else: a union with the real in all its offshoots—a seamless blurring of boundaries.

Horacio isn't the only one who's climbing Diotima's ladder—I'm right behind him, even if I can hardly tell which end is up. To me it's less a ladder than a seesaw: it pivots between the body and the mind, till they form a continuous arc.

I've absorbed you limb by limb: I am your communicant. You're the flesh of all my thoughts, the blood of all my words. I enshrine you, as in a monstrance. You make me long for the silent retreats I've missed. Soon I'll take them up again, and worship you from afar.

Every day, I inscribe you in my notebooks. After you leave, I write down what you blurted at climax: as if it were a gospel, a testament. 'Take the milk.' 'What a wave.' 'Now you're a woman.' 'Don't make me laugh.'

I thumb through that scripture at random, in my internal twilight: the 'light-between.' I summon scattered memories from dawn and dusk; I weave them into one.

I've accreted chairs, tables, mirrors, pictures, books. But the house seems bare and hollow: a whale's 'bonehouse'—the Norse expression for 'body.' The relentless sun has bleached it to chalk, crumbled it to dust.

Wall against wall, the courtyard collapses. Deep in the tropical blaze, it's a well where the light tumbles headlong and drowns. Stranded, I lose all impulse, all future, all present, and all past.

Nothing is left but the palms in the square, swaying outside my door... and beyond them, the listless drone of traffic. The city dissolves like a sea without a shore.

It rained for a while, but now the evening has cleared. Breakable as glass, I cross the irised asphalt and rough cement, threading my way through the neighborhood. A stray look might shatter me.

I've never felt lonely, in all these hours without direction, without regrets. But after the novels and plays about people I might have been, I realize again: I have a life. It can never be deserved or explained away. Each of my friendships, each of my loves is like a stone in that riverbed of solitude.

The prison of love can also set us free. On this urban square, I summon up the fireflies at El Silencio, blameless and mute in the darkening trees. Their signals multiply until they roll me in their surf, the pure throb of process.

This is 'beauty': even here, I submit to the cannibal of love. I give myself up to the eating and the eaten, the seeing and the seen. I notice, and I notice not to notice. Ending it will not help us. Beginning again, oh yes... beginning again.

Not a question of need, but of the absolutely singular. The way you look at me now as I hold your shoulders, rocking you back and forth. Each time is only once—once, as it has to be: this instant we can never call our own.

We're always standing in the stream of our good-byes. Your face is a reflection on the surface. But when I touch it, the water overflows. You have a life: you also have a life.

I live you as an axis far from suffering, a long vacation on the earth. The lines we've learned unreel in time allotted, time removed. But what we mean, we'll never say in so many words—or in so few.

The past comes back again, but now as if eternal. After we made love you asked: Paraíso, cómo se dice? Paradise, I answered. The shifting stairs eliminate our differences. We shed them like breaths—till they fuse as a single breath.

All we give up is a point of view. Our changes occur at once, repeat after me. The opening closes in on us, the closing opens out of us. 'I' and 'love' and 'you' make sense for a moment: a stitch in time, a bird in hand, proverbs that keep us alive.

I go back home, lie down on my bed: our bed, you always call it. Wordlessly, our syllables persist, a shimmer at the confines of our sleep. We hover where only dreams start and stir.

All the ancient children are knowable in you, all their sly, harmless, cruel little games. Their bruises reappear on your face and arms, like the markings on a moth. Your eyebrows, your hair, the down on your chest, brush by me in the dark.

I have to wonder why we've come this close. For you, every question is an answer. Here is the night, not of our making. Here is the moon. Here are our bodies, the shadows of light.

Amado, San Sebastián, May 1989

I don't know what got into Chiara this winter. I thought we were doin pretty good, goin on eight or nine years together now. Toda una vida, a whole life! But she had to go and fuck it all up. Coño!

Catulo hooked us up, about a year after she came down here on vacations. He thought he was doin her a favor, handin me off to her. Always says he discovered me. Huh, que me descubrió? I never say a word, but he's not the first score I ever made, and not the only one back then! Ni hablar, no way!

I met Catulo when I was seventeen, but I'd been around the block. I already knew a lot. A couplea years later, he set up that date with me and Chiara. He was already workin at the Playa Hermosa hotel, and I hardly ever saw him anymore. So he didn't give me up so she could have me. Qué va, bullshit!

I was kinda ready for somethin by then. Sure, I was already hitched to Reina, but she's a wife. Children and all, it's not the same, no es lo mismo. Chiara was shoppin around too when she got here. So I found what I wanted and she found what she wanted. I'm not talkin about money. Sure, she gave me a job, but they all do that, women and men, todas y todos. When they have a thing for me, that's how they try to keep me around.

She's ok with Reina, ok with the chicks I screw for fun. Hombres too, like Catulo, Héctor, or any other dude. Guys, so what's the big deal? I don't care where I stick my dick. If I'm on toppa one, he's a woman to me. Chiara is kinda like a man cause she's never jealous. She's always been glad I have a wife, a lotta hot mamacita chicks and a lotta dudes. Practice makes perfect, she says. She cracks me up!

If she's not jealous it could be cause of her age, ten years more than me. But it's not just that. Héctor's her age, and a guy, and even that didn't stop him from being like Reina. Wacko jealous! He was so mad when I switched from him to Chiara he spread all kindsa dumbass talk. How she jinxes people and makes em die from a fucú, a curse, and how she's a spy for the CIA. Huh? A Italian? Héctor went off his rocker.

With Chiara it was different. Things were goin so good for us up to last winter. She was raised by a buncha nuns, and sometimes she acts like one. Not in bed, but everywhere else. If she's here, it's the same as before, and we screw like fuckin animals, como animales. But she won't hang here for long. She spends months and months on stupid retreats. It's what the priests call retiros, I guess. But I'm not a Catholic, or a Protestant Evangélico neither, anymore.

Sometimes she goes off to places in India. She calls em ashrams. Ass-rams is what I call em, cause I get fucked. No sex with Chiara from that far away. Ni en pintura, not even in a picture. Or sometimes she goes to temples in Japan. She used to hang in places like that when I first met her, and now she's at it again.

She's always very responsible. She sends my salary straight to my account, if she's here on the island or not. Not that I've done much to earn it, lately, almost nada. Except for puttin up with that maldita Luz Divina. The old perra never lets me have a minute's peace. Thinks she can boss me around the way she does with Chiara. The dried-up bitch!

For a long time I stayed busy with repairs and paintin here in the capital. Then I built the cabaña on Playa Grandota. But once I finished with that, there wasn't much to do but a kinda routine, there and here the same. Chévere turned out bein a better encargado than I thought. He looks after the cabin on the beach and the finca in El Silencio too. Chiara keeps sayin I oughta go back to school, to the universidad. Or get my training for some kinda trade. But I say fuck, I always hated the teachers, the libros and exams. Can you see me takin orders from a boss, a patrón?

Coño!

That's when she came up with the taxi idea. Yeah, in a way it sounded good. She never had much use for a car in Puerto Indio, since there's so many cheap taxis. But last year every time she took em she started askin the driver about the business, el negocio. You know, how they make out. They said the money was pretty good. Most of em rent their car from the owner by the week, and keep what's left over. After the rent, gasolina, and repairs, they still have enough to get by. Chiara decided she'd buy a car, and rent it to me for a good price. Then we'd both be doin ok.

But hey, I told her, I don't even have a license! About time you did, she said.

She bought a Ford Escort, I don't know why except she said it sounded sexy. She joked how an Escort's so square she's gotta be a puta seria, a real whore, not some stuck-up call girl. After that Chiara stayed for a couplea months, to make sure I was goin to my driving class. I kept tellin her why not just buy a fake license like a lotta people do, but she said no, it's too risky if I don't learn to drive. Peligroso. She went on a trial run with me one day, and she was pissin herself we'd end up dead, I did so bad. I got better, though, in a hurry!

At first I kinda hated changin my routine of morning gym and her house after lunch. But once the lessons got goin, I kinda enjoyed em. Gave me the feelin I'm really somebody, sitting behind the wheel of a brand new car, a carro. Dark green, yeah: verde, her favorite color. After I passed the test, I made good dough. I supported my family, my children I mean, and I put the car rent every week in Chiara's account at the bank.

That only lasted a couplea months. I had extra expenses, children sick and that kinda stuff. And I knew Chiara wasn't payin attention, in India or Japan or wherever she was. One after one, I fell off on the pagos to the bank. It was the easy way out. If Chiara turned up now and then, I just told her business was slow, or there was a emergencia. No importa, doesn't matter, she always said.

She's sweet, yeah for sure. But she just never knows what our life's really like. Our goddam life. She wanna know, but being a gringa she can't. I gotta make somethin outta me, right? But not by slavin for my dad. He just likes to humiliate me, always has. I needa go back to the States if I really wanna make some plata, some dough, and I'm almost thirty now. Hard to believe! And I'd never tell Chiara, but the reason I don't have a visa to Nueva Yol anymore is I got deported. A dumb fuckin thing. I was only waitin outside while a shitass amigo robbed a bodega in Queens. His stupid idea, but he's a citizen and I'm not, so I paid for it big time. Deported, back to the island.

The only way I can go to the States now is without a visa. Like an illegal. So I've been raisin money to buy a place on a yola, one of the boats crossin from here to Puerto Rico. At night, hidden like. It costs a lot cause the captain can end up in the jail, la carcel. But one of em told me he'd take the Escort for half the fare. The rest I've been raisin from anywhere I can think of. People are givin me loans and one day I'll pay em back when I start makin dollars. Sincerely, sinceramente. Plus I gotta pawn somea Chiara's things in her house, and I pawned mosta the junk in me and Reina's house too.

I've been tryin to get help from Esperanza, mi novia, my girlfriend. But she can't causea her boss. Su patrón. She's livin in an apartment he lets her have, but what if he noticed somethin missin? Yeah, she let me sell all the jewelry I gave her. The bracelets and necklaces. She's been afraid anyway he'd see em and find out she's got a boyfriend. So far she's keepin him fooled. Must be a butthead, a real bruuuto!

Chiara's not onto her yet, but Reina is. She's always sniffin round about other women. My girlfriend came up with the yola plan. I'm goin on the boat first, then she's gonna follow me, soon as I get a job in Nueva Yol, the Apple. I wish she'd go with me now, she turns me on so much. But we just had a baby, Lucita. And she's gotta take care of her, she's so small. Nobody knows about Lucita but the boss, and he thinks the baby is his. What a dickhead! Well good, if it makes him give more to my girlfriend on accounta her.

I'm gonna tell Chiara everything now. The truth, la verdad! I'm writin her a letter. I won't be here when she gets back, but she'll find it on her desk. I know she's such a chicken she's gonna think the worst. She'll worry about the yola might sink and I'll get drowned, or they'll arrest me before I make it to my mom's house in Queens. I know she'll go through hell, but she'll understand when I explain in my letter.

I love Chiara more than anybody, even my girlfriend. But I gotta get ahead for my children, mis hijos! And coño, I gotta live my life.

Chiara, Plaza Drake, over the next six weeks

My long meditation retreat in Bodh Gaya was useless, once I returned to Puerto Indio. So much for the 'imperturbable mind.' All sorts of things ran through my head when I read Amado's letter. Pulling at straws, I tried to dwell on the positive. Maybe he'd been arrested on US territory. In that case, he'd be deported back to Canuba soon enough.

Or the local police might've uncovered the yola ring. It's human trafficking, after all. Normally, they would've been in cahoots with the gang themselves; but if they weren't getting their cut, they'd make trouble. So maybe Amado was holed up in the countryside till things simmered down.

I couldn't help envisaging the worst scenarios, too.

Amado might've been shipwrecked. He might've gone under, or been mauled by sharks. He might've been whacked by the same thugs who'd promised to send him to Puerto Rico.

His letter alluded to some 'friends' who'd left five days before, and who'd called to confirm they'd reached New York. Probably they were stooges, phoning from Esmeralda, Barlovento, or some other town, to make their voices sound faraway. At times Amado—the worldly-wise macho—is still a credulous little boy.

I felt numbed, but I tried to get a handle on the facts. I tracked down everyone who might have an inkling of his whereabouts. I started with Reina, but all she did was harp on her marital gripes. 'Whatever happened to that fuckin guy, he had it coming'—and so on. Did she know something she wasn't telling me? Or was she flying blind, like me? Amado hadn't even called to talk to his children, she said. An ominous sign, I thought, since he loves them so much. But Reina didn't seem upset at all, except by the loss of her only chair. 'And here we are, thanks to that creep, with nothin to sit on but a soda-pop crate!'

Her unconcern gave me a glimmer of hope. I rang the taxi service where Amado had been working these past few months. The dispatcher snarled: Yeah, I'd like to getta holda that goddam jerk, and punch him in the nose, the fuckin cheat! He said Amado had left a few weeks back, after racking up debts with all the other drivers.

Screwing up my courage, I paid a call on Héctor—my self-appointed enemy. He had a similar story to tell. Like a bolt from the blue, Amado had asked him for a loan—something about an operation for one of his children. And then he'd promptly vamoosed. I must've looked crushed, since even Héctor consoled me.

In desperation, I sought out Amado's father, though I'd never met him before. At the flagship Paniagua store, posing as a family friend, I wangled my way into his office. A robust man in his early fifties, he was almost as athletic as his son. He wasn't hostile or self-righteous, as I'd expected; he said he approved of my 'friendship' with Amado. He blamed Reina for the strife between him and his 'boy,' as he called him.

The more Sr. Paniagua rambled on, the softer his voice became, until his affection overwhelmed him. He wept for a minute or two, and so did I. That broke the chill, and now we saw to the matter at hand. He'd heard the whole saga, except the part about the mafiosi and the car. He said he also knew where Amado was lying low: those were the words I wanted to hear.

My dumbbell son is still in this country. He's on his grandfather's farm. And he's still driving that Ford of yours. He's nothing but a crook for trying to trade it in, and it would serve him right if you threw him in jail.

I assured him I wouldn't press charges. He vowed Amado would report to me the following morning, 'or else.' We parted with a handshake. He even kissed me on the cheek.

Well... now I've been waiting since breakfast. Sure enough, the Escort pulls up at Plaza Drake around eleven AM. Through the window, I watch Amado strut toward my house with his trademark bravura. Gruffly, he bursts into the sala, acting as if I were in the wrong.

You got some kinda nerve talkin to my father, mi padre! He was pissed off at me already. But now you go blabbin about my deal with the agente de viajes!

Travel agent? Despite my other emotions, I have to roll my eyes. The absurdity of the term tickles Amado, too, and we both start laughing. Luz Divina skulks nearby, eavesdropping as usual. Under my breath, I suggest we go to the tower.

Amado thinks he's in the clear. Yeah, there's lotsa things to discuss, amiga. I've got a propuesta for you, you know, business.

A business proposal? I squint at him noncommittally.

We walk across the square without a word, pausing only to glance at the Ford. I note he's jazzed it up with tacky decals and a wide orange stripe down each side—to enhance the 'trade-in' value, no doubt.

As soon as we enter the circular room and close the door, his frosty insolence melts away. He locks me in a vise-like embrace, hoisting me into the air. Then he sets me down again, without relaxing his grip, and chants a kind of litany: I'm sorry, lo siento, forgive me, perdóname!

I'm sorry, lo siento, forgive me, perdóname!

Strangely, I recall Torquato Tasso in Goethe's play; in the last scene, he cleaves to the Duke 'as to a crag in a stormy sea.' Has my strength overtopped Amado's? Impossible—physically, anyway: but as we know, men are fragile. I'm flabbergasted when I realize he's crying. His broad chest heaves with sobs, like a mountain roiled by aftershocks. His hot tears trickle down my neck. Whatever he does, it's always excessive.

I pry myself away. — Of course, I forgive you, I tell him. Laying my hands on his shoulders, I stare deep into his eyes. What I see there is remorse. — So you do know what love means, after all.

He yields to his grief again. I dive with him into the wave—but then I pull back. — I repeat: I forgive you. But Amado, tell me this: *what* am I forgiving?

He chews his lower lip, like a guilty ten-year old. Seconds later, his cockiness rebounds. — I didn't leave after all. No me fui!

Good! You've seen the light. This whole scheme was insane.

No, Chiara, you're dead wrong! Estás equivocada!

He confesses that at the last minute, the 'travel agent' refused to accept the car—that was all. — Up to then, I hadn't shown him anything but the insurance papers. Remember, you put em in my name. In case of a accident.

When the gangster asked him to sign over the ownership, he saw the title belonged to me: Chiara Trigona. — The bastard said he didn't wanna get his whole outfit in trouble, just cause of a stolen car. He was mad as hell, and that's why I've been hiding.

Thank God. You could've been shark bait by now. Or they might've rubbed you out before you even left. That guy was a swindler.

No, Chiara, he seemed ok. Simpático. This is the only way I can get to Nueva Yol, ever since I lost my visa.

You can wait. Go through the regular channels, like everybody else.

That's harder now—don't you know? And I've been wasting my time, hangin around here.

I agree, Amado. I've been saying for years you should learn a trade. Electrician, mechanic—you decide.

He jumps down my throat. That's easy for *you* to say. I won't be able earn much here. Nothin, nada! And I gotta take care of my children.

I feel sorry for them, too, Amado. You should've thought about that before you opened your fly. Anyway, you could've gone back to the States long ago, when you still had your residence card.

He's visibly flustered. — Ummm, Reina didn't want me to. But Esperanza does. And now we've got a baby together! A little girl, Lucita.

What? Are you bonkers? You can't even feed Reina's children! That's the most ridiculous thing I've ever heard.

Esperanza! Whoever she is, she's taking you for a ride. She got pregnant on purpose, I bet. All she wants is money. And you fell for that? You're a total numbskull.

Amado clenches his fists, and takes a deep breath. — Esperanza, she's not a puta, some kinda whore. She does fine without my dough, bendito. She's a bilingual secretary, a secretaria bilingüe. Get a loada this: she just went on a trip to Chile with her boss, a few months back. He's a honcho executive, fuckin bigtime.

I'm unimpressed, so he takes another another tack. — Look at it this way. You don't have to worry about me anymore. You know I love you more than anybody except my children, mis hijos. More than Esperanza. A lot more than Reina. All I need is one little favor. For the love of God! Just loan me the same dinero they promised me for the car, and I'll pay it back when I find a job in Nueva Yol. But first I gotta make the yola trip to Puerto Rico. Is it a deal?

What can I say to Amado after this? My joy at finding him safe and sound has soured. I've always loved his gutsy Engspan, but now it grates on my ears. I make an effort to control myself.

You pawned my belongings. You stole my car. And now you expect me to foot the bill for your suicide? Just because some floozy wants you to take her to the States? That's what this is about: it's in that moronic letter you wrote. Once you're set up, you'll bring her over as your wife. *If* you survive the trip. Forget it, amigo. I don't need another death on my conscience.

He doesn't have to ask me what I mean. Years ago, Héctor schooled him in my 'leyenda negra': 'Touch Chiara and die.' The 'black legend' of how I hexed Ramsés and Hamlet... Halfheartedly, Amado tries a few more arguments, then turns to leave.

Before he can cross the room, I demand the car keys. — I'll be selling the Ford tomorrow.

He's stunned. Cómo? What'll I live offa, huh?

I'm adamant. — That's your problem. And Esperanza's.

Amado's father must have stressed he'd better cooperate, or else he might go to jail. Woodenly, he forks over the keys.

When I try to unload the Escort the following day, the dealer says: I'll give you a break, and take it off your hands. He offers me less than half of what it's worth. At several other lots, I hear the same rigamarole. In the end, I hide the car from Amado in a long-term garage.

For a month or so, we face off in the time-honored game. Who'll be the first to get in touch? Dismally, I send Luz Divina to recoup my stereo, as well as several other things Amado hocked. The toaster, the iron, the video-player. As if this weren't bad enough, I receive a massive phone bill, chockablock with long-distance calls to Chile.

Luz Divina stokes my indignation with rumors about his other misdeeds—always capped by the same refrain: Now if *I'd* been running things, none of this would've happened! She's right, of course. I shouldn't have let Amado mind the house. But after a while I get sick of her palaver. I ask her never to bring up his name again.

She seizes on this in triumph: Yes! It's just like he's dead and buried!

From now on, she refers to him as 'el difunto'—the deceased. Unwittingly, I fall into the trap. 'What did el difunto do with the corkscrew?' 'Did el difunto make off with the tablecloth, too?'

After four or five weeks, my longings get the best of me. I pick up the phone. Does Amado remember where he stored… the paintbrushes? He sounds so happy to hear my voice! Paintbrushes? He's not sure where they are. He'll have to sort through the storage room. When can he come over?

That's the only pretext we need. I hire him to retouch the peeling walls—a job he's done every year. We're taking up where we left off, with no limits in sight.

Horacio, Callejón del Platero, November 1989

I have been in a dither whether I should telephone Chiara straightaway. Or should I procrastinate until she retrogresses? Such horrendous tidings… So lamentable, to abbreviate her expedition. But if I fail to communicate with her, she might truncate our amity. I am cognizant she voyaged to Greenland on assignment, and then she was ruminating a sojourn with some acquaintances in Vermont. She should be there now, according to this peripatetic agenda. I remain obliged to the empyrean that she always entrusts me with her itinerary: I have consummated my objective in that respect, during our coeval duration as intimates. At any juncture in sublunary existence, emergencies can transpire.

And this is urgent, incontrovertibly. Let me see, here is the numerical codification. Multitudinous digits! How befuddling… I am always astounded when contraptions like this actually function. But there you are: a ringtone. Bling—bling—bling—bling…

Chiara vocalizes. Hello, yes?

I am dumbstruck… Ultimately, through a monumental exercise of self-composure, I elocute. Ch-ch-chiara? This is Horacio. — I am stuttering, how unfortunate: it is psychogenic in this instance, not neurogenic. I never anticipated that she would respond herself.

What a surprise! she trills, in her equable contralto. A pleasant one, Horacio!

How was your perambulation of G-g-greenland? I catechize.

My article is really about Nuuk, so I didn't stray too far. It's a quaint town, with multi-colored buildings. Fine and dandy, if you don't mind the freezing weather, which

I do. That's why I live in the tropics! Greenland was frigid, but it's almost as cold here in Vermont. We've had an early blizzard, and the snow has piled up sky-high. All the way to the windowsills! I can't hope for much relief in New-foundland, where I'll be spending a week at the Dogen Zen Retreat, before I fly home from New York.

She is loquacious, as ever. My instinct is to extricate myself from her garrulity with the utmost alacrity. I can recommence this colloquy posteriorly, when I feel some-what more mettlesome. — I suppose you are frenetically occupied with your cohorts. Presumptively, this is not an opportune occasion to converse. — My stammer has dis-sipated, at least.

Oh no, it's an ideal moment, she cachinnates. Every-body else in the house has gone cross-country skiing. No thanks, I told them, winter sports are not for me. I'm sit-ting here alone beside the fire in the hearth, with a mug of hot cider in my hand. All I see outside is snowdrifts and ice-covered trees. Hearing you warms me up—a balmy breeze from Puerto Indio!

What you characterize seems almost surrealistic, Chiara. Here we are laboring under a calefaction bane! Nevertheless, I would not exchange our clime for yours: refrigeration is noxious to my constitution. I would probably contract bronchitis—or even pneumonia. To coronate everything else!

She bristles when I enumerate my latest maladies, so

I omit the subject posthaste. How are her mater, her pater, her frater? Inquiring after the family is an age-old Canuban custom, a mode of circumlocuting any indelicate directness.

After a while, she cannot tolerate the suspense. What's wrong, Horacio? Something must've happened. Otherwise you wouldn't have called.

I tergiversate. — This is difficult to formulate in vocables.

Just tell me! Please!

Very well. No, not very well! Something befell your soulmate, Amado. Something catastrophic.

Her voice falters. — The worst?

At last, I summon up my valor. As we say, 'from our viscera we must fabricate a heart': 'de tripas corazón.' — Yes. He has gone the way of all flesh. — There: now it is irreversible.

I hear a minor cascade, as she ululates. — Wait! — She has discharged scalding appley extract on her extremities: she lucubrates aloud about the pandemonium. She is marshaling her fortitude, no doubt, so she will not hyperventilate.

After a protracted interval, she produces the ineluctable query: How did he die?

He was conducting a vehicle, and it careened into an edifice. Reina declaimed the complete causal sequence to Catulo: it was an accident.

She does not hesitate: No, it wasn't an accident. It was murder.

Preposterous, Chiara. That does not concord with reality at all.

Yes it does. I should know. I'm the murderer.

Now I am thoroughly nonplussed. — How ludicrous! You did not attend upon the calamity; he was not even piloting your automobile!

I can't talk about it now.

Catatonically, she expresses her gratitude, just as the receiver eludes her possession. It percusses on a plethora of adamantine superficies. Could they be nugatory furnishings, or the parquet flooring below? Such obstreperous clunks and thuds! They almost puncture my auditory timpanum. I keep reiterating hello, hello, hello? Chiara? And then, demoralized, I abdicate.

Luz Divina, Plaza Drake, two days later

Chiara blew in last night. I wasn't expecting her. She came back as soon as she heard. She could've warned me! What a lack of respect…

Today she tried to turn herself in to the police. Keeps claiming she's a 'murderer.' Loonier than ever! She's always been kinda screwy, but this is the living end. At three different stations, the policemen ran her off. They said her passport proved she wasn't even *on* the island!

So now it's way past four. I plunk a dish of breadfruit and beans in front of her. Thank God I stewed these, I tell her, in case you showed for lunch. I would've made that baked macaroni you like, if I'd known for sure. The one from Sillily.

She doesn't answer. Last night she sent me home and went straight to bed. This morning she left at the crack of dawn, before I got here. I haven't had time to tell her what's been going on. She always calls it gossip—chismes—but it's just the facts.

I stay near the table. All she does is pick at the grub. She's only pretending to eat. I've had enough of this. I have to fill her in, whether she wants to listen or not. — I don't know why you're going on like this. What happened to the difunto is his fault, not yours.

She perks up. Please! Don't use that word, Luz Divina. You were calling Amado that long before he died.

So were you! For a while you were mad at him, then you made up. You even put him in charge of the house again. Soon as the wreck happened, Horacio sent for me. Or else *nobody* would've been here.

Thank you for your help, she says—like she doesn't really mean it.

Never mind. You can always count on me. You should've seen how he treated me while you were gone!

He kept using ugly words like perra, telling me to beat it.

Maybe you provoked him.

Some nerve she's got! But I stay polite. — He said I'm too bossy, too mandona, but I was just trying to help. If you're going to fix a lamp or paint a wall, you can't do it any old way!

She clams up, so I switch to something else. — I don't know why you locked yourself in that tower before you left. You didn't even open the door when I carried your meals up there. All those stairs! You said gracias through the keyhole, and told me to set the tray on the top step. Humpf! Sittin up there like a knot on a log.

I was meditating.

That's just a word she uses for doing nothing. But I have to be nice. — Don't feel sad, Señora Chiara. The difunto got what was coming to him. I'm the only person you can trust: I guess you know that now! You should've left me taking care of the house instead of him when you ran off. Six weeks! It's up to me to stay here when you're gone, even if you're only in that tower. But no, you let him grab my place!

Chiara's always disrespecting me. Like with Marino, that dirty Bono. He wanted to cheat me out of my job, and so did the difunto. One of them's a drunk and the other one's dead. I guess that fixes them!

If I let her have a piece of my mind, it's for her own good! — Don't think cause he's a real difunto now he's some kinda saint. While you were gone the neighbors saw him do lots of terrible stuff, lots of maldades. He was even shacking up here with a puta! A whore! Black as a crow! She slept *in your bed, in your sheets.* Your sheets I keep so clean and *white*! What could be worse than that? She was so soot-face, she must've been a Bono. And another thing: Amado was driving all over town with that puta *in your car.* Somebody else told me they *even have a baby*! A bebé!

Chiara oughta be jealous, but I guess she doesn't care. Yes, she says, I know. Esperanza: that's the woman's name.

There's plenty more the difunto did! I tell her a whole bunch of stories. People who bumped into him and that woman! People who watched her nurse the baby! And there's a big lesson Chiara could learn from that, if she had any brains. But instead of talking it over, she drops her fork and bolts for the door like a rabbit, a conejo!

I chase after her, and point to one of the rocking chairs. — That's where he sat and cried for hours, the difunto. He was writing you a letter, he said. He left it up in the tower. He wanted me to give you this key.

That gets her attention! I pull it out of my pocket, and stick it in her hand.

For once, Luz Divina delivered a message—only because it suited her. She must think the letter will discredit poor Amado, even more than her scuttlebutt. Another letter! It's as if history is repeating itself. But this time around, his words will come to a stop...

I've always prized this silver key to the tower's upper room. I asked Amado to treat it with care. The landlord says it's the original from 1901, when the building was constructed. As I clutch it now, going up the stairs, I remember a line from Borges: he marveled that 'a slender key could open an entire house.' What about an entire love? An entire life?

I must be losing it... I'm not on the stairs anymore. I'm peering through the window in Vermont, after Horacio called. Snowflakes have started swirling again. They dance lightly, an alphabet with graceful serifs. Then they multiply, thickening into a blizzard.

In the mudroom, I put on a parka and snowshoes. Time for my afternoon walk, no matter what the weather. Beyond the threshold, a howling wind sears my face, slashing it like a whitehot sword. Expelled, as bewildered as Eve, I blunder through gates of snow...

Suddenly I'm back in the tower, hobbling up the last flight of stairs. I turn the silver key in the rattly lock. In the cylindrical room, Amado created a shrine: he placed a table under each of three windows, overlooking the sea. At this hour, their louvered shutters slice the daylight into hard-edge, refulgent bands. Here I find the letter Luz Divina must've meant, along with scores of others from previous years.

On the table to the left, there's a sheaf of pages in his hand, culled from my filing cabinets. In his typical style, they mesh Spanglish with Engspan. By alternating words from either language, he felt sure he'd hammer home his point. As to everyday idioms, he frequently got them skewed. Instead of tit for tat, tit for tit; instead of chip on your shoulder, chip on your chin.

His spelling in English was fairly standard, but less so in Spanish. He dropped some *s*'s, mimicking Canubano phonetics. He confused *s* with *c* and *z*, and *v* with *b*—so *cerveza*, the Spanish for beer, was warped into *serbesa*. Accents disappeared. Ah well, that's neither here nor there: pedantic details have paled to insignificance. At least his English teachers did well by him in Queens. I was touched when he showed me his diploma one day, beaming with pride.

I remember each and every one of these notes. The first one—dated 24 December, 1984—came with a Christmas gift:

Really realmente Chiara, I don't know how to thank you, you're so good to me. I know you're thanking me too, tu

me agradece so many things but it's that life is so, la vida
es asi, since we're one for the other. No lying, sin men-
tirte, you are a very pretty lady. For the next year I desire
you te deseo the best, todo tu te merece you deserve it all
for you, and so I leave you a kiss and a strong abraso with
both my arms and so much happiness and felicidades,
and all things coming the way you want.
señora I love you tanto, Amado

He drew hearts at the bottom, with 'I love you' and 'Te
quiero' inside them. It used to annoy me when he called
me 'señora': after all, he was only ten years younger. But
the honorific seems endearing to me now.

The next letter is also adorned with hearts—some of
them pierced by arrows. Amado clipped it to the envelope,
postmarked January 1987. He sent it to the Princeton Club
in New York, where I was staying for a couple of weeks
to hobnob with editors. The return address was written
in his nonchalant Spanish. Though he lived in the shod-
dy slum of San Sebastián, his street was named for the
motherland's most eminent painter, Velázquez. In Amado's hasty scrawl, he becomes 'Belasque': a well-deserved
gut-punch to imperial prestige... But I kick myself for even
noticing; it's always the sentiment that counts. And here,
his love for me shines through:

Dear Chiara, Hola
For amistad and friendliness we are one, and I remember
you mucho, I think about you. Even with the distancia

that separates us in this momento I always remember and recuerdo the great momentos I spent with you when we were talking, when we went to travel viajando in the campo, when we were looking at films and pelicula. So many things make me think of you, really realmente we are very buenos amigo. We already have good relation a long time, and in all that time we know each other we never have a problem.

I can say we've been a pair a real pareja of best amigo with a good AMISTAD so few friends can say they have, and have for so much time like you and me, TU Y YO. Chiara, I hope in this momento you and all your familia are well in health and especially you and I give you a big kiss and a strong abraso in my two arms.

Chiara, now thanks to God I am better in my leg and soon I hope I'll see you again. I strange you te extraño mucho, and it's too bad you're not here cause I want to see you, and God keep you and Adiós amiga your friend who I love you mucho

Amado

He 'stranges' me: meaning he misses me. As I miss him, now more than ever... The line about his leg refers to the time he was sideswiped by a motorbike. Even when he wasn't at the wheel himself, he was always accident-prone—landing in one mishap after the next. Long before the fatal wreck, he smashed up the Harley that Héctor gave him.

There are many messages about household matters, reminders Amado left for me to buy this or that. Their narrow scope, focused on our daily routine, makes them all the more wrenching. Through them, I recapture him; I almost embrace him again...

With a shiver, I turn to the table on the right. All it holds is a manila envelope, decorated with a large winged heart and neatly labeled in Amado's bold print: SEE YOU IN ESTADOS UNIDOS, USA! Inside is a lengthy letter, no doubt the one Luz Divina watched him compose:

Chiara,

It's very hard to tell you all this but I really did change the car for a trip to Puerto Rico and New York. I did it for Esperanza. You know, illegal. This time it worked! I don't know how to explain you but I hope you understand me since she's wanting to move there and I couldn't get a legal visa, and I'm not married to Reina so I don't need a divorce to marry Esperanza now. But we woulda had to wait two years for me to bring her to Estado Unido on my residencia visa, if I could get it again. Sabes? You know? So the yola boat was the only way. The yola to Puerto Rico and plane to Nueva Yol were costing me fifteen thousand escudos and they accept the carro for twelve thousand. But I had to add three thousand more. Desesperado I sold your radio and had to pawn your video player again for raising money, and also pawn all Reina's stuff. Esperanza was already going to make this trip on thursday but I worried and not let her go. But then the trip gettin there was fine and our friends they called us from Nueva Yol, and then I decided to go first and let her go on the next yola with our baby. I hope you understand me and forgive me, with your pardón, but I swear I don't want to fail you since I never failed you.

I know I did really bad since the correct was to call you and explain what I was doing, llamandote for sure. But I never had the courage since it's not so easy for me and now you and me we have so much time together junto, but I never nunca failed you and you know it tu lo sabe. I'm failing you now but with my heart roto and broke in many pieces of pedazos. Cause it hurts me what I do to you now, mucho. You don't know how much I'm thinkin of you and how much I'm crying, llorando y llorando. In moments now writing you it's hard, duro cause of tears and lagrima. I'm llorando like never in the life. Chiara I love you and I'm hopin you'll pardon me perdonarme one day. And if you can't forgive me God will pardon me because he knows why I do all this, todo esto. God and you know why I don't want Esperanza and mis hijos my children to suffer what I suffer from when I was small and I'm suffering now.

I know you think all this is just a vanity of me, a vanidad.

I don't want help from my father but I still want somethin in this life. You know I realize now in this country you can't make it since here aqui a Canubano can break his back for 20 years trabajando and always we stay in the same place, el mismo lugar. Why? Porqué? Cause the money you earn here is nothin and gives you nothin, it only gives for rice and beans and some little bit carne, meat. It's like we say the pay here is only to give you for those three things and to rent a house not yours, no tuya. Chiara the principal for me is the dos muchachos I've got with Reina. I am their father su padre and I want a house una casa where they can make their vida when they're big.

Esperanza she is takin care of our little girl, the chiquita, but you're right I shoulda stayed in Nueva Yol with my mamá but now I'll go back some way. But I say to myself if I stayed there before, I woulda never met Esperanza or you, ni Esperanza ni tu.

Chiara I hope I'll be payin you pagandote back everything when I can. In case of something happens to me now on the trip to Nueva Yol I ask you on my knees de rodilla to your feet that you will be helping my children however you can. Cause one thing is for sure, if I can't pay you if yo no puedo ever pagarte

GOD WILL PAY YOU, TE PAGARA DIOS

I say goodbye crying llorando with pain and mucho dolor, me who loves you quien te quiere and will always love you,

Your friend tu amigo Amado

Once again, his signature is framed by hearts, with 'I love you' and 'Te quiero' in flowery script. Then there's a jarring comment labeled 'Comentario Luz Divina':

Chiara you know Luz Divina more than me, you know all the things she's always trying to cause. One time I surprise her with your closet open where you keep your things and she's takin somethin out, I don't know what, que tipo de cosa. But I don't say a word, nada, and I put 100 escudo under her chair to see if she's stealin, robando. Results that she took the dinero and didn't tell me, and me waitin and nada. So I ask her what about my 100 escudos and what about Chiara's closet, and she gets real nerviosa and starts up cryin, llorando. The thing bein I don't want to accuse but I don't wanna be accused of what more things you find gone in your house en tu casa, since I have only put my hand on your aparato stereo and video player. If something else is gone she stole it lo robó ella to try accusing me.

Send Luz Divina to the pawn place compraventa, the direction is on this receive, where she can pay back the video and musica. You have to send her with 1500 escudos. Pardona me please por favor, and by God por Dios. Amado

Shaking my head despondently, I leaf through the album on the center table, bound in oxblood velour. It contains photos of boyfriends and pick-ups I've taken over the years. My house served as the backdrop for some, but others were snapped in the tower. As for the models, they run the gamut of every size and hue. Besides their youth, all they have in common is an impressive physique, ranging from limber Apollo to chiseled heavyweight. Here's Hamlet, here's Ramsés, and so on down the list.

Amado left the tome splayed open to his pictures, which fill it by three quarters or more. They portray 'the deceased' in all his moods: impish, sultry, sardonic, but never camera-shy. So much vitality, extinguished at the age of twenty-nine! It hardly seems possible. 'El difunto…' Now that he's really dead, that nickname makes me shudder with remorse.

He and I had united again: I fooled myself that we

could go on forever. But it wasn't so; it wasn't so. These past few months were only a reprieve. Our long vacation on earth had almost ended.

Shoving the table aside, I unlatch the shutters and lean out. For several hours, I sail with the clouds across the sky. They trundle above the sea, slowly at first, then faster and faster... Topheavy with rain, they run aground on the darkening shoals of twilight... Finally they rip apart, ship-wrecked in a gulf of blackness... The moonrise, I know, is far away—and the sunrise, farther still.

Catulo, the shop on Callejón del Platero

Chiara will be aghast to hear Bruckner when she drops by, not Gibbons or Byrd. She and my brother listen to mincing madrigals, whereas I prefer Late Romantic balderdash! I've raised the oriel, and the *Eighth* is thundering forth, full metal jacket. That should give her a hint of what to expect—a chance to prepare for the onslaught of... me. Ah, tragical Queen Dido: my favorite thespian role! But I'll control myself. After all her felicity, now she's languishing in a fairyland forlorn, and I wouldn't want to stoke her désarroi.

Knock, knock, who's there? I knew she would gravitate to our Gallic lane this AM. I can be prescient at times:

masculine intuition! Besides, who phoned her with the cataclysmic news? My brother Horacio. And who's always minding the store? Right again: the churchy little wizard. At night, I may use the sofa in a pinch, but I'm never here by day. The fact is, I have a lot more to impart than he does: the nitty-gritty, the whole enchilada. I'll try to show her clemency, too, even if it goes against my forthright grain. Hahaha, some have denounced me as brutally frank.

When I open the door, her eyes go snap, crackle, and pop. I guess she didn't discern my musical cue. Poor thing, she's too confused: still reeling from the shock.

I enfold her tenderly. — I know you're looking for Horacio. Alack, he went stone-collecting with Virgilio in Piedras Blancas. Their artisans need new rocks to paint, since the stock on the shelves is running low. I guess you'll have to settle for me.

She mentions Amado's letter. She strives to be brave, but soon she flies into smithereens. With another hug, I sweep up the pieces, and ease her into a comfy chair. I lower the volume of Anton B. to a backstage whisper. — I've been bopping to the city fairly often of late, girlfriend. Amado rumbaed into my purview several times while you were gone. Davvero, this disaster has been impending for months.

Crestfallen, she searches my face. — Please promise you won't make fun of me. Or drool over the randy bits.

Oh yes, she's disconsolate: I'm not feigning my compassion. — Chiara, I could never love anyone as much as you loved Amado. The years have tempered me into a blade of steel; but I won't be churlish today—not to you.

I believe you, she gulps; and then she starts blubbing in earnest.

I drape my arm around her shoulders. — Grief is like a dam. Go ahead, let it burst.

I fetch her a tea-towel: five teary minutes ensue. Once she gets a grip, I tune my lyre. As she hearkens to my dulcet chords, maybe they'll comfort her at last—even if I'm only whistlin' Dixie.

I launch my monologue with a bold cliché. Everything is about sex and money, I pontificate: more often, a messy omelette made from both. By his own admission, some time ago Amado relapsed into his periodic vice, gambling. He was feeding another habit, too: a fatal attraction called Esperanza.

I happened upon them together one day, tooling around in the Ford, and I waved Amado over to the curb. He lowered the window and gave me five. His joy in touting his wheels (and almost as an afterthought, his squeeze) was blithely infectious. I could tell she didn't come cheap. Black and statuesque, with sleek, taffeta skin, she was so enticing I felt tempted, too.

About a month later, I bumped into Reina. I've known her ever since I first seduced Amado—long before Héctor blipped across the screen. Now, trussed up in curlers on a Saturday afternoon, she wanted to vent her grievances: over an icy jumbo Papagayo—or three or four! She's normally a deaf-mute, but with me she's a Chatty Cathy. By the way, amica, the bottles of beer have endowed her with a budding embonpoint. Right up my alley, so to speak—or hers!

As I suspected, 'that bitch Esperanza' had proved a daunting rival. Like any jealous spouse, Reina posted her spies all over town. One of them overheard the 'monkey-face whore' bragging to a girlfriend. 'Amado's the man for me! He's zero-cool! A *big* fuckin guy, in every way! And he's as horny for me as I am for him. His family's loaded, and he's got a super-ass car. I bet ya anything he's gonna take me to the Apple! His mother owns a business in Nueva Yol, where he grew up. Visa, here I come!'

Whoaaaa, cara Chiara! When I met her, Esperanza didn't shoot off her mouth. Quite the opposite: she seemed downright genteel. Reina and her friend must have mucked up her words with their own cucaracha lingo—if she ever uttered them at all.

Truth or fiction, Reina was livid. She vowed she'd chew the trollop up and spit her out. — Amado won't marry me, oh no! But he's plannin to hitch up with that prieta hussy and take her to Nueva Yol! Over my dead body! — She flexed her muscles to illustrate the point. — I even hear the cunt is knocked up!

I was puzzled by one factoid, bubbling from the beery

suds: per Reina's informants, Esperanza came equipped with a stalwart protecteur. Reina raised her fist. — Why does that black-face slut need to ride around with Amado, when she's got a car of her own? Why does she suck up his taxi fares when she's whorin her ass in a fancy condo? She's already gettin paid to fuck a rico who keeps her in style. Amado's dough oughta go to me and our two kids, our muchachos! And now he's having a baby with her too!

I smirk at Chiara, in a brief aside: Who would've thunk it, girlfriend? She never mentioned your dibs on the funds.

Anyway, as I sauntered home, a row of tsk-tsks filed through my head. Honestly, dearheart, after all these years on the island, how could you be such a sap? Did you really think you could gift our boy a car, and not set off a chain reaction?

She looks so woebegone! I pet her once more to atone for my sass.

There, there, carissima. Just wilt into the cushions and chill out... Not long ago, I chanced on Amado again, at a jeweler's. He was leaving the shop with a tiny box, very lavishly wrapped. Aha! I japed. So you found a woman who can swallow the whole thing, like an hombre! Weren't Reina and Chiara skillful enough?

He grinned at me complicitly. Listen, you fuckin puta. Maybe you're good, ok. But this bitch got a throat on her, even wider and deeper than yours.

We shot the breeze for a while at a sidewalk café. Wisecracks aside, I chided him for his fickleness: Get real, Superboy. If you buy her presents, you're eating away at your children's food.

Huh! I can tell you've been talkin to Reina. She's always yappin about how I oughta do more for my children with her. Not true.

I swooped. What do you mean, your children *with her*?

Sheepishly, he blushed. Esperanza and me, we've got a baby girl, Lucita. But don't tell Reina, or Chiara neither. — Then he recovered his bravado. — And you know what? I don't pay a centavo for Lucita. Nada! Esperanza takes care of everything.

I deadpanned. And all that moola, how does she rake it in?

He wasn't duped. I bet Reina told you Esperanza's got a sugar daddy. Mentira: that's just a lie. Sure she's got a boss, an executive. But she works hard. She's a bilingual secretary.

I couldn't resist. One tongue for him, and one for you?

Chuckling dude to dude, Amado loosened up. He complained you'd been away too long, Chiara. He'd lost the knack of talking freely. He could only do that with his two best friends: you and me. Reina's bloodhounds stalked him day and night, so he had to second-guess his every move. But since I was a man of the world, and one of his oldest pals, I would understand. He loved Esperanza, and she loved him. That's why they were willing to tough it out, as long as they could do it together.

'Brahmskovsky' was oozing from the soundtrack, amica: the turgid strings of a Hollywood film. — How romantic, I jeered. And what a hardworking girl!

Verdad! he insisted, she did have a job. She reported to her office every morning. Her magnate had also doled out a bijou flat in Loma Linda. Amado winked. — You know—sabes? He picks up the tab: he can visit her anytime he wants.

So there was some sugar in daddy's pot, after all... and in hers. But I kept those aperçus to myself.

Amado unbosomed, fingering his pecs. He said Mr. Bigwig usually phoned, to make sure Esperanza would be at home. But one day, he appeared without any notice. Amado had no choice but coitus interruptus, and a kangaroo-leap into the closet. What a bummer! He could hear her having sex with her patron, only a few feet away. He could even watch them through the louvers of the door. But manfully, he didn't budge an inch; this proved how much he adored Esperanza. Because of the baby, they couldn't afford to lose her salary. Otherwise, he would've clobbered the SOB. Sometimes Esperanza cried, she felt so morose. That's why he bought her a coral pendant just now, to cheer her up.

Well, what *about* the baby? I objected. Doesn't that tip her 'employer' off?

Lucita looks just like her mother, and the dickhead

thinks she's his. So he chips in more than ever! Get it? Entiendes?

Several more months went by... As you know, Chiara, I've snagged a prime position at a ritzy new resort, much farther away than Hermosa. While I was learning the ropes, I cameoed here in Puerto Indio almost as rarely as you. On the one occasion when we had lunch together, you were irate. Amado had endeavored to barter your car for a yola cruise to Puerto Rico—and not in a stateroom. But as it turned out, that was only the dress rehearsal. Woe is you!

Not long ago, I coincided with him at La Cumbre: the lofty Summit or Summum Bonum, as I dub it in my Thomist moods. Over the screeches of queens and other nocturnal raptors, we had a lengthy heart-to-heart. I'll fill you in on that anon, if you can bear up. The next day, I was intrigued when he phoned me. For many years now, we've tacitly agreed never to get in touch. We've depended on serendipity to bring us together, like ships passing in the night. But without any hanky-panky, Chiara, rest assured! What, don't you trust me?

When Amado called, I flirted a tad, I must own up. But I swear it was all in jest. What's wrong? I razzed him. Did your girlfriend get braces, or come down with strep? Hunting for a substitute sub?

I was blown away when he asked me for a 'loan'—Canuban parlance for a lagniappe, as we know. Everybody is au courant that I live beyond my means, somewhere over the rainbow. I owe my German employers a mint in advances on my salary. But for my birthday, Aunt Alba Iris had given me a tidy sum, so I offered him a thousand escudos: to wit, a hundred dollars, in our devalued currency. When he skipped by for the stash, I traded it for the low-down.

He hemmed and hawed, then blurted out the truth. I told you last night at La Cumbre. I'm hard up, ombe. I've gotta make it to Nueva Yol as soon as I can.

His residence visa had run out eons ago, he said; it would take a month of Sundays to get it renewed. He'd decided to take his chances on a boat to Puerto Rico. He was rustling up the fare as best he could. All this you've heard about, presumably.

Now I was really worried, carissima Chiara. Like any sensible earthling, I share your dim view of human trafficking. I shot him a petulant look: Come off it, Amado! You've been through the same malarkey before. Chiara told me you tried to pull a fast one with her car a while back; it didn't pan out, so why should this?

That's the problem, man. Like I was sayin at La Cumbre, ever since Chiara got mad and took away the car, I don't earn shit: no hay na. Unless it's from a odd job, a trabajito. I've gotta borrow from every fuckin body I know. Esperanza's helpin some, but her jefe might wise up if she lifts dinero from his pockets. Especially since he's been snoopin around, askin about me.

When I voiced my misgivings again, Amado changed his tune. He would forget about the trip, he vowed. But anyway, he needed a high-priced antibiotic for one of his children. Most likely, he invented that fable on the spot. With my usual frivolity, I handed over the cash—for auld lang syne!

As we said good-bye, I tried to encourage him. Buck up, sweetheart—mi corazón. The car wasn't wolfed down by a hungry Bacá! Our Canuban yeti lurks only in the mountains. Chiara assured me she never sold the thing: she's just waiting till she trusts you again. Then she'll redeem it from the garage, you can man the wheel, and all will be well!

Chiara seems unglued, but there's no time to pray tell. Just at that moment, some tourists pound on the door. Heavens to Betsy, girlfriend! I forgot to hang out the CERRADO sign. — I gauge them through the casements: the gals are wearing swim-togs in the midst of town; the menfolk waggle plastic mariconeras, schlocky handbags for males. — As soon as I dispose of this Euro-trash, I'll be right back. Cross my heart!

No hurry, she sighs with a chapfallen mien. Let me duck out for a bit. I need some air.

As if they'd met Melpomene herself, the beach-bunnies stand aside to let her pass.

Catulo's quip about the car made me sick, and now I feel totally derailed. So it had all come down to that: a thoughtless, throwaway line. I'm haunted by another phrase, from the King James Bible I used for my thesis at Princeton: 'My soul is exceeding sorrowful, even unto death.'

So far it had been a conundrum, one I couldn't unknot. On this second go-round, how had Amado taken the car from the parking garage? How did he realize it hadn't been sold? The papers were still in a locked drawer, right where I'd left them.

I asked at the car park. Chawing on a toothpick, the attendant stonewalled. — Hmmm, I think I remember a green Ford. Si, si, an Escort. But that was months ago. When the owner never shows, a car can get stolen. Bendito! Who knows how? You sure you come to the right garage?

I showed him the receipt, proof positive. He cocked his head toward a sign. 'Abandoned vehicles: at your own risk.'

I couldn't blame Catulo for letting the cat out of the bag; after all, I hadn't sworn him to secrecy. For Amado, one offhand comment had been enough; all he had to do was check every garage near my house until he found the Ford.

He probably asked the traffickers to steal the car themselves, since he was well-known in the neighborhood. No problem: for a moderate tip, the attendant would look the other way. Since the owner would be gone for several months, no one would get into trouble. By the time I reported the theft, the police would dismiss it as a 'cold case,' impossible to solve.

There's no rational link between the Ford and Amado's death. Horacio said he wasn't driving it when the accident occurred. Then why do I recoil, as if one thing led to the other? Somehow, the car is the essential link in a lethal chain... or as Borges wrote, the slender key to an entire house.

Catulo, in the shop

Once the tourists waddle off, Chiara mopes back into the store. Now she desperately wants to change the subject. I guess she'd rather reminisce about the days of wine and roses—of Shangri-La and splendor in the grass.

You mentioned the Summit. Way back when, I saw Amado and Reina do an uproarious striptease there. We were all so carefree then.

Shelving her agony for a sec, I go her one better: I can't even count the times I watched them do that act! They were dynamite!

She blanches. I'm ready, Catulo. Tell me about your

meeting with Amado at La Cumbre.

I forge ahead with my verbal choreography—albeit in more guarded battements and jetés. Carissima, the club was dour that night: the whole rookery of 'birds' was blue—a sullen, midnight blue. Reina never showed at all, though she's a regular. Around one AM, Amado straggled through the door, listless and down at the mouth.

His face lit up when he saw me lounging by myself. He didn't have to ask if he could join me; we've been best buds for umpteen years. He knew I'd listen to his troubles, and spot him a string of Canuba Libres, his Ariadne's thread.

After the first round, he yammered about his money bind—tight as a tourniquet, he whinged. After the third round, he kvetched that his woman's boss had caught them 'in flagrante'—and so that cash flow might run dry. By the fifth round, our alpha machote was chomping on humble pie. All he'd scared up was part-time employment, driving a battered truck for an iron workshop. As he drained another glass, he rattled off the expenses he couldn't meet.

By this time, he'd downed a quart of rum. From now on, he soliloquized about you—and you alone. Why does that surprise you, girlfriend?

Chiara still won't trust me, he blabbered. That's what hurts me the most. I love her more than anybody else. You know that, amigo, lo sabes muy bien. She's always treated me so good. Always teaching me somethin, jawin about books, countries I've never been to, stuff like that. Not anymore. I guess she just sees me as some kinda animal, only good for sex. Even when she's in town, we fuck but she hardly talks.

His expression was hard to construe. Heartbreak, rage, disgust? He knocked the table back, spilling my Absolut and ice all over my lap. As soon as he reared up, the customers bayed like a pack of werewolves. Amado, Amado! Take it off! Quítalo todo! Take it all off!

The shrillest of them all were the 'drag empresses,' high as Mt. Everest on hooch and drugs. I've prattled to you before about that coven. Their ringleader is a fag-hag called Chuchu: a biological woman—what's left of her. She was slumped against the back of her chair, spineless as a beanbag. After a tumbler or three of whisky, and machine-gun hits of crack, she'd rafted down the river of no return.

Amado staggered onto the stage. He reminded me of a clown who's forced to satisfy his fans, though he's used up all his gags. He boogied with clumsy steps, out of synch with the disco beat. As he dropped his clothes, I noticed his body had lost its peerless shape: he'd gone from Praxiteles to gummy bear. He couldn't cover the gym fees anymore, I suppose.

At the end of his lame routine, everybody gasped. He'd tossed his underwear aside! Mechanically, he jacked his penis to a full corncob erection. For a minute or two, the DJ was too gobsmacked to cut the music. Bucking in a parody of sex—in and out, in and out—Amado stumbled off the stage and headed for Chuchu's table. He was stroking his tool to the tune of 'Stop! In the Name of Love.' Her harpies-in-waiting snatched at it hungrily, pumping it up and down.

Swatting them off, he plunged his cock into Chuchu's slackjawed mouth. Her eyes were glassy, almost sightless. She barely knew what was happening. As the semen gushed down her throat, she almost choked. The remix suddenly ground to a halt. Amado's member sagged, limp and dejected. When it slid from Chuchu's lips, cum dribbled down her chin.

He threw on his clothes and walked out, not even waving good-bye.

Chiara, a while later

I never drink before noon. But this morning I'm glad Catulo keeps a cache of Stolly in the shop. We pause for a couple of shots—what he dubs a 'Godunov interlude.' I hope he's almost through with his account; my endurance is about to snap.

Fortified, he says that Reina turned up, a week after Amado's funeral. Foisting the children on one of her sisters, she'd made the trip to Playa Cerrucho, where Catulo manages the main hotel. It's a three-hour bus ride from

Puerto Indio; but she hankered to chat with someone who'd share a laugh or two about his scrapes—someone who'd really known him well.

She'd never resented their 'dalliance.' Like most Canubanas, she didn't consider men a serious threat. After all, they couldn't produce a second family, or cause a financial strain; sometimes they even replenished the household piggy-bank. Catulo was the couple's oldest friend: that was all. Through liter after liter of Papagayo, she cursed 'that pendejo bastard, Amado'—and then, unburdened, she 'skedaddled back to the capital,' in the dancer's words.

Did she know he was planning to hop a boat to Puerto Rico?

No. From what you said about his letter, he must've been gearing up to leave. But he didn't tell her squat.

I've already heard about the pickup Amado was driving when the accident took place. Horacio alluded to it when he rang me in Vermont. Now Catulo fills me in on the details—'the *final* details,' as he gingerly calls them.

According to Reina, her brother Sigfrido needed to move to a new apartment. Amado offered to help him, with his usual generosity—and recklessness. His foreman at the iron workshop had warned him: he should never overload the ramshackle truck, and he was strictly forbidden to borrow it. To stymie any wise ideas, after hours the keys were locked in a safe.

For Amado, that amounted to a double dare. Not only

did he sneak into the lot that evening and jump-start the jalopy, he piled it high with Sigfrido's belongings. The clunker had faulty brakes; and with all the extra weight, when Amado cut a hairpin turn, they completely gave way.

Sigfrido was riding in the passenger seat. After the wreck, he told Reina the pickup had shimmied out of control, slewing quickly toward a hospital wall. Amado could've saved himself by exiting just before impact. Instead, he thought only of his brother-in-law, who was paralyzed by fear. Reaching over, he threw open the door and pushed him out. Sigfrido survived with nothing more than a broken arm.

Amado had sacrificed those last few seconds he needed for his escape, and so he bore the full brunt of the crash. Pulling him from the wreckage, some passers-by carried him to the emergency room. His mighty heart was still beating; but a few minutes later, he gave up the ghost.

The morticians didn't try to reconstruct his face, it was so badly shattered. They nailed the casket lid shut, once and for all.

After a cursory service, attended solely by Reina and her children, he was buried in an unmarked grave.

Once Virgilio and I have triaged the stones we garnered, I promenade to Chiara's residence. Festina lente, quoth Augustus. Yet Luz Divina does not subscribe to the imperial maxim. I descry her ricocheting back and forth on Plaza Drake, conferring excitedly with her sanitation colleagues—the curler-diademed ladies who char at the dwellings nearby.

Espying me, she hastens towards Chiara's commorancy. I have hardly adumbrated the threshold, when her logorrhea attains its apogee. Yesterday afternoon, she clamors, Chiara inserted some apparel into a rucksack; she delineates each article of raiment in excruciating detail. Then, without any whys or wherefores, our Sicilian Athena accelerated through the portal, and promptly dematerialized.

Subsequently, Chiara's mater and pater telecommunicated. Alas, what with the linguistic impediment, comprehension desiccated on the proverbial vine.

The marchese visited Puerto Indio by aeolian propulsion last year, yachting over from the Virgins with a British earl. Chiara was absent, so I apportioned the honors. Since then, Luz Divina has often interrogated me about the gentleman—in particular, whether 'he knows how to talk yet.' He does expectorate some macaronic English; but in Castilian all he can emit is 'hola'—and his spouse is likewise unversed.

Lugubriously, I peruse Chiara's index of coordinates, and excavate their tele-ciphers. When I aspired to embark on holy orders, I sojourned for a trimester at the Pontificia Universitatis Gregoriana in Rome; as it betided, for me it was merely an urban villeggiatura. But my Italian is still serviceable—a sight better than Catulo's snippets from Puccini, at any rate—even if in the present circumstances, a *Tosca* aria might be dolorously apropos.

The marchesa responds straightaway, courtly but distraught. She divulges that her daughter left a 'strambissimo' recording on the communiqué machine. — Yes, very strange! She claims she murdered somebody, Horacio. Stupidaggini, total nonsense! And what's this about doing penance? Has she really gone off to live in a cave?

Eureka! That is the lone indication I necessitate. — Do not aggrieve yourself, I placate the marchesa, I divine where she is: merely on a transient, arcadian digression. Chiara will be safe and sound, sana e salva! Beyond the umbrage of a dubiety, she is not homicidal. She is inculpating herself because a valued confederate expired. Amongst the psychotherapists, 'survivor's guilt' would be the nomenclature, or so I hypothesize… Till ere long, nobile signora!

Without further ado, I confabulate with Torsten at his auberge. — Sure enough, he corroborates, Chiara stayed here last night. She hired a car and driver to bring her from the capital—must've cost a frigging fortune. Now she's hoofing it to her cabin on Playa Grandota, I guess. Or maybe to the cave.

A propitious augury, I muse, however simplistically couched; she suspires for a measure of solitude, in order to excogitate. Even if the notion of such a peregrination smites me with infirmity!

Before regressing to our mercantile establishment, I alleviate Luz Divina. — Chiara is in Barlovento, on sabbatical for several days—I mean, resting. Never mind, my dear, everything will be all right.

Chiara, November 1989 to June 1991

After hearing Catulo out, I shambled home in bewilderment. Hollowness. Fury. I imagine soldiers must go through this, in the bedlam of battle. A comrade shields you when you cross the line of fire; his torso is scythed in two instead of yours. This isn't war, and I shouldn't overstate the simile. But what good does courage do? How long will the world remember? The hero's valor lasts no more than an instant, brief as an exploding star...

For me, the strand west of Palma Verde has always been a map of Eden: now, my earthly paradise has shriveled and turned to ash. As I trudge here, I'm one of the damned in Dante's hell, my feet stepping forward while tears drip down my back. I stare at the past that lies behind me, and this shore is the happiness I've lost. Its magnificence seems ghastly, a mockery worse than despair.

Starting from the village, a scraggly path winds along the coast, then angles up a boulder-strewn slope. At its edge, a promontory claws the sea with splayed-out fingers, lichened and gnarled. A webbing of secluded beaches connects them, each in a different tint and texture of sand: khaki and rough; white and pebbly; pink and finely sifted; greenish and pocked with shells. Locals call this crag the Mano de Dios, the Hand of God; it's the nearest point to the whale-shaped islands. Amado and I often swam to them from these coves, lured by the dazzling sun. This afternoon, no one would dare: the sea hurtles against its cage like a maddened beast, slobbering fragments of coral and kelp.

At its endpoint, Playa Caracol swerves into a wide spit of honey-dark sand, streaked with grey and white. No matter how overcast my mood, I've always been elated when I round the bend and catch sight of the view: the mountains, the inlets, the serrated cliffs of Dutchman's Bay; the mist brimming from low-keeled clouds. But today, the marvels of the landscape seemed tarnished and dull. Unavoidably, Coleridge comes to mind: 'I see, not feel, how beautiful they are.' Only Amado was able to tether me to earth, to force me to incarnate. Now I'm no more than a phantom again, melting into thin, thin air.

I continue to the cabin, no longer even noticing the curves of the palm-fringed bight. I haven't returned in almost a year, so I expect to find the place run-down... Yes, the screen-wire on the ground floor hangs in tatters, and the octagon's green paint has peeled. There's no sign of the caretaker, Chévere—or of Rosy, the mare. Amado always worried that someone would rustle her, sooner or later; but maybe Chévere rode her off on an errand of some kind. Without the horse, I can't afford to stop and rest. I need to reach El Silencio by dusk: the final leg of the trek is too dicey in the dark.

Playa Grandota extends for a mile and a half beyond the pagoda; I plod along, but the soggy sand impedes my progress. Around the next point lies another deserted beach, severed by two creeks that mingle before they join the sea. Black with sediment from the mangroves, one is called Río Negro: this is where I went birding with Amado in Don Eneldo's skiff, several years ago. Its crystal twin is Río Blanco, and both are easy to ford along their saltwater shoals.

After Playa Dos Ríos—Two Rivers Beach—the coast fans out in uneven arcs, patchworks of mica-speckled pebbles and powdered sand. There must be a storm in the offing; the ocean heaves along the horizon in broad-backed swells. The clammy stillness where I slog is oppressive—though far above, in the tropopause, a wind shreds the clouds into banners of ebbing light.

A couple of miles further west, Río Frío wells from a cave; nearby, the torrent has sculpted a trapezoidal pool, ringed by sedges and reeds. This is where Amado and I made love beneath the moon—and where by day, we cooled off after our languid swims. Surging over limestone blocks to the sea, the frigid current grapples with lukewarm waves that always win. Here we would paddle for hours in the surf, bathe in the icy creek, and dry off on the sun-scoured sand.

Now the foam glitters at me spitefully. Every rock reminds me of Amado. His memory crushes me, as if he's straddling my back. I come close to slipping on the mossy stones where Río Frío meets the tide; on the other bank, I lie down for a while to recoup my strength.

A mile more, and the strand peters out. Eroded cliffs, the stumps of the primal sierra, ram the ocean full tilt. The headlands mount in cyclopean steps, furred by tenacious ferns; the beaches narrow to fragile hems, darkening under overhangs of rock. As I climb into the hills, a volley of stars riddles the sky like grapeshot.

I'm already starting to trip on splintered roots and snaggy stones. For now, this is irksome enough; but it could be deadly if I pitched over the drop-off beside the path, into the maelstrom of churning seas and jagged boulders far below. I feel a rush of relief when Chévere lopes toward me, equipped with a flashlight; Rosy tags along behind him, more docile now. He's heard about Amado's accident, he tells me. After that, he holds his tongue.

I swing into the saddle, and he leads me to the border of the farm; his cousin Wilfrido, who's only twelve years old, takes over from here. Several months ago, I gave him permission to live in one of the shacks the Medinas left. I'm glad I also said he could plant some crops, since a few supplies will come in handy now. I spread my sleeping bag on his packed-dirt floor, and immediately black out.

The next morning, he invites me to share his cabin, for as long as I want. Bleakly, I tell him I'll stay in the cave from now on. Voluble as ever, he tries to change my mind: the cave is too lonely; no, too spooky; anyway, it's full of bats. In the end, he relents. He agrees not to disturb me, except in an emergency.

With Wilfrido toting the backpack, we clamber up the rugged goat-trail to the cave. When he says good-bye, I'm already posted at my look-out, on a worn shelf of rock at the cavern's mouth, framed by strangler fig trees. Here I renounce the human race, 'and all its works, and all its pomps.'

Amado, killing a man is much easier than I thought: a careless slip of the hand, and it's done. Under the archway of this cave, you exist wholly within my mind. If I don't take care, I'll whittle you down to nothing but a figment of my grief. The past will destroy your present, sapping the life you still nourish inside my own. I refuse to degrade you to that grim phrase from Yeats: 'my heart's victim, and its torturer.'

Could it have been any different? Could I have intervened to save you from yourself? The path you chose wasn't random, picked out of a hat. I hurried you over the edge, bent on denying my fulfillment. I was too headstrong to be like other women, reliant on a man for completeness—too arrogant to accept that between you and me, gender and power balanced out.

Even before your death, I'd gone back to my nunlike ways; after our lengthy elopement, the convent reclaimed me. When I lived where the seasons change, I hated the spring. Black spring, I always called it: a shroud of leaves that blots out the sky. In the tropics, I'm buried in a tomb where summer never ends—a damp mausoleum of green.

I'd like to believe you never gave up faith in yourself. No, death just overtook you unawares. But as hard as I try, I can't let myself off the hook. In spite of all you did to free me, I hadn't truly reformed. You *were* the flesh, Amado, and that's why I neglected you—why I murdered you in the end. The car I bought was a weapon: I used it to mow you down like a defenseless child.

Without me, you would never have learned to drive. Athletes feel compelled to raise the bar, to trump their own benchmarks. Weights, stamina, speed—it's all the same. Knowing your yen for excess, your parents kept you safe from engines of any kind. When Héctor bought you a motorbike, it wasn't long before you totaled it. You outlived the crash by a miracle—thrown loose before you slammed into a tree.

This time you weren't so lucky—if luck played a role. You never lost control, I lost it for you: I was the banshee at the wheel, the demon I've always been. Learning to drive, what does that mean? You strap your body into a metal box; you become a machine yourself. I divorced you from nature, the source of your strength. Like a derelict guardian, I left you exposed to the abuser who did you in.

Esperanza happened to be a woman; she could equally as well have been a man. Like a succubus, she drained you dry and threw away the husk. You forfeited everything you had—but worse than that, everything you were, without and within. After your first attempt to steal the car, you asked for my forgiveness. But now, how can you forgive me in return?

She and I both blighted you: entrapped by our wiles, you atrophied and decomposed. If she was a vampire, I was an incubus. The last time we had sex, I was the one who penetrated you; despite my games with other boyfriends, I'd never entered you before. Swallowing your macho pride, you submitted to my caprice. As I harnessed the dildo to my pelvis, your eagerness to please me was abject. You pulled your knees to your chest and let me screw you—without a whimper, 'like a man.'

From a tremendous height, I looked down at your eyes: I saw nothing there but surfaces, insubstantial glints. I fucked you till you spewed like a geyser. Soundlessly, your face an impassive mask, you flecked my breasts with a slurry of rancid cream.

When I showed you to the door, for a moment you held back. You were waiting for my usual fond good-byes. But instead of embracing you, I laid my hands on your chest. I sent you off with an indifferent nudge: I willed you to vanish. Two months later, you were dead.

As in those evil videos I've read about, I raped you before I snuffed you. Maybe Héctor was right; maybe I have a genius for butchering young men. First Ramsés, then Hamlet, now you. What no one understands is how the slaughter doubles back on me. I'm a black widow who's ensnared in her own web. Each time I succumb to the same corrosive torment, the 'sorrow unto death.'

I envy people with the gumption to take their own lives. My mother suffers from bouts of depression. She defines the syndrome precisely: you don't wish you were dead, you wish you'd never been born.

To me, the 'sorrow unto death' is an inner dearth. Not the detachment of a saint but a drab privation, a leaden inanition. I'm robbed of sleep, hunger, thirst, even breath. I try to breathe, but what I breathe isn't air. It's the dregs of air, a room gutted by fire—an invisible prison I carry wherever I go. A glass case encloses me, a vacuum where no one hears me gag.

Before I mangled you, I thought I'd vanquished the past. I no longer nurse that delusion. After centuries, an ancient tree ceases to grow: my barren twig serves no purpose. Soon enough, in a gust of wind, I'll snap and plummet to earth. Until then, I'll stretch a little further towards the light—or towards the dark.

My love for you, and yours for me, was a clearing without a center: it rippled through the woods, leaf by leaf. But here my days are dreary, a lineage of overlapping shadows. I'm falling through a rift in time, a bottomless crevasse. Night wheels against the cavern like a juggernaut, sealing me off from the world.

For Wilfrido, it's a vapid routine: every day, he slinks up the trail to my lair. Nearby he deposits some tasteless food and a gallon of water, for drinking and cat-baths. No matter what the weather, I'm still perched on this stone. It's shaped like a natural bench, and I've become part of it.

If he breaks a stick underfoot, I never stir. My eyes are focused on the Humpback Islands—swimming in a trinity, but motionless. Though now they seem eternal, the waves will grind them imperceptibly to sand. After humans become extinct, they may even seed a desert.

How many weeks have gone by? Ten, eleven, twelve? Wilfrido is at the end of his rope: he makes louder and louder noises when he climbs up the path. He must wonder if I'm dead, since I never budge. I know I've lost weight, and my hair is turning grey. Do I still have a face at all?

One morning he sends for Chévere, his older cousin. When he inches closer, he looks horrified. Am I really that gaunt? I ask him where Wilfrido is. Chévere whistles, and the younger boy steps from behind a tree.

They're amazed I'm talking again, and so am I. It's as if I'm a child, entranced by my surroundings. I prate about some cinnamon-throated swallows, nesting where they never did before. I gabble about a plant with velvety leaves, silver-green on top and maroon below. They tell me its Taíno name, self-evident to them. I notice that both of them have slightly pointed ears, like fauns. Soon we're chatting as freely as ever.

Before they go, I promise to leave the cave. Mañana? Tomorrow? All right. I've given in to them without a second thought. It's true I should resurface. Like a whale, I must come up again for air—and endure the light of living, for better or worse.

I miss the sound of the surf: I've stared too long at the far-off islands, the voiceless sea. But I won't deny the value of that deafness. I'll bring it with me into the future, whatever that future holds. From my solitary cliff, the ocean seems immobile, a vast slab of bluegreen stone. No currents, no breakers, no foam. Here in the silence, I no longer need a shore.

It's hard for me to tear myself away. Wilfrido badgers me from the crack of dawn. When I scrabble down from the cave, it's almost noon. After months without any exercise, hiking to the coast is a tedious grind. I barely make it to the nearest beach by twilight.

Thank God the full moon is rising in the east. I tramp along beneath its otherworldly radiance, keeping the sea always to my right. From the marshes, I hear familiar bird calls: the whistles of tree ducks; the screeches of hobgoblin owls; the melancholy plaints of potoos; the quequerequés of nighthawks.

I ford Río Frío at its shallowest point, where the chilly stream runs counter to the waves. This is the trickiest part of the trek, as I know from previous injuries to shins and knees. The rocks are slimy, as always. In the dimness, I plot my footing by trial and error; my Swiss river-sandals are a godsend in the maze.

Unscathed, I take them off and pad down the two-mile shore to Dos Ríos. On this swath of beach, any pitfall will be minor, no more than a protruding pebble or shell. Quickening my pace, I fall into step with the moon's reflections; platinum stripes glide beside me on the sodden, immaculate sand.

Laced with phosphorescence, rivulets uncurl from the quiet sea; its roar has abated now to a faint, continuous sigh. The offing is a crisp black band on the sky's farthest rim. There's no wind now—not even a breeze. The palms to my left stand transfixed, like mourners around a grave; waiting for words of solace, they mutely bow their heads.

Since there aren't any rocks in the rivers of Dos Ríos, wading them poses no challenge. Before long, I've arrived at the octagonal cabin on Playa Grandota. After lugging my rucksack up the stairs to the second floor, I secure the folding doors as snugly as I can. All the same, I can't shut out the moonlight… On nights like this, it pierces the enormous roof: seeping through the tiles, it pulses to the slow syncopation of the clouds.

The ceiling looms above me like a monster moon itself, a gargantuan lunar disk. I try to sleep, but I've grown too accustomed to the blackness of the cave. Ragged halos of light crawl across my face, teasing me awake. Crickets, katydids, and frogs chirr or thrum in the marshes close by. It's no use: around three in the morning, I go for a stroll along the beach.

On half the horizon, a squall blurs the sky, while the other half spotlessly glows. The moon blazes at its zenith, a pockmarked face partially veiled by filmy clouds. Spellbound, I move forward, as if I were crossing a threshold. It's then that I see the double moonbow, for the first time in my life—the only time, no doubt.

Over the whole dome of night, a rainbow in grisaille begins to form, in spectral shades of white and bone, silver and grey, charcoal and black. Shimmering, the arch redoubles farther out; and now two moonbows span the limitless, violet blue... Like a lesson on perspective from an antique book, they plunge into infinity: portals to a void that breathes with ghostly life.

I invented 'moonbow' on the spur of the moment, since I'd never heard of one before. But I should've known there's nothing new under the sun—or the moon. The next morning in Palma Verde, a crusty fisherman tells me he's seen a moonbow from his boat several times. An 'arcoiris de la luna,' he calls it: a 'rainbow of the moon.'

By a fluke of good fortune, that afternoon I catch a ride to Puerto Indio with one of Torsten's guests. He's a Finnish stockbroker, eager to burble on about the island; after my months of isolation, I'm too taciturn for his taste...

Amado, are you here? As I skirt the shores of Barlovento Bay, I summon up our whale-watching trip. The beach scene on the key between you and Catulo floods my memory; much as I try to curb myself, every detail awakens my libido. A current surges through underwater canyons; lava-flows reopen the seabed's scars, still unhealed.

On that day, I watched myself make love with you by proxy: I experienced the out-of-body trance often evoked by survivors. Was it voyeurism, onanism, or something in between? Isn't sex a flickering burst of images—remembered or imagined—as much as an act in the here and now? Perversely, almost like a necrophile, I sense my desire kindling. Or maybe just the opposite: a posthumous lust sweeps over me, as if I were already dead.

The impression is still vivid when I reach Plaza Drake. It's a hand-grenade about to go off; I need to throw it far away. Like it or not, I have to learn the truth of Schiller's threnody. 'Auch das Schöne muss sterben': even the beautiful must die.

Riffling through my bookshelves, I dredge up all I can on moonbows. They appear in certain waterfalls—though even there, they're scarce. There's a painting by Caspar David Friedrich, a poem by Marianne Moore. But a double moonbow? Not a trace. Could I have seen the only one on earth?

Three months earlier, I'd done little more than drop off my luggage; now bills and repairs demand my attention. First-off, I ring my parents. Indignantly, my mother says she's grateful to Horacio: *he* keeps her apprised of my whereabouts. 'Bedda Matri, sei impossibile!' she exclaims. 'For heaven's sake, you're impossible!' But after a while, she makes light of my 'camping trip'—as Horacio had blandly dubbed it. My father, distant as always, never picks up the phone.

The next year goes by in a fog. If I took refuge in El Silencio to do penance, I needn't have bothered. Life always exacts the price we're meant to pay—whether we're willing to cough it up, or not.

Maybe it all started with the nervous strain, or the

sketchy diet during my time on the cliff. Since then, I've been beset by chronic indigestion, anemia, and a host of other ills. Though the doctors run test after test, they can detect no cause for my symptoms. With milquetoast solicitude, Horacio is exultant: at last he has a companion in his misery, a fellow valetudinarian.

At the amusement park of Puerto Indio, nothing has changed. The merry-go-round of politics whirls as giddily as ever—from the zebra to the tiger, from the lion to the giraffe. Ángel María has gained full ascendancy; he leads Espinosa through his dotage with a kid-gloved, iron hand. Our multifaceted friend is the regime's éminence grise—and some would crown him the heir apparent. Yet even he can't halt the escudo's debasement; in less than a decade, it's lost nine tenths of its worth. In fact, foreign watchdogs accuse him of 'adjusting' it for selfish ends. Rumor has it that he's tripled his in-laws' fortune, as well as his own. As for Leandra, she consoles herself with her growing family: she can already boast two healthy infants, and I've heard she's hoping for more.

In the past months, I've followed the events mainly from abroad, since I never stay in Canuba for long. When I do, I rent a car and drive to Palma Verde. After a night at Torsten's inn, I lick my wounds in the cabin on Playa Grandota. Though I take long walks on the beach, I haven't had the heart to return to El Silencio.

I never look up Lamia or Catulo—much less Frederica.

Every now and then I phone them on a scratchy connection, from remote locales like Borneo or Ladakh, safely out of reach. Lamia vaunts her sexual feats, Catulo satirizes his beach resort, and Frederica fills me in on the social set. Horacio's chamber orchestra has made him the toast of the town. I allow only him to follow my movements; but thanks to my entreaties, he keeps them under wraps. I send him a monthly sum for Luz Divina, since she doesn't believe in banks. She stashes her money in a sock.

My assignments keep me spinning, almost as much as Ángel María: not on a government carrousel, but on the roulette-wheel of travel. That game of chance may seem exciting to some; to me it's only a ploy to evade my sadness. Passively, I feed on my profession like a remora attached to a whale.

Writing about small-scale farmers in faraway places—often called 'peasants' in their languages—I develop a subgenre all my own. I chronicle their lives in Magude, Anatolia, Sichuan, Preah Vihear, or Boquerón, wherever I find a rural outback. My articles home in on individuals—on the minutiae of their daily habits, as they till their fields and harvest their crops. I sleep in huts that are theirs, attend village meetings that are theirs, transcribe words that are theirs. One by one, they've replaced me: as a separate being, I no longer exist.

My vocation has morphed into substance abuse; I'm as dependent as any other addict. To buy the numbness I crave, I've mortgaged my soul.

It's just like Chiara to fall out of the sky, after four months who knows where. She could've called me beforehand. She shows me no respect—as always, como siempre!

Like every morning, I've been up since six. As soon as Chiara traipses in, about a quarter to nine, I put the water on to boil. She always wants tea, like in Chinatown, when any normal person drinks coffee. I set the table on the patio for her breakfast. All I've got is some crackers she left in a tin; but she never eats much, anyway.

She tries to butter me up, wanting to know how I've been—as if she cared. She grabs me around the waist, and I have to hug her back.

Why did you stay away so long? I stare her down.

She looks guilty, like she might apologize. But her face goes sour when she hears a meow. She wasn't expecting that! There she is, Cirenea, perched on the ledge over the door. She's waving her tail at me. She's cute as a peluche, an animal toy, with her long fur and orange eyes.

Luz Divina, Chiara says, there's a cat in here.

I just shrug. — Sure there's a cat. She's a female. A gata, not a gato.

Chiara's smart about some things, but not what people care about. Like telling a gata from a gato.

She sits down at the table. — You always shoo off stray cats.

You're the one who tells me not to hit them with my broom.

That doesn't mean I want them hanging around. Remember, my mother is allergic to cats, so I didn't grow up with them. She used to gasp for air whenever one got close. Maybe that's why I don't like them.

I ignore her. She'll shut up after a while! It's time for my kitty's breakfast. — Cirenea, Cirenea! Kitty kitty kitty!

Stop cooing to her, please. Cirenea? Is that her name?

It's what I call her.

Aha! You gave her a 'resguardo' name, to protect her. Do you mean you've adopted this cat?

Always making trouble! — No, I tell her, Cirenea adopted me. One morning she peeked over the roof, licked her paws, and curled up where she is right now.

She plops down to the ground, and circles my ankles.

Chiara doesn't take to her—not yet. — Oh, she just wants food.

It's not because of food. She knows I'll give her plenty. Cirenea needs me, and I need her. That's what her name means, helper.

Chiara is fit to be tied. — Don't tell me you've been feeding her! Now it'll be hard as hell to get rid of that cat.

We don't want to get rid of her.

Yes 'we' do! And please don't include me in any 'we' this or 'we' that. I won't have any cats here—that's final.

I've been planning for this. I know just what to say: I

kept her because of you, Doña Chiara. How about those mice? Since Cirenea came, I haven't seen a single one.

That should do the trick! Chiara hates it when mice gnaw her books. To kill them, I scatter bits of cheese on the floor, caked with Tres Pasitos, a killer poison. They only make 'three little steps' after eating it. When their corpses turn up, I sweep them away, pim-pam-pum. Or sometimes I set out sheets covered with glue, and the mice get stuck. The next morning I brain them with a stick and scrape the cadavers off, so I can use the traps again.

She hesitates: That Tres Pasitos stuff is awful. But the way they squeak all night on those glue-traps is even worse... You're sure she's a good mouser?

The best. And Cirenea isn't noisy, like other cats. She hardly makes a peep. Look what a pretty color she is, just like a papaya.

I'm winning now! Chiara loves colors, and she's noticed Cirenea's coat. I've never seen anything like it: part brown, part black, with orange stripes. Her eyes are like that too—dark brown with orange sparkles.

Chiara hushes up. She's sipping her tea and munching her crackers, reading a newspaper she brought along. Happy as a baby sucking on a pacifier, a bobo. I guess she's fine with Cirenea now. She yaps a lot, but I can handle her.

This spring I accepted a glut of contracts from the high-end glossies. They'd had enough of my pieces about subsistence farmers in the boondocks. They told me to return to the basics: Victoria Falls, Macchu Pichu, Angkor Wat—destinations on the bucket list. After South Africa and Indonesia, I did a lengthy stint in Egypt, and now I'm completely wiped out.

As soon as I reach the house on Plaza Drake, I leave my bags in the tall front-room and step into the courtyard. Enclosed by its massive Colonial walls, my hidden garden slumbers as sedately as ever. Bronze bells wrangle in nearby campaniles, and mockingbirds stitch their tunes to the rising light.

I've phoned Luz Divina now and then, but I didn't tell her I was arriving today. Might as well keep her on her toes... She pretends to be offended, but soon she goes back to her tasks. Pottering around the patio, she waters the plants she's already watered, and sweeps the flagstones she's already swept. She wants to be near me, I realize—not without a twinge of gratitude.

Here's the anomaly. Inexplicably, that dream of hers drew us closer than ever. She stood there like a sovereign as she told it, holding her broom for a scepter. But her vision of walking on water, of sublime self-reliance, also opened a chasm between us. She rings the changes of her daily routine, washing the dishes and ironing the clothes. Then at times, all of a sudden, I glimpse her far away—a power unto herself.

I sit down at the wrought-iron table, pour myself a cup of tea, and skim through the paper. To my left, a bougainvillea's twigs flutter and take wing: flambeau butterflies. Despite the storied grandeur of Hogsback, Borobudur, and the Valley of the Kings, I've missed my Caribbean nook. This breakfast on the patio is a ritual, unchanged for over a decade. Maybe I'm getting too set in my ways…

The cat confronts me with a novelty, and not a welcome one. Luz Divina believes I've given in to her, but all I feel is resignation. Stubbornness has always been her strong suit, and I'm too tired to put up a fight—at least for now.

I may be in for an uphill battle. She's treating the pussy like a loved one—even guarding her with a moniker, a 'resguardo'. In Canuba this isn't a nickname, much less a diminutive; it varies widely from the name received at birth. If you were christened Carlos, you might be dubbed Pedro or Juan. The fake name works as a decoy, to shield you from the evil eye. Enemies can't cast a spell on you, without invoking your true name.

As far as I can tell, the custom harks way back. It might be a legacy of African slaves, who toiled in the cane fields under European whips. It might be an offshoot of Taíno beliefs—all we can do is speculate. Her alias makes the cat like a daughter to Luz Divina, whose own secret name I'll never know.

I've slipped to second place in the pecking order, no doubt about that. Luz Divina hardly clears the breakfast things away, before she scurries off on Cirenea's behalf. The impertinent malkin examines me. Who is this interloper? she seems to ask. Nettled, I turn back to the news: Ángel María and Espinosa, what are they up to now?

After a while, a furry head rubs against my legs. Is she looking for a handout? Or is she being friendly, as Luz Divina claims? To test the tabby, I reach down and pat her nose. She bites my thumb: she doesn't break the skin, but it hurts.

Ow!

Meow! she echoes. No doubt she has an answer for everything, like Luz Divina herself.

An hour later my housekeeper comes back, clutching a plastic bag. To my distaste, she sloshes the contents into a bowl. She beams as her darling devours the bloody offal. — Poor little gatica, you must've been starving. The carnicero didn't have any innards for you today, so I walked all the way to the market.

I protest. — You walked that far, to get this ugly mess? You say it's too much trouble to go there for me.

Luz Divina doesn't rise to the bait. When hand-to-hand combat fails her, she resorts to a war of attrition. She centers all her attention on Cirenea, who's gobbling up the entrails. Then the glutton naps in a shady corner, while Luz Divina speeds through her chores.

Not even her pussycat can keep her from rushing away at the self-appointed hour: two in the afternoon—much earlier than most domestics. Now it'll be my turn to wear the apron. Before leaving, Luz Divina curtly informs me there's a dish in the fridge for Cirenea. — See you tomorrow, hasta mañana.

I scarcely look up from my desk. *Travel World* needs a feature on felucca trips down the Nile, and I'm scrambling to meet the deadline. But at seven or so, an imperious tail swishes against my feet. — All right, all right. — I head for the kitchen.

Hmmm, this Ginori soup bowl belonged to my grandmother; only an heirloom is worthy of Cirenea. The florid porcelain dish holds a scoop of Bumblebee Tuna in oil. Luz Divina rightly guessed it would repel me less than poultry guts: I can see the web she's trying to weave.

The feline snoozes again after her supper, and everything quiets down. About eleven, I climb into bed, planning to read for an hour. From my bedroom, two French doors open out on the patio. As a rule, the garden makes for a tranquil scene, dimly lit by low-wattage lamps; but tonight, all hell breaks loose. Yowling comets flash across the flagstones, in frenzied pursuit of Cirenea. To Luz Divina, she may be a pet; to tomcats, she's a babe.

There's a blossoming vine that sheds its fragrance only after dark. Canubans call it 'dama de día, puta de noche'—'lady by day, whore by night.' The expression fits Cirenea to a tee: from midnight to dawn, her couplings never cease. She and her johns zoom down the stairs and up to the roof, caterwauling as they go. I can only quell the fracas by closing the shutters and doors; but then the house swelters—and their shrieks still pierce the walls.

The next day, when I condemn the orgy to Luz Divina, she guffaws in my face. — You must be kidding! I stayed here for several months, all alone with Cirenea. I never noticed any noise!

Of course not, you sleep so soundly. Besides, you shut the house as tight as a drum. You even stuff rags under the doors.

She always refutes what I say, no matter how trivial. — That's not true, I'm a very light sleeper.

Now and then, Luz Divina takes a siesta in the spare room, even when I'm in town. She snores like a buzz saw. I've tried to wake her up, to no avail.

She presses on: And I keep the windows wide-open at night, so the house can cool off.

If I arrive impromptu on a red-eye flight, the house is bolted like a fortress, with all the windows sealed. She's scared the slightest crack will let 'evildoers' in.

I persevere: I'm only telling you what I heard and saw last night. If you contradict me, you're calling me a liar. That pussycat of yours is as loose as they come.

Avoiding outright denial, she opts for a subtler tack:

Well, I'm sure she has lots of suitors. But she wouldn't let them go too far. Cirenea is a señorita, a virgin!

How can you say that? She's play-acting: se da por señorita, that's all.

The turn of phrase applies to girls who live with their parents, seemingly as pure as the driven snow—and who screw on the sly in 'love-motels.' In her youth, Lamia was the archetype, though now she no longer pretends.

Luz Divina snorts: I can tell just by looking at her. She has innocent eyes.

She's no virgin. For heaven's sake, now you've got me doing it! We're talking about an animal, not a person! It's a cat's nature to roam around at night and mate with all comers. What if she gets pregnant—then what will you do? How about those kittens in the plaza last year? It was pitiful, the way they mewled until the dogs polished them off. That's what happens to a litter nobody wants.

She crinkles her brow. If those kitties were dumped in the street, por algo será, there was a reason. You saw how ornery they were. — She pauses cagily. — Suppose Cirenea had babies. Not now, she's still a virgin señorita! But suppose she did have children someday… they wouldn't be like that.

I'm thunderstruck. — Whatever they'd be like, they couldn't stay here. Cirenea is already one cat too many. If you want to keep her, you'll have to get her spayed.

I flip through the yellow pages. — Here's a vet, only five

blocks away. — I copy out the address on a scrap of paper; since Luz Divina can't read, I also make her a map. — I'm writing a big article, and the deadline is two weeks away. I don't have time to leave the house. Anyway, she's your pet—and your responsibility!

She turns her back on me. — Cirenea hasn't had any babies yet. She's too young to get 'preparada.'

In Canuban, the term means 'tying the tubes.' — Let me remind you one last time, we're talking about an animal. And either she goes to the vet, or you take her home with you.

She caracoles like a horse, with a scornful air. — No, it's much nicer for her here.

All that means is, you want me to feed her. You're paying for her gourmet food with my household funds. Here's your choice. Spayed, she stays here. Knocked up, you take her home!

She sulks the rest of the day. The next morning, she alleges she has no time for the vet—and so on, for two more weeks.

I begin to observe swelling pimples on Cirenea's belly, and she's also gaining weight. She's beginning to look a bit bulbous. Luz Divina laughs off my qualms.

She's always had those spots! She was much too skinny, poor little thing. I'm fattening her up with whipped cream.

What can I do but wince and bear it? With all these

distractions, I miss my deadline, and have to beg for extra time. I've done too much field-research, darn it—six trips on six different boats. Frantically, I grub through piles of disorderly notes. My scribbles have run together, smudged by the waters of the Nile.

Let's see, was the temple of Kom Ombo on the left bank or the right? Who built Abydos, Seti I or Ramses the Great? Did that fast-talking Ahmed pilot the *Mizrah* or the *Fatima*?

All night, stately feluccas swan through my dreams, their sails bleached white by the desert sun. Bored with their own divinity, supercilious cats recline on the decks, cooled by eunuchs with peacock fans. Silky gastronomes, they disdain the people's offerings: spiced rats on wooden trays; ewe's milk in earthenware cups; wicker baskets full of smelt, round and shiny as coins.

Later, once the boat docks, a psychopomp takes my hand in her velvet paw. She guides me down basalt ramps and granite stairs, deep into a pyramid. Now we enter the hall where a leonine judge will roar my secret name, and weigh the ultimate value of my ka…

Cirenea absconds from view: she never tiptoes down from the roof anymore, even for meals. Luz Divina cabals with her up there every morning, then leaves her a dish of pellets for supper. Chained to my computer, all I register is distant muttering. They seem to be conspiring—but so discreetly, I can't make out a word… At the witching hour, no yelps disturb my rest. Do the frolics still go on? Worn-out as I am, I could sleep through anything...

But on one occasion, I do wake up, just before dawn. In my nightmare, I'm still in my Sicilian middle school, the scuola di primo grado. Weirdly, the building has expanded: with its gigantic, flaring pillars, it's more like a temple in Karnak. I haven't attended my courses all year, and now I've flunked my exams. An ibis-headed scribe shows my record to the principal, who twitches her tail disapprovingly...

When I come to, I hear a high-pitched sound, like the faint keening of mice stuck in glue. But ever since the pussycat appeared, there've been no rodents—and no songbirds either, to my chagrin. Is Cirenea inside the house somewhere? Soon enough, I trace the whines to my small spare-room.

When I peer under the bed, Cirenea isn't startled by the flashlight. Instead of reflecting its beam, her eyes seem to radiate from within. She's surrounded by six balls of fluff, ranging in color from jet to marmalade. They mewl at the tops of their lungs, till each of them locates a teat; as she suckles the kittens, she flexes her paws contentedly.

Despite myself, I'm overawed by this tondo of feline motherhood. For the first time in my life, I wonder if I've missed out on something vital. I ask myself a series of idle questions. What if I'd had a child with Amado? Girl or boy? How old would the toddler be today? But I quickly suppress such fatuous thoughts...

Cirenea's tranquility reminds me of another scene, from several weeks ago. Reading in bed, I glanced up at the garden. On that still, breezeless night, the courtyard shimmered like a stage: a lucent penumbra, etched by dark-green leaves. Cirenea entered from the left, crossing the flagstones with her tail held high, slowly and majestically. A yellow tomcat approached her from the right, as hieratic as a figure in a frieze. Was he a brother, a friend, a lover—or all three? Advancing step by step, they finally converged. No bites, swipes, or hisses marred their ceremonial. Solemnly, their muzzles met, in what can only be described as a kiss of peace...

After watching Cirenea and her kittens for a while, I return to bed and try to sleep. I drop off for only a minute or two, just long enough for another disturbing dream.

I've often pictured Amado as a tiger, prowling through the forest in search of boars, muntjacs—and above all, she-cats. But now I'm a tigress myself, sprawled out under succulent plants. Not long ago, I've given birth to a naughty male cub. He clambers along my belly with mischievous delight. Growling and nuzzling, he tortures my teats. I luxuriate, tantalized by pain: Amadito is making love to me. Meanwhile his adult incarnation stands beside us—playing a pan flute, emerald and soft. Its pipes wiggle prehensilely, like the fingers of a hand...

I sit up in a panic. Eerily, Amado has paid me a visit.

But where does he want to lead me? To what kind of world? A shiver races up my spine, as I joggle the image off.

In the harsh light of day, stern measures are called for. How can I cope with seven cats? This is Luz Divina's headache, not mine.

She arrives bright and early. — Marvelous! Que maravilla! Cirenea's first babies! Aren't you glad?

I'm overjoyed *you* like them—since they're going home with you.

But they're better off here!

I feel like I could scream: First, your cat and her boyfriends gave me no rest. Now her kittens will be climbing all over the place. You only want her around in the morning, when she's on good behavior.

She's always on good—

I cut her off: You knew damn well she was pregnant all along. Cirenea the virgin! I warned you what would happen. Now make up your mind! Are these cats going home with you, or somewhere else?

Where else could they go?

Oh, I'll come up with a place for them!

All morning, Luz Divina drudges with a tragic, hangdog look. At one o'clock she tries to sneak away, even earlier than usual. When she's halfway through the door, I stop her in her tracks. — Wait a minute! What have you decided?

Nothing. Nada! It's all up to you. — She glares at me

long and hard, then scoots down the street.

A few minutes later, Padre Flores drops by, cadging donations for his charities. Querida Chiara! Dear friend! he greets me warmly. I haven't seen you for several months.

I've been traveling, from here to Timbuktu. After all this time, I suppose you're expecting a pretty penny.

He chuckles, unapologetically. — It's not for me, as you know. Just do what you can. — His cassock drips with perspiration. He must've been galumpfing in the sun for hours: no small task for such a delicate man. As always, he carries himself with dignified benevolence.

I invite him to rest his bones on one of my rocking chairs—but I also have an ulterior motive. When I ask for his advice, he seems quite familiar with Cirenea. Someone else has confessed to him already, I infer. Right on cue, the inquisitive feline pokes her head into the room.

I just don't understand, I tell the priest. If Luz Divina is so fond of that cat, why won't she take her home?

He tilts forward, his leathery face beaded with sweat. — I minister to lots of people like her, in the slum where she lives. Most of them are gardeners, cooks, or maids. But I've never met anyone so devoted to her employer.

Devoted? That's hardly the word I'd use.

He smiles ironically, stroking his beard. — I didn't say her devotion was well-placed. Her brothers have left the island to look for employment. On top of that, in her divorce she lost her husband and her child. So you're her family now—for better or worse. — His tone leaves no doubt that he leans toward 'worse.' — She doesn't want to have the cat at all, unless you're the official 'aunt.'

Two women making a home together... a vintage Canuban alliance. Often, they bring up children as well: either from a former marriage, or 'on loan' from their relatives. So that's how Luz Divina regards our workaday link; to me the notion seems absurd, as silly as my dream about a baby. There are far too many humans already in this crowded, polluted world. As for kittens, the sky is raining cats and and dogs, as the saying goes.

Padre Flores can tell I'm no longer listening. He clears his throat, and speaks more loudly: Luz Divina's road has been a rocky one. But then Cirenea came along, to help her on her way.

Hmmm... She did say the name means 'helper.'

That's right; all she did was add a feminine ending. He appears in the Fifth Station of the Via Crucis, as you'll recall. You can consult St. Matthew if you like, or St. Luke. But now I have to run along.

As soon as he leaves, I reach for my King James Bible; at Princeton, it was a primary source for my thesis on Ben Jonson. Revised By His Majesty's Special Command. The other editions on my shelves don't have a concordance, but this one does. I jump to 'the Cyrenean' in St. Matthew.

And after that they had mocked him, they took the robe

off from him, and put his own raiment on him, and led him away to crucify him. And as they came out, they found a man of Cyrene, Simon by name: him they compelled to bear his cross.

I hadn't realized I was standing at Pilate's gate. Luz Divina must have seen St. Simon's statue at the cathedral: he's one of the figures in the Taíno Way of the Cross. Priests often use the sculptures as teaching aids for communicants like her. I'd forgotten he was from Cyrene. Well, maybe I can mobilize a Cyrenean of my own...

Sigfrido Pérez, heading for Plaza Drake, July 1991

I'm glad Señora Chiara called me today. The money sure comes in handy. They don't pay a policeman much. I've asked her for odd jobs a few times, chiripeos. Last time I left her my number at the station. That was smart, cause I don't work her beat anymore. How else would she get a holda me, especially now Amado's dead? He was more than a cuñado to me. More than a brother even. We spent all our time together, and he even taught me English, inglés. That helped me get ahead, move up a rank. And he saved my life! Most guys woulda worried about their own skin insteada somebody else.

Find a home for cats? I tell her. Sure, ombe. That's as easy as pie. I'll run right over in the squad car.

Ten minutes later, I'm knockin on the door. When she opens it, she laughs. Caramba, Sigfrido. You've certainly slimmed down!

Yeah, Señora Chiara. I've been workin real hard. Maybe I lost a few pounds. — I feel kinda embarrassed, since my uniform's too big and I look like a bum. — Sorry I didn't shave today.

Who cares? You're practical and fast. That's what I'm after.

Right. I gotta report back to my sergeant on the double, so I got no time to waste. Where's the cats? — She shows me the whole bunch under a bed. I jerk my thumb. — You wanna get rid of the mama cat too, or just the kittens?

Get rid of them, no! They need a new home.

Right, right. That's what I mean. — She's tryin to trip me up! — I know a old lady, a viejita, who's loony about cats. She's on my new beat.

You think she might have a mother cat who'd adopt these kittens?

No problem! She's got heaps of mama cats.

But wouldn't Cirenea miss her kittens?

I gotta hoot at that. — Nooo-ooo. She-cats have litters all the time! After a minute or two, she won't remember this batch.

How can you be so sure?

Take it from me. My grandma kept a lotta cats. Gatos? Cats? I know em inside out. — Señora Chiara's futzin too much, and I gotta scram; the sergeant might discharge me. — You got a cardboard box?

She lets me scrounge around through her closets. Hey, here's a box for shoes, that'll do. I pour some milk in a tin pan and hold it up to the mama cat's nose. Then I set it on the patio. She ditches her kittens and goes for la leche, the milk. Just like that!

Now Doña Chiara's convinced. — I guess you're right. Cats only care about their meals.

While the mama's busy feedin, I stick the sleepy kitties in the box. They don't even squeal. I nod my head at the door. — I'm outta here. That'll be four hundred escudos.

Isn't that a bit steep?

Most of the dough goes to the old lady, la viejita. — I grin at her friendly, amistoso. — It's kinda like sendin your kids to school. You gotta pay the tuition. Come on, señora. I gotta get goin!

Rich people's always wonderin, I know. Is this guy cheatin me or not? I coulda charged her more. But Amado and her had a thing between them, I bet. I don't think my sister Reina knew. Anyway, her husband and Chiara were close. He'll always be my main man, mi pana, after what he did for me. My number one!

I hand the gangly cop his escudos, and off he goes. He may be bumptious, but he knows how to cut to the chase.

Slightly dazed, I shuffle to the patio. Cirenea is lapping up the last of the milk. She licks some droplets from her whiskers and pads back to the bed. I trail along behind her. Maybe I should distract her a bit longer. Would she like some ribbon, or a piece of twine? But she doesn't react as Sigfrido predicted—not at all. When she sees her kittens are missing, she does a double take. Then another. Where are they?

It's going to be a long, anguished evening—I can tell. Cirenea scuds round and round the spot where she gave birth. I try everything. Canned salmon, cream, spools of thread: nothing sidetracks her anymore. In her capers on the roof, the males did most of the screeching; by day she mainly dozed, too tired to raise her head. But now her meows escalate into wails.

I give up on writing, and the hours drag by. Even after midnight, she won't let me sleep. When I crumple onto the bed in sheer exhaustion, she hops up beside me. Every time I drift off, she thumps my chest with her paws. Why don't I hunt for the kittens? She doesn't seem to blame me for what's happened. I'm upset they disappeared; that much she can sense. Sometimes she snuggles against my collarbone and lets me hold her: a fleeting consolation. After a while, she howls all over again, tapping on my ribs.

By the time Luz Divina reports for duty the next morning, the cat and I are both in a shambles. My housekeeper is much less glum than I expected. Seeing her darling malkin still here makes up for the kittens' absence.

When I recap the whole saga, she scoffs at me. Old lady, huh? And you believed him? Ese policía! — She spits out the word like a curse. — He probably backed over those kittycats with his car. What an easy way to gyp you out of your dough!

To Canubans, afflicted by corrupt policemen, 'cop' equals liar and thief. Maybe Luz Divina is right... I ring up the station, catching Sigfrido just in time: he's about to set out on his beat. Take it easy, he says. The kitties are doin great at the old lady's house. You wanna talk to her? Here's her number.

When I call, an elderly woman replies. Yes, she's glad to have the kittens. Oh yes, another cat has adopted them. One who had a 'short litter' several days ago... Si, si, si.

Luz Divina is skeptical, but strangely unconcerned. Slyly, she lets drop: Even if you don't bring those babies back home, Cirenea can have some more.

We're back to square one! — No, there won't be any kittens here, I tell her. Not now, not ever. Either Sigfrido can carry them to your house, along with Cirenea. Or she can join them where they are. I made a mistake—

You sure did, she chops me off in mid-sentence. You

can't take children away from their mother. — Her voice quavers. — It's the worst thing you can do.

Now it comes back to me. When her husband jilted her, he carted off their little girl to his new wife. I've never understood how Luz Divina could have let this happen. Was her maternal instinct too feeble, or did he force the issue? Maybe he threatened to beat her, for all I know... She almost never talks about her daughter. Does she feel bitter towards the girl for siding with her father? Or angry with herself for not defending her rights? Either way, the rift has left an indelible scar.

I make a last-ditch attempt to cajole her. — Well, Cirenea can have her kittens back. At the old lady's, why not? Or you can take them all to live with you. Then you can give the babies to your friends and neighbors, as soon as they're big enough. After that, Cirenea can come back here, to keep you company when I'm away. — I don't tell her so, but I intend to have the cat spayed for sure, if she ever returns.

Now Cirenea orbits us both, mewing hoarsely. She's on her last legs. Luz Divina doesn't say a thing. She looks like she's just been slapped. Her pop-eyed expression has frozen on her face. Her upraised hand doesn't move. She resembles a statue I've seen in my dreams, guarding the shrine of the cat-goddess Bast. The Egyptians bred orange cats for sacrifice, fiery-golden like the sun god, Ra...

I gaze at my computer screen, watching blue squiggles

on a backlit lake. All of a sudden, Luz Divina bounces back, restarting her usual routine. Cirenea's puling doesn't let up. I can't stand it anymore: unless things come to a head, I'll never finish my article.

I'm calling Sigfrido, I announce. — I was sure Luz Divina would react. But instead, all she does is dust and sweep, deaf to the world.

The policeman swings by in a jiffy. This time, he pockets his fee in advance. Then he bustles about, organizing 'Operation She-Cat,' as he dubs it. He selects another box and chucks some sardines inside; before long, Cirenea climbs into the trap. After all these hours of fretting, she must be famished.

I'm determined. — This is it, Luz Divina. Either you say adiós, or you go with your pet to collect the kittens. I'll be happy to give you a few days off, to get them settled in. Plus a weekly allowance for their food.

I'm stunned when she drops her broom, marches up to the box, and pats Cirenea on the head. — Good-bye, gatica. Don't be afraid. That's how it is. El mundo es así. — The cat stares back at her and floats a question mark: an inflected, querulous meow. Her protective name has failed.

There's a moment of silence. Then Luz Divina addresses her in a low-pitched voice, quiet and self-possessed. She seems to be intoning a shibboleth, but I can't quite catch it. Something like 'Nyanga' or 'Mionga,' in an accent that isn't Hispanic. It sounds like a word from an African tongue, spoken by slaves long ago… or a Taíno dialect, centuries-old and now extinct… or a language from the dawn of time, buried under desert sand and rocks.

The cat pricks her ears. She listens to every syllable. This is what Luz Divina calls her, when nobody else can hear: her secret name, that's hers and hers alone.

Sigfrido closes the flaps over her head. She doesn't resist. Stumping off with the box, he clangs the door behind him.

Luz Divina sighs from a million miles away, picking up her broom: That's the end of her!

We never mention the cat again, by any name.

Luz Divina, Plaza Drake, January 1992

I can't help it if I let out a squeal, a chillo! Chiara should've treated Cirenea with respect, like she deserved. But what does Chiara know? She's a suitcase, not a woman. She couldn't even love a cat.

When you're mean to one animal, the others will come after you. I'm disturbing her breakfast, but it's not my fault. She's reading the news and slurping tea, lazy as ever. She must've been born in the Barrio Chino!

She barely looks up from the paper. — What's wrong? Another centipede?

She might've been right most days. Those enormous critters scare me to death: they're slinky and flat, and they can grow ten inches long. Sometimes they wriggle up from the drains. Chiara's not afraid of them, maybe because they haven't bitten her yet. She snaps their backs with a shoe, pim-pam-pum.

No, I tell her. It's not a centipede, it's a crab, a cangrejo!

That's a new one. It must be pretty small, if it squeezed through the grate.

I wouldn't call it small. Come and look.

She gets up and goes round the corner to the sink, where I'm washing the clothes. That crab is huge! she says. Blue with red edges. Looks like the ones they serve in restaurants.

The crab rears up and waves its front legs, ready to fight. Chiara almost jumps out of her skin. — What a laugh! Now it's your turn to be the fraidy-cat!

I've told you before, Luz Divina. Snakes and insects don't bother me, but I'm terrified of spiders. The way their legs spread out and move in a row gives me the willies. Crabs are even worse. They're like tarantulas with shells! Who cares if they go forwards or sideways?

So you're leaving the problem to me?

Why don't you scoop up the crab in your bucket and throw it over the wall?

All right. Maybe the neighbors will cook it. I don't like creepy-crawlies, but something you can eat is different. Crabs don't taste good to me, or else I'd take this one home!

Too bad we'll be doing those filthy Bonos a favor. They're our neighbors, next door. Their patio is more like an orchard, right in the center of town. They've got avocados, tamarindos, mangoes. Grapefruits, zapotes, oranges, nísperos, limones. Do they ever share them with me? Never, jamás!

How can they see with all those branches blocking the sun? I guess they keep the rain off, too. Their house is a ruin, the old-timey kind. Chiara calls houses like that 'Colonial.' She says the Matrimonio Nacional protects them—keeps em from getting knocked down. It's an office up the street from here, a useless oficina! All they do is sit around, just like her.

Thank God we've got Espinosa. When rich people leave for Miami, he takes away their houses and rents them to the poor. He's a fox, a zorro. He knows we'll keep voting for him, especially at twenty escudos a vote. His campaign leaders hand out the money from trucks. But the rich people complain, the ones that have stayed. For them, the rent he lets them charge isn't worth the effort to collect it. That's what they say! Hah, they sure make *me* pay every month.

I've heard the couple who own that house could use the dough. They're over eighty, and they live in a leaky shack in San Sebastián. Their children in Miami wouldn't believe how much a heap of busted bricks is worth. If you can get rid of the tenants, los inquilinos!

But those Bonos won't scram any time soon. They've got a bunch of brujería altars, in between the trees and rocks. Brujos make a lotta money by casting evil spells. They can kill you by looking at you cross-eyed. I bet that's why the landlords never come around. And why Espinosa doesn't bug em, even if they can't vote for him—and even if he hates all the prietos. Yeah, and there's something else, much worse! I've heard how a long time ago some nuns got pregnant and left their babies there to die, so the place is cursed by God Almighty. Dios Todopoderoso!

Right around noon, I find another crab in the back bathroom. It's blue too, and even larger than the first one. I push it into my bucket with the broomstick and toss it over the wall. That's that! I go home, hungry for rice, beans, and chicken stew. When I've had my fill, I sleep for twelve hours straight.

The next morning, Chiara tells me a funny story. After I left, she finds three more cangrejos on the patio, crabs with shells eight inches wide—not counting their legs. To keep em out of her bedroom, she closes all the doors. She hears em bumping against the flowerpots, but at least she feels safe inside.

She's been up to her neck in that garbage she writes. Past midnight, she cracks open a door and peeks out. Five or six crabs, fighting on the patio bricks. She can see them in the moonlight. Disgustada, she takes a shower and goes to bed. But now comes the craziest part!

Around four in the morning, she hears a noise right over her head. Click-click-click. Like spoons clacking together. Click-click-click. She turns on the light over her bed. There's the biggest crab of all, the size of a plate, a plato! It's hanging from the lamp by one of its claws, three or four inches from her face!

I slap my knees and laugh till I cry. When I catch my breath, I tell her she was lucky: Don't you know crabs like to eat people's eyes? You coulda ended up blind, ciega!

Bah, she says. That's what you Canubans call a Chinese story—an unbelievable yarn. But if he'd fallen onto my face, he might've cut my forehead or cheeks. And sure, with one of his jabs, he might've blinded me—by accident.

She doesn't know cangrejos like me! Anyway, she jumps out of bed and grabs that steel pipe I keep in the closet, in case any evildoers break into the house. I could've told her a broomstick would be enough. Crabs are weak. She lobs the cangrejo to the floor, and he skits around from room to room. She scars several chairs whacking at him. What stupidity! Pretty soon he's a pile of bits, with icky juice running out. Just more gunk for me to clean up this morning…

Now I look outside and the whole patio is full of crabs. I tell her I've only got two arms, I can't trap em all. So she calls up that Sigfrido again. Damn policeman! Over the next few days, he catches about three dozen cangrejos and takes em home. After boiling the crabs alive, he and his family gobble them up.

He keeps asking me why don't you like cangrejos and I tell him we had lots of jaibas in the river when I was little. A jaiba is a sweetwater crab. My mamá cooked em with coco milk all the time. We ate so many I got sick of em. For life!

Meanwhile I sniff around and find out what happened. It was all the Bonos' fault to begin with. I should've known. The dirty prietos! A crab-stew restaurant was paying them to keep the crabs. They built four pens under a tamarindo tree. But Bonos know less about cangrejos than evil spells. They didn't put cement under the cages. So all the crabs dug their way out. Three hundred of em escaped. Then it was easy to climb up the vines on the walls and go everywhere else.

They're still crawling around the Barrio Antiguo. It's a plague, una plaga. Today a kindergarten had to close down. When the cangrejos popped out of the closets, they seemed six times bigger to those little children than to us. I bet it'll be a long time before Chiara opens her patio doors at night. Me, I'm not afraid of crabs, or anything else. That's how I am! Así soy yo! Well, maybe I'm scared of criminals breaking in, and centipedes.

After my battles with cats and crabs, I decided to take a rest from travel assignments. Still in mourning over Amado's death, I had to force myself to resume my former life. First, I paid a call on Horacio at the shop; we listened quietly to madrigals by Byrd and Gesualdo. A week later, I weathered a lunch at El Mediterráneo with the irrepressible Lamia. Then Catulo joined me one night for drinks on my roof terrace, and kept me in stitches with his madcap repartee. I even attended one of Frederica's parties, a farewell shindig for the Italian ambassador. This morning, Ángel María asked me to write the English narration for a documentary about 'our' whales. Day by day, I've tried to 'return to normal'; but as I should've known, there's no such thing as normal in Canuba.

When I was small, my favorite Bible story was the Plagues of Egypt, from the book of Exodus. My grandmother's cousin, the Bishop of Tragusa, used the Vulgate to teach me Latin. I often begged him to read the passage aloud, when he stayed with us at the villa. Every time, he would cluck his tongue at my morbid streak: I love you, dear, but you're a little bit daft—'un pò mala abbirsata.'

Grimly, the Lord progresses from frogs, lice, flies, and locusts to the decimation of cattle. He ends up by slaying the Egyptians' firstborn—'from Pharaoh's son to the captive's in the dungeon.' After scourging me with cats and crabs, the island demiurge soon sought a human victim—though without wholly giving her the axe.

The northeast corner of Plaza Drake is paved with uneven, abraded stones; they resemble the molars of a mastodon. Supposedly, they're vestiges of a Renaissance brothel—the oldest in the hemisphere. A month ago, Luz Divina tripped on the rocks and fell, injuring her kneecap. I rushed her to the emergency room in a taxi. The X-rays showed she'd need surgery, or else she'd be crippled for life.

The operation was slated for the following week, on the next date available. In the meantime, her neighbor Griselda agreed to look after her. The patient would need to stay off her feet, to prevent the fracture from worsening. Luz Divina is so pig-headed, the doctor had to hammer his message home; Griselda swore she'd force her to keep still.

The procedure took place as scheduled, at the best private clinic in town. Luz Divina bragged about the luxury to her brothers. They're well off, thanks to the black market: they smuggle merchandise from Curaçao to Canuba, where Espinosa has restricted foreign imports. But needless to say, they didn't offer to help with the medical bills.

On the anaesthetic, Luz Divina soared through the roof. Before they wheeled her away in the gurney, she grabbed my hand and raved incoherently: Mi amor, te quiero, te quiero. My love, I love you, I love you.

I'd never seen her so demonstrative. To Luz Divina, was 'Chiara' merely a pseudonym? Was 'mi amor' my secret name, known to her alone? No wonder she'd resented Marino and Amado so much...

She also jabbered about the Bonaventurans next door, and how they'd cast a spell on her: 'el mal de ojo,' the evil eye. Why had they zapped her with a curse? Because Sigfrido had snitched their crabs. The nurses asked me what the gibberish was all about. But I told them: Never mind!

After rehab, though she has a slight limp, she feels no discomfort at all. Armed with her broom, she's ready to wage war on 'Bonos,' crabs, policemen, Chiaras, or any other enemies that come her way. She hasn't carped on sorcery, ever since she left the clinic. Thank God! Let's hope we've had enough 'brujería' for a while.

But in Canuba, you can't foresee what will happen next, and this evening I'm in for a jolt. It's been several years since Amado's death, and in all this time I haven't heard a peep from Reina. Now, like a deflated zeppelin, she droops on my doorstep. I hardly recognize her at first. Most bodybuilders' muscles turn to flab when they give up weights, but Reina's brawn has shrunk: her eyes are like the buttons on a shriveled snow man. In a monotone, she states the obvious: I don't go to the gym anymore.

She has no time, she explains, since she works two shifts at Fiesta Pollito. It's a Canuban fast-food chain, often misnamed 'Party Chick' in the ads that target tourists: a bad calque with a racy subtext. I've never sampled the cuisine, but at least the franchise holds its own against invaders like Popeye's and KFC.

When I migrated to Puerto Indio, street fare consisted of local dishes, sold by vendors from tricycle carts. I'm too dyspeptic to eat nanimachos, marikekis, camburicos, or cimarrones—much less drink iced hielo-hielos to wash them down. But I was proud my adopted country had fought off Burger King, Pizza Hut, Wendy's, and their ilk.

That was then. These days, when I go to the modern parts of town, I cringe at the 'golden arches' and other eyesores. So this is 'globalization'! More like Americanization. In major urban centers, from Milan to Palermo, they even deface my native Italy.

I'm not sure why Reina dropped out of sight for so long. I fully expected her to ask me for money after Amado died; I would've been more than willing to lend a hand. But unaccountably, she vaporized.

I passed by her house in San Sebastián a few months later, to check on her and the children. A garrulous neighbor told me they'd left for the countryside, 'never to return.' All Sigfrido would let on about his sister was the wary tag: 'tá en el campo, feliz'—'she's out in the country, just fine.' Clearly, she didn't want to be bothered. Amado's family had always spurned her as a campesina, I remembered; and in moments of misfortune, we often draw strength from our roots.

For whatever reason, here she is again, framed by my door jamb. Cordially, I steer her towards a rocking chair.

'Cuanto tiempo!' Puffing out the Spanish for 'long time no see,' she slouches on the seat.

Where have you been the past few years? I ask.

At my mother's. Now I'm back.

Time hasn't loosened her tongue. By dint of a dozen more questions, I piece things together. As I guessed, she'd gone back to the one-horse farm where she'd been raised. It's near Coyambaya—an hour or so southwest of Puerto Indio.

I'm not the only one she's left out of the loop: she hasn't kept up with Catulo, either—much less Amado's parents. I'm sure the Paniaguas would've supported the children, for their son's sake. But maybe she worried they'd woo them away from her with their wealth, a frequent occurrence in island families.

In recent months, the price of staple crops like coffee, tobacco, and chocolate has sharply declined. The crisis obliged Reina to try her luck in Puerto Indio, and she landed a job at Fiesta Pollito. Before long, she teamed up with another chicken-frier; they share a cabin in the slum of Quita Sueños, on the outskirts of the city. Soon she and her partner plan to move to a larger shack, so her children can join them. For now, true to Canuban custom, they subsist on the farm with their grandma, and Reina sends whatever she can spare.

I sum up. — So you need some help?

Yeah.

How much?

Dinero? Money… no.

Maybe a small loan?

I'm not a beggar.

I admire her self-sufficiency: the rural ethic of yore. — What can I do for you, then?

It's about Amado. He won't go away.

I'm mystified. — But he's dead and buried.

No, he's not.

What on earth do you mean?

He comes to see me.

Well, I'm sure he's harmless. — I try not to sound condescending.

She brings me up short. — He visits my mother. The children, too. We have to lay him to rest.

How?

I went to Coyambaya, to ask the picture. There's an old man there. He hears San Francisco talk. He said I've got to look for a woman. The one who killed Amado. She can keep him underground.

This is the longest speech I've ever heard her deliver— and the most baffling! If nothing else, I know which picture she consulted. Coyambaya is an antiquated town, famed for its 'miraculous' painting of St. Francis. Worshippers

366

make an annual pilgrimage to the Baroque chapel that houses it. The church was built by a seventeenth-century bishop, who'd been the first to 'hear San Francisco talk.'

Amado took me to Coyambaya once to watch the procession. If their prayers have been answered, supplicants fulfill their vows to the saint. Some crawl on their knees for miles; others march with gifts of cash pinned to their backs. Many parade in gaudy cross-dress, inviting public ridicule as a penance. But since this is Canuba, they earn more approval than blame, and jauntily salute the cheering crowds. Some even prance in cakewalks, or lock their arms in rip-roaring cancans.

When I reminisce, Reina lapses into terseness. — Nobody does that shit anymore.

What, no more pilgrimage? Not even the old man?

He's the only one left. A few nuns, maybe.

St. Francis speaks to him, and nobody else?

Yeah.

Who's the woman he mentioned? — For a moment, my lingering guilt assails me. Am I the murderer? I wonder.

Reina is adamant. — You know who: Esperanza.

You were jealous of her, weren't you? But Amado died in a wreck.

She did it to him, though. That's what San Francisco says.

Some kind of spell, you mean?

Sure, a hechizo. — Now she quizzes me in turn. —

Where is she?

Esperanza? How should I know? I've never met her.

But you met the bruja. Amado told me.

Diana?

Right. She can track her down.

What makes you so sure?

That's what the picture said. 'The witch knows everything. A woman killed your husband. Find her, and he can
rest.'

So you believe the witch is Diana, and the woman is
Esperanza?

Who else? Diana's the only bruja Amado knew. And
the woman is either me or Esperanza. So it has to be her.

Reina has made up her mind on that score. As far as
she's concerned, I'm not in the running. She leaves me her
number at Fiesta Pollito, and tells me to keep her posted. In the whole exchange, her face hasn't betrayed an iota
of emotion. Jumping up, she hurries away as if she'd only
popped by to borrow some sugar or salt.

Alone again, I repair to the roof and brood, as night
streams around me. You're on the move, all right, Amado;
your disquiet has affected me, too. Over the past few
months, your urgency has intensified. I haven't seen you as
an apparition, like your family. But I've been jotting down
memories of the moments we shared: the baseball game,
the whale-watching trip, the pagoda by the sea, the cavern

on the cliff.

My pen coils across the page, as if another hand were guiding my own. You haunt me in a thousand different guises, through a hundred people's eyes. That's how I envision you, in sentences I'm forced to write—even if I know they're only illusions. Aging and deranged, the black widow tautens her web into a cocoon. But the male she has beheaded doesn't change into a chrysalis. Blown from the branch, his carcass tumbles on sterile ground.

For me you were a sacred landscape: I explored every hill, every valley, every plain of skin. Now your topography blurs, like an atlas left to molder in the rain. The palpable becomes a faded icon; the timbre of your voice, a barely audible rasp. The message you carved on tablets of flesh has crumbled to dust. Could any simulacrum ever revive what your presence once was?

Walking on the road to Emmaus, I meet a man without a face. He breaks bread at a rustic table, and everyone is you—refracted in every mirror, on every wall. Only a wonderworker can perform such a trick: the alchemy of nature transmuted into deceit. Until the trumpet sounds, you wander through my solitude like the 'ríos sonorosos,' the 'sonorous rivers' in their forested ravines. Apostle and traitor, evangelist and thief, I echo and distort St. John of the Cross: 'these words are my Beloved for me.'

I had a dream about Chiara last night... I'm sure she'll barge in on me today. Ça va de soi! No doubt about it! We haven't crossed paths in many years, ever since Amado introduced us. She won't recall how to reach my temple: it's not in the classy part of town. But it won't be hard for her to find me. All she has to do is turn to Padre Flores. He's told me he calls on her often, drumming up donations. Since he ministers to Bonaventurans, too, we sometimes join forces.

Ah, voilà! There she is! I open the door and kiss her on both cheeks. I suppose she'll want to chitchat, before we get down to brass tacks.

I hope I'm not intruding, she chirps. I'm delighted to see you again, thanks to Padre Flores. He was doing desk work for once, instead of his pastoral rounds. I gather you and he run several charities together.

Mais oui! Oh yes! He calls me his 'Bonaventuran mambo.' But don't let the Archbishop know; he abhors us 'heretics,' no matter how well-meaning we may be. I wouldn't want to cause the good padre any trouble.

Yes, he's always so kind. Just now he sent his assistant along to guide me. What a labyrinth.

Teófilo isn't much of a bodyguard: too scrawny—and gun-shy, too. You probably feared for your life. Anyway, no more small talk—enough bavardage! You want to ask about Amado's visitations. Well, go ahead.

Chiara is taken aback. — How did you know?

Because he's been telling me to expect you. He's been hounding Reina and her family, so you'll come pester me.

Why doesn't he 'hound' me directly?

I raise my chin. All I can muster is a wintry smile. — Because you don't believe in such things. You're too rational. I had to go through a long apprenticeship, before I could listen to the dead. The loas, the mysteries… I had to travel far into our past to comprehend them. I learned the rites of the Gagá, and how to speak with spirits. But simple folk, who live in the countryside, encounter them often. And not just in their dreams: Amado comes to his children in broad daylight.

Does he visit you, too?

Oh yes. De plus en plus, more and more. He's becoming very insistent. He longs to sleep the eternal sleep, and grant you your freedom. — I arch my brows disdainfully. — Not that I care about you.

Chiara frowns; I've hurt her to the quick. — Please help Amado, at least! Reina says Esperanza killed him, so only she can lay him to rest. She claims that you know where she is.

Esperanza? She has nothing to do with any of this. What an idiotic idea! I've never laid eyes on the woman.

Chiara backpedals, peeved by my contempt. — I wonder what happened to the baby girl she had with Amado. What was her name? Lucita? Let's hope somebody's looking after her.

Don't worry. From what I've heard about her mother, she hustles plenty of money for the child. Anyway, Reina's birdbrain is only a jumble. That's why people like her need people like me.

Now Chiara's really piqued. — All right, then. If you're so wise, can *you* quiet him down?

Maybe. But I didn't 'kill' him either. All I did was remove the protection I'd given him.

Some kind of spell?

A blessing. To call it something you might understand.

Why would you take it away? I thought you were fond of him.

I was. But my love went unrequited. I had to put up with Reina, and that whore Esperanza. They were no competition, though: sex-machines, that's all. He was much more wedded to you. I've always despised you, Chiara, with every fiber of my being. That's why the loas punished you as well. They did it for me, whether I wanted them to or not. They let Amado die, and they pinned the guilt on you.

Chiara bridles. — So they put me under a curse? Nonsense. Let's look at the facts. Esperanza wanted Amado to take a yola to the States, despite the risk to him. He tried to sell my car to pay for the trip. I guess you were pleased, since that destroyed the trust between us. Wasn't that enough to break our bond? Why attack a second time, and do Amado in? Not that I believe you could. It's all hocus-pocus to me.

Can she really be so blind? — You're an ignorant fool. I can't justify what the loas do. They're beyond human control. I dismissed them too, when I was a schoolgirl in Bonaventure. The nuns at the Lycée Saint-François taught us to reason like Descartes; they were more French than the French. But Pascal had an inkling of mystical powers in his 'Nuit du Feu,' his 'Night of Fire'—even if that vision came to him only once. Only once! I enter into trances every day. I've lived a thousand lives! The loas have ridden me, over and over. I've galloped through their nights of fire, and their days of parching thirst. I've foamed at the mouth like a demented mare. The spirits of Petró mount me whenever they will. You can't imagine where they take me. Fields of shattered glass. Rivers of blood...

I'm veering far away; Chiara will write me off as mad. But she has no choice: she has to go along with me now.

Can't you intercede for Amado? she pleads. You have to release him, so he'll leave us all in peace. He must be in torment himself.

I'm struggling: should I give in? My head sinks to my chest. — Maybe Amado has been trapped here long enough. All right... all right. The time is ripe. I'm ready now to liberate his soul.

And what about me?

She meant to sound derisive, but I see straight through

her. — Everything is connected in the spirit world. When Amado departs, you'll experience a deep relief. — Chiara seems humbler now, more chastened than before.

Is there anything I can do?

Finally! Finalement! I have her where I want her. — Yes. Tell me more about his family. To carry out a certain ritual, I'll need a relative. Not his children: this is only for adults.

What about Reina?

No. Even if she weren't a cretin, she doesn't share his blood.

Chiara mulls it over. — As you know, Amado had no siblings, and his parents are strict Protestants. They'd never pitch in. Besides Reina, there's her brother, Sigfrido. Amado must've felt very close to him: he saved him in the last seconds before the crash. But he's not a blood relation, either.

I pounce on this. — That *is* a 'blood relation,' for us. I never heard about the details of the accident. From what you say, Amado gave his friend life itself. Now Sigfrido owes him that gift in return. I'm sure he wants to send Amado to Guinea, the Promised Land. Over the centuries, we've never forgotten that we come from Africa. Amado used to make fun of Reina. He called her 'tall, white, and dumb.' But if he can visit her now, it's because she still feels the pull of the 'other side': our ancestors, our gods. No matter what color they are, Canubans are Africans, too.

Chiara agrees. — Reina happened to turn out white, in the dice roll of the genes. Her brother is dark, and so is one of her children. The other one is wheat-colored, 'trigueño,' like their father. From what Amado told me, the little girl Lucita is black. But it's not about race. It's about tradition.

I spread my arms. — What is race, quand même? Does it really exist, after all? For that matter, what is tradition? It's not about either of them. It's about belief, even if some of us don't know it. — Chiara seems to sense what I'm driving at. Maybe I've misjudged her.

I grew up in Sicily. Northern Italians often discount us as 'gli africani.' They're right, Diana, but I take it as a badge of honor.

Yes! You're African, too! I tell her. That's why you're at home with us. That's why I've reached you *here*. — I jab at her heart. — That's why Amado pursues you. Don't delude yourself. He's not just a memory. Isn't he more alive to you now than ever before?

Sigfrido, Plaza Drake, a week later

In a big green jeep, Diana's people hauled me away from that temple joint and left me on the plaza. I can hardly walk, but thank God I made it to the door. I lean on it a while before I knock. I've gotta get a holda myself.

A couplea months ago Doña Chiara called me about the crabs. An easy way to make some dough, and stew a buncha cangrejos into the bargain. But this time! Maybe God needed to punish me, for Amado dying instead of me. Or maybe because I'm greedy. Ever since I got my promotion to sergeant, I've been playin the game. Stopping turistas on the road. When she called me at the station yesterday, I told her my fee's gone up.

Sure I wanna help if it's for Amado, I told her. But I have to charge a fee, como quiera, no matter what. Bigger than before. Make up for the time away from my job. Si, señora. I earn a lot off traffic fines.

That's the game. I nab people for a small violation. Or say I'm goin to. Sometimes it's real, sometimes it's only make believe. Especially with the tourists. I tell em this is my birthday today, and they get the hint. If they give me a present, I don't fill out a ticket. There's a lotta money in that, believe me!

When I asked her for six hundred escudos, she lost her cool. Started talkin about the principle of a thing.

Call it inflación, I said, inflation. I oughta charge you more, but I wanna do what I can for Amado. He was a helluva guy. I'd like to be there for his last adiós, if that's what this is. For the past few months my mother and sister's been bitchin and bitchin about his fantasma, his ghost. I don't believe in that crap, but I'm sicka hearin about it. To me it's kinda creepy, know what I mean?

She agreed to my terms, just like I knew she would. Then she gave Diana my number. Not the other way around! She has to keep cops from snoopin her up. I bet that charity bullshit at her temple is for illegals. Immigrants comin to Canuba by boat. Goddam Bonos!

She said Diana was askin her if I'm squeamy, quisquilloso. After seein me handle the jumbo crabs, Chiara told her I've got nerves made from iron. Yeah, but she didn't know what Diana was up to. I'm still shaking, and I must be breathin hard, cause Chiara hears me now and opens the door. I kinda fall inside the house, and then before I know it I'm babbin like a loco, a crazy man.

Doña Chiara, you shoulda warn me. Rayos! That woman is worse than a bruja, a witch: she's a fuckin demon. Excuse my bad talk, my palabrota. What she made me do to that chicken! A big rooster with a red head. While it still had a head. When I got there, she tied a red bandana round my forehead. Said I'm sposed to look like the rooster. I was afraid she'd chop my head off too. She put some strings of beads, all kindsa colors, around my neck. Then she kept singin, in words that don't make sense. After a while I forgot what time it was. Hell, I forgot what year it was! I dunno where the fuck I am, or what I'm doin anymore. She gives me some kinda super strong rum she calls clairin or clerán—somethin like that. When we finally get outta there, I'm covered with blood, and she is too. She cleans me off with a towel, and slaps me hard to make me leave.

I'm leanin on Chiara's shoulder. I feel my eyes flippin back in my head. I can't stand up. She pulls a chair over and makes me sit down. After a minute, I start jawin again.

I saw him. Amado. I still see him now. Layin on the table. There was nothin there before but a sheet and four black candles in the corners, cuatro velas negras. Then he's layin on toppa the sheet, just like that. Breathin still and regular, like he's fast asleep. He's not wearin any clothes. There's not a single scar from the wreck—I swear. No mark on him anywhere, even on his face.

His hands are folded on his chest, and his arms are thick and strong. And his legs. Remember when he used to go to the gimnasio, the gym? That's what he looks like. Fuerte, strong as ever! That bruja Diana puts some salt on his lips, and he smiles. A sonrisa. Damndest thing I ever saw. Then I musta blacked out, for maybe ten seconds. When I come back to, he's gone and disappeared, and the table's empty like before.

Doña Chiara's lookin at me like it's her fault. Sigfrido, she says, I'm sorry I got you into this.

I try standing up, but it's so fuckin hard. Coño! I hold on to her shoulder, and she steadies me. I guess she's afraid I might pass out again.

All a sudden that bitch Luz Divina comes bustin outta the kitchen, swingin her broom. I thought I heard your ugly voice! she screams. Murderer! Asesino! You better get outta here, or I'll kill you like you killed my Cirenea!

She's hittin my ankles and knees, cause she knows I'm so wasted I can't punch back. Chiara sticks the money in my pocket and shoves me into the street. Luz Divina keeps wavin her fuckin broom at me, still shoutin. That'll teach you, you damn policeman, maldito policía! Get the hell outta here!

I open my mouth, but nothin comes out. Like when you're havin a nightmare, a pesadilla! I start runnin as fast as I can, anywhere away from here, hoping to God I don't fall down and bust my ass.

Chiara, Plaza Drake to Hiroshima, that night

When Sigfrido tottered into the room, I realized what I'd put him through. He was as gabby as ever; but Diana had sapped his braggadocio. His skin had turned the chalky black of frozen chocolate. He was trembling from head to foot: in his baggy brown uniform, he looked like a pup tent lashed by a gale.

While he babbled, Luz Divina was sweeping the roof-terrace upstairs. She'd still be crowing over his terror, if she'd eavesdropped on the gory parts. I won't tell her, that's for sure: the notion of Diana hacking up a rooster gives me the heebie-jeebies.

After Sigfrido's account, I'd rather not go to the cemetery tonight, as I promised her I would on the phone. Maybe my superstitious nursemaids warped me more than I thought, with their jitters about ghosts—the 'fantàsimi' of Nodica. If I'm lucky, Diana will forget about our rendez-vous.

But at eleven o'clock, her chauffeur raps on my door. To my bemusement, she awaits me in a dark-blue Lexus. Did one of her followers lend her the car? Usually, I'd question her, like any proper journalist. Right now, I'm only concerned about what's in store.

The other day, her yellow cotton dress was plain but elegant. This evening, she's wearing a sapphire turban and white linen robe, as when Amado introduced us years ago. She doesn't say a thing as I slip in beside her, though she does press my hand. I take the gesture for more than a hello—a sign of reassurance.

As we speed away from the Barrio Antiguo, I ponder what she said last week. Amado visits me, all right... through my remorse, my memories, my words. Maybe I'm partly African, after all. It's a far stretch from Sicily to Nigeria, but not as far as from Iceland: I have to grant her that.

Diana's face is inscrutable, like a polished Benin bronze. She seems serene for now, but how long will her calmness last? Her moods pivot quickly, from hermetic arrogance to amorous spite. Her beauty must have inflamed Amado, no matter what she claims: in retrospect, it's odd that he rarely brought her up. Despite myself, I'm stirred by her as well. She must be an expert dissembler; when I met her at the temple, I never guessed she was in love with Amado herself.

The Lexus weaves through slum after slum, far from the city center. We glide past thousands of shacks, cobbled from plywood, cardboard, and tin. Electric wires twist along the roofs like manmade lianas.

After more than a decade, I still have to wonder: why am I here? I've been selfishly aloof from the masses, in this jerrybuilt metropolis—even more estranged than the plutocrats, who share the local culture, at least. Though I live cheek by jowl with these islanders, I haven't fully mastered their sprightly creole. As a rule, I avoid their food; I stick to baked pasta when I'm at home, like any good Sicilian. I don't listen to their music, unless a radio assaults my ears: I find their songs too schmaltzy, too loud. But then, I dislike Italian pop just as much. My tastes are limited to classical composers, the older the better…

What effort have I made, in all these years, to absorb the Canuban point of view? In my articles, I write about farmers in far-off lands, but not the campesinos here— much less the urban poor. The truth is, I've never thought of them as indigent, but simply as indigenous: they're rich in something I could never have. Acceptance, equanimity—or a meditative blankness?

In my chimerical realm, I am the sole inhabitant. Columbus was convinced he'd sailed to East Asia. Like him, I've traveled to a fictive island, a mirage. At best, I'm merely a colonist; while those around me truly live, all I do is fantasize. As Catulo says: 'Canuba doesn't exist. Canuba is you.' Long ago, Amado derided my unreality—an exile more mental than geographic. It seems fitting, almost symbolic, that he had a child called Luz, with a woman named Esperanza. Not 'light divine,' but human light, the light of an earthly hope…

Like most Canubans, he feared that migrants from Bonaventure would 'Africanize' this island. Italians rail against the 'African invasion,' too, now more than ever— not just from the South to the North of our peninsula, but from the vast continent itself. What of it? We all originate in Africa, the anthropologists say, so we're only being re-plenished by our roots. Constant flux has always been the source of humanity's strength…

Throughout our journey past rushing images—as much within me as without—Diana's silhouette gleams against the window. Her profile is as placid as Nefertiti's, reflected on the glass of her display case in Berlin. Im-perturbable, mysterious… even beneficent. The chauffeur slows his pace. 'Hiroshima,' he announces matter-of-fact-ly.

Diana addresses me in French. Is this so the driver won't understand? Or so he will? — You're probably not familiar with this neighborhood, Chiara. Only the most wretched end up here. Developers stick nice labels on the ritzy quarters of town: Cuesta India, Colina del Sol, Arroyo Hermoso, Loma Linda. It's part of the sales pitch. In the worst of the barriadas, why bother to lie?

You're right. I went to a slum once with Padre Flores, a bidonville as squalid as this. You must know it: Quita Sueños. I've always found the name sadly poetic.

Poetic? Those 'sueños quitados,' those 'stolen dreams,' what do you suppose they are? Dreams of a decent life? The fat cats always strip them off your body, even if they're the last rags you have. To the residents there, that name isn't wistful: it's no metaphor to them. Their huts lie next to the railroad where they work. Every morning at five, the sugarcane wagons roll by, and 'take their sleep away.'

Oh, I see. — Her description stung me like an accusal; instinctively, I beat around the bush. — Isn't it telling that Spanish relies on the same word for 'sleep' and 'dream'? Without the fundamentals, without food and sleep, you can't afford the luxury of dreams. — Diana seems receptive, so I rattle on. — It's like the word 'ilusión': it means illusion, but it can also mean excitement, or even hope. The language itself seems to declare that hope is an illusion. There's nothing similar in Italian, French, or German— though there's something fairly close in English. 'High hopes' always end in disappointment. The difference is, English reminds you not to aim for much; Spanish warns you not to aim for anything.

Diana looks me full in the face. She appears to take my comments to heart. — I never knew an Italian could be so 'réaliste'—so realistic.

When you say 'réaliste,' it's what we'd call 'pessimista'—pessimistic. Underneath it all, we're more cynical than you, though we dismiss our fate with a laugh. We don't say 'the more things change, the more they stay the same.' We don't grumble and analyze like the French. We say things will never change—that they'll always be impossible. Notice the tense we use: 'che sarà sarà,' 'what will be will be.' The future is predestined, so why worry at all? You're not French, of course, any more than I'm Italian…

Yes and no! We're both Southerners—and Southerners are more aware of the bitter truth. We've all been colonized. I imagine Sicilians, like Bonaventurans, have resisted what our masters called 'la mission civilisatrice'—'the civilizing mission.' As though we were savages! Northerners have always sold us short and beaten us down, but they can't deprive us of our despair.

Her solidarity surprises me. I've only been chattering away my anxiousness—buying time. But now the car rolls to a stop before a rusty, wrought-iron gate. The chauffeur opens Diana's door, and I slide out behind her. A blind wall dominates the street, stretching off for a hundred meters. On the opposite side of the fissured pavement, a shanty town creaks in the wind.

She curtseys. Welcome to the cemetery of Hiroshima.

How in the world did the neighborhood get that name?

The story goes that some Japanese refugees were stranded here, on their way to Brazil after World War II. But I've never unearthed any trace of them. The Caribbean is rife with old wives' tales like that. The campesinos who filled this slum must have heard about Hiroshima on the radio. It was another place where people had suffered; the shoe fit, and the label stuck. There's war here, too, every day of the week: drug-traffickers fighting over their turf.

A shudder rockets up my back. — I've heard this country is a clearinghouse for narcotics, between Colombia and the States.

C'est vrai! That's right. Even between Mexico and Europe.

The driver hops back into the Lexus; he locks the doors with a resounding click. I feel a lump in my throat. — Are you sure it's safe for us to be here this late?

It's all right if you're with me. But I wouldn't advise you to come here by yourself. Midnight is when I make my rounds: I go to every graveyard in the city, at least once a month. Don't ask me why. My calling demands it.

A wizened codger appears at the portal, dressed in a black trilby and tattered vest. Dragging the gate ajar, he greets us in Bonavent.

'Bonswa, Dantès,' Diana replies. 'Good evening, Dantès. Mèsi anpil. Thanks very much.'

His gas lantern flickers fitfully, as he leads us forward into the gloom. The moon is waning, but it sheds enough light for me to discern the graves on either side. — Most of these are freshly dug, I whisper.

Diana shrugs her shoulders. — Not because they're new: they get looted again and again. Nobody's creating zombies, by the way: I've watched a few of those asinine horror films. Addicts want money for their habits. If they can't steal gold teeth or jewelry from the dead, they dump the corpses out and hawk the coffins. There's always a market for those, what with the rival gangs. They shoot it out night and day.

My consternation goads her on. — Or else they sell the cadavers to the medical school, if they're still juicy enough. They're like archaeologists, in fact. Officially, this cemetery bears the name of a Taíno clan, the Nanoris. God knows Indian tombs have been pillaged, down through the centuries. In Canuba, in Bonaventure—all over the Americas. Hardhearted whites, who don't value native beliefs, carry skeletons off from ancient burial grounds. They ship them to museums in London or Paris, Washington or New York. No sacrilege could be more terrible. Here in Hiroshima, the bodies aren't as old as in the Taíno mounds. But at least they've stayed on the island where they belong. Even in a landfill, once the med students have sawed them to bits, the bones remain in Canuba.

Were Diana's religious tenets overblown? I often

suspect Catholic priests of this—Buddhist monks and Vedic teachers, too. We all need more humility, more emptiness, more light: nothing special... I start to bring up 'the benefits to science,' but that would only ring hollow. Every now and then I glance over my shoulder—as I've been doing ever since Sigfrido's report. I have to struggle to keep my voice from quaking. — The grave-robbers must be dangerous.

They're armed to the teeth. But they know better than to tangle with me. I have weapons much more lethal than theirs. — Her claim comes across as a statement, not a boast.

I guess that means you've 'protected' Amado's tomb. I'd hate to think...

Oh yes! Though they all avoid it anyway; they've even marked it so there's no mistake. He's the most powerful spirit for miles around. They've discovered what he can do if they provoke him. Soon he'll sleep forever; but that won't dawn on them for some time yet. He never wore jewelry, and his pinewood coffin has rotted away. So there's nothing left for them to steal.

A few steps further on, Diana comes to a halt before a rough slab of concrete. There's a catch in her voice. — Here he is. — She takes me by the arm, and we stand in silence. After a while, she murmurs softly. — You know, when the accident happened, Reina had him buried the following day. I never had a chance to give him the graveside service—even if I'd wanted to. My followers in San Sebastián tipped me off about his death. Through one of them who lives nearby, I tracked down his cemetery plot.

I don't recount that Reina went to see Catulo, or that Horacio phoned me. There's no purpose in riling Diana up again. All I volunteer is that Reina didn't even call Amado's parents; his employer let them know, several days later. She left town before telling anyone where he was laid to rest.

'Rest'? Not yet. — Diana almost seems to sympathize with Reina. — She probably didn't want to get in touch with his parents; they never condoned her 'marriage.' And she approved of Esperanza even less, from what Amado told me. That's why he hardly ever referred to his friendship with me; it would've only aroused her jealousy. In Amado's world, I didn't exist. Strange, how he always offended everyone who loved him.

Including me, I add timidly.

She tosses her head, though her tone is still mild. — We wouldn't want to forget you! Let it go, as the Americans say—let *him* go... Oh well, if I'd known about the crash right away, I might've scraped some money together. I could've found a better place for Amado than this.

If the wreck caught Diana off guard, she's not as clairvoyant as she pretends. — I was traveling, I tell her, and didn't get back in time. Not that it mattered. I suspect Reina meant to keep his funeral to herself, since she'd always had to share him with the rest of us.

I fear I've been too outspoken; but Diana only waves me aside. — Yes, we're all in this together.

On the primitive tombstone, I pick out some letters. They must have been traced in the cement while it was wet. 'Amado, Querido Padre, Querido Hijo, Querido Esposo.' 'Amado, Dear Father, Dear Son, Dear Husband': a trite inscription, written by a workman who hadn't known him, almost as an afterthought. Here at least, he and his family are reconciled.

The epitaph swims before my eyes. Yes, everything that rises must converge… The father, the son, the husband are one and the same: this is the trinity I worship in you, too… You are all of them, Amado, our Beloved…

Diana rouses me from my reverie. She's distant from me now, in a hinterland beyond my ken. — You promised to help me with the final rite. You're dreading the worst, after Sigfrido's tall tales; but this is all. — She reaches into her robe and scatters a few red feathers on the headstone. Then she sprinkles the ground with drops from a tiny flask.

Don't worry: it's holy water, not blood. Now we'll repeat the words together, in whatever language you want. — She intones a chant of some kind, in her solemn, rhythmic Bonavent.

After a phrase or two, I grasp that she's saying the Credo. As in my childhood, I recite it too. In Spanish and

English for your sake, Amado; in Italian and Latin, for my own. — Dios de Dios, Luz de Luz. God from God, Light from Light. Dio da Dio, Luce da Luce. Deum verum de Deo vero. True God from true God.

Midnight has come and gone. But there's a shining all around us, and it isn't just the moon. On the grave, your outline glistens. You're stronger than ever—glorious and intact... And now I see you vanish, like a whale-calf into the sea.

*A*s I related in the 'Foreword,' Sailing to Noon *owes its origins to a scuffed, leather briefcase packed with notebooks. Artemisia Vento, a Sicilian travel writer, entrusted them to me in 2016. Familiar with my efforts as a translator and editor, she'd sent a message to my website, shortly before she moved to Asia. She took it as a sign when she discovered I was living on her native island, in the historic center of Palermo. She was there too, by chance, at an elderly aunt's palazzo on the Via Paternostro. On a radiant day in early October, we met at a sidewalk café, shaded by the towering trees of the Giardino Garibaldi.*

This would be her 'last week in the West,' Artemisia confided. She'd already made a farewell visit to her parents, south of Siracusa. On a whim, she'd decided to leave me her 'scribbles': for many years, she'd been drafting a lengthy narrative. 'It's not exactly a grab-bag, but the three divisions differ widely. If you care to give them a glance, you'll see what I mean. Who knows? Maybe you could turn them into a trilogy.'

Was it her reassuring gaze? Her even-tempered charm? Whatever the reason, I took to her on the spot. After skimming through the manuscript, I asked her a number of questions, as we strolled through the city over the next few days.

Though she'd split the first section among nine voices, wasn't her sequential approach a bit old hat? 'Do you teach creative writing?' she joked. Jetting around the globe for her articles, she'd read tons of novels on her endless flights, so she was well aware of shifting fashions. When she'd started her project, in the late seventies, straightforward plots were still the rule; but then they'd morphed and morphed again, as in a hall of funhouse mirrors. 'Some might say they underwent a metastasis,' she quipped. 'But I believe the fade-ins, fade-outs, and parallel stories are merely copied from the visual media: well and good.' In her initial phase, she'd naively tried to portray the world 'as she found it—or misconceived it.' She loved insoluble mysteries, temporal ricochets, myopic details, alternate endings, molting personae, and meta-fictions. But why retrofit them like hidebound rules?

Even so, why had she opted for a blow-by-blow chronology? Despite some flashbacks, she replied, her linear method flowed from the daily entries in her journal. After completing a first series of segments, she'd toyed with stringing them in reverse, from the future to the past. 'Forward or backward, the whales appear at the center, and that's where they belong.' But she'd decided a gimmick like this might seem gratuitous—though readers were welcome to try it on their own. 'Label my approach "archaicizing," if you like; or call it "The New Simplicity," if that rings up to date. I couldn't care less. The next two panels are more contorted; they warped organically as I wrote them, to fit their misshapen themes. Anyway,' she added, 'a thousand modes of story-telling can coexist. Isn't eclecticism a hallmark of the "postmodern"? Sorry to use such a trendy word!'

Hadn't she overdrawn her protagonists, verging on parody? 'You don't know the Caribbean very well! In fact, I toned them down.' From early on, the characters in Dickens, Trollope, or Balzac (and later in her reading life, Goncharov, Vargas Llosa, or Galdós) had amused her with their zany tics. All the same, satire should never be dismissed as reductive; members of a class, nationality, or any other cohort are individuals, not stereotypes. 'Who's to dictate how others should sound and behave, much less think? Doesn't this depend on factors like their age, education, and experience? Don't Anglos vary widely among themselves, and Italians, too? On the other hand, foreigners often understand us better than we like to imagine. It might be a matter of distance—the greater inclusiveness of a panoramic lens.'

Wasn't her mimicry of 'Spanglish' or 'Germglish' condescending, even offensive? 'I don't see why, if that's how some of us actually talk. Isn't your question patronizing in itself?' No social circle is inferior, she went on—and no speech-pattern, either. From the dawn of humanity, translingual hybrids have been the norm, not the exception. Like the Sicilian 'dialect' of her childhood, she considered them fully-fledged languages, equal to any other. 'Oxford English,' 'newscast American,' 'peninsular Spanish,' 'Hochdeutsch,' 'Parisian French,' and 'standard Italian' are variants, too. As an amateur linguist, she'd always aimed for accuracy; she'd even *made tape-recordings of her models. But she doubted that they revealed any universal traits. 'We all develop an idiom of our own, as unique to us as our fingerprints. More than anything, we need to listen to each other, with empathy and respect.'*

Why had she created Canuba, instead of depicting an actual place? In her case, she felt, 'hyper-realism' made no sense. She'd spent her youth on several continents, never staying put for long. As a reporter, she'd crisscrossed the planet—though the Caribbean had always lured her back. Her island was an amalgam of Venezuela, coastal Colombia, Hispaniola, Cuba, and Puerto Rico, with other elements thrown in. Canuba's creole was a potpourri; its flora and fauna, too—wryly bogus at times. Readers could liken the island to their own countries, or deny any similarity; in either case, they'd be right. In its own modest way, Canuba resembled Macondo or Yoknapatawpha: both there and not there. She'd never presume to carve a local backdrop in stone, even her hometown; her subjectivity would interfere. Her sister Nina's 'Nodica' was alien to hers, though they were raised side by side.

I tried to pin her down: wasn't Chiara her alter ego? 'No, not at all! I'm too much of a prude; besides, she's hooked on romantic illusions. I fused several friends to write her script—just as I did with the rest of my vaudeville troupe.' When I smiled, she explained: 'Catulo, Lamia, and Horacio are performing artists, don't forget. Amado and Reina boogie for the disco crowd. Ángel María wears many masks to attain his goals. Luz Divina stars in her own domestic skits. Frederica impersonates a grande dame. Even Cirenea poses as a virgin. Chiara stages her "pathetic fallacy" toward nature, but also toward mankind. Far more deeply, Diana enacts religious rites...'

Then all your characters are playing roles? 'Oh yes, unconsciously or consciously, to the point of "camp." Drama: in the Caribbean, it's everywhere—even more than in Italy, and that's saying quite a lot! Each island is a small proscenium, where the actors loom larger than life. They stylize themselves into caricatures; they emote at a histrionic pitch. Once you're addicted to that intensity, the outside world seems drab... But after four decades, I've had enough. For me, the show is over.'

Ironically, by now we'd meandered to the Teatro Massimo. 'Baroque playwrights knew precisely what I mean,' Artemisia laughed, nodding toward the colossal facade. 'My Nodica might be Noto or Modica, under the twilight of a scrim. My Tragusa echoes Ragusa, with its Deus ex machina behind the Duomo's crimson drapes. If you climb the hill and open them, there's nothing there!'

She gave me a brusque, double kiss on the cheeks. This would be our last conversation, she announced. 'Do as you please with "our" notebooks; it's entirely up to you. My only request is that you burn them in the end.' We said goodbye on the theater's steps, between the two huge lions cast in bronze; their Art Nouveau riders, Opera and Tragedy, had never looked more precarious. With profound regret, I watched her stride down the Via Maqueda, unswerving and determined. Her flight was due to leave in several hours; I'm convinced I'll never see her again.

Artemisia's firmness of purpose had inspired me: I accepted her challenge then and there. Sifting through the welter of pages, I perceived how the first novel might fit into a well-established scheme. At the antipodes of Canuba, Samuel Butler welded New Zealand into a dyad: itself but also Erewhon, a faulty palindrome of Nowhere. During our chats in Palermo, Artemisia alluded to Barataria, the 'insula' Sancho Panza misgoverned—as ineptly as Columbus ruled the Spanish Main. Prospero's island, where he demotes Caliban to a Taíno slave, is cut from the same bloodied cloth. As these works affirm, while we'll never expiate our colonial past, we can disavow its triumphalist screeds—though as Chiara comes to recognize, her 'easy conquests' are neocolonial, too. Humanity's anchor, too heavy to raise, drags destructively across the ocean floor. Seen through a whale's eye, every corner of Europe has also been a colony, even if the overlords have switched command.

Beavering away, I began to wonder whether Artemisia's 'quaint' techniques weren't ahead of their time. Strangely, they combined the outmoded and the avant-garde. Horacio's Latinisms look backward to Montaigne, but forward to Bolaño's Xosé Lendoiro, who quotes from Roman authors in Latin. Catulo, Lamia, and Frederica, with their jumpy antics and hard edges, their capitals, hyperboles, and exclamation marks, cavort like cartoons from a manga. In another twist, the idyll between Chiara and Amado blends a romance—bodices and jockstraps frankly ripped—with a nature documentary. When extreme opposites attract, they couple like separate species, defiantly belying our practical age. Yet despite all their passion, they can't swim upstream to the Taíno past: its environmental harmony has dwindled to an obsessive mirage. They self-identify with animals, in their longing for that primal oneness; but like the rest of us, they're swept down a river of change.

In the tongue-in-cheek 'seminar' at the crux of the tale, library shelves bookend a mock colloquium. Ruined civilizations coalesce within the island's seabound edges, compressing and compressed. Amerindians, Africans, and Europeans honeycomb its restless population, constantly transformed. Like Castilian itself, the Canuban language recycles borrowed words. Ancient Greek, Latin, Hebrew, and medieval Arabic jostle with imported slang, just as they do in the Spanish classics. The erotic analogues of Middle Eastern cults bluntly undercut the biblical Song of Songs. Defaced by Christian bigotry, pagan columns can barely uphold the Church's fissured roof. The gender-blurring of the novel fleshes out these metamorphoses in the most blatant terms. The only 'orientation' is disorientation. Personality can alter at any moment: the self is a circumstance. Gener-

alizations swirl and clash, but no one takes them seriously—much less abides by them. 'Hypertexts' like mine gratefully collapse.

As I suggested in the prologue, this afterword could also be a foreword. Between them is the 'interword,' the present that shuttles back and forth—through our memories, our hopes. Artemisia invited us to read her chapters in reverse, or to skip around them at will, as in the random musings of a balmy afternoon. If we take her hint and read the first episode last, we'll embark on a reverie that each of us has known—careening from trepidation to joy, and from anguish to confidence.

We often walk a tightrope of dread: stretched across the 'two infinities,' it hovers between the atoms and the stars. When human love recedes beyond our reach, we shut ourselves off: no keys will unlock our solitary door. But the 'divine light' we fear may simply be a benign ordinariness—an unblinking acceptance of the here and now. In that frame of mind, we second Chiara's belief at the close of her daydream. Amado will return, she assures herself, and so she looks forward to a restful sleep. Sleep is the twin of death; but also, she concludes, 'what a treat.' Her question at the outset of the book—'why did I come here'—seems like an answer that soothes and consoles.

—HR

A Note on the Type

Sailing to Noon is typeset in Minion, which was designed by Robert Slimbach in 1990 for Adobe Systems. Minion was an early member of the well-regarded Adobe Originals program: it featured a set of type families derived from classical typographic styles. Minion is based on typefaces such as Jenson and Bembo that appeared in Venice in the late 16th century. It exhibits the graceful proportions, harmonious contrast between thick and thin strokes, and sculpted serifs for which these typefaces are known. Despite its venerable lineage, Minion works well for contemporary typography, and is widely used in current book design.

Notes on the Contributors

Hoyt Rogers has published his fiction and poetry in a wide range of periodicals, including *The New England Review*, *AGNI*, and *The Fortnightly Review*. As a prize-winning translator, editor, and essayist, he has worked with Viking, Knopf, Farrar Straus, Yale, Seagull, and various presses large and small. He has collaborated with Paul Auster, Yves Bonnefoy, Lincoln Kirstein, Philippe Claudel, and many others. He is the author of a poetry collection, *Thresholds*, as well as a study of the Late Renaissance. Please visit hoytrogers.com.

Artemisia Vento is the pseudonym of a travel journalist whose work appeared in countless magazines from 1978 onward, under different bylines. She specialized in writing about islands, above all in the Caribbean and Mediterranean, with a focus on village traditions and nature. At the end of 2016, she abandoned her career and withdrew from the world; she now lives a cloistered existence somewhere in Asia. The location of her community, and whether it is Buddhist, Christian, Vedic, interfaith, or secular, are secrets she keeps to herself.

Frank Báez has published six books of poetry, a short story collection, and three non-fiction works. He belongs to the Spoken Word band El Hombrecito, which has produced three albums. In 2006, he received the Short Stories Prize of the Santo Domingo International Book Fair for *You'll Have to Pay the Shrinks Yourself*; and in 2007, the Salomé Ureña National Poetry Prize for *Postales*. He was selected for the Hay Festival in 2017 as a member of Bogota 39, the best Latin American writers under forty. His work has been widely translated.

Mary Heebner's artworks belong to many collections both private and public, including the British Library and the Getty Center. Her numerous books combine her paintings with her writing, or pair her art with authors ranging from Shakespeare to Eshleman. Harper Collins published two volumes of Pablo Neruda's poetry accompanied by her paintings, with translations by Alastair Reid. Her fascination with antiquity informs her artworks and artist books on Lascaux, Angkor, and Classical sculpture. Please visit maryheebner.com.

Joan Tapper was the founding editor of *National Geographic Traveler*; she then moved on to *Islands* magazine, which she headed up for thirteen years. She is the author of *Island Dreams: Caribbean*, a comprehensive work on the archipelago, with photographs by Nik Wheeler. She has written many other popular books on travel, culture, and history, working with such publishers as Thames & Hudson and Random House Penguin. She is also a well-known editorial consultant, for writers of both fiction and non-fiction. Please visit joantapper.com.

John Balkwill is a book designer, publisher, and artist. He studied with the master printer Gabriel Rummonds, as well as with the wood engravers John DePol and Akira Kurosaki. He has collaborated with various authors on edition projects, including Gary Snyder, Daniel Boorstin, James McPherson, and Wole Soyinka. He has produced artist's books with Jacquelyn McBain, Mark Ryden, and Peter Goin, among many others. His books and prints, amply exhibited, figure in both private and public collections. Please visit luminopress.com.

The Caribbean Trilogy

But this new world here sought, is stranger far
than his, who stretched his vans from Palos.

— Melville

Though it stands fully on its own, *Sailing to Noon* is
the first volume of *The Caribbean Trilogy*, three novels by
Hoyt Rogers (with Artemisia Vento and Frank Báez). The
second and third books, *Midnight at Sea* and *Return to
Day*, are forthcoming; a sequel is also in preparation, *The
Caribbean Farewell*.

penetrates her mysterious form of possessiveness and love—reading the signs. The cat story is brilliant. I really felt this book: I entered its geography, saw and smelled and moved in it, which is a tribute to its vivid intimacy. But the novel has important dollops of irony and the ludicrous too, without which it would lose its comedic edge and wisdom.

—Siri Hustvedt

On an expansive canvas, Hoyt Rogers has portrayed a sense of life that is freewheeling and all-forgiving. Rich and multifarious, *Sailing to Noon* has enormous vitality and texture: it is a big performance—the epic myth of Canuba. I greatly admire the atmospherics, tonal shifts, and drive of this book.

—Jonathan Galassi

I was totally engaged with the novel *Sailing to Noon* from start to finish. I think it fully captures the ethos of the Spanish Caribbean, and the poetry of our islands: chaotic and sensual, pure and depraved, almost surreal. A truly unique world! The language is beautiful, and the tone extremely varied. There are many elements of satirical farce and magic realism; but there's also a tragic undertone, especially in the last third of the book—though true to Caribbean form, even here it's blended with high comedy. These days when I read the 'current novel,' it often puts me to sleep; but not this one, because it's too exciting: the characters, the pace, the humor. I like how Hoyt Rogers divides the text into narratives by distinct personae, who convey delicious vignettes of island living, funny and absurd at times. In addition, we get to know how they really think: what's going on in their minds. Overall, this book is an eloquent plea for pansexuality and liberation.

Chiara is a humanist full of curiosity, a cultivated intellectual who feels the pull of this 'other' island, which resembles and yet differs from the Sicily of her childhood. She is also a nature-lover, enthralled by the exuberance of the tropics. Undaunted by the dark forces that begin to loom, she opens herself to the new experiences that Canuba can bring. She embraces her spiritual journey on the island, her dream of a paradise attained, a place close to the earth and its creatures, shaped by instincts and the natural flow. Amado is Chiara's mentor in her quest for amorous bliss. He's a good boy/bad boy, lost and restless and yet a kind, sensitive soul. Self-assured and self-indulgent, he's ruled by his raw and intense sexuality. He's surrounded by figures who try to use him, though he continues to be a fighter.

Paradoxically, he struggles in a harsh milieu that coexists with a sphere where beauty reigns. He embodies Canuba—that defective utopia—and his imperfect love changes Chiara forever.

Sailing to Noon is dominated by nature, and death is simply a part of nature. The whale-calf Chiara meets in the middle of her adventure reappears at the end. The book concludes on a positive note which stresses the preciousness of life, the randomness of destiny and how loved ones can be unexpectedly taken away from us. Yet what we remember is that they made us grow and brought us happiness; and so they become an enduring part of the place where we live, and of ourselves.

—Ricardo Bernardo

I think *Sailing to Noon* will have a lasting impact on readers worldwide. Not only is it a great literary work, with a prodigious versatility of language, it is also accessible to everyone. Whether you catch each and every allusion or not, the energetic plot moves you forward, like a play or a film.

The narrators speak for different levels of society, instead of limiting our experience to only one. As soon as we absorb a couple of the monologues, the various voices start to come alive inside our heads. That diversity and heterogeneity are the essence of the Caribbean.

The characters are fabulous—especially Amado, who incarnates so many elements of island life. He undergoes an evolution, almost a kind of redemption: that must be why the others yearn for his resurrection. My favorite episode is the one about the cat; I admire the way everyday events become transformed into a metaphor for deeper layers of human exchange.

Another achievement here (and a discovery for me) is how Hoyt Rogers illustrates the idea of love; I'd say that this is the overarching theme of the novel. It generates a range of secondary topics: longing, solitude, anxiety, eroticism, jealousy, violence, tenderness, and so on. Skillfully, magic realism is woven into the amorous web.

The multifaceted afterword also serves an important role, by expanding the field of intertextuality even further, and preparing us for the novels to come.

—Frank Báez